BOOKS BY
THE SAME AUTHOR:

NOVELS:
Cloned Lives
The Sudden Star
Watchstar

ANTHOLOGIES:
Women of Wonder
More Women of Wonder
The New Women of Wonder
Bio-Futures

SHORT FICTION:
Starshadows

THE NEW WOMEN OF WONDER

THE NEW WOMEN OF WONDER

RECENT SCIENCE FICTION STORIES BY WOMEN ABOUT WOMEN

EDITED, WITH AN
INTRODUCTION AND NOTES, BY

VINTAGE BOOKS
A Division of Random House, New York

A Vintage Original, January 1978
First Edition
Copyright © 1977 by Pamela Sargent

All rights reserved under International and Pan-American Copyright Conventions. Published in the United States by Random House, Inc., New York, and simultaneously in Canada by Random House of Canada Limited, Toronto.

Library of Congress Cataloging in Publication Data
Main entry under title:

The New women of wonder.

Bibliography: p.
CONTENTS: Dorman, S. View from the Moon station.—McIntyre, V. N. Screwtop.—Arnason, E. The warlord of Saturn's moons. [etc.]
1. Science fiction, American—Women authors.
2. Women—Fiction. I. Sargent, Pamela.
PZ1.N4448 1978 [PS648.S3] 813′.0876 77-76577
ISBN 0-394-72438-0

Manufactured in the United States of America

Since this copyright page cannot accommodate all acknowledgments, they can be found on the following page.

ACKNOWLEDGMENTS

"View from the Moon Station" by Sonya Dorman. Copyright © 1977 by Sonya Dorman. By permission of the author and her agent, John Schaffner.

"Screwtop" by Vonda N. McIntyre. Copyright © 1976 by Vonda N. McIntyre. First published in *The Crystal Ship*. Reprinted by permission of the author.

"The Warlord of Saturn's Moons" by Eleanor Arnason. Copyright © 1974 by Eleanor Arnason. First published in *New Worlds 6*. Reprinted by permission of the author.

"The Triumphant Head" by Josephine Saxton. Copyright © 1970 by Anne McCaffrey. First published in *Alchemy & Academe*. Reprinted by permission of the author and her agent, Virginia Kidd.

"The Heat Death of the Universe" by Pamela Zoline. Copyright © 1967 by Pamela Zoline. First published in *New Worlds*. Reprinted by permission of the author.

"Songs of War" by Kit Reed. Copyright © 1974 by Kit Reed. First published in *Nova 4*. Reprinted by permission of Brandt & Brandt.

"The Women Men Don't See" by James Tiptree, Jr. Copyright © 1973 by Mercury Press, Inc. First published in *The Magazine of Fantasy & Science Fiction*. Reprinted by permission of the author and her agent, Robert P. Mills, Ltd.

"Debut" by Carol Emshwiller. Copyright © 1970 by Damon Knight. First published in *Orbit 6*. Reprinted by permission of the author and her agent, Virginia Kidd.

"When It Changed" by Joanna Russ. Copyright © 1972 by Harlan Ellison. First published in *Again, Dangerous Visions*. Reprinted by permission of the author.

"Dead in Irons" by Chelsea Quinn Yarbro. Copyright © 1976 by Chelsea Quinn Yarbro. First published in *Faster Than Light*. Reprinted by permission of the author.

"Building Block" by Sonya Dorman. Copyright © 1975 by Sonya Dorman. First published in *Analog*. Reprinted by permission of the author and her agent, John Schaffner.

"Eyes of Amber" by Joan D. Vinge. Copyright © 1977 by the Condé Nast Publications, Inc. First published in *Analog*. Reprinted by permission of the author.

*To Marion Collins
and Marion Thorstensen*

CONTENTS

INTRODUCTION
PAMELA SARGENT

I

Women have been writing science fiction ever since its beginnings, which some critics date to the year 1818, when Mary Shelley published her novel *Frankenstein*. Since then, women have written every kind of sf, from the so-called hard science story based on extrapolation from known scientific facts to the more speculative and stylistically experimental story.

In the 1930s, C. L. Moore wrote fantasy stories with a strong female protagonist, Jirel of Joiry. Moore later collaborated with her husband, Henry Kuttner, on many sf stories. Leigh Brackett, who has written many film scripts, began writing science fiction adventure stories during the 1940s; her works were not only colorful but also contained stronger characterizations than most adventure sf. Judith Merril, a writer and editor, had enormous influence in the late fifties and early sixties with her anthologies, and was largely responsible for introducing American readers to the more experimental British sf being written during the sixties. Cele Goldsmith Lalli, editor of the magazines *Amazing* and *Fantastic* during the late fifties and early sixties, published early work by Thomas M. Disch, Roger Zelazny, Ursula K. Le Guin, R. A. Lafferty, and many others. Joanna Russ brought feminist concerns to the attention of many sf readers for the first time. By the beginning of the seventies, Ursula K. Le Guin was being honored by many as one of the best sf authors writing today. There are others—authors who have been popular all along or who are now finding a wider readership: Marion Zimmer Bradley, Anne McCaffrey, Zenna Henderson, Kate Wilhelm, Katherine MacLean, Carol Emshwiller, and many others.

At the same time, women have remained a minority in sf, perhaps no more than 10 to 20 percent of writers and readers. As a result, most sf has been conservative in its depiction of future roles for women or has ignored them altogether. Male writers, aware that the audience for their work was primarily male, tended to write about men. Women writers generally did the same; during the fifties, when more women were writing sf, many used female protagonists but usually depicted them in traditional roles, thus mirroring the mores of the society at that time.

The turmoil of the 1960s was reflected in science fiction. Just as the forties had "after the bomb" tales and the fifties saw many anti-McCarthy stories, the sixties had its share of anti–Vietnam War stories as well as overpopulation and "ecology" stories. Science fiction during the sixties was also largely dominated by a debate between those who wanted sf to remain more traditional in its writing and its use of ideas and plots, and those who sought to write about different themes and used innovative techniques to explore those themes; this debate occasionally surfaces even now.[1]

The proponents of innovation, who encouraged writers to believe that sf could be different, greatly influenced female as well as male authors. More women began writing; not coincidentally, many of them wrote for the British magazine *New Worlds* (edited by Michael Moorcock) and the American anthology *Orbit* (edited by Damon Knight), two places where new approaches were encouraged. One contribution by women writers was a more overt emphasis on characterization, which in turn may have encouraged more interest in the roles of women.

Even so, most science fiction to this day has remained conservative in its sociological extrapolations. In pointing out this flaw, one is likely to be accused of seeking to impose an ideological test on the genre, rejecting works that do not measure up. But in fact I am asking why the overwhelming majority of science fiction books limit female characters to traditional roles. We should have more diversity, not less. As Mary Kenny Badami put it:

> I do not want fans to stop arguing about whether Larry Niven's Ringworld system is possible, or whether Arthur C. Clarke's Rama could accelerate around the sun, or whether H. G. Wells' Cavorite is a plausible antigravity method. I do not want us to stop debating the ethics of *Starship Troopers*, the consequences of genetic manipulation, the politics of first contact, the uses of mythology in Delany and Zelazny. But even as we discuss those questions, I do want us to see the issue of sex roles and sexism as fair game for discussion as well. Feminism isn't the only topic we should be talking about, but in sf we haven't talked about it at all until comparatively recently.[2]

II

What has been happening recently? During the late 1960s, Anne McCaffrey became the first woman sf writer to win both the Nebula Award (given annually by the members of the Science Fiction Writers of America) and the Hugo Award (given annually by the members of the World Science Fiction Conventions). She was given the Hugo for her novella "Dragonrider," and the Nebula for the novella "Weyr Search"; "Dragonrider" later became part of *Dragonflight* (Walker, 1968), a novel with a female protagonist.

In 1970, Ursula K. Le Guin's novel of a world where the inhabitants combine both male and female traits, *The Left Hand of Darkness* (Walker, 1969), won the Nebula and Hugo awards for the best novel of the year.[3] Joanna Russ's "When It Changed" (1972) and James Tiptree, Jr.'s "Houston, Houston, Do You Read" (1976), two strongly feminist stories about all-female societies, have also won Nebula awards. Other award-winning works with either feminist elements or innovative characterizations of women are Le Guin's *The Dispossessed* (Harper & Row, 1974), Joe W. Haldeman's *The Forever War* (St. Martin's, 1974), and Vonda N. McIntyre's "Of Mist, and Grass, and Sand" (1973). Lisa Tuttle, a talented young writer, won the John W. Campbell Award for Best New Writer in 1974 and C. J. Cherryh won it in 1977 (the award, set up to honor the memory of influential editor Campbell by the Condé Nast Publications, is voted on annually by members of the World Science Fiction Conventions). Phyllis Eisenstein, Tanith Lee,

Cherry Wilder, Marta Randall, Sally A. Sellers, Ruth Berman, Jacqueline Lichtenberg, and other young women are publishing sf and fantasy.

Other writers have had success with works that take account of women. Samuel R. Delany, one of the most honored sf writers of the past ten years, has portrayed male and female characters in untraditional ways in much of his work. In *Triton* (Bantam, 1976), he writes about a future society which emphasizes and encourages the freedom to live in many different ways. One has to obey only the set of laws one voted for and there are many different legal systems, as well as one area where there are no laws. A person may be heterosexual, homosexual, bisexual, or have any number of possible orientations at different times. Even one's gender is not fixed; a person can change from one sex to the other, and several different sexes are recognized.

The central character in the novel is Bron Helstrom, who has particular difficulty in dealing with Triton and its people:

> The particular psychology Delany has chosen for his study (Bron's) might be called that of a garden variety 20th-century misogynist, but in fact this is an oversimplification which skirts the book's central accomplishment. Bron is in all too many ways far more *enlightened* than most 20th-century misogynists. In his particular universe, he cannot help but be. He is constrained in a multitude of subtle and pervasive ways by his world; by its language, so that "E-girls" may be either men or women, and "boymade" may be the word applied to articles of war; by its social structure, so that his boss may be a woman and he may even, under a variety of social pressures, like her; by its

political structure, so that Bron's problem is rare enough to preclude encounters with any group with like interests . . .[4]

Delany's future society is in fact so fluid that no generalizations can be made about it or the people in it, who are so highly differentiated that even their past lives are irrelevant when one meets them; one must judge a person for what he or she is at that moment. In fact, it is considered rude to ask about a person's past.

Bron, with his peculiar (for Triton) notions about maleness and his propensity for making generalizations, is constantly pitted against that world. His mistaken assumptions about people create problems in his personal life. His conviction that there is some inherent difference between males and females finally leads him to become a woman; it is the only way he can express the qualities and characteristics he sees as female, since he has no conceptual way of dealing with his problem.

Delany's complex novel shows us a completely different future society. The setting of Cecelia Holland's *Floating Worlds* (Knopf, 1976) bears more of a resemblance to past human experience. Two thousand years from now, Earth's society is anarchic and people live communally, in cities covered by domes to protect people from the environmental damage that has made much of the planet's surface uninhabitable. The only "government" is a committee, which settles disputes by negotiation. Mars is a democracy; the Moon is ruled by a military dictatorship. Uranus and Saturn are ruled by mutants, the Styths, whose civilization is based on war and conquest. The Styths firmly believe that they should rule everyone.

Though Earth is egalitarian, the Styth Empire is patriarchal and its people own slaves; women have few rights. Yet the novel's main character, a strong Earthwoman named Paula Mendoza, manages to rise to a position of influence among the Styths. Chosen by Earth's committee to negotiate with them, Paula allies herself with one of the Styth warlords, Saba, wins the friendship of this difficult and violent man, and tries to affect history. Paula is one of the tougher heroines in sf, and the novel is a well-written adventure with depth.

Marion Zimmer Bradley's *The Shattered Chain* (Daw, 1976) is part of a series of novels about the planet Darkover. But unlike many of her previous novels, it is concerned with the role of women in this society. The women of Darkover are little more than chattels; in the planet's "Dry Towns" they even wear chains. But the planet is also the home of the Free Amazons, who choose to live outside of these restrictions. Bradley is saying that, at least in part, one may *choose* to remain enslaved; many Darkovan women, knowing that an alternative exists, are too fearful of the difficulties of freedom to become Amazons.

Each Free Amazon must swear an oath promising to defend herself if necessary, never to marry except as an equal to her mate, never to be known by a man's name (but only as the daughter of her mother), and to bear children only by choice. An Amazon's allegiance is to the band of women; she must renounce other loyalties and never appeal to a man for protection or support. Interestingly, although a Free Amazon must be able to defend herself, engaging in sword-play over trivial insults is frowned upon as an unnecessary display.

The people of Darkover, descendants of settlers from Earth, have forgotten their Terran origins. Though they trade with Terra, they have little contact with its people. An agent of Terra, Magda Lorne, born and raised among the Terrans but trained from birth in Darkovan customs, must rescue the kidnapped Peter Haldane, another Terran agent and Magda's former husband as well. The novel is told from the viewpoints of three different women: Magda, the Free Amazon Jaelle n'ha Melora, and the Darkovan noblewoman Rohana Ardais. The differing roles of these women and the conflicts that result make this vivid novel considerably more than an adventure story. Magda in particular must reconcile being a Terran with her training as a traditional Darkovan woman and her later bond with the Free Amazons.

Kate Wilhelm's *The Clewiston Test* (Farrar, Straus & Giroux, 1976) concerns a chemical researcher, Anne Clewiston. Anne and her husband Clark Symons have discovered a pain suppressant. Their employer, a pharmaceutical firm, wants to use the suppressant on human subjects, even though animal experimentation has shown that there may be dangers; several chimps used in the tests have begun to act irrationally. At the beginning of the novel, Anne is recovering from a serious car accident. As the book progresses those around her, including Clark, begin to suspect that she may have used the pain suppressant on herself and is going mad.

This plot provides a framework in which Wilhelm can examine the problems inherent in many male-female relationships. Anne's situation forces her to examine her life with her husband, which is complicated by the fact that she is more gifted than Clark and feels some ambivalence about this.

At one point in the novel, after Anne's doctor has told her she has recovered enough to resume sexual relations, Clark tries to force himself on her. Anne attempts to express her resentment:

> "I took it for granted that we were equals in all ways. At work, here around the apartment. All ways. But I was kidding myself. All I have to do is say something. Tonight I said something and you went on anyway. Always your way. You know best. If there's something we do that you don't like, don't enjoy, it's simple, you just don't initiate that again, and if I start to, you ignore me. It has to be your way . . ." [5]

Clark, hurt by Anne's later assertion that he tried to rape her and her expression of disgust at his action, comes to believe she has used the suppressant because it allows him to comfort himself by thinking she was not rational. This novel skillfully combines science-fictional elements with characters that illuminate human experience and the relationships between men and women.

Even as newer writers are making their mark, older writers are being rediscovered. This is partly because there is a widespread interest in sf in general among readers, and because of a growing interest in the genre and its past. Some attention is being paid to the contributions of women writers

such as Francis Stevens, C. L. Moore, Leigh Brackett, and Andre Norton. Moore's memorable female
characters include the swashbuckling Jirel and Di-
erdre, a cyborg whose brain has been transferred to
a metal body (in "No Woman Born," 1944).

Andre Norton has been a widely popular writer
of sf for many years. She has written more than
seventy books, has many readers, and yet little critical attention has been paid her within the sf community. She has won no awards and her numerous
books for young people are rarely commented upon.
Much of her early work was written from the view-
point of male characters, at least partly because this
was more salable, but later books have strong female characters as well. One series of novels, dealing with an alien planet in another time and space
called the Witch World, utilizes both female and
male characters. As Sandra Miesel writes:

> The least discussed aspect of the Witch World
> series is its feminist viewpoint . . . The consis-
> tently unflattering portraits of conventional
> women make the virtues of the nonconformists
> shine more brightly.[6]

Several women characters in these books are concerned with personal freedom and are willing to
endure hardships for it; clearly, Norton realizes that
freedom, worth having, is not easy to find. In
"Toads of Grimmerdale" (1973), a recent novelette
which takes place on the Witch World, Hertha, a
young woman who has been brutally raped, seeks
her attacker. She has not seen his face but can recognize him by a metal bowguard he wore on his
wrist. Though Hertha wants vengeance, by the

story's end she has found something quite different, with the help of a man she meets on her journey.

Obviously the notion shared by many that science fiction was basically a man's (or boy's) genre was not entirely true, yet it was also not entirely false. While offering women the chance to write about scientific possibilities, future societies, or exotic alien places, there were also restrictions of sorts; some were editorial, others were commercial, still others were self-imposed. Many authors, men and women, felt restricted at least in part because sf was often seen as an escapist literature or as books for children and young people.

In spite of this, many writers did defy restrictions and succeeded. There are more female writers entering the field than ever before, though they are still outnumbered by men. Now it is commonplace to hear older sf writers and critics say that the most interesting new writers of science fiction are women. Sf author Vonda N. McIntyre offered a possible explanation:

> As to why many of the best sf writers are women, out of proportion to their representation in the field, the selection process works at a different level for women. Many women who might make good or adequate writers have too little self-confidence even to submit stories to potential markets. Of stories of equal quality, those with male-sounding bylines are more likely to be thought "good" than those with female-sounding bylines (studies have been done that prove this). One rather expects that the same thing happens in a professional slushpile. The fact that the mediocre stories . . . are almost all written by men, that

the bad stories are virtually *all* written by men, is
good for the egos of women writers who have succeeded . . . but it doesn't do much for women
who might make perfectly competent if somewhat
uninspired writers (let's face it, that's what most
stories published these days are, competent [usu-
ally] and uninspired) but can't share in the rather
freer and more self-deterministic life of a writer
because women have to be twice as good as men
at what they do to get half as far.

We'll know the millennium has arrived when a
woman can be only competent at her job, just
like most men, without having to endure dis-
paraging remarks.[7]

More idealistically, perhaps, one can hope that as
more women of talent write sf and men of ability
continue to do so, there will be less room for the uninspired and the bad, and less of it published. Sf,
like many fields of endeavor, has only drawn on little more than half of the available talent.

III

In recent years there has been talk in sf circles of
a longing for the "golden years" of science fiction, a
nostalgia for traditional stories with familiar trap-
pings. There are many reasons for this. The academic interest in the genre has stimulated interest
in the accomplishments of the past. There is much
to be learned from older works and a lot of enjoy-
ment to be found in reading them. Because more
people are reading sf, publishers have more reason
to reissue older novels or to make short fiction by
well-known authors available to this new audience.

There is nothing wrong with that. But some readers and editors go further, wanting science fiction written *now* to embody these old virtues. It is good to encourage strong extrapolation, interesting characters, good story structures, and the rest. But often a derivative new work with stereotyped characters and old ideas is seen as a fine example of a book with these "older virtues." Work that attempts to be innovative is seen as suspect.

This situation affects women and men who wish to attempt something new in their fiction. One author of a successful first novel had her second rejected by the same publisher because the book was about an all-female world and there were no male characters in it.[8] Other authors have reported difficulties in seeing work published that defied conventional canons, either because of its style or because of its subject matter.

Some of this is to be expected (though not appreciated) when one is writing in a "popular" genre and asking publishers, who have to show a profit, to print the finished work. Some of it may be the result of a growing conservatism in the society as a whole. Part of it, within sf, is that the audience is still seen as being largely male, much of it relatively conservative as well. Any difficulties an innovative or unconventional male writer may face are multiplied for an unconventional female writer. It is one of the paradoxes of science fiction as a whole that it is seen as "free-wheeling" and "speculative," while in reality it is so conservative.[9]

Even so, many within sf have published discussions about women and science fiction. Editors of "amateur" or small press publications, such as Janice Bogstad, Jessica Amanda Salmonson, Jeffrey D.

Smith, Amanda Bankier, Denys Howard, and others, have devoted time and energy to printing these discussions.

But many are tired of the topic. Some are perhaps "battle-scarred" after arguing for so long. Some persist in thinking that feminists are trying to impose a "party line." Others may be bored, wanting to get back to the "serious" business of hunting for scientific errors or implausibilities in a plot. A few probably believe the issue is settled.

Raising the issue has had an effect. If one is going to write about a future patriarchal world, one at least has to explain why it is that way instead of taking it for granted. The author falling back on old assumptions about biological differences will show a certain lack of creativity at the least; the writer who insists that "the unconscious dictates the story" will reveal that the conscious mind has not been dealing too much with issues, or something of it might have penetrated to the unconscious depths. Part of the reason usually is that the author depicts certain types of societies or believes, for example, that future societies *will* be imperialistic, capitalistic, or barbaric in the wake of a disaster or during the settling of a new planet. It may reasonably follow that men will be dominant in such worlds, though not necessarily; a future capitalism or barbarism need not resemble the past or present.

Some writers are introducing stronger female characters, which is a step forward even if such a character often seems isolated, without supportive relationships with other women, or a token. Others are trying to portray egalitarian worlds where equality is taken for granted or to show the problems women may have in societies where it is not. Women may have a greater stake in writing about worlds that are different in radical ways from our own, and it is refreshing to conceive of societies in which strong independent women are the norm rather than the exception. But male writers such as John Varley, Hal Clement, Joe W. Haldeman, Alexei Panshin, James H. Schmitz, P. J. Plauger, Samuel R. Delany, Thomas M. Disch, John Wyndham, and others have broken or are now trying to break with standard ways of writing about women in their sf.[10]

Marion Zimmer Bradley, in an essay describing the ways in which she has dealt with female characters in her own work, ended by saying:

> I think science fiction is being greatly enriched by its expansion. My favorite editor tells me that a full half of the manuscripts on his desk now have recognizably female names, and that all the good new writers seem to be women. If any woman still believes that science fiction and fantasy publishers are closed to women, she is either gravely misinformed, or she is making excuses for her own incompetence by attributing her failure to editorial prejudice. The prejudice simply is no longer there . . .[11]

In spite of the problems any innovative writer may face if he or she is seen as "uncommercial" by a publisher, and the occasional bias that can still be encountered,[12] this is generally true. *Analog*, the most popular sf magazine, recently published a women's issue; Robert Silverberg's *The Crystal Ship* (Thomas Nelson, 1976) is an anthology of short novels by women. *The Magazine of Fantasy & Science Fiction* has long been receptive to stories by

women. The popular writer James Tiptree, Jr., has
admitted she is in fact Alice Sheldon; she has published sf under the name Raccoona Sheldon recently.[13] The fine historical novelist Cecelia Holland
entered sf in 1976; Doris Lessing and Lois Gould
have used sf and fantasy techniques in their work
(Lessing in particular has had a long-standing interest in sf). The well-known poet Marilyn Hacker
has worked within sf in the past as an editor and
has contributed to the discussion of women in sf
(most notably in her introduction to the Gregg
Press edition of Joanna Russ's *The Female Man*,
published in 1977). But more important, women are
contributing more to sf magazines and anthologies;
their works are more numerous on library shelves
and in bookstores. Some bookstores specializing in
science fiction and fantasy report that books by
women generate a lot of interest.

This is all part of progress toward what I hope
will be the end result: women and men being fairly
represented in sf as a whole. If works by women
simply become a genre within sf, with male-au-
thored works regarded as its main body, we will all
lose.

Let me describe the situation in another way. In
systems engineering, it is known that all parts of a
system must work efficiently and be planned according to what one wishes the entire system to do.
Planning piecemeal results in jury-rigging; the thing
may get by or it may fail. The same is true of biological systems, as people in medicine are learning,
and of the ecological sphere as well; an isolated
incident may have far-reaching effects.

Science fiction writers, like all writers, deal in fictional systems. In the case of sf, these works may be extrapolative and realistic, fantastic and far-fetched, satirical, based on probabilities, possibilities, or completely imaginary constructions that exist only in the author's mind and may never exist elsewhere. The task of the sf writer is to create a coherent imaginary system which is an artistic whole, without ignoring some elements in favor of others. Each writer does this in a distinctive way.

The criticism most often leveled at sf is that too many of its works are jury-rigged and the elements —societal, scientific or imaginary, characters, plots, literary techniques, and all the rest—do not quite hold together. Perhaps the genre as a whole, having often ignored women—as well as the old, the middle-aged, the non-white, and the non-Western—does not quite hold together. It is within this context that we can view the role of women in sf. By adding their voices, they enrich the entire fictional system of science fiction. A fuller picture of future possibilities can result. By attracting more readers, they may encourage other women to engage their imaginations.

Kurt Vonnegut, Jr., in an interview, spoke eloquently about the writer and society:

> Writers are specialized cells doing whatever we do, and we're expressions of the entire society —just as the sensory cells on the surface of your body are in the service of your body as a whole. And when a society is in great danger, we're likely to sound the alarms. I have the canary-bird-in-the-coal-mine theory of the arts. You know, coal miners used to take birds down into the

mines with them to detect gas before men got
sick. The artists certainly did that in the case of
Vietnam. They chirped and keeled over . . . I
continue to think that artists—all artists—should
be treasured as alarm systems.[14]

A few of the alarm systems are sounding in this
collection. Some of the writers are new voices in
science fiction; others have written longer but have
new things to say about women in a science-fictional
context. All are worth listening to, and all will en-
tertain the reader as well.

NOTES

1. This debate can be characterized by the following examples. During the 1960s, the magazine *Analog* (edited by
John W. Campbell, Jr.) sought stories with intriguing ideas,
active characters, and straightforward conventional narra-
tion; some stories published there suffered from a pedestrian
style, cardboard characterization, standard plotting, and an
uninspired development of ideas. The magazine *New Worlds*
(edited by Michael Moorcock) and the anthology *Dangerous Visions* (edited by Harlan Ellison) encouraged new
stylistic innovations and an adult approach to topics (such as
sexuality) that had only rarely been treated by sf writers;
they sometimes printed overly pretentious pieces, need-
lessly obscure stories, and a few topical tales that seem
dated today. A debate, called the "New Wave versus Old
Wave" argument by its participants, began.

Some claimed that the innovators would rob science fiction of the elements (adventure, wonder, or new ideas)
that distinguished it from other types of fiction; the experimental writers were accused of wallowing in decadence
or emphasizing the sordid side of life. Others accused the
"old-fashioned" writers of imposing outdated limits on the
genre and of preferring pulpy writing and standard plots.
An undercurrent of political debate was present as well,
with conventional writers often seen as conservatives, capi-
talists, imperialists, or warmongers and innovative writers
viewed as radicals, socialists, communards, or degenerates.
In reality, some good writing of all kinds was published
and the argument served to expand the potential of the
genre. Many writers could not easily be placed on one side

or the other (three examples that come to mind are Harry Harrison, who has unconventional social ideas but regularly wrote for *Analog*; John Brunner, who has written both conventional and experimental novels; and R. A. Lafferty, a Catholic conservative whose stories are wildly innovative both in style and subject matter). Throughout this debate, no one seemed to question the legitimacy of a good story well-told that did not need to aspire to anything beyond itself. However, the predominance of this kind of tale, both ill-written and well-written, was rightly called into question, since it threatened to drown out every other voice.

What was really behind this argument? Many writers were tired of what might be called the trivialization of the genre; they wanted more than adventure stories or sociologically naïve idea exercises. The best sf had always been more than simply entertainment, but the needs of the market had obscured this, surrounding the good stories with many poor ones.

The trivial story was a story in which there were no real problems, where the hero always won and every question had a clear answer. Innovative writers wanted sf stories that took account of real human problems. Later, more conventional sf writers, perhaps with some justice, accused the experimental writers of too much concern with style, of seeking only to shock rather than enlighten the reader, or of "solving" problems by having the protagonist give up and surrender to despair or nihilism. Those on both sides were capable of producing trivial stories on occasion.

Sf author and critic James Blish, in a speech he gave in 1960, may have opened this debate. In his speech, later published as an essay, he asked what science fiction should do:

> The writer or reader who still thinks an exploding star is inherently more wonderful than the mind and heart of the man who wonders at it is going to run out of these peripheral wonders sooner or later, and then perhaps he will blame the readers or the writers or the editors or the benighted public—we have seen this process going on for a long time. What he is now seeking from fiction of all kinds, science fiction included, is not the sense of wonder, but the sense of *conviction*. That is the feeling that the story you are reading is about something that is worth your adult attention, and that the author approached it in that light. (James Blish, "A Question of Content," in William Atheling, Jr., *The Issue At Hand*, Chicago, Advent, 1964, p. 127.)

Author Ursula K. Le Guin commented on the same issue recently:

> Genuine newness, genuine originality, is suspect. Unless it's something familiar rewarmed, or something

experimental in form but clearly trivial or cynical in content, it is unsafe. And it must be safe . . .

The almost limitless freedom of form available to the modern artist is, I think, a function of this trivialization of art. If art is taken seriously by its creators or its consumers, that total permissiveness disappears, and the possibility of the truly revolutionary reappears. If art is seen as sport, without moral significance, or if it is seen as self-expression, without rational significance, or if it is seen as a marketable commodity, without social significance, then anything goes . . .

When art only shows how and what, it is trivial entertainment, whether optimistic or despairing. When it asks why, it rises from mere emotional response to real statement, and to intelligent ethical choice. It becomes, not a passive reflection, but an act. (Ursula K. Le Guin, "The Stalin in the Soul," in *The Future Now*, ed. by Robert Hoskins, Greenwich, Conn., Fawcett, 1977, p. 14 and 19.)

This issue, then, the question of whether or not science fiction was to be about important things or trivial things, was at the root of the vociferous debating during the '60s, though it was often obfuscated by arguments about literary techniques, political differences, or subject matter. In a more muted form, the argument is continuing. A concern with women in sf is of course part of this demand for non-trivial science fiction.

2. Mary Kenny Badami, "A Feminist Critique of Science Fiction," in *Extrapolation*, Vol. 18, No. 1 (December 1976), p. 16.

3. A precursor of Le Guin's novel was Theodore Sturgeon's *Venus Plus X* (Pyramid, 1960), which depicted a future world of androgynous human beings. Sturgeon's protagonist, a man of our time, attempts to be sympathetic until he discovers that these people, through genetic manipulation, have *chosen* to be this way.

4. Jean Mark Gawron, Introduction to Samuel R. Delany, *Triton* (Boston, Gregg Press, 1977), p. xi.

5. Kate Wilhelm, *The Clewiston Test* (New York: Farrar, Straus & Giroux, 1976), p. 143.

6. Sandra Miesel, Introduction to Andre Norton, *Witch World* (Boston, Gregg Press, 1977), p. xxii.

7. Vonda N. McIntyre, "Women in Science Fiction: A Symposium," in *Khatru*, edited by Jeffrey D. Smith (Phantasmicon Press Publication #41, Issues 3 and 4, November 1975), p. 6. Another problem has been a traditional one: the family responsibilities of women have delayed their entrance

into sf (as in everything else) until they are older. A few have mentioned, in various publications, the difficulty in writing while young children are still at home. Male writers have solved this problem by living alone or having wives willing to keep distractions out of the work area, two solutions more difficult for women until recently. Men often have more self-confidence and more moral support from those around them.

Many male sf writers began writing and publishing while still in their teens or barely twenty: C. M. Kornbluth, Robert Silverberg, Hal Clement, Isaac Asimov, Michael Moorcock, Harlan Ellison, Frederik Pohl, Samuel R. Delany, Gardne R. Dozois, and many others have done so. A list of female writers of equal quality would show women who started later, many at thirty or close to it. There are of course exceptions: Robert Heinlein stated writing near the age of thirty, R. A. Lafferty in his late forties; Lisa Tuttle published stories while in her teens. But one of the most noted facts about sf authors as a group—their relative youth when they began to publish—has not applied to women until recently.

Happily, there are also cases of successful marriages between sf writers: C. L. Moore and Henry Kuttner, Leigh Brackett and Edmund Hamilton, E. Mayne Hull and A. E. van Vogt, Kate Wilhelm and Damon Knight.

8. Reported in *Janus* Vol. 2, No. 4, 1977 (edited by Janice Bogstad), and in *Windhaven*, Issue 1 (Atalanta Press, 1977, edited by Jessica Amanda Salmonson). The editor who rejected the novel is a woman. The publisher seems to have no qualms about books which are male-oriented and unlikely to appeal to women.

9. At a recent science fiction convention, organizers of a panel on women in sf were asked by a member of the convention's committee to avoid having "radical" types on the panel. The panel was then scheduled at the same time as a "belly-dancing" exhibition was being given elsewhere in the hotel.

10. Vonda McIntyre has said that while editing *Aurora: Beyond Equality*, a collection of non-sexist sf by women and men, she found that "virtually all non-sexist cultures portrayed included not only equality of men and women as a given, but reverence for other life and biological systems as well. The societies are basically communal and relatively nonmaterialistic." (*Khatru* 3 and 4, p. 119)

McIntyre and her co-editor, Susan Janice Anderson, also received less inspiring works. According to McIntyre: "We knew we would get lots of 'exotic means of getting pregnant' stories, and we did, from people who should have known better. Also a sprinkling of illegal pregnancy stories (a plot that has my vote for stupidest sf cliché of the century) . . .

"Some of the stories we got were unbelievable. 'My goodness aren't we all equal' lecture stories in which everyone talks about equality and acts like 1955. Joke stories: a man wants to sue the government because the ERA outlaws discrimination and he can't have children. (Translation: hahaha, isn't the very idea of the ERA funny?) One about trading wives, one about how women on welfare should have to serve as prostitutes. I've repressed as many as possible." (*Khatru* 3 and 4, pp. 38–39)

11. Marion Zimmer Bradley, "An Evolution of Consciousness," in *Science Fiction Review* (Issue 22, August 1977), edited by Richard E. Geis, p. 45.

12. Samuel Delany, in *Khatru* 3 and 4, cited a British editor who held the statement "women sf writers don't sell" as a given. The editor had purchased books by Ursula Le Guin; during the course of the conversation, the editor alternated between using the masculine and feminine pronouns when referring to Le Guin.

13. The degree to which stereotypical thinking can rule us was illustrated by comments made about Tiptree before her identity became known. One male author, in an introduction to a book of stories by Tiptree, wrote: "It has been suggested that Tiptree is female, a theory that I find absurd, for there is to me something ineluctably masculine about Tiptree's writing . . . [H]is . . . keen knowledge of the world of hunters and fishermen . . . would appear to prove him male." A female author, in a symposium on women and sf, criticized Tiptree for doing male "guilt-trips"; another participant, in response to one of Tiptree's remarks, said: ". . . now that's somebody's *son* speaking." Part of this can be seen as a tribute to Tiptree's skill in creating male characters. In our society, it may be close to impossible to avoid stereotypical thinking.

14. Kurt Vonnegut, Jr., *"Playboy* Interview," in *Wampeters, Foma & Granfalloons* (New York, Delacorte Press–Seymour Lawrence, 1974), p. 238.

THE NEW WOMEN OF WONDER

VIEW FROM THE MOON STATION

Planet, memory that floats
with white sails of cloud,
you buried my first shoes
in seaweed and my tears
ran into your storm drains.

Blueberries came down
from your hills to drink
among Sunday bells in town.

I wouldn't take back
one flame from the lantern,
one second iced white
on winter streets, not one
hurricane's howl when I lost
my fear of blowing away,
a stripped shingle.

On the far side
of an old globe you stand
traditional as a light
in the window,
blue beacon always visible.

—*Sonya Dorman*

∞

SCREWTOP
VONDA N. McINTYRE

*Vonda N. McIntyre received a B.S. from the
University of Washington, where she also
did graduate work in genetics. She won a
Nebula Award for her novelette "Of Mist,
and Grass, and Sand" and has published a
novel,* The Exile Waiting *(Fawcett-Gold
Medal); a second novel,* Dreamsnake, *will
be published by Houghton Mifflin. She was
also co-editor, with Susan Janice Anderson,
of* Aurora: Beyond Equality *(Fawcett-Gold
Medal), an anthology of feminist science fiction. In "Screwtop," she shows us a young
woman struggling to survive in a prison on
a distant world.*

Hot and wet from the fine, steamy rain, Kylis sat
on her heels at the top of the drilling pit and
waited for the second-duty shift to end. She rubbed
at a streak of the thick red mud that had spattered
her legs and her white boots when she walked
across the compound. Redsun's huge dim star altered colors; white became a sort of pinkish gray.
But among the forest's black foliage and against the
Pit's clay, white uniforms stood out and made prisoners easier for the guards to see.

A few other people waited with Kylis at the south
end of the deep slash in the earth. Like them, she
crouched unsheltered from the rain, strands of wet

hair plastered to her cheeks, watching for friends she had not seen in forty days.

Below lay two completed generator domes; above them rose the immense delicate cooling towers, and the antenna beaming power along the relay system to North Continent. Fences and guards protected the finished installations from the prisoners. Kylis and the rest worked only on clearing the fern forest, extending the Pit, drilling a third steam well—the dirty, dangerous jobs.

Paralleling the distant wall of volcanoes in the east, the drill pit extended northward. Its far end was invisible, obscured by the rain and by clouds of acrid smoke that billowed from the trash piles. The Pit was being lengthened again to follow the fault line where drilling was most efficient. Another strip of frond forest had been destroyed, and its huge primitive ferns now lay in blackened heaps. The stalks never burned completely, but until the coals died, a bank of irritating smoke and sticky ash would hang over the prison camp. The fine rain sizzled into steam when it fell on glowing embers.

Kylis started at the long shrill siren that ended the second shift. For an instant she was afraid the hallucinations had returned, but the normal sounds of the prison responded to the signal. The faraway roar of bulldozers ceased; the high whine of the drill slipped down in pitch and finally stopped. People left their machines, threw down their tools, and straggled toward the trail. They passed beneath the guards' towers, watched and counted by the Lizard's crew. One by one and in occasional pairs they started up the steep slope of clay and debris and volcanic ash, picking their way around gullies and across muddy rivulets. Screwtop seemed very quiet now, almost peaceful, with no noise but the hum of turbines in the two geothermal power plants, and the rhythmic clatter of the pumps that kept the drill pit unflooded.

Kylis could not yet see Jason. She frowned. He and Gryf, who was on the third shift, had both been all right when she got off duty. She was sure of that, for news of accidents traveled instantaneously between working crews. But Kylis had been alone, sleeping much of the time, in the nine hours since the end of her shift. Anything could happen in nine hours. She tried to reassure herself about her friends' safety, because the pattern and rhythm of the work just ended had been too normal to follow a really bad accident.

She could not put aside her anxiety and knew she would not until she had seen and spoken to and touched both Gryf and Jason. She still found herself surprised that she could care so much about two other human beings. Her past life had depended on complete independence and self-sufficiency.

Below, Gryf would be standing in the group of prisoners near the drilling rig. She tried to make him out, but the only person she could distinguish at this distance was the guard captain, called by everyone —when he was out of earshot—the Lizard, for his clean-shaven face and head gave him a smoothly impervious reptilian appearance. He was standing alone, facing the prisoners, giving orders. He wore black, as if in defiance of the heat, as a symbol of his superiority over everyone else in the camp. Even so, he was conspicuous now only because he was separated from the others. Gryf was conspicuous in any crowd, but the rig was too far away for Kylis to identify even Gryf's astonishing ebony-and-tan calico-patterned skin. The first time she had seen him, his first day at Screwtop, she had stared at him so long that he noticed and laughed at her. It was not a ridiculing laugh, but an understanding one. Gryf laughed at himself, too, sometimes, and often at the people who had made him what he was.

Gryf was the first tetraparental Kylis had ever seen or heard of, and even among tetras Gryf was unusual. Of his four biological parents, it happened that two of them were dark, and two fair. Gryf had been planned to be a uniform light brown, only his hair, perhaps, varicolored. Genes for hair color did not blend like those for skin. But the sets of sperm and ova had been matched wrong, so the mixture of two embryos forming Gryf made him his strange paisley pattern. He still had all the selectable intellectual gifts of his various parents. Those qualities, not his skin, were important.

New tetraparentals were special; the life of each was fully planned. Gryf was part of a team, and it was inconceivable to the government of Redsun and to the other tetras that after all the work of making him, after all the training and preparation, he would refuse his duty. When he did, he was sent for punishment to Redsun's strictest prison. If he changed his mind, he could at a word return to the tetras' secluded retreat. He had been at Screwtop half a year and he had not said that word.

Kylis was no Redsun native; she was oblivious to the others' awe of Gryf. She was curious about him. Neither because of nor in spite of the pattern of his skin, he was beautiful. Kylis wondered how his hair would feel, the locks half black and wiry, half blond and fine.

He was assigned to a nearby crew. Kylis saw immediately that he had been given hard and dirty jobs, not the most dangerous ones but those most tiring. The guards' task was not to kill him but to make life so unpleasant that he would return to the tetras.

Kylis waited to speak to him until she would not risk discipline for either of them. Without seeming to, the Lizard was watching Gryf closely, padding by every so often in his stealthy, silent way, his close-set eyes heavy-lidded, the direction of his gaze impossible to determine. But eventually his duties took him to another part of the camp, and Kylis left her own work to tell Gryf the tricks experience had taught her to make the labor a little easier.

Their first night together was Gryf's first night at Screwtop. When the shift ended, it seemed natural to walk back to the prisoners' shelters together. They were too tired to do much more than sleep, but the companionship was a comfort and the potential for more existed. They lay facing each other in the darkness. Starlight shone through a break in the clouds and glinted from the blond locks of Gryf's hair.

"I may never be let out of here," Gryf said. He was not asking for sympathy, but telling her his future as best he knew it. He had a pleasant, musical voice. Kylis realized these were the first words she heard him say. But she remembered his thanking her for her advice—and recalled that he had thanked her with his smile and a nod and the look in his eyes.

"I'm in for a long time," Kylis said. "I don't think there's that much difference between us." Screwtop could kill either of them the next day or the day before release.

Kylis reached up and touched Gryf's hair. It was stiff and matted with sweat. He took her hand and kissed her grimy palm. From then on they stayed together, growing closer but never speaking of a future outside the prison.

Several sets later Jason arrived and changed everything.

Kylis brought herself back to the present. She knew Gryf was below somewhere, though she could not make him out in the blotch of dirty white. She had been on the last shift during a previous set and she knew the schedule. The prisoners still working would not be exposed to much more danger today. Instead, they would have the dullest and most exhausting job of the period. During the last shift before the free day, once every forty days, all the equipment was cleaned and inspected. Anything done wrong was done over; the shift could drag on long past its normal end. Kylis hoped that would not happen this time.

At the bottom of the slope, Jason emerged from the bright cancer of machinery. He was muddy and grease-spattered, gold-flecked with bleached hair. He was very large and very fair, and even on Redsun where the light had little ultraviolet he sunburned easily. Though he had been working from dusk to mid-morning his legs were horizontally striped with sunburn, darkest at the top of his thighs and lightest just below his knees, marking the different levels to which he had pulled the cuffs of his boots. Right now they were folded all the way down.

He glanced up and saw Kylis. His carriage changed; he straightened and waved. His blond beard was bristly and uncombed and his hair was plastered down with sweat. The waistband of his shorts was red with mud spattered onto his body and washed down by perspiration and rain. As he came closer she saw that he was thinner, and that the lines around his eyes had deepened. They had been lines of thought and laughter; now they were of fatigue and exposure. He hurried toward her, slipping on the clay, and she realized he, too, had been worried.

He heard I was in sensory deprivation, she thought, and he was afraid for me. She stood motionless for a few seconds. She was not quite used to him yet; his easy acceptance of her and his concern seemed innocent and admirable compared to the persistent distrust Kylis had felt toward him for so long. She started forward to meet him.

He stopped and held out his hands. She touched him, and he came forward, almost trembling, holding himself taut against exhaustion. His pose collapsed. Bending down, he rested his forehead on her shoulder. She put her hands on his back, very gently.

"Was it bad?" His voice was naturally low but now it was rough and hoarse. He had probably been directing his crew, shouting above the roar of machinery for eighteen hours.

"Bad enough," Kylis said. "I've been glad of the work since."

Still leaning against her, he shook his head.

"I'm okay now. I've quit hallucinating," she said, hoping it was true. "And you? Are you all right?"

She could feel his breath on her damp shoulder.

"Yes. Now. Thanks to Gryf."

Jason had started this set on first day shift, which began at midnight and ended in the afternoon. Its members worked through the hottest part of the day when they were most tired. Halfway through his third work period Jason had collapsed. He was delirious and dehydrated, sunburned even through his shirt. The sun drained him. Gryf, just getting off when Jason fell, had worked through his own sleep period to finish Jason's shift. For them to switch shifts, Gryf had worked almost two of Redsun's days straight. When Kylis heard about that, she could not see how anyone could do it, even Gryf.

Gryf had broken the rules, but no one had made Jason go back to his original shift. The Lizard must never have said anything about it. Kylis could imagine him standing in shadow, watching, while Gryf waited for a confrontation that never came. It was something the Lizard would do.

Jason's shoulders were scarred where blisters had formed in the sun, but Kylis saw that they had healed cleanly. She put her arm around Jason's waist to support him. "Come on. I found a place to sleep." They were both sticky with sweat and the heat.

"Okay." They crossed the barren mud where all the vegetation had been stripped away so the machines could pass. Before they turned off the path they drew rations from the mechanical dispenser near the prisoners' quarters. The tasteless bars dropped through a slot, two each. There were times in Kylis' life when she had not eaten well, but she had seldom eaten anything as boring as prison rations. Jason put one of his bars into his belt pouch.

"When are you going to give that up?"

Jason nibbled a corner of his second ration bar. "I'm not." His grin made the statement almost a joke. He saved part of his food against what Kylis thought ludicrous plans of escape. When he had saved enough supplies, he was going to hike out through the marsh.

"You don't have to save anything today." She slipped her tag back into the slot and kept reinserting it until the extra points were used and a small pile of ration bars lay in the hopper.

"They forgot to void my card for the time I was in the deprivation box," Kylis said. In sensory deprivation, one of the prison's punishments for mistakes, she had been fed intravenously. She gave Jason the extra food. He thanked her and put it in his belt pouch. Together they crossed the bare clay and entered the forest.

Jason had been at Screwtop only three sets. He was losing weight quickly here, for he was a big-boned man with little fat to burn. Kylis hoped his family would discover where he was and ransom him soon. And she hoped they would find him before he tried to run away, though she had stopped trying to argue him out of the dream. The marsh was impassable except by hovercraft. There were no solid paths through it, and people claimed it held undiscovered animals that would crush a boat or raft. Kylis neither believed nor disbelieved in the animals; she was certain only that a few prisoners had tried to escape during her time at Screwtop, and the guards had not even bothered to look for them. Redsun was not a place where the authorities allowed escape toward freedom, only toward death.

The naked volcanoes cut off escape to the north and east with their barren lava escarpments and billowing clouds of poison gas; the marsh barred west and south. Screwtop was an economical prison, requiring fences only to protect the guards' quarters and the power domes, not to enclose the captives. And even if Jason could escape alive, he could never get off Redsun. He did not have Kylis' experience at traveling undetected.

The fern forest's shadows closed in around them, and they walked between the towering blackish-red stalks and lacy fronds. The foliage was heavy with huge droplets formed slowly by the misty rain. Kylis brushed past a leaf and the water cascaded down her side, making a faint track in the ashes and mud on her skin. She had washed herself when she got off duty, but staying clean was impossible at Screwtop.

They reached the sleeping place she had discovered. Several clumps of ferns had grown together and died, the stems falling over to make a conical shelter. Kylis pulled aside a handful of withered fronds and showed Jason in. Outside it looked like nothing but a pile of dead plants.

"It isn't even damp," he said, surprised. "And it's almost cool in here." He sat down on the carpet of dead moss and ferns and leaned back smiling. "I don't see how you found it. I never would have looked in here."

Kylis sat beside him. A few hours ago she had slept the soundest sleep she had had in Screwtop. The shade alleviated the heat, and the fronds kept the misty rain from drifting inside and collecting. Best of all, it was quiet.

"I thought you and Gryf would like it."

"Have you seen him?"

"Only across the compound. He looked all right."

Jason said aloud what Kylis feared. "The Lizard must have had a reason for letting him take my shift. To make it harder on him." He too was worried, and Kylis could see he felt guilty. "I shouldn't have let him do it," he said.

"Have you ever tried to stop him from doing something he thinks he should?"

Jason smiled. "No. I don't think I want to." He let himself sink further down in the moss. "Gods," he said, drawing out the word. "It's good to see you."

"It's been lonely," Kylis said, with the quiet sort of wonder she felt every time she realized that she did care enough to miss someone. Loneliness was more painful now, but she was not lonely all the time. She did not know how to feel about her newly discovered pleasure in the company of Gryf and Jason. Sometimes it frightened her. They had broached her defenses of solitude and suspicion, and at times she felt exposed and vulnerable. She trusted them, but there were even more betrayers at Screwtop than there were outside.

"I didn't give you those extra rations so you could save them all," she said. "I gave them to you so you'd stop starving yourself for one day at least."

"We could all get out of here," he said, "if we saved just a little more food." Even at midmorning, beneath the ferns, it was almost too dark to make out his features, but Kylis knew he was not joking. She said nothing. Jason thought the prisoners who

fled into the marsh were still alive there; he thought
he could join them and be helped. Kylis thought
they were all dead. Jason believed escape on foot
possible, and Kylis believed it death. Jason was an
optimist, and Kylis was experienced.

"All right," Jason said. "I'll eat one more. In a
while." He lay down flat and put his hands behind
his head.

"How was your shift?" Kylis asked.

"Too much fresh meat."

Kylis grinned. Jason was talking like a veteran,
hardened and disdainful of new prisoners, the fresh
meat, who had not yet learned the ways of Screwtop.

"We only got a couple new people," she said.
"You must have had almost the whole bunch."

"It would have been tolerable if three of them
hadn't been assigned to the drilling rig."

"Did you lose any?"

"No. By some miracle."

"We were fresh once too. Gryf's the only one
I ever saw who didn't start out doing really stupid
things."

"Was I really that fresh?"

She did not want to hurt his feelings or even
tease him.

"I was, wasn't I?"

"Jason . . . I'm sorry, but you were the freshest
I ever saw. I didn't think you had any chance at
all. Only Gryf did."

"I hardly remember anything about the first set,
except how much time he spent helping me."

"I know," Kylis said. Jason had needed a great

deal of help. Kylis had forgiven him for being the cause of her first real taste of loneliness, but she could not quite forget it.

"Gods—this last set," Jason said. "I didn't know how bad it was alone." Then he smiled. "I used to think I was a solitary person." Where Kylis was contemptuous of her discovered weaknesses, Jason was amused at and interested in his. "What did you do before Gryf came?"

"Before Gryf came, I didn't know how bad it was alone, either," she said rather roughly. "You'd better get some sleep."

He smiled. "You're right. Good morning." He fell asleep instantly.

Relaxed, he looked tireder. His hair had grown long enough to tie back, but it had escaped from its knot and curled in tangled, dirty tendrils around his face. Jason hated being dirty, but working with the drill left little energy for extras, like bathing. He would never really adjust to Screwtop as Gryf and Kylis had. His first day here, Gryf had kept him from being killed or crippled at least twice. Kylis had been working on the same shift but a different crew, driving one of the bulldozers and clearing another section of forest. The drill could not be set up among the giant ferns, because the ground itself would not stand much stress. Beneath a layer of humus was clay, so wet that in response to pressure it turned semiliquid, almost like quicksand. The crews had to strip off the vegetation and the layers of clay and volcanic ash until bedrock lay exposed. Kylis drove the dozer back and forth, cutting through ferns in a much wider path than the power plants themselves would have required. She had to make room for the excavated earth, which was piled well back from the Pit's edges. Even so the slopes sometimes collapsed in mud-slides.

At the end of the day of Jason's arrival, the siren went off, and Kylis drove the dozer to the old end of the Pit and into the recharging stall. Gryf was waiting for her, and a big fair man was with him, sitting slumped on the ground with his head between his knees and his hands limp on the ground. Kylis hardly noticed him. She took Gryf's hand, to walk with him back to the shelters, but he quietly stopped her and helped the other man to his feet. The new prisoner's expression was blank with exhaustion; in the dawn light he looked deathly pale. Hardly anyone on Redsun was as fair as he, even in the north. Kylis supposed he was from off-world, but he did not have the shoulder tattoo that would have made her trust him instantly. But Gryf was half carrying the big clumsy man, so she supported him on the other side. Together she and Gryf got him to their shelter. He neither ate nor drank nor even spoke, but collapsed on the hard lumpy plat-form and fell asleep. Gryf watched him with a troubled expression.

"Who is that?" Kylis did not bother to hide the note of contempt in her voice.

Gryf told her the man's name, which was long and complicated and contained a lot of double vowels. She never remembered it all, even now. "He says to call him Jason."

"Did you know him before?" She was willing to

help Gryf save an old friend, though she did not quite see how they would do it. In one day he had spent himself completely.

"No," Gryf said. "But I read his work. I never thought I'd get to meet him."

The undisguised awe in Gryf's voice hurt Kylis, not so much because she was jealous as because it reminded her how limited her own skills were. The admiration in the faces of drunks and children in spaceport bazaars, which Kylis had experienced, was nothing compared to Gryf's feeling for the accomplishments of this man.

"Is he in here for writing a book?"

"No, thank gods—they don't know who he is. They think he's a transient. He travels under his personal name instead of his family name. They are making him work for his passage home."

"How long?"

"Six sets."

"Oh, Gryf."

"He must live and be released."

"If he's important, why hasn't anybody ransomed him?"

"His family doesn't know where he is. They would have to be contacted in secret. If the government finds out who he is, they will never let him go. His books are smuggled in."

Kylis shook her head.

"He affected my life, Kylis. He helped me understand the idea of freedom. And personal responsibility. The things you have known all your life from your own experience."

"You mean you wouldn't be here except for him."

"I never thought of it that way, but you are right."

"Look at him, Gryf. This place will grind him up."

Gryf stared somberly at Jason, who slept so heavily he hardly seemed to breathe. "He should not be here. He's a person who should not be hurt."

"We should?"

"He's different."

Kylis did not say Jason would be hurt at Screwtop. Gryf knew that well enough.

Jason had been hurt, and he had changed. What Gryf had responded to in his work was a pure idealism and innocence that could not exist in captivity. Kylis had been afraid Jason would fight the prison by arming himself with its qualities; she was afraid of what they would do to Gryf. But Jason had survived by growing more mature, by retaining his humor, not by becoming brutal. Kylis had never read a word he had written, but the longer she knew him, the more she liked and admired him.

Now she left him sleeping among the ferns. She had slept as much as she wanted to for the moment. She knew from experience that she had to time her sleeping carefully on the day off. In the timeless environment of space, where she had spent most of her life, Kylis' natural circadian rhythm was about twenty-three hours. A standard day of twenty-four did not bother her, but Redsun's twenty-seven hour rotation made her uncomfortable. She could not afford to sleep too much or too little and return to work exhausted and inattentive. At Screwtop inattention was worth punishment at best, and at worst, death.

She was no longer tired, but she was hungry for anything besides the tasteless prison rations. The vegetation on Redsun, afflicted with a low mutation rate, had not evolved very far. The plants were not yet complex enough to produce fruiting bodies. Some of the stalks and roots, though, were edible.

On Redsun, there were no flowers.

Kylis headed deeper into the shadows of the rain forest. Away from the clearings people had made, the primitive plants reached great heights. Kylis wandered among them, her feet sinking into the soft moist humus. Her footprints remained distinct. She turned and looked back. Only a few paces behind her, seeping water had already formed small pools in the deeper marks of her bootheels.

She wished she and Gryf and Jason had been on the same shift. As it was, half of their precious free time would be spent sleeping and readjusting their time schedules. When Gryf finally got off, they would have less than one day together, even before he rested. Sometimes Kylis felt that the single free day in every forty was more a punishment than if the prisoners had been forced to work their sentences straight through. The brief respite allowed them to remember just how much they hated Screwtop, and just how impossible it was to escape.

Since she could not be with both her friends, she preferred complete solitude. For Kylis it was almost instinctive to make certain no one could follow her. Unfolding the cuffs of her boots, she protected her legs to halfway up her thighs. She did not seal the boots to her shorts because of the heat.

The floor of the forest dipped and rose gently, forming wide hollows where the rain collected.

Kylis stepped into one of the huge shallow pools and waded across it, walking slowly, feeling ahead with her toe before she put her foot down firmly. The mist and shadows, the reddish sunlight, and the glassy surface created illusions that concealed occasional deep pits. Where the water lay still and calm, microscopic parasites crawled out of the earth and swarmed. They normally reproduced inside small fishes and primitive amphibians, but they were not particular about their host. They would invade a human body through a cut or abrasion, causing agonizing muscle lesions. Sometimes they traveled slowly to the brain. The forest was no place to fall into a water hole.

Avoiding one deep spot, Kylis reached the far bank and stepped out onto a slick outcropping of rock where her footprints would not show. When the stone ended and she reentered the frond forest, the ground was higher and less sodden, although the misty rain still fell continuously.

The ferns thinned, the ground rose steeply, and Kylis began to climb. At the top of the hill the air stirred, and the vegetation was not so thick. Kylis found some edible shoots, picked them, and peeled them carefully. The pulp was spicy and crunchy. The juice, pungent and sour, trickled down her throat. She picked a few more stalks and tied the small bundle to her belt. Those that were sporing, she was careful not to disturb. Edible plants no longer grew near camp; in fact, nothing edible grew close enough to Screwtop to reach on any but the free day.

Redsun traveled upright in its circular orbit; it had no seasons. The plants had no sun-determined clock by which to synchronize their reproduction, so a few branches of any one plant or a few plants of any one species would spore while the rest remained asexual. A few days later a different random set would begin. It was not a very efficient method of spreading traits through the gene pool, but it had sufficed until people came along and destroyed fertile plants as well as spored-out ones. Kylis, who had noticed in her wanderings that evolution ceased at the point when human beings arrived and began to make their changes, tried not to cause that kind of damage.

A flash of white, a movement, caught the edge of her vision. She froze, wishing the hallucinations away but certain they had come back. White was not a natural color in the frond forest, not even the muddy pink that passed for white under Redsun's enormous star. But no strange fantasy creatures paraded around her; she heard no furious imaginary sounds. Her feet remained firmly on the ground, the warm fine rain hung around her, the ferns drooped with their burden of droplets. Slowly Kylis turned until she faced the direction of the motion. She was not alone.

She moved quietly forward until she could look through the black foliage. What she had seen was the uniform of Screwtop, white boots, white shorts, white shirt for anyone with a reason to wear it. One of the other prisoners sat on a rock, looking out across the forest, toward the swamp. Tears rolled slowly down her face, though she made no sound. Miria.

Feeling only a little guilty about invading her privacy, Kylis watched her, as she had been watching her for some time. Kylis thought Miria was a survivor, someone who would leave Screwtop without being broken. She kept to herself; she had no partners. Kylis had admired her tremendous capacity for work. She was taller than Kylis, bigger, potentially stronger, but clearly unaccustomed to great physical labor. For a while she had worn her shirt tied up under her breasts, but like most others she had discarded it because of the heat.

Miria survived in the camp without using other people or allowing herself to be used. Except when given a direct order, she acted as if the guards simply did not exist, in effect defying them without giving them a reasonable excuse to punish her. They did not always wait for reasonable excuses. Miria received somewhat more than her share of pain, but her dignity remained intact.

Kylis retreated a couple of steps, then came noisily out of the forest, giving Miria a few seconds to wipe away her tears if she wanted to. But when Kylis stopped, pretending to be surprised at finding another person so near, Miria simply turned toward her.

"Hello, Kylis."

Kylis went closer. "Is anything wrong?" That was such a silly question that she added, "I mean, is there anything I can do?"

Miria's smile erased the lines of tension in her forehead and revealed laugh lines Kylis had never noticed before. "No," Miria said. "Nothing anyone can do. But thank you."

"I guess I'd better go."

"Please don't," Miria said quickly. "I'm so tired of being alone—" She cut herself off and turned away, as if she were sorry to have revealed so much of herself. Kylis knew how she felt. She sat down nearby.

Miria looked out again over the forest. The fronds were a soft reddish black. The marsh trees were harsher, darker, interspersed with gray patches of water. Beyond the marsh, over the horizon, lay an ocean that covered all of Redsun except the large inhabited North Continent and the tiny South Continent where the prison camp lay.

Kylis could see the ugly scar of the pits where the crews were still drilling, but Miria had her back half turned and she gazed only at unspoiled forest.

"It could all be so beautiful," Miria said.

"Do you really think so?" Kylis thought it ugly— the black foliage, the dim light, the day too long, the heat, no animals except insects that did not swim or crawl. Redsun was the most nearly intolerable planet she had ever been on.

"Yes. Don't you?"

"No. I don't see any way I ever could."

"It's sometimes hard, I know," Miria said. "Sometimes, when I'm tiredest, I even feel the same. But the world's so rich and so strange—don't you see the challenge?"

"I only want to leave it," Kylis said.

Miria looked at her for a moment, then nodded. "You're not from Redsun, are you?"

Kylis shook her head.

"No, there's no reason for you to have the same feelings as someone born here."

This was a side of Miria that Kylis had never seen, one of quiet but intense dedication to a world whose rulers had imprisoned her. Despite her liking for Miria, Kylis was confused. "How can you feel

that way when they've sent you here? I hate them,
I hate this place—"

"Were you wrongly arrested?" Miria asked with
sympathy.

"They could have just deported me. That's what
usually happens."

"Sometimes injustice is done," Miria said sadly.
"I know that. I wish it wouldn't happen. But I de-
serve to be here, and I know that too. When my
sentence is completed, I'll be forgiven."

More than once Kylis had thought of staying on
some world and trying to live the way other people
did, even of accepting punishment, if necessary, but
what had always stopped her was the doubt that
forgiveness was often, or ever, fully given. Redsun
seemed an unlikely place to find amnesty.

"What did you do?"

Kylis felt Miria tense and wished she had not
asked. Not asking questions about the past was one
of the few tacit rules among the prisoners.

"I'm sorry . . . it's not that I wouldn't tell you, but
I just cannot talk about it."

Kylis sat in silence for a few minutes, scuffing the
toe of her boot along the rock like an anxious
child and rubbing the silver tattoo on the point of
her left shoulder. The pigment caused irritation and
slight scarring. The intricate design had not hurt
for a long time, nor even itched, but she could feel
the delicate lines. Rubbing them was a habit. Even
though the tattoo represented a life to which she
would probably never return, it was soothing.

"What's that?" Miria asked. Abruptly she grimaced. "I'm sorry, I'm doing just what I asked you
not to do."

"It doesn't matter," Kylis said. "I don't mind. It's a spaceport rat tattoo. You get it when the other rats accept you." Despite everything, she was proud of the mark.

"What's a spaceport rat?"

That Miria was unfamiliar with the rats did not surprise Kylis. Few Redsun people had ever heard of them. On almost every other world Kylis ever visited, the rats were, if not exactly esteemed, at least admired. Some places she had been actively worshiped. Even where she was officially unwelcome, the popular regard was high enough to prevent the kind of entrapment Redsun had started.

"I used to be one. It's what everybody calls people who sneak on board starships and live in them and in spaceports. We travel all over."

"That sounds . . . interesting," Miria said. "But didn't it bother you to steal like that?"

A year before, Kylis would have laughed at the question, even knowing, as she did, that Miria was quite sincere. But recently Kylis had begun to wonder: Might something be more important than outwitting spaceport security guards? While she was wondering, she came to Redsun, so she never had a chance to find out.

"I started when I was ten," Kylis said to Miria. "So I didn't think of it like that."

"You sneaked onto a starship when you were only ten?"

"Yes."

"All by yourself?"

"Until the others start to recognize you, no one will help you much. It's possible. And I thought it was my only chance to get away from where I was."

"You must have been in a terrible place."

"It's hard to remember if it was really as bad as I think. I can remember my parents, but never smiling, only yelling at each other and hitting me."

Miria shook her head. "That's terrible, to be driven away by your own people—to have nowhere to grow up. . . . Did you ever go back?"

"I don't think so."

"What?"

"I can't remember much about where I was born. I always thought I'd recognize the spaceport, but there might have been more than one, so maybe I have been back and maybe I haven't. The thing is, I can't remember what they called the planet. Maybe I never knew."

"I cannot imagine it—not to know who you are or where you come from or even who your parents were."

"I know *that*," Kylis said.

"You could find out about the world. Fingerprints or ship records or regression—"

"I guess I could. If I ever wanted to. Sometime I might even do it, if I ever get out of here."

"I'm sorry we stopped you. Really. It's just that we feel that everyone who can should contribute a fair share."

Kylis still found it hard to believe that after being sent to Screwtop Miria would include herself in Redsun's collective conscience, but she had said "we." Kylis only thought of authorities as "they."

She shrugged. "Spaceport rats know they can get caught. It doesn't happen too often and usually you hear that you should avoid the place."

"I wish you had."

"We take the chance." She touched the silver tattoo again. "You don't get one of these until you've proved you can be trusted. So when places use informers against us, we usually know who they are."

"But on Redsun you were betrayed?"

"I never expected them to use a child," Kylis said bitterly.

"A child!"

"This little kid sneaked on my ship. He did a decent job of it, and he reminded me of me. He was only ten or eleven, and he was all beat up. I guess we aren't so suspicious of kids because most of us started at the same age." Kylis glanced at Miria and saw that she was staring at her, horrified.

"They used a child? And injured him, just to catch you?"

"Does that really surprise you?"

"Yes," Miria said.

"Miria, half the people who were killed during the last set weren't more than five or six years older than the boy who turned me in. Most of the people being sent here now are that age. What could they possibly have done terrible enough to get them sent here?"

"I don't know," Miria said softly without looking up. "We need the power generators. Someone has to drill the steam wells. Some of us will die in the work. But you're right about the young people. I've been thinking about . . . other things. I had not noticed." She said that as if she had committed a crime, or more exactly a sin, by not noticing. "And the child . . ." Her voice trailed off and she smiled sadly at Kylis. "How old are you?"

"I don't know. Maybe twenty."

Miria raised one eyebrow. "Twenty? Older in experience, but not that old in time. You should not be here."

"But I am. I'll survive it."

"I think you will. And what then?"

"Gryf and Jason and I have plans."

"On Redsun?"

"Gods, no."

"Kylis," Miria said carefully, "you do not know much about tetraparentals, do you?"

"How much do I need to know?"

"I was born here. I used to . . . to work for them. Their whole purpose is their intelligence. Normal people like you and me bore them. They cannot tolerate us for long."

"Miria, stop it!"

"Your friend will only cause you pain. Give him up. Put him away from you. Urge him to go home."

"No! He knows I'm an ordinary person. We know what we're going to do."

"It makes no difference," Miria said with abrupt coldness. "He will not be allowed to leave Redsun."

Kylis felt the blood drain from her face. No one had ever said that so directly and brutally before. "They can't keep him. How long will they make him stay here before they realize they can't break him?"

"He is important. He owes Redsun his existence."

"But he's a person with his own dreams. They can't make him a slave!"

"His research team is worthless without him."

"I don't care," Kylis said.

"*You*—" Miria cut herself off. Her voice became much gentler. "They will try to persuade him to follow their plans. He may decide to do as they ask."

"I wouldn't feel any obligation to the people who run things on Redsun even if I lived here. Why should he be loyal to them? Why should you? What did they ever do but send you here? What will they let you do when you get out? Anything decent or just more dirty, murderous jobs like this one?" She realized she was shouting, and Miria looked stunned.

"I don't know," Miria said. "I don't know, Kylis. Please stop saying such dangerous things." She was terrified and shaken, much more upset than when she had been crying.

Kylis moved nearer and took her hand. "I'm sorry, Miria, I didn't mean to hurt you or say anything that could get you in trouble." She paused, wondering how far Miria's fear of Redsun's government might take her from her loyalty.

"Miria," she said on impulse, "have you ever thought of partnering with anybody?"

Miria hesitated so long that Kylis thought she would not answer. Kylis wondered if she had intruded on Miria's past again.

"No," Miria finally said. "Never."

"Would you?"

"Think about it? Or do it?"

"Both. Partner with me and Gryf and Jason. Not just here, but when we get out."

"No," Miria said. "No, I couldn't." She sounded frightened again.

"Because we want to leave Redsun?"

"Other reasons."

"Would you just think about it?"

Miria shook her head.

"I know you don't usually live in groups on Red-sun," Kylis said. "But where I was born, a lot of people did, even though my parents were alone. I remember, before I ran away, my friends were never afraid to go home like I was. Jason spent all his life in a group family, and he says it's a lot easier to get along." She was skipping over her own occasional doubts that any world could be as pleasant as the one Jason described. Whatever it was like, it had to be better than her own former existence of constant hiding and constant uncertainty; it had to be better than what Gryf told her of Red-sun, with its emphasis on loyalty to the government at the expense of any family structure too big to move instantly at the whim or order of the rulers.

Miria did not respond.

"Anyway, three people aren't enough—we thought we'd find others after we got out. But I think—"

"Gryf doesn't—" Miria interrupted Kylis, then stopped herself and started over. "They don't know you were going to ask me?"

"Not exactly, but they both know you," Kylis said defensively. She thought Miria might be afraid Kylis' partners would refuse her. Kylis knew they would not but could not put how she knew into proper words.

The rain had blurred away the marks of tears on Miria's cheeks, and now she smiled and squeezed Kylis' hand. "Thank you, Kylis," she said. "I wish I could accept. I can't, but not for the reasons you think. You'll find someone better." She started up, but Kylis stopped her.

"No, you stay here. This is your place." Kylis

stood. "If you change your mind, just say. All right?"

"I won't change my mind."

"I wish you wouldn't be so sure." Reluctantly, she started away.

"Kylis?"

"Yes?"

"Please don't tell anyone you asked me this."

"Not even Gryf and Jason?"

"No one. Please."

"All right," Kylis said unwillingly.

Kylis left Miria on the stony hillside. She glanced back once before entering the forest. Miria was sitting on the stone again, hunched forward, her forearms on her knees. Now she was looking down at the huge slash of clay and trash heaps, the complicated delicate cooling towers that condensed the generators' steam, the high impervious antenna beaming power north toward the cities.

When Kylis reached the sleeping place, the sun was high. Beneath the dead fern trees it was still almost cool. She crept in quietly and sat down near Jason without waking him. He lay sprawled in dry moss, breathing deeply, solid and real. As if he could feel her watching him, he half opened his eyes.

Kylis lay down and drew her hand up his side, feeling bones that had become more prominent, dry and flaking sunburned skin, and the scabs of cuts and scratches. He was bruised as though the guards had beaten him, perhaps because of his occasional amusement at things so odd that his reaction seemed insolence. But for now, she would not notice his new scars, and he would not notice hers.

"Are you awake?"

He laughed softly. "I think so."

"Do you want to go back to sleep?"

He reached out and touched her face. "I'm not that tired."

Kylis smiled and leaned over to kiss him. The hairs of his short beard were soft and stiff against her lips and tongue. For a while she and Jason could ignore the heat.

Lying beside Jason, not quite touching because the afternoon was growing hot, Kylis only dozed while Jason again slept soundly. She sat up and pulled on her shorts and boots, brushed a lock of Jason's sunstreaked hair from his damp forehead, and slipped outside. A couple of hours of Gryf's work shift remained, so Kylis headed toward the guards' enclosure and the hovercraft dock.

Beyond the drill-pit clearing, the forest extended for a short distance westward. The ground continued to fall, growing wetter and wetter, changing perceptibly into marsh. The enclosure, a hemispherical electrified fence completely covering the guards' residence domes, was built at the juncture of relatively solid land and shallow, standing water. It protected the hovercraft ramp, and it was invulnerable. She had tried to get through it. She had even tried to dig beneath it. Digging under a fence or cutting through one was something no spaceport rat would do, short of desperation. After her first few days at Screwtop, Kylis had been desperate. She had not believed she could survive her sentence in the prison. So, late that night, she crept over to the electrified fence and began to dig. At dawn she had not reached the bottom of the fence supports, and the ground was wet enough to start carrying electricity to her in small warning tingles.

Her shift would begin soon; guards would be coming in and going out, and she would be caught if she did not stop. She planned to cover over the hole she had dug and hope it was not discovered.

She was lying flat on the ground, digging a narrow deep hole with a flat rock and both hands, smeared all over with the red clay, her fingernails ripped past the quick. She reached down for one last handful of dirt, and grabbed a trap wire.

The current swept through her, contracting every muscle in her body. It lasted only an instant. She lay quivering, almost insensible, conscious enough to be glad the wire had been set to stun, not kill. She tried to get up and run, but she could not move properly. She began to shudder again. Her muscles were overstimulated, incapable of distinguishing a real signal. She ached all over, so badly that she could not even guess if the sudden clench of muscles had broken any bones.

A light shone toward her. She heard footsteps as the guards approached to investigate the alarm the trap wire had set off. The sound thundered through her ears, as though the electric current had heightened all her senses, toward pain. The footsteps stopped; the light beam blinded her, then left her face. Her dazzled vision blurred the figure standing over her, but she knew it was the Lizard. It occurred to her, in a vague, slow-motion thought, that she did not know his real name. (She learned later that no one else did either.) He dragged Kylis to her feet and held her upright, glaring at her, his face taut with anger and his eyes narrow.

"Now you know we're not as easy to cheat as starship owners," he said. His voice was low and raspy, softly hoarse. He let her go, and she collapsed again. "You're on probation. Don't make any more mistakes. And don't be late for duty."

The other guards followed him away. They did not even bother to fill in the hole she had dug.

Kylis had staggered through that workday; she survived it, and the next, and the next, until she knew that the work itself would not kill her. She did not try to dig beneath the fence again, but she still watched the hovercraft when it arrived.

By the time she reached her place of concealment on the bank above the fence, the hovercraft had already climbed the ramp and settled. The gate was locked behind it. Kylis watched the new prisoners being unloaded. The cargo bay door swung open. The people staggered out on deck and down the gangway, disoriented by the long journey in heat and darkness. One of the prisoners stumbled and fell to his knees, retching.

Kylis remembered how she had felt after so many hours in the pitch-dark hold. Even talking was impossible, for the engines were on the other side of the hold's interior bulkhead and the fans were immediately below. She was too keyed up to go into a trance, and a trance would be dangerous while she was crowded in with so many people.

The noise was what Kylis remembered most about coming to Screwtop—incessant, penetrating noise, the high whine of the engines and the roar

of the fans. She had been half deaf for days afterward. The compartment was small. Despite the
heat the prisoners could not avoid sitting and leaning against each other, and as soon as the engines
started, the temperature began to rise. By the time
the hovercraft reached the prison, the hold was
thick with the stench of human misery. Kylis hardly
noticed when the craft's sickening swaying ceased.
When the hatch opened and red light spilled in,
faintly dissipating the blackness, Kylis looked up
with all the others, and, like all the others, blinked
like a frightened animal.

The guards had no sympathy for cramped muscles or nausea. Their shouted commands faded like
faraway echoes through Kylis' abused hearing. She
pushed herself up, using the wall as support. Her
legs and feet were asleep. They began regaining
sensation, and she felt as if she were walking on
tiny knives. She hobbled out, but at the bottom of
the gangway she, too, had stumbled. A guard's
curse and the prod of his club brought her to her
feet in a fury, fists clenched, but she quelled her
violent temper instantly. The guard watched with
a smile, waiting. But Kylis had been to earth, where
one of the few animals left alive outside the game
preserves and zoos was the possum. She had learned
its lesson well.

Now she crouched on the bank and watched the
new prisoners realize, as she had, that the end of
the trip did not end the terrible heat. Screwtop was
almost on the equator of Redsun, and the heat and
humidity never lessened. Even the rain was luke-
warm.

The guards prodded the captives into a compact

group and turned hoses on them, spraying off filth and sweat. Afterward the new people plodded through the mud to the processing dome. Kylis watched each one pass through the doorway. She had never defined what she looked for when she watched the new arrivals, but whatever it was, she did not find it today. Even more of them were terribly young, and they all had the look of hopelessness that would make them nothing more than fresh meat, new bodies for the work to use up. Screwtop would grind them down and throw them away. They would die of disease or exhaustion or carelessness. Kylis did not see in one of them the spark of defiance that might get them through their sentences intact in body or spirit. But sometimes the spark only came out later, exposed by the real adversity of the work.

The hatch swung shut and the hovercraft's engines roared to full power. No one at all had been taken on board for release on North Continent.

The boat quivered on its skirts and floated back down the ramp, through the entrance, onto the glassy gray surface of the water. The gate sparked shut. Kylis was vaguely disappointed, for the landing was no different from any she had seen since she was brought to Screwtop herself. There was no way to get on board the boat. The familiar admission still annoyed her. For a spaceport rat, admitting defeat to the safeguards of an earthbound vehicle was humiliating. She could not even think of a way to get herself out of Screwtop, much less herself and Gryf and Jason. She was afraid that if she did not find some chance of escape, Jason might really try to flee through the swamp.

She ran her fingers through her short black hair and shook her head, flinging out the misty rain that gathered in huge drops and slipped down her face and neck and back. The heat and the rain—she hated both.

In an hour or two the evening rain would fall in solid sheets, washing the mist away. But an hour after that the faint infuriating droplets would begin again. They did not seem to fall, but hung in the air and collected on skin, on hair, beneath trees, inside shelters.

Kylis grabbed an overhanging plant and stripped off a few of its red-black fronds, flinging them to the ground in anger.

She stood up, but suddenly crouched down in hiding again. Below, Miria walked up to the fence, placed her hand against the palm lock, and waited, glancing over her shoulder as if making certain she was alone. As the gate swung open and Miria, a prisoner, walked alone and free into the guards' enclosure, Kylis felt her knees grow weak. Miria stopped at a dome, and the door opened for her. Kylis thought she could see the Lizard in the dimness beyond.

Almost the only thing this could mean was that Miria was a spy. Kylis began to tremble in fear and anger, fear of what Miria could tell the Lizard that would help him increase the pressure on Gryf, anger at herself for trusting Miria. She had made another mistake in judgment like the one that had imprisoned her, and this time the consequences could be much worse.

She sat in the mud and the rain trying to think, until she realized that Gryf would be off work in only a few minutes. She did not even have time to wake Jason.

When Kylis turned her back on the guards' domes, Miria had not yet come out.

Kylis was a few minutes late reaching the drill pit. The third shift had already ended; all the prisoners were out and drifting away. Gryf was nowhere around, and he was nothing if not conspicuous. She began to worry, because Gryf was frequently first out, never last—he did not seem to tire. Certainly he would wait for her.

She stood indecisively, worried, thinking, He might have wanted something in the shelter.

She did not believe that for a moment. She glanced back toward the bottom of the Pit.

Everything happened at once. She forgot about Miria, Lizard, the prison. She cried out for Jason, knowing her voice would not carry that far. She ran downhill, fighting the clay that sucked at her feet. Two people she knew slightly trudged up the hill— Troi, skeletal, sharp-featured, sardonic, and Chuzo, squarely built and withdrawn. Both were very young; both were aging quickly here.

They supported Gryf between them.

Ash and grease disguised the pattern of his paisley skin. Kylis knew he was alive only because no one at Screwtop would spend any energy on someone who was dead. When she was closer, she could see the ends of deep slashes made by the whip where it had curled around his body. Blood had dried in narrow streaks on his sides. His wrists were abraded where he had been tied for the punishment.

"Oh, Gryf—"

Hearing her, Gryf raised his head. She felt great relief.

Troi and Chuzo stopped when Kylis reached them.

"The Lizard ordered it himself," Troi said bitterly. Screwtop held few amenities, but people were seldom flogged on the last day of the shift.

"Why?"

"I don't know. I was too far away. Anything. Nothing. What reason do they ever have?"

Kylis quieted her anger for the moment. She took over for Chuzo. "Thank you," she said, quite formally.

Troi stayed where he was. "Get him to the top, anyway," he said in his gruff manner.

"Gryf? Can you make it?"

He tightened his hand on her shoulder. They started up the steep path. When they finally reached the top, the immense sun had set. The sky was pink and scarlet in the west, and the volcanoes eastward glowed blood red.

"Thanks," Kylis said again. Chuzo hesitated, but Troi nodded and left. After a moment Chuzo followed him.

Gryf leaned heavily on her, but she could support him. She tried to turn toward the shelters and their meager stock of medical supplies, but he resisted weakly and guided her toward the waterfall. If he wanted to go there first, he must think his wounds had been contaminated.

"Gods," Kylis whispered. Clumsily, they hurried. She wished Jason had heard her, for with him they could have gone faster. It was her fault he was not there. She could not hold Gryf up alone without hurting his back.

Gryf managed a smile, just perceptible, telling her, I hurt but I am strong.

Yes, Kylis thought, stronger than Jason, stronger than me. We'll survive.

They continued.

"Kylis! Gryf!"

Gryf stopped. Kylis let him, with relief. Jason splashed toward them.

Gryf's knees buckled. Kylis strained to keep him out of the mud, away from more parasites. Jason reached them and picked Gryf up.

"Could you hear me?" Kylis asked.

"No," Jason said. "I woke up and came looking. Where are you taking him?"

"To the overflow pipe."

Jason needed no explanation of the dangers of infection. He carried Gryf toward the waterfall, swearing softly.

The cooling towers from the steam wells produced the only safe water the prisoners had for bathing. It spewed from a pipe to a concrete platform and spilled from there to the ground, forming a muddy pool that spread into the forest. The water was too hot for anyone to go directly beneath the cascade. Jason stopped in knee-deep hot water. They were all standing in heavy spray.

Jason held Gryf against his chest while Kylis splashed water on Gryf's back from her cupped hands. She washed him as gently as she could and still be safe. She found no parasites and none of their eggs. The water swept away mud and sweat, turning Jason bright pink and Kylis auburn and Gryf all shades of dark brown and tan.

Kylis cursed the Lizard. He knew he would look bad in the eyes of the tetra committee if Gryf were crushed or bled to death or went home with everything but his brain. But he would look worse if he could not force Gryf to go home at all.

Gryf's eyelids flickered. His eyes were bright blue, flecked irregularly with black.

"How do you feel?"

He smiled, but he had been hurt—she could see the memory of pain. They had touched his spirit. He looked away from her and made Jason let him turn. He staggered. His knees would not support him, which seemed to surprise him. Jason held him up, and Gryf took the last thin flake of antiseptic soap from Kylis' hand.

"What's the matter?" she asked.

Gryf turned her around. For a moment his touch was painful, then she felt the sharp sting of soap on raw flesh. Gryf showed her his hand, which glittered with a mass of tiny, fragile eggs like mica flakes. Gryf used up her soap scrubbing her side, and Jason got out what soap he had left.

"This cut's pretty deep but it's clean now. You must have fallen and smashed a nest."

"I don't remember—" She had a kinesthetic memory, from running down into the Pit. "Yes, I do . . ." It hit her then, a quick shock of the fear of what might have been—paralysis, senility, agony—if Gryf had not noticed, if the eggs had healed beneath her skin and hatched. Kylis shuddered.

They returned to the compound, supporting Gryf

between them. The wall-less, stilt-legged shelters were almost deserted.

Jason climbed the slanted ladder to their shelter backward, leaning against it for stability while he helped Gryf. The steps were slick with yellow lichen. Kylis chinned herself onto the platform. In their floor locker she had to paw through little stacks of Jason's crumbling ration bars before she found their mold poultice and the web box. She had been very hungry, but she had never eaten any of her friend's hoarded food. She would not have had such restraint a year ago.

Jason put Gryf down between the makeshift partitions that marked their section of the shelter. Gryf was pale beneath the pattern of tan and pigment. Kylis almost wished Troi and Chuzo had left him in the Pit. The Lizard might then have been forced to put him in the hospital. She wondered if Troi or Chuzo might be helping the Lizard make Screwtop as hard on Gryf as they could. She did not want to believe that, but she did not want to believe Miria was an informer, either.

Their spider—Kylis thought of it as a spider, though it was a Redsun-evolved creature—skittered up the corner post to a new web. Kylis often imagined the little brown-mottled creature hanging above them on her tiny fringed feet, hating them. Yet she was free to crawl down the stilt and into the jungle, or to spin a glider and float away, and she never did. In dreams, Kylis envied her; awake, she named her Stupid. Kylis hoped the web box held enough silk to soothe Gryf's back.

"Hey," Jason said, "this stuff is ready."

"Okay." Kylis took the bowl of greenish mold paste. "Gryf?"

He glanced up. His eyelashes and eyebrows were black and blond, narrowly striped.

"Hang on, it might hurt."

He nodded.

Jason held Gryf's hands while Kylis applied first the mold, then delicate strips of spider silk. Gryf did not move. Even now he had enough strength to put aside the pain.

When she was done, Jason stroked Gryf's forehead and gave him water. He did not want to eat, even broth, so they kissed him and sat near him, for his reassurance and their own, until he fell asleep. That did not take long. When he was breathing deeply, Jason got up and went to Kylis, carrying the bowl.

"I want to look at that cut."

"Okay," Kylis said, "but don't use all the paste."

The poultice burned coldly, and Jason's hands were cool on her skin. She sat with her forearms on her drawn-up knees, accepting the pain rather than ignoring it. When he had finished treating her, she took the bowl and daubed the mold on his cuts. She almost told Jason about Miria, but finally decided not to. Kylis had created the problem; she wanted to solve it herself if she could. And, she admitted, she was ashamed of her misjudgment. She could think of no explanation for Miria's actions that would absolve her.

Jason yawned widely.

"Give me your tag and go back to sleep," Kylis said. Since she had been the first to get off work this time, it was her turn to collect their rations. She took Gryf's tag from his belt pouch and jumped from the edge of the platform to the ground.

Kylis approached the ration dispenser cautiously. On Redsun, violent criminals were sent to rehabilitation centers, not to work camps. Kylis was glad of that, though she did not much like to remember the stories of obedient, blank-eyed people coming out of rehab.

Still, some prisoners were confident or foolish or desperate enough to try to overpower others and steal. At Screwtop it was safest to collect neither obligations nor hatreds. Vengeance was much too simple here. The underground society of spaceport rats had not been free of psychopaths; Kylis knew how to defend herself. Here she had never had to resort to more serious measures. If she did, the drill pit was a quick equalizer between a bully and a smaller person. Mistakes could be planned; machines malfunctioned.

The duty assignments were posted on the ration dispenser. Kylis read them and was astonished and overjoyed to find herself and her friends all on the same shift, the night shift. She hurried back to tell them the news, but Jason was sound asleep, and she did not have the heart to wake him. Gryf had gone.

Kylis threw the rations in the floor locker and sat on the edge of the platform. A scavenger insect crawled across the lumpy floor of fern stalks. Kylis caught it and let it go near Stupid, barricading it until the spider, stalking, left her new web and seized the insect, paralyzed it, wrapped it in silk to store it, and dragged it away. Kylis wondered if their spider ever slept, or if spiders even needed sleep. Then she stole the web.

She grew worried. She knew Gryf could take care of himself. He always did. He had probably never really reached his limits, but Gryf might overestimate even his strength and endurance. He had rested barely an hour.

Kylis fidgeted for a little while longer. Finally she slid down into the mud again.

Water seeped quickly into new footprints in the battered earth around the shelters; Gryf had left no trail that she could distinguish from the other marks in the clay. She went into the forest, with some knowledge and some intuition of where he might be. Above her, huge insects flitted past, barely brushing clawed wingtips against the ferns. It was dark, and the star path, streaked across the sky like the half-circular support of a globe, gave a dim yellow light through broken clouds.

Kylis was startled and frightened by a tickling of the short hair at the back of her neck. She flinched and turned. Gryf looked down at her, smiling, amused.

"Kylis, my friend, you really needn't worry about me all the time." She was always surprised, when he spoke, to remember how pleasant and calming his voice was.

His eyes were dilated so the iris was only a narrow circle of light and dark striations.

Every few sets, someone died from sucking slime. It grew in the forest, in small patches like purple jellyfish. It was hallucinogenic, and it was poisonous. Kylis had argued with Gryf about his using it, before her sentence in the sensory deprivation chamber showed her what Screwtop was like for Gryf all the time.

"Gryf—"

"Don't reproach me!"

"I won't," Kylis said. "Not anymore."

Her response startled him only for a moment; that it startled him at all revealed how completely drained he really was. He nodded and put his arms around her.

"Now you know," he said, with sympathy and understanding. "How long did they make you stay in the box?"

"Eight days. That's what they said, anyway."

He passed his hand across her hair, just touching it. "My poor friend. It seems so much longer."

"It doesn't matter. It's over for me." She almost believed the hallucinations had stopped, but she wondered if she would ever be certain they would never return.

"Do you think the Lizard sentenced you because of me?"

"I don't know. I guess he'd use anything he could if he thought it'd work. Never mind. I'm all right."

"I would have done what they want, but I could not. Can you believe I tried?"

"Do you think I wanted you to?" She touched his face, tracing bone structure with her fingers like someone blind. She could feel the difference between the blond and black hair in his striped eyebrows, but the texture of his skin was smooth. She drew her fingers from his temples to the corners of his jaw, to the tendons of his neck and the tension-knotted muscles of his shoulders. "No one should make friends here," she said.

He smiled, closing his eyes, understanding her irony. "We would lose our souls if we did not."

He turned away abruptly and sat down on a large rock with his head between his knees, struggling against nausea. The new scars did not seem to hurt him. He breathed deeply for some time, then sat up slowly.

"How is Jason?"

"Fine. Recovered. You didn't have to take his shift. Lizard couldn't let him die like that."

"I think the Lizard collects methods of death."

Kylis remembered Miria with a quick shock of returning fear. "Oh, gods, Gryf, what's the use of fighting them?"

Gryf drew her closer. "The use is that you and Jason will not let them destroy you and I believe I am stronger than those who wish to keep me here, and justified in wishing to make my own mistakes rather than theirs." He held out his hand, pale-swirled in the darkness. It was long and fine. Kylis reached out and rubbed it, his wrist, his tense forearm. Gryf relaxed slightly, but Kylis was still afraid. She had never felt frightened before, not like this. But Miria, uncertainty, seeing Gryf hurt, had all combined to make her doubt the possibility of a future.

Gryf was caught and shaken by another spasm of retching. This time he could not suppress it, and it was more severe because he had not eaten. Kylis stood by, unable to do anything but hold his shoulders and hope he would survive the drug this time, as he had all the times before. The dry vomiting was replaced by a fit of coughing. Sweat dripped from his face and down his sides. When the pitch of his coughing rose and his breath grew more ragged, Kylis realized he was sobbing. On her knees beside him, she tried to soothe him. She did not know if he was crying from the sickness, from some vision she would never see, or from despair. She held him until, gradually, he was able to stop.

Sparkles of starlight passed between the clouds, mottling Gryf with a third color. He lay face down on the smooth stone, hands flat against it, cheek pressed to the rock. Kylis knew how he felt, drained, removed, heavy.

"Kylis . . . I never slept before like this . . ."

"I won't go far."

She hoped he heard her. She sat cross-legged on the wide rock beside him, watching slow movements of muscle as he breathed. His roan eyelashes were very long and touched with sweat droplets. The deep welts in his back would leave scars. Kylis' back had similar scars, but she felt that the marks she carried were a brand of shame, while Gryf's meant defiance and pride. She reached toward him, but drew back when her hand's vague shadow touched his face.

When she was certain he was sleeping easily, she left him and went to look nearby for patches of the green antibiotic mold. Their supply was exhausted. It was real medicine, not a superstition. Its active factor was synthesized back north and exported.

Being allowed to walk away from Screwtop, however briefly, made remaining almost endurable, but the privilege had a more important purpose. It was a constant reminder of freedom. The short moment of respite only strengthened the need to get out, and, more important, the need never to come back. Redsun knew how to reinforce obedience.

Kylis wandered, never going very far from Gryf, looking for green mold and finding the rarer purple hallucinogenic slime instead. She tried to deny that it tempted her. She could have taken some to Gryf —she almost did—but in the end she left it under the rocks where it belonged.

"I want to talk to you."

She spun, startled, recognizing the rough voice, fearing it, concealing her fear badly. She did not answer, only looked toward the Lizard.

"Come sit with me," he said. Starlight glinted on his clean fingernails as he gestured to the other end of an immense uprooted fern tree. It sagged but held when he sat on it.

As always, his black protective boots were pulled up and sealed to his black shorts. He was even bigger than Jason, taller, heavier, and though he had allowed his body to go slightly to fat, his face had remained narrow and hard. His clean-shaven scalp and face never tanned or burned, but somehow remained pale, in contrast to his deep-set black eyes. He licked his thin lips quickly with the tip of his tongue.

"What do you want?" She did not approach him.

He leaned forward and leaned his forearms on his knees. "I've been watching you."

She had no answer. He watched everyone. Standing there before him, Kylis was uneasy for reasons that somehow had nothing to do with his capacity for brutality. The Lizard never acted this way. He was direct and abrupt.

"I made a decision when sensory deprivation

didn't break you," he said. "That was the last test."

The breeze shifted slightly. Kylis smelled a sharp odor as the Lizard lifted a small pipe to his lips and drew on it deeply. He held his breath and offered the pipe to her.

She wanted some. It was good stuff. She and Gryf and Jason had used the last of theirs at the end of the previous set, the night before they went on different shifts. Kylis was surprised that the Lizard used it at all. She would never have expected him to pare off the corners of his aggression out here. She shook her head.

"No?" He shrugged and put the pipe down, letting it waste, burning unattended. "All right."

She let the silence stretch on, hoping he would forget her and whatever he wanted to say, wander off or get hungry or go to sleep.

"You've got a long time left to stay here," he said.

Again, Kylis had no answer.

"I could make it easier for you."

"You could make it easier for most of us."

"That's not my job." He ignored the contradiction.

"What are you trying to say?"

"I've been looking for someone like you for a long time. You're strong, and you're stubborn." He got up and came toward her, hesitated to glance back at his pipe but left it where it was. He took a deep breath. He was trying so hard to look sincere that Kylis had an almost overwhelming urge to laugh. She did not, but if she had, it would have been equally a laugh of nervous fear. She realized suddenly, with wonder: The Lizard's as scared as I am.

"Open for me, Kylis."

Incredulity was her first reaction. He would not joke, he could not, but he might mock her. Or was he asking her an impossibility, knowing she would refuse, so he could offer to let her alone if Gryf would return to the tetras. She kept her voice very calm.

"I can't do that."

"Don't you think I'm serious?"

"How could you be?"

He forced away his scowl, like an inexperienced mime changing expressions. The muscles of his jaw were set. He moved closer, so she had to look up to see his eyes.

"I am."

"But that's not something you ask for," Kylis said. "That's something a family all wants and decides on." She realized he would not understand what she meant.

"*I've* decided. There's only me now." His voice was only a bit too loud.

"Aren't you lonely?" She heard her words, not knowing why she had said them. If the Lizard had been hurt, she would revel in his pain. She could not imagine people who would live with him, unless something terrible had changed him.

"I had a kid—" He cut himself off, scowling, angry for revealing so much.

"Ah," she said involuntarily. She had seen his manner of superficial control over badly suppressed violence before. Screwtop gave the Lizard justifiable opportunities to use his rage. Anywhere else it would burst out whenever he felt safe, against anyone who was defenseless and vulnerable. This was the kind of person who was asking her for a child.

"The board had no right to give him to her instead of me."

He would think that, of course. No right to protect the child? She did not say it.

"Well?"

To comply would be easy. She would probably be allowed to live in the comfort and coolness of the domes, and of course she would get good food. She could forget the dangerous machines and the Lizard's whip. She imagined what it would be like to feel a child quickening within her, and she imagined waiting to give birth to a human being, knowing she must hand it over to the Lizard to raise, all alone, with no other model, no other teacher, only this dreadful, crippled person.

"No," she said.

"You could if you wanted to."

So many things she had discovered about herself here had mocked her; now it was a claim she had once made to Gryf: I would do anything to get out of here.

"Leave it at that," she said quietly. "I don't want to." She backed away.

"I thought you were stubborn and strong. Maybe I made a mistake. Maybe you're just stupid, or crazy like the rest of them."

She tried to think of words he would understand, but always came up against the irreconcilable differences between her perception of the Lizard and what he thought of himself. He would not recognize her description.

"Or you want something more from me. What is
it?"

She started to say there was nothing, but hesitated. "All right," she said, afraid her voice would
be too shrill. Somehow it sounded perfectly normal. "Tell Gryf's people to set him free. Get Jason
a parole and a ticket off-world." For a moment she
almost allowed herself to hope he had believed
her offer was sincere. She was a very good liar.

The Lizard's expression changed. "No. I need
them around so you'll do what I say."

"I won't."

"Pick something else."

For an instant's flash Kylis remembered being
taunted like this before, when she was very small.
Anything but that. Anything but what you really
want. She pushed the recollection away.

"There isn't anything else," she said.

"Don't hold out. You can't bribe me to let them
go. I'm not a fool."

He needed no officially acceptable reason to hurt
her. She knew that. Fear of his kind of power was
almost an instinctive reaction for Kylis. But she
whispered, "Yes, Lizard, you are," and, half blind,
she turned and fled.

She almost outran him, but he lunged, grabbed
her shoulder, pulled her around. "Kylis—"

Standing stiffly, coldly, she looked at his hand.
"If that's what you want—"

Even the Lizard was not that twisted. Slowly, he
let his hand fall to his side.

"I could force you," he said.

Her gaze met his and did not waver. "Could
you?"

"I could drug you."

"For seven sets?" She realized, with a jog of alienness, that she had unconsciously translated the time from standard months to sets of forty days.

"Long enough to mess up your control. Long enough to make you pregnant."

"You couldn't keep me alive that long, drugged down that far. If the drugs didn't kill it, I would. I wouldn't even need to be conscious. I could abort it."

"I don't think you're that good."

"I am. You can't live like I did and not be that good."

"I can put you in the deprivation box until you swear to—"

She laughed bitterly. "And expect me to honor that oath?"

"You'd have children with Gryf and Jason."

This was real, much more than a game for the Lizard to play against Gryf. He wanted her compliance desperately. Kylis was certain of that, as certain as she was that he would use his own dreams to help fulfill his duty to Redsun. Still she could not understand why he felt he had some right to accuse her.

"Not like this," she said. "*With* them—but not *for* one of them. And they wouldn't make themselves fertile, either, if you were a woman and asked one of them to give you a child."

"I'm quitting. I'd take him out of here. I'd give him a good home. Am I asking that much? I'm offering a lot for a little of your time and one ovulation." His voice held the roughness of rising temper.

"You're asking for a human being."

She waited for some reaction, any reaction, but he just stood there, accepting what she said as a simple statement of fact without emotional meaning or moral resonance.

"I'd kill a child before I'd give it to you," she said. "I'd kill myself." She felt herself trembling, though it did not show in her hands or in her voice. She was trembling because what she had said was true.

He reacted not at all. She turned and ran into the darkness, and this time the Lizard did not follow.

When she was sure she was not being watched, she returned to Gryf's rock in the forest. Gryf still slept. He had not moved from the time he fell asleep, but the gray rock around him gleamed with his sweat. Kylis sat down beside him, drew up her knees and wrapped her arms around them, put her head down. She had never felt as she felt now—unclean by implication, ashamed, diminished—and she could not explain the feeling to herself. She felt a tear slide down her cheek and clenched her teeth in anger. He will not make me cry, she thought. She breathed deeply, slowly, thinking, Control. Slow the heartbeat, turn off the adrenaline, you don't need it now. Relax. Her body, at least, responded. Kylis sat motionless for a long time.

The heavy, moist wind began to blow, bringing low black clouds to cut off the stars. Soon it would be too dark to see.

"Gryf?" Kylis touched his shoulder. He did not move until she shook him gently; then he woke with a start.

"Storm's coming," Kylis said.

In the dimming starlight, a blond lock of Gryf's hair glinted as he rose. Kylis helped him up. Dead ferns rustled at their feet, and the sleeping insects wrapped themselves more closely in their wings.

At the edge of the forest Kylis and Gryf picked their way across a slag heap and reached the trail to the prisoners' area. A faint blue glow emanated from their shelter, where Jason sat hunched over a cold light reading a book he had managed to scrounge. He did not hear them until they climbed the stairs.

"I was beginning to get worried," he said mildly, squinting to see them past the light.

"Gryf was sick."

"You okay now?" Jason asked.

Gryf nodded, and he and Kylis sat down in the circle of bioluminescence that did not waver in the wind. Jason put his book away and got their rations and water bottles from the locker. The stalks Kylis had picked were by now a bit wilted, but she gave them to Gryf anyway. He shared them out. The meal was slightly better and slightly more pleasant than most at Screwtop, but Kylis was not hungry. She was ashamed to tell her friends what had happened.

"What's the matter?" Jason asked suddenly.

"What?" Kylis glanced up at him, then at Gryf. Both were watching her with concern.

"You look upset."

"I'm okay." She leaned back gradually as she spoke, so her face was no longer in the light. "I'm tired, I guess." She searched for words to put into the silence. "I'm so tired I almost forgot to tell you we're all on night shift."

That was good enough news to change the subject and take her friends' attention from her. It was even good enough news to cheer her.

Later they returned to the hiding place in the forest and slept, lying close with Gryf in the middle. In the distance the sky flashed bright, then darkened. Only a faint mutter reached them, but the lightning revealed heavy clouds and the wind carried the sound closer. Kylis touched Gryf gently, taking comfort in his deep and regular breathing. Lightning scarred the sky again, and seconds later thunder rumbled softly. The wind rustled dry fronds.

Gryf stroked Kylis' tattooed shoulder. He touched her hand and their fingers intertwined.

"I wish you could get out," she whispered. "I wish you would." The lightning flashed again, vivid and close, its thunder simultaneous. Jason started in his sleep. During the brief flare Gryf looked at Kylis, frowning.

It began to rain.

In the morning Kylis woke by reflex, despite the absence of the siren. The whole day was free, but she and her friends had to rest, for the night shift was first on duty.

Gryf was already sitting up. He smiled in his it's-all-right way.

"Let's see," Kylis said.

He turned. The welts were silver-gray down their lengths, even where they crossed. They were uninfected and the ends had begun to heal. Gryf stretched his arms and looked over his shoulder. Kylis watched his face, the fine lines at the corners of his eyes, but he did not flinch. Biocontrol was one thing Kylis had proper training in, and she knew Gryf could not stretch human limits indefinitely. This time, though, he had succeeded.

"How much better are you?" she asked.

He grinned and Kylis laughed in spite of herself. She forced away the thought and worry of the Lizard. Together she and Gryf woke Jason.

But all the rest of the day her apprehension grew. She was certain the Lizard would not accept her refusal easily. Now Kylis had to look twice at the little movements in her peripheral vision, once to make sure they were not hallucinations and again to make sure they were not the Lizard. By evening she was taut with acting out a pose of normality and maintaining an artificial calm, and she was affecting Jason and Gryf with her agitation. She would not speak of the reason. She could be nearly as stubborn as Gryf.

Kylis was almost relieved when the siren shrieked and they had to return to the installation to gather their rations and the set's allowance of medicinal soap. She had tried being angry, and sullen, and heedless, but under it all she was frightened.

They walked past the guard stations, across the lengthening shadows of afternoon. At the top of the Pit they stopped, looking down. But they could not delay; they descended.

The heat from the unworked day seemed to pool in the center of Screwtop. The sides of the Pit reflected heat; the metal of the machinery radiated it. The effects of temperature and noise combined synergistically.

Kylis and Gryf and Jason were all assigned to the probe crew. Across the Pit, Kylis saw the Lizard watching her with no expression at all. She looked away. Miria was on this shift, too, but Kylis did not see her.

They dragged out the new drill bit and raised it; it hung suspended above the shaft, taller than a person, narrow and dangerous. It frequently seemed to recognize the absurdity of its domestication by weak human beings, and rebelled. At Screwtop it was all too easy to ascribe personality and malevolent intentions to inanimate objects.

Shaft sections lay in racks like giant petals around the stem of the drill, fanning out in rays opposite the bubble-covered works of the first two generators. The hum of turbines spread across the floor of the Pit, through bootsoles, reaching flesh and blood and bone. To Kylis, the vibration seemed to be the anger of the wounded earth, unwillingly giving up the secrets and the energy of its interior, helpless in its resentment.

When this shaft was finished, the temperature at its bottom would approach 800 degrees C. When the crew broke through the caprock and released the pressure, that temperature was enough to turn the water below into superheated steam. It was enough to drive another generator. It was enough, if they did not seal the caprock properly, to kill them all instantly. They would seal it, tap it, and build an air-conditioned bubble over it. Then engineers, heavily protected, would move in and build the machinery. The prisoners, who were not trusted anywhere near the generators, would move farther on to drill another well.

This was a clean way of generating power, and cheap in all but human terms. The wells eventually ran dry and power needs for North Continent grew greater. Redsun had no fossil fuel, few radioactive elements, too many clouds to use the energy of its dim star.

Gryf's job was to guide the shaft sections to the drill. Some concession was made to his value; he was not put on the most dangerous jobs. The command to begin was given, and the small contrived delays and grumblings ceased.

The work turned the prisoners almost into automata. It was monotonous, but not monotonous enough. Complete boredom would have allowed daydreams, but danger hung too close for fantasizing. Sweat slid into Kylis' eyes when she was too busy to wipe it away. The world sparkled and stung around her. The night passed slowly. The Lizard watched from a distance, a shade like any other shadow. While he was near, Kylis felt alone and, somehow, obscenely naked.

At midnight the prisoners were allowed to stop for a few minutes to eat. Gryf eased himself down the control tower ladder. At the bottom, Kylis and Jason waited for him. They sat together to eat and swallow salt tablets. The break gave them time to rest against the morning.

Kylis sat on the ground, her back against metal, half asleep, waiting for the bell. The floor of the Pit was set and muddy and littered with broken rock and ash, so she did not lie down. The Lizard had kept his distance all evening. Kylis thought he

was unlikely to do anything direct while she was
among so many people, though they could do nothing against him.

"Get up."

She started, frightened out of a light doze by the
Lizard's voice. He and his people had their backs
to her; they moved between her and Gryf and en-
circled him. He rose, emerging from the shadows
like a tortoiseshell cat.

The Lizard looked at him, then at Kylis. "Take
him," he said to his people.

"What are you going to do?" Hearing the note
of panic in her own voice, Kylis clenched her fists.

"The tetras want him back. They need him.
They're getting impatient."

"You're sending him home?" Kylis asked in disbelief.

"Of course," the Lizard said. He looked away
from Kylis, at Gryf. "As soon as he's had enough
of the deprivation box."

Beside Gryf, Jason stood up. Gryf put his hand
on Jason's arm. The Lizard's people were moving
nearer, closing in, should the Lizard need aid. A
few of the prisoners came closer to see what was
happening. Miria was among them. Kylis watched
her from the shadows, unseen. As the guards led
Gryf away, Miria half smiled. Kylis wanted to
scream with rage.

"How will they like it if you kill him?" Jason
shouted.

"They take that chance," the Lizard said.

"It won't work," Kylis said. The deprivation box
would never make Gryf go back to the tetras, and
it could not force Kylis to do what the Lizard

wanted. Even for Gryf she could not do that.

"Won't it?" The Lizard's voice was heavy and angry.

"Don't do this to him," Kylis said. "Gryf is—just being here is like being in the box. If you put him in a real one—" She was pleading for Gryf; she had never begged for anything in her life. The worst of it was she knew it was useless. She hoped bitterly that Miria was still human enough to understand what her spying had done.

"Shall I take you instead of him?" Without waiting for an answer, laughing at her, the Lizard turned away.

"Yes," Kylis said.

He swung around, astonished.

"You can put me in the box instead of him."

The Lizard sneered at her. "And send the tetras you instead of him? What use do you think you'd be to any of *them*? You could be a pet—you could be a host mother for another little speckled baby!"

Leaning down, scooping up a handful of mud, Kylis took one step toward the Lizard and threw the sticky clay. It caught him in the chest, spattering his black uniform and pale skin. Kylis turned, bending down again. This time the clay was heavy and rocky.

"Kylis!" Jason cried.

"And *you*!" Kylis shouted. She flung the mud and stones at Miria.

As the Lizard's people grabbed her, Kylis saw Miria fall. Under the spotlights the clay was red, but not as red as the blood spurting from Miria's forehead.

The Lizard, scowling, wiping clay from his chin,

barely glanced at Miria's unmoving form. He gestured to Kylis.

"Put her where she can't hurt anyone else."

They marched her away, leaving Jason behind, alone.

They put Kylis in a bare cell with one glass wall and a ledge without corners and ventilation that did not temper the heat. They stripped her and locked her in. The room passively prevented self-injury; even the walls and the window yielded softly to blows.

From inside, she could see the deprivation box. It was the correct shape for a coffin, but larger, and it stood on supports that eliminated the vibration of the generator.

The guards led Gryf into the deprivation room. He, too, was naked, and the guards had hosed him down. He looked around quickly, like a hunted animal alarmed from two sides at once. There was no help, only Kylis, pressed against the window with her fists clenched. Gryf tried to smile, but she could see he was afraid.

As they blindfolded him and worked to prepare him, Kylis remembered the feel of the soft padding packing in around her body, restraining head and arms and legs, preventing all movement and all sensation. First it had been pleasant; the box was dark and silent and gave no sensation of either heat or cold. Tubes and painless needles carried wastes from her body and nourishment in. Kylis had slept for what seemed a very long time, until her body became saturated with sleep. Without any tactile stimulation she grew remote from the physical world, and shrank down as a being to a small spot of consciousness behind the place her eyes had been. She then tried to put herself in a trance, but they had expected that. They prevented it with drugs. Her thoughts had become knit with fantasies, at first such gentle ones that she did not notice. Later they separated themselves from reality and became bizarre and identifiable. Finally they were indistinguishable from a reality too remote to believe in. She remembered the encompassing certainty of madness.

Kylis watched them lock Gryf into the same fate. They turned on the monitors. If he tried to ask to be let out, the subvocalization would be detected and his wish would be granted.

After that no one came near them. Kylis' sentence in the box had been eight days, but the sensory deprivation had overcome her time sense and stretched the time to weeks, months, years. She spent her time now waiting, almost as isolated. At intervals she fell asleep without meaning to, but when she awoke, everything was always the same. She was afraid to think of Gryf, afraid to think what might be happening to Jason alone outside, afraid to think about herself. The hallucinations crept back to haunt her. The glass turned to ice and melted in puddles, and the walls turned to snow clouds and drifted away. Her body would begin to shiver, and then she would realize that the walls were still there, quite real, and she would feel the heat again. She would feel Gryf's touch, and turn to embrace him, but he was never there. She felt herself slipping into a pit of confusion and visions and she could not gather strength or will to pull herself out. Sometimes she cried.

She lay in the cell and felt herself change, felt her courage dissolve in the sterile whiteness. The floor of the cell cradled her, softly, like a soothing voice telling her she could do what was easiest, anything that would ensure her own survival.

She sat up abruptly digging her nails into her palms.

If she believed all that, she should yell and beat her fists on the glass until the guards came, beg them to take her to the Lizard, and do what he had asked. If she did that, everything Gryf was going through and everything she had endured would be betrayed. If she decided now to let another person make her decisions for her, or if she lost herself so completely that she could not make them herself, then she had only trivial reasons for what she had done.

Her reasons were not trivial; she could not force herself to believe they were, not for Gryf's sake or Jason's or her own. Gryf had found the strength to gamble coming to Screwtop on the chance of his own freedom; Jason had found the strength to stay alive where by all rights he should have died. Kylis knew she would have to find the same kind of strength to keep her sanity and her control.

She wiped the back of her hand across her eyes, put her right hand on the point of her left shoulder, leaned against the wall, and very slowly relaxed, concentrating on the reality of each individual muscle, the touch of plastic beneath her, the drop of sweat sliding down between her breasts.

When a cool draft of air brushed her legs, she opened her eyes. The Lizard stood in the doorway, looking down at her, a black shape surrounded by concentric rings of color. She had never seen him with such a gentle expression, but she did not return his expectant smile.

"Have you decided?"

Kylis blinked and all the bright colors dispersed, leaving a stark black-clothed figure. His expression hardened as Kylis gradually returned to Redsun's hell and made the connections she needed to answer him. Her fingers were half curled. She turned her hands over and flattened them on the floor.

"You haven't changed . . . you haven't changed me."

The Lizard glared at her, his expression changing to disbelief. Kylis said nothing more. She did not move. The Lizard made a sound of disgust and slammed the door. The cool air stopped.

He did not return, but Kylis did not try to convince herself she had beaten him.

She stared through the window and willed the tetras to come and free her friend. They must keep track of what was done to him. She could not believe they did not realize what such isolation would do to one of their own kind.

She had been staring at the same scene for so long that it took her a moment to realize it had changed. Four guards came in and began to open the sensory deprivation chamber. Kylis leaped up and pressed her hands to the glass. The deprivation chamber swung open. Kylis remembered her own first glimpse of light as the guards had pulled the padding from her eyes and disconnected tubes and needles. Gryf would be trying to focus his black-flecked blue eyes, blinking; his roan eyelashes would brush his cheeks.

The guards lifted him out, and he did not move. His long limbs dangled limp and lifeless. They carried him away.

Kylis sank to the floor and hugged her knees, hiding her face. When the guards came, they had to pull her to her feet and shake and slap her to force her to stand. They led her through their compound and pushed her through the exit, locking the gate behind her. They did not speak.

Kylis stood in the harsh illumination of spotlights for a few blank moments, then walked slowly toward the comforting shadows of night. She had needed darkness for a long time. Everything seemed more than real, with the absurd clarity of shock.

She saw Jason before he heard her; he was a pale patch on the edge of the light, sitting with his knees drawn up and his head down. Kylis was afraid to go to him.

"Kylis?"

She stopped. Jason's voice was rough, almost controlled but breaking. She turned around and saw him peering at her over his folded arms. His eyes were very bright. He pushed himself to his feet.

"I was afraid," he said. "I was afraid they'd take you both, and I didn't want to stay here alone."

"Go away."

"What? Kylis, why?"

"Gryf's dead." Desperation made her cruel. She wanted to go to him, and mourn with him, but she was afraid she would cause his destruction too. "And Gryf's the only thing that kept us together."

Stunned, Jason said nothing.

"Stay away from me," Kylis said, and walked past him.

"If Gryf is dead, we've got to—"

"No!"

"Are you sure he's dead? What happened?"

"I'm sure." She did not face him.

He put his hands on her shoulders. "We've got to get out of here before they kill us too. We've got to get north and tell people what's going on."

"Crazy!" She pulled free.

"Don't do this to me, Kylis."

His plea sliced through her grief and guilt, and even through her fear for him. She could not stand to hurt him. There was no fault in Jason, and no blame to assign to him. His only flaw was a loyalty she hardly deserved. Kylis looked around her, at the bare earth and the distant machines and the soft black ferns, all so alien. She turned back.

"I'm sorry," she said.

They held each other, but it was not enough comfort. Jason's tears fell cool on her shoulder, but she could not cry.

"There's something more than Gryf and the tetras," Jason said. "Please let me help. Tell me why all this is happening."

She shook her head. "It's dangerous for you to stay with me."

Suddenly he clenched his fingers around her arm. She pulled back, startled, and when she looked up, he scared her. She had never seen cruelty in Jason, but that was how he looked, cruel and filled with hatred.

"Jason—"

"I won't kill him," he said. "I won't . . . let me go—" He looked down and realized he was gripping Kylis' arm. "Oh, gods." He let her go and turned and walked into the forest.

Rubbing the bruise he had left, Kylis slowly looked behind her. What Jason had seen was the Lizard watching them from the gateway of the guards' enclosure. He did not move. Kylis ran.

The thick band of multicolored stars, shining through breaks in the clouds, lighted the way only where the ferns did not close in overhead. Kylis stumbled through the darkness, not even slowing for pools of rainwater. Her legs ached from fighting the suction of wet clay. Suddenly her shoulder rammed a rough stalk and her momentum spun her, flinging her against another. She stopped, gasping for breath, the air burning her throat.

Kylis straightened and looked around, getting her bearings. The stars glittered like sparks in the surface of standing water. She walked more carefully among the ferns. Her footsteps spread ripples out around her and the water sloshed gently from her boots. Only when she reached the shelter of dead ferns did she realize how silly and unnecessary it had been for her to be careful not to fall.

Inside the cool nest she lay down and composed herself. When she finally caught her breath, she began breathing slowly and regularly, counting her heartbeats. Gradually she extended the number of beats for each inhalation, for each exhalation, then she slowed her heart as well. She thought about Gryf, dying deliberately rather than giving his life to those he hated. And she thought about Jason, who would never kill even in vengeance. She was certain of that. If she were gone, he at least would be safe.

She felt the gasp reflex growing stronger and set her perception of it aside. Her breathing had ceased now, and her heartbeat would stop soon. Her thoughts slowed, her memory drifted to more pleasant times. She found herself with Gryf again, kissing him, standing in the clean hot lake, touched by spray from the overflow pipe. She smiled. A bright yellow star glittered through a gap between the ferns. Kylis let her eyes close, shutting out the last light.

Insistent hands shook her. She was dimly aware of them and of a voice calling her name. She concentrated more strongly on dying. A fist pounded her chest and she gasped involuntarily. Someone leaned down and breathed into her mouth, holding her chin up and her head back, forcing air into her lungs. Her heart pounded. Pushing the person away, Kylis sat up angrily and almost fainted.

Miria caught her and made her lie down again. "Thank gods, I found you. I could hear you but then you disappeared."

Kylis did not answer, but only blinked her eyes against the light Miria carried. She tried to be angry at her, but it seemed too futile.

"Kylis!" Miria's voice rose in panic. "Are you there? Can you hear me?"

"Of course I'm here," she said. She felt dizzy. She wondered why Miria had asked such a silly question. "What do you mean, am I here?"

Miria relaxed and brightened her lantern. "I was afraid I'd come too late." She had a bad scar, pink and new, on her forehead.

"Get away from me. Why couldn't you let us

alone?" Kylis knew she would not be able to try to kill herself again for quite a while; she had used up too much strength.

"Gryf's all right," Miria said.

Kylis stared at her. "But I saw— How do you know? You're lying!"

"He's all right, Kylis. I know. Please trust me."

"Trust you! You told the Lizard about Gryf and Jason and me! He never knew before how much he could hurt us! And now he'll go after Jason, too, so I'll—" She stopped.

"The Lizard knew you were together, but I never told him your plans. You honored me with a request to join your family. Do you think your judgment of me was so wrong?"

Kylis sighed. "It wasn't very good about the kid who turned me in." She had to rest and breathe a moment. "I saw you go inside the fence without any guards. And after that, the Lizard—"

"What was he trying to make you do?"

"Have a child and give it to him."

Miria sat back on her heels. "To *Lizard*? Gods." She shook her head in disbelief, in sympathy for Kylis, for anyone, particularly a child who would come under the Lizard's control. The yellow lantern glow glinted from the dark and lighter brown strands of Miria's hair. Kylis suddenly saw the two distinct colors for the first time. The lighter brown was not sun streaked—it grew that way naturally.

"You're a tetra, aren't you?"

Miria looked up, and Kylis knew she would not lie. "Yes. Anyway," she said sadly, "I used to be."

"They let you go?"

"No!" She ran her hand across her hair and spoke

more calmly. "No. I was never like Gryf. I never understood what he wanted, at least until a few days ago. After you and I talked . . ." She drew in a long breath. "I was in an accident. I was foolish. I took chances I had no right to take, and I nearly drowned. I died for several minutes. No oxygen could get to my brain." She looked away, fiddling with the control on the lantern. "I can remember who I used to be, but I'm not her any more. I cannot do the work I was meant for. I feel so *stupid*. . . . I was afraid you'd done that to yourself, damaged your brain."

"I'm all right, Miria." Kylis pushed herself up on her elbow, suspicion and anger forgotten for a moment. "They sent you here because you had an accident? I think that's awful."

"They could have—they should have, for what I did. But I'm here to watch Gryf."

"To protect him? And you let them put him in the box?"

"You know enough about Gryf to know . . ." Miria's voice faltered. "I was not here only to be sure he lived. I wanted to force him to go back to his team. I wanted him . . . to make up for my failure."

"Why should he be responsible?"

"Because we're the same."

"Miria, I don't understand."

"He had the same place I did, on a different team. For important projects we make two groups and keep them separate, so they will confirm each other's research or develop alternate lines. Gryf is my trans-brother. That is what we call tetras with the same parents in opposite couples." She rubbed her

tawny forearm. "He was never meant to be a trans,
of course, but it made no difference for the work.
I crippled my team—I felt I had to keep Gryf from
crippling his. I felt responsible."

"What's going to happen now?"

"Now . . ." Miria grasped Kylis' hands. "I'm not
a tetra any more, Kylis. I have no vote. But I have
a say, and I will do my best to persuade them to
set him free."

"Miria, if you can—"

"I may do no better than keep them from sending him back here."

"Why did you change your mind?"

"Because of what you told me. I thought about
it all the time Gryf was in deprivation. What I
was doing to him to force him to share my loyalties
—I almost killed him! I allowed the Lizard to torture him. You knew better than I what that could
mean."

"But he's all right—you said he's all right."

"He is," Miria said quickly. "He will be. He over-
came the drugs and put himself in a deep trance.
I haven't lied. But I had nothing to do with freeing
him before he died. I understand now what happened. After two days I realized Gryf must be let
go, but the Lizard would not come out and he
would not reply to my messages. He hoped to
break you to his will and Gryf to mine. When he
could not—finally he was afraid to keep Gryf in
there any longer." Her voice was strained. "I've
caused you so much pain. I hope some day you will
all be together, and happy, and will be able to
forgive me."

"Miria, I wish—"

The roar of a plane drowned out her words. Kylis glanced up reflexively. In all the time she had been at Screwtop, she had never heard or seen a plane. The North Continent was too far away, and here there was no place to land.

"I've got to go. I shouldn't have left Gryf, but I had to talk to you." Miria helped Kylis to her feet and out of the shelter. Kylis accepted the help gratefully. She felt wobbly.

They waded through shimmering shadows as Miria's light swung on her hip.

"Kylis," Miria said slowly, "I don't know what will happen. I hope I can free Gryf. I will try to help you. And Jason. But the Lizard serves the government well. They may decide he was right and I was wrong. Whatever happens will take time, and I may not be able to do anything at all. I don't want to deceive you."

"I understand." Jason was in no less danger now, nor was she. But at least Gryf was safe. For a few moments Kylis could set aside her fear in the joy that he was alive.

They entered the compound's long clearing and reached the path that led toward the prisoners' shelter. Kylis saw the vertical takeoff plane hanging in midair. It slowly lowered itself, straight down, until it was out of sight behind the bank. Its engines slowed, idling.

"I can't take you to your shelter," Miria said. "I'm sorry—"

"Can I come the rest of the way—just to be sure —?"

"Gryf will already be on the plane, Kylis. You wouldn't be allowed to see him."

"All right," she said reluctantly. "I can get back myself from here."

"Are you sure? Will you be all right?"

Kylis nodded. "For now."

"Yes . . ." Miria shifted her weight back and forth, reluctant to leave her alone but anxious to meet the plane.

"Go *on*," Kylis said.

"Yes. I must . . ." She hesitated a moment more, then leaned quickly forward and embraced Kylis. "This is such a terrible place," she whispered. "Somehow I'll change it." She turned abruptly and hurried away.

Miria walked silhouetted against the lights and lantern. Kylis watched her go. At least she could hope now. She realized she must find Jason and tell him everything, but most particularly that Gryf was alive and out of the prison. Perhaps to be free. Then he could contact Jason's family—

"Oh, gods," Kylis groaned. "Miria! Miria, wait!" She ran toward the enclosure, stumbling from exhaustion.

She reached the bank above the fence just as Miria put her palm against the lock. The gate swung open.

"Miria!" Kylis cried. She was afraid Miria would not hear her over the engines of the plane, now inside the enclosure. But she cried out once more, sliding down the hill, and Miria turned.

She met Kylis between the bank and the fence, taking her elbow to support her as she struggled for breath.

"Jason's family," Kylis said. "Redsun thinks he's just a transient but he's not. If his people knew he was here, they'd ransom him." She remembered most of Jason's name, his family name, and told it to Miria. "Can you tell them? Just send a message?"

Miria's eyes widened. "Is that who he is?"

Kylis nodded.

"It will have to be done carefully, to keep his identity a secret, but I can do that, Kylis, yes." Then she sobered. "You'll be alone—"

"I'm all right alone. I've always been alone before. I can protect myself, but I can't protect Jason from the Lizard. Will you do it? Will you promise?"

"I promise."

Kylis clasped Miria's hands for an instant and let her go. Miria went inside the enclosure and boarded the plane. The engines screamed, and the aircraft rose, sliding forward like a hovercraft through the gateway. Clear of the fence, it rose higher until it had cleared the height of the marsh plants. It accelerated straight north.

Kylis watched it until it was out of sight. She wished she had seen Gryf, but now she believed Miria; she could believe he was alive.

In the eerie gentle light of dawn, as Kylis started away, the harsh spotlights dimmed one by one.

∞

THE WARLORD OF SATURN'S MOONS

ELEANOR ARNASON

*Eleanor Arnason lives in Minneapolis,
Minnesota, where she works in a museum.
She has written a number of radio spots on
facts from American history and worked
on another radio series about inventors.
Her stories have appeared in* Orbit *and*
New Worlds. *"The Warlord of Saturn's
Moons" is a humorous yet poignant story
about a science fiction writer and the two
worlds in which she lives.*

Here I am, a silver-haired maiden lady of thirty-
five, a feeder of stray cats, a window-ledge
gardener, well on my way to the African violet and
antimacassar stage. I can see myself at fifty, fat
and a little crazy, making cucumber sandwiches
for tea, and I view my future with mixed feelings.
Whatever became of my childhood ambitions:
joining the space patrol; winning a gold medal at
the Olympics; climbing Mount Everest alone in
my bathing suit, sustained only by my indomitable

will and strange psychic arts learned from Hindu mystics? The saddest words of tongue or pen are something-or-other what might have been, I think. I light up a cigar and settle down to write another chapter of *The Warlord of Saturn's Moons*. A filthy habit you say, though I'm not sure if you're referring to smoking cigars or writing science fiction. True, I reply, but both activities are pleasurable, and we maiden ladies lead lives that are notoriously short on pleasure.

So back I go to the domes of Titan and my redheaded heroine deathraying down the warlord's minions. Ah, the smell of burning flesh, the spectacle of blackened bodies collapsing. Even on paper it gets a lot of hostility out of you, so that your nights aren't troubled by dreams of murder. Terribly unrestful, those midnight slaughters and waking shaking in the darkness, your hands still feeling pressure from grabbing the victim or fighting off the murderer.

Another escape! In a power-sledge, my heroine races across Titan's methane snow, and I go and make myself tea. There's a paper on the kitchen table, waiting to tell me all about yesterday's arsons, rapes and bloody murders. Quickly I stuff it into the garbage pail. Outside, the sky is hazy. Another high-pollution day, I think. I can see incinerator smoke rising from the apartment building across the street, which means there's no air alert yet. Unless, of course, they're breaking the law over there. I fling open a cabinet and survey the array of teas. Earl Grey? I ponder, or Assam? Gunpowder? Jasmine? Gen Mai Cha? Or possibly an herb tea: sassafras, mint, Irish moss or mu. Deciding on Assam, I put water on, then go back to write an exciting chase through the icy Titanian mountains. A pursuer's sledge goes over a precipice and, as my heroine hears his long shriek on her radio, my tea kettle starts shrieking. I hurry into the kitchen. Now I go through the tea-making ceremony: pouring boiling water into the pot, sloshing the water around and pouring it out, measuring the tea in, pouring more boiling water on top of the tea. All the while my mind is with my heroine, smiling grimly as she pilots the power-sledge between bare cliffs. Above her in the dark sky is the huge crescent of Saturn, a shining white line slashing across it—the famous Rings. While the tea steeps, I wipe off a counter and wash a couple of mugs. I resist a sudden impulse to pull the newspaper out from among the used tea leaves and orange peelings. I already know what's in it. The Detroit murder count will exceed 1,000 again this year; the war in Thailand is going strong; most of Europe is out on strike. I'm far better off on Titan with my heroine, who is better able to deal with her problems than I am to deal with mine. A deadly shot, she has also learned strange psychic arts from Hindu mystics, which give her great strength, endurance, mental alertness and a naturally pleasant body odor. I wipe my hands and look at them, noticing the bitten fingernails, the torn cuticles. My heroine's long, slender, strong hands have two-inch nails filed to a point and covered with a plastic paint that makes them virtually unbreakable. When necessary, she uses them as claws. Her cuticles, of course, are in perfect condition.

I pour myself a cup of tea and return to the story.

Now my heroine is heading for the mountain hide-out where her partner waits: a tall, thin, dour fellow with one shining steel prosthetic hand. She doesn't know his name and she suspects he himself may have forgotten it. He insists on being called 409, his number on the prison asteroid from which he has escaped. She drives as quickly as she dares, thinking of his long face, burned almost black by years of strong radiation on Mars and in space, so the white webbing of scars on its right side shows up clearly. His eyes are grey, so pale they seem almost colorless. As I write about 409, I find myself stirred by the same passion that stirs my heroine. I begin to feel uneasy, so I stop and drink some tea. I can see I'm going to have trouble with 409. It's never wise to get too involved with one's characters. Besides, I'm not his type. I imagine the way he'd look at me, indifference evident on his dark, scarred face. I could, of course, kill him off. My heroine would then spend the rest of the story avenging him, though she'd never get to the real murderer—me. But this solution, while popular among writers, is unfair.

I go into the kitchen, extract a carrot from a bunch in the icebox, clean it and eat it. After that, I write the heroine's reunion with 409. Neither of them is demonstrative. They greet each other with apparent indifference and retire to bed. I skip the next scene. How can I watch that red-headed hussy in bed with the man I'm beginning to love? I continue the story at the moment when their alarm bell rings, and they awake to find the warlord's rocket planes have landed all around their hideout. A desperate situation! 409 suggests that he make a run for it in their rocket plane. While the warlord's minions pursue him, my heroine can sneak away in the power-sledge. The plan has little chance of success, but they can think of none better. They bid farewell to one another, and my heroine goes to wait in the sledge for the signal telling her 409 has taken off. As she waits, smoking a cigar, she thinks of what little she knows about 409. He was a fighter pilot in the war against the Martian colony and was shot down and captured. While in prison something happened to him that he either can't remember or refuses to talk about, and, when the war ended and he was re-leased, he became a criminal. As for herself, she had been an ordinary sharpshooter and student of Hindu mysticism, a follower of Swami Bluestone of the Brooklyn Vedic Temple and Rifle Range. Then she discovered by accident the warlord's plot to over-throw the government of Titan, the only one of Sat-urn's satellites not under his control. With her information about the plot, the government may still be saved. She has to get to Titan City with the microfilm dot!

The alarm bell rings, and she feels the ground shake as 409's plane takes off. Unfortunately I'm writing the story from my heroine's point of view. I want to describe 409 blasting off, the warlord's rocket planes taking off after him, chasing him as he flies through the narrow, twisting valleys, the planes' rockets flaring red in the valley shadows and missiles exploding into yellow fireballs. All through this, of course, 409's scarred face remains tranquil and his hands move quickly and surely over the plane's con-trols. His steel prosthetic hand gleams in the dim light from the dials. But I can't put this in the story, since my heroine sees none of it as she slides off in

the opposite direction, down a narrow trail hidden
by overhanging cliffs.

I am beginning to feel tense, I don't know why.
Possibly 409's dilemma is disturbing me. He's certainly in danger. In any case, my tea is cold. I turn
on the radio, hoping for some relaxing rock music
and go to get more tea. But it's twenty to the hour,
time for the news, and I get the weekend body
count: two men found dead in suspected westside
dope house, naked body of woman dragged out of
Detroit River. I hurry back and switch to a country
music station. On it, someone's singing about how he
intends to leave the big city and go back down
south. As I go back into the kitchen, I think:

> Carry me back to Titan.
> That's where I want to be.
> I want to repose
> On the methane snows
> At the edge of a frozen sea.

I pour out the old tea and refill the cup with tea
that's hot.

The radio begins to make that awful beepity-
beep-beepity sound that warns you the news is coming up. I switch back to the rock station, where the
news is now over. I'm safe for another fifty-five minutes, unless there's a special news flash to announce
a five-car pile-up or an especially ghastly murder.

The plan works! For my heroine, at least. She
doesn't know yet if 409 got away. She speeds off un-
pursued. The power-sledge's heating system doesn't
quite keep her warm, and the landscape around her
is forbidding: bare cliffs and narrow valleys full of
methane snow, overhead the dark blue sky. Saturn

has set, and the tiny sun is rising, though she can't see it yet. On the high mountains the ice fields begin to glitter with its light. On she races, remembering how she met 409 in the slums of The Cup on Ganymede, as she fled the warlord's assassins. She remembers being cornered with no hope of escape. Then behind the two assassins a tall figure appeared and the shining steel hand smashed down on the back of one assassin's head. As the other assassin turned, he got the hand across his face. A moment or two more, and both the assassins were on the ground, unconscious. Then she saw 409's twisted grin for the first time and his colorless eyes appraising her.

There I go, I think, getting all heated up over 409. The radio is beginning to bother me, so I shut it off and re-light my cigar. I find myself wishing that men like 409 really existed. Increasingly in recent years, I've found real men boring. Is it possible, as some scientists argue, that the Y chromosome produces an inferior human being? There certainly seem to be far fewer interesting men than interesting women. But theories arguing that one kind of human being is naturally inferior make me anxious. I feel my throat muscles tightening and the familiar tense, numb feeling spreading across my face and my upper back. Quickly I return to my story.

Now out on the snowy plain, my heroine can see the transparent domes of Titan City ahead of her, shining in the pale sunlight. Inside the domes the famous pastel towers rise, their windows reflecting the sun. Her power-sledge speeds down the road, through the drifts that half cover it. Snow sprays up on either side of the sledge, so my heroine has trouble seeing to the left and right. As a result, it's

some time before she sees the power-sledges coming
up behind her on the right. At the same moment
that she looks over and sees them, their sleek silver
bodies shining in the sunlight and snow-sprays
shooting up around them, her radio begins to go
beep-beep-beep. She flicks it on. The voice of Janos
Black, the warlord's chief agent on Titan, harsh and
slurred by a thick Martian accent, tells her the bad
news: 409's plane has been shot down. He ejected
before it crashed. Even now the warlord's men are
going after the ejection capsule, which is high on a
cliff, wedged between a rock spire and the cliff wall.
Janos offers her a trade: 409 for the microdot. But
Janos may well be lying; 409 may have gotten away
or else been blown up. She feels a sudden constric-
tion of her throat at the thought of 409 dead. She
flicks off the radio and pushes the power-sledge up
to top speed. She realizes as she does so that 409 is
unlikely to fare well if Janos gets ahold of him. Janos'
wife and children died of thirst after the great Martian network of pipelines was blown apart by
Earther bombs, and Janos knows that 409 was a
pilot in the Earther expeditionary force.

I write another exciting chase, this one across the
snowy plain toward the pink, green, blue and yellow
towers of Titan City. The warlord's power-sledges
are gaining. Their rockets hit all around my heroine's
sledge, and fire and black smoke erupt out of the
snow. Swearing in a low monotone, she swings the
sledge back and forth in a zig-zag evasive pattern.

I stop to puff on my cigar and discover it's gone
out again. My tea is cold. But the story's beginning
at last to interest me. I keep on writing.

As my heroine approaches the entrance to Titan

City, she's still a short distance ahead of her pursuers. Her radio beeps. It's Janos Black again. He tells her his men have gotten to the ejection capsule and are lowering it down the cliff. Any minute now, they'll have it down where they can open it and get 409 out.

Ignoring Janos, she concentrates on slowing her sledge and bringing it through the city's outer gate into the airlock. A moment or two later, she's safe. But what about 409?

Frankly, I don't know. I stand and stretch, decide to take a bath, and go to turn the water on. The air pollution must be worse than I originally thought. I have the dopey feeling I get on the days when the pollution is really bad. I look out the window. Dark grey smoke is still coming out of the chimneys across the street. Maybe I should call the Air Control number (dial AIR-CARE) and complain. But it takes a peculiar kind of person to keep on being public-spirited after it becomes obvious it's futile. I decide to put off calling Air Control and water my plants instead. Every bit of oxygen helps, I think. I check the bathtub—it's not yet half-full—and go back to writing. After a couple of transitional paragraphs, my heroine finds herself in the antechamber to the Titan Council's meeting room. There is a man there, standing with his back to her. He's tall and slender, and his long hair is a shade between blond and grey. He turns and she recognizes the pale, delicate-looking face. This is Michael Stelladoro, the warlord of Saturn's moons. His eyes, she notices, are as blue as cornflowers and he has a delightful smile. He congratulates her on escaping his power-sledges, then tells her that his men have gotten 409 out of the

ejection capsule. He is still alive and as far as they
can determine uninjured. They have given 409 a
shot of Sophamine. At this my heroine gasps with
horror. Sophamine, she knows, is an extremely
powerful tranquilizer used to control schizophrenia.
One dose is enough to make most people dependent
on it, and withdrawal takes the form of a night-
marish psychotic fugue. The warlord smiles his delightful smile and turns on the radio he has clipped
to his belt. A moment later my heroine hears 409's
voice telling her that he has in fact been captured.
He sounds calm and completely uninterested in his
situation. That, she knows, is the Sophamine. It
hasn't affected his perception of reality. He knows
where he is and what is likely to happen to him,
but he simply doesn't care. When the Sophamine
wears off, all the suppressed emotions will well up,
so intense that the only way he'll be able to deal
with them will be to go insane, temporarily at least.

The warlord tells her he regrets having to use the
Sophamine, but he was certain that 409 would refuse to talk unless he was either drugged or tortured,
and there simply wasn't enough time to torture him.

"You fiend!" my heroine cries.

The warlord smiles again, as delightfully as before, and says if she gives the microdot to the Titan
Council, he will turn 409 over to Janos Black, who
will attempt to avenge on him all the atrocities committed by the Earthers on Mars.

What can she do? As she wonders, the door to the
meeting room opens, and she is asked to come in.
For a moment, she thinks of asking the Titanians to
arrest the warlord. Almost as if he's read her mind,
he tells her there's no point in asking the Titanians

to arrest him. He has diplomatic immunity and a warfleet waiting for him to return.

She turns to go into the meeting room. "I'll tell Janos the good news," the warlord says softly and turns his radio on.

She hesitates, then thinks, a man this evil must be stopped, no matter what the cost. She goes into the meeting room.

I remember the bath water, leap up and run into the bathroom. The tub is brim-full and about to overflow. I turn off the tap, let out some of the water, and start to undress. After I climb into the tub, I wonder how I'm going to get 409 out of the mess he's in. Something will occur to me. I grab the bar of soap floating past my right knee.

After bathing, I put on a pink and silver muumuu and make a fresh pot of tea. Cleanliness is next to godliness, I think as I sit down to write.

My heroine tells her story to the Titan Council and produces the microdot. On it is the warlord's plan for taking over the government of Titan and a list of all the Titanian officials he has subverted. The president of the council thanks her kindly and tells her that they already have a copy of the microdot, obtained for them by an agent of theirs who has infiltrated the warlord's organization. "Oh no! Oh no!" my heroine cries. Startled, the president asks her what's wrong. She explains that she has sacrificed her partner, her love to bring them the information they already had. "Rest easy," the president says. "Our agent is none other than Janos Black. He won't harm 409."

Thinking of Janos' family dying of thirst in an isolated settlement, my heroine feels none too sure of this. But there's nothing left for her to do except hope.

After that, I describe her waiting in Titan City for news of 409, wandering restlessly through the famous gardens, barely noticing the beds of Martian sandflowers, the blossoming magnolia trees, the pools of enormous silver carp. Since the warlord now knows that the Titan Council knows about his schemes, the council moves quickly to arrest the officials he's subverted. The newscasts are full of scandalous revelations, and the warlord leaves Titan for his home base on Tethys, another one of Saturn's moons. My heroine pays no attention to the newscasts or to the excited conversations going on all around her. She thinks of the trip she and 409 made from Ganymede to Titan in a stolen moon-hopper, remembering 409's hands on the ship's controls, the way he moved in zero-G, his colorless eyes and his infrequent, twisted smile. Cornball, I think, but leave the passage in. I enjoy thinking about 409 as much as my heroine does.

After two days, Janos Black arrives in a police plane. 409 is with him. Janos comes to see my heroine to bring her the news of their arrival. He's a tall man with a broad chest and spindly arms and legs. His face is ruddy and Slavic, and his hair is prematurely white. He tells her that he kept 409 prisoner in the warlord's secret headquarters in the Titanian mountains till the Titanian police moved in and arrested everybody.

"Then he's all right," she cries joyfully.

Janos shakes his head.

"Why not?"

"The Sophamine," Janos explains. "When it wore

off, he got hit with the full force of all his repressed feelings, especially, I think, the feelings he had about the war on Mars. Think of all that anger and terror and horror and guilt flooding into his conscious mind. He tried to kill himself. We stopped him, and he almost killed a couple of us in the process. By we I mean myself and the warlord's men; this happened before the police moved in. We had to give him another shot of Sophamine. He's still full of the stuff. From what I've heard, the doctors want to keep giving it to him. They think the first shot of Sophamine he got destroyed his old system of dealing with his more dangerous emotions, which are now overwhelming him. The doctors say on Sophamine he can function more or less normally. Off it, they think he'll be permanently insane."

"You planned this!" she cries.

Janos shakes his head. "The warlord gave the order, miss. I only obeyed it. But I didn't mind this time. I didn't mind."

I stop to drink some tea. Then I write the final scene in the chapter: my heroine's meeting with 409. He's waiting for her in a room at the Titan City Hospital. The room is dark. He sits by the window looking out at the tall towers blazing with light and at the dome above them, which reflects the towers' light so it's impossible to look through it at the sky. She can see his dark shape and the red tip of the cigar he smokes.

"Do you mind if I turn on the lights?" she asks.

"No."

She finds the button and presses it. The ceiling begins to glow. She looks at 409. He lounges in his chair, his feet up on a table. She realizes it's the first time she's seen him look really relaxed. Before this, he's always seemed tense, even when asleep.

"How are you?" she asks.

"Fine." His voice sounds tranquil and indifferent.

She can't think of anything to say. He looks at her, his dark, scarred face expressionless. Finally he says, "Don't let it bother you. I feel fine." He pauses. She still can't think of anything to say. He continues. "The pigs don't want me for anything here on Titan. I think I'll be able to stay."

"What're you going to do here?"

"Work, I guess. The doctors say I can hold down a job if I keep taking Sophamine." He draws on the cigar, so the tip glows red, then blows out the smoke. He's looking away from her at the towers outside the window. She begins weeping. He looks back at her. "I'm all right. Believe me, I feel fine."

But she can't stop weeping.

Enough for today, I think and put down my pencil. Tomorrow, I'll figure out a way to get 409 off Sophamine. Where there's life there's hope and so forth, I tell myself.

∞

THE TRIUMPHANT HEAD

JOSEPHINE SAXTON

Josephine Saxton lives in England. She is the author of the novels The Hieros Gamos of Sam *and* An Smith *and* Group Feast *(both published by Doubleday). A collection of her short fiction,* Vector for Seven *(Doubleday), has also been published. Her stories have appeared in* New Worlds, *Orbit,* New Dimensions, *and* Again, Dangerous Visions. *Her gift for depicting the alien and unusual in the everyday world is displayed in "The Triumphant Head."*

M y eyes are open and I am awake. There can be no doubt that I am physically awake. He was awake before I stirred in the sun-scarred sheets, I can hear him in the dressing room next door, splashing about, walking about, singing about, full of it all, and if shaving lotion has a sound, then that too reaches me . . . but I must not allow that to distract me in this way.

Having washed all the important crevices and the bits that show of myself (good bath last night, reeking with essence of pine), I sit here in my comfortable chair, re-upholstered by myself in dark green cut velvet, and as I sit naked on it a pattern of acanthus leaves will grow on my backside, but hold hard, who sits here, looking into the mirror, and why, and *what* is this I see?

So, awake. I question, how awake is that?

Each day at this time I can by my own efforts reveal images.

I utter the challenge.

Beginning with the body, one leg, then the other, one arm, the other, and then the back, oh those acanthus leaves, up through the body the stream should flow, should it not, confirming the fact of being awake, so that I experience that . . . there was some of that cut velvet left over, I wonder if it would make a hit, sort of Garboish perhaps.

That noise? His chest expander. Christ, get on with it, the image, it has to come; what will it be today?

I face the mirror. A Georgian mirror, black and gilt, the corners elegantly encrusted, mended with evil-smelling glue, the cracks masked with cheap gold paint, a good job if I may say so, only the marks of celluloid butterflies placed on its heavy glass by some thin hand now dead, meant to reflect the miraculous patterns seen in nature at the height of summer, a celluloid wonder, and here on my mirror the horrid blur of its pseudopod, marring my beauty unless I lean to the right which I now do, the better to see you with, my dear . . .

Begin again—Bruce knew nothing, he was just a student of Arachnida.

To be more than awake, for however short a time.

Look in the mirror.

Come to me, two-legged being who will live the day as some dim zombie with the ticket "Anonymous member Dramatis Personae Planet Earth" stuck on me unless I can pull this off, this fantastic act, to see myself, not as others see me, but as I am. Preferably before that other thumping being, next door, push-ups now perhaps, strains a pectoral fibre, and for what may I ask? No, I may not ask, he never questions me as to what I do in here each morning. He will be in here though, asking about breakfast before I've half begun. He will know it is me sitting here by the fact that I shall answer "yes dear, orange juice in the fridge, kidneys to follow." Nobody else could say that to him at eight in the morning, in this room. It is outside his experience.

Be still then, choose a small spot on which to rest the eyes, fix it, not with a vibrant glare, but with a steady gaze, seeing and not seeing, and make of that gaze an anchor, so that reality may pervade; one cannot force this process—but you are way off beam again. Thoughts think, body live. If I could say: "Somebody, help me."

I am sitting here, a normal-enough practice for a human being, exploring, and what are little girls made of? Bones and blood and skin and hormones, and a reliable heart to keep things going until I get things in perspective.

Who is here today, hiding in my living corpse. There must be somebody there, always it is so, but which one?

Supposing *he* came in at this moment, just as my image appeared. Would he notice, see it for himself? An interesting supposition, and, at the back of my mind, Robbie Burns, making love wholesale on beds of heather, and the seas have not yet run dry, and a bloody good thing too, leave that . . .

I suddenly find I have released an amount indefinable of the source of my energy and do not quite know what to do with it; at this point I must achieve the miracle of stopping thinking at the same time as allowing my thoughts to think themselves, and then, given grace, things might begin to shape up; I may turn this mass of meat into a person, and within that person will be recognisable another, like Chinese boxes, known only to that person next door who is doubtless dressing himself in his chalk-stripe and two tones, he being a male cognisant of what goes on in the scene, as "wife," or, in his cups, as "the wife," the words implying a certain uniqueness and superiority over all other wives, but understood nevertheless to mean "her," the wife, we all have them, like heads. Heads.

Through the relaxed channels of my flesh flow, life, and run, but never to waste, bring me into focus; who is there today, nok nok nok, who is it, welcome friend, plenty of room in my body, have your say for twenty-four hours, but do not deter me from my aim, that is our bargain. You live, I live.

Things are jumping now, the acanthus leaves are doing fine, and the mirror is still as still, waiting, only a clothes moth hovers expectantly over my cashmere sweater which I shall presently wear for the role I shall play today; my body lives, it glows, molten it glows, and my arms, they glow, and my feet, they draw something up through them and resist and glow like the element on the heater that is now singeing that unfortunate moth. My chest passes on the message into my clavicles, otherwise known as right collarbone, left collarbone, up through my neck and chin, to my lips which sing as if a fraction from a kiss, and my nose, tingling, working against me and into an orgasmic sneeze—later, the sneeze, it will keep. Now for my eyes, the right and the left and through the unknown quantities that lurk behind the bones of THE TRIUMPHANT HEAD.

So it is you today, is it, I half suspected it. Surly, insentient, woman of dusty antimony, mineral lady, butter would not melt, and gaze unseeing into the black depths of space (we all have our off days), and for a moment I saw, before the going and going away of it, in the wordless moments, the image in the mirror.

"Hullo dear, not dressed yet, what about breakfast?"

For a split second the powers of speech refuse the carefully held orbicularis, clinging to the delicate pleasure of a moment ago, but that is nonsense, of course you can speak, you are in command now, you know your lines.

"I'm almost ready, just got to throw on a few clothes. Juice is in the fridge, kidneys to follow."

"Pity about the clothes, you look nice like that."

I stand up and lean over closer to the mirror, staring at my face. He sniggers. It is the acanthus leaves. I snigger back at his reflection in the mirror, thinking, "Does he deduce from this elegant imprint that I have been sitting on this chair for at least ten minutes?"

He goes away, clumping athletically downstairs to forage for the orange juice.

Clothes on, and a little Ultima II will do wonders for these pores, deceiving the eye over the matter of the odd wrinkle. And face powder.

God, what a marvellous sneeze that was, most satisfactory. Powder, there's powder over everything, every crevice of this mirror frame holds a delicate blur of triple-milled silk. Lovely dark eye liner, green shadow, and the mascara, a touch on the eyebrows, then with a brush and with care, the lips, dewy is the word. I brush with vigour my short hair and cover it with a wig, an expensive foible, but a fantastic transformation. I the gold beauty. My own mother would not recognise me, nor I either, were it not for the fact that I saw the act of putting on the wig, and not only that, beneath that ... and beneath that ...

Stay with me during this day, mineral lady, you are ugly, but at least I know you, a bit.

If you were the outer image, we would be locked away in some psychiatrist's cupboard along with other freaks, those with birthmarks over the entire epidermis, deep like rose-coloured leather; I have seen them, spoken with them, and without fail have smelt ineradicable and unhealthy pain in the soul, and have suspected great beauty locked within.

But there is no cause for depression or despair; I have my face to hide in, and my mask of make-up, and other's ideas of what I am to screen me, until perhaps I become indeed something else, that need not fear showing itself only for a brief moment, coaxed and cajoled to appear, and then retire behind the veil.

Dust off a bit of this powder with a face tissue, put the lid on the jar of cream, set the chair straight, switch off the heater element, and go to make breakfast. Looking at the mirror as I leave, I murmur: "See you tomorrow."

∞

THE HEAT DEATH OF THE UNIVERSE

PAMELA ZOLINE

Pamela Zoline is a writer and painter. She was born in Chicago and now lives in London with her husband, artist John Lifton, and their daughter, Abigail. Her paintings have been exhibited at the Tate Gallery; both her art and her fiction have appeared in New Worlds. *She is completing a novel, tentatively called* Dream-Work; *a portion of the book will be published in Harlan Ellison's anthology* The Last Dangerous Visions. *Her artistic and literary talents are expertly combined in "The Heat Death of the Universe," which was her first published story.*

1. ONTOLOGY: That branch of metaphysics which concerns itself with the problems of the nature of existence or being.

2. Imagine a pale blue morning sky, almost green, with clouds only at the rims. The earth rolls and the sun appears to mount, mountains erode, fruits de-

cay, the Foraminifera adds another chamber to its shell, babies' fingernails grow as does the hair of the dead in their graves, and in egg timers the sands fall and the eggs cook on.

3. Sarah Boyle thinks of her nose as too large, though several men have cherished it. The nose is generous and performs a well-calculated geometric curve, at the arch of which the skin is drawn very tight and a faint whiteness of bone can be seen showing through, it has much the same architectural tension and sense of mathematical calculation as the day-after-Thanksgiving breastbone on the carcass of turkey; her maiden name was Sloss, mixed German, English and Irish descent; in grade school she was very bad at playing softball and, besides being chosen last for the team, was always made to play center field, no one could ever hit to center field; she loves music best of all the arts, and of music, Bach, J. S.; she lives in California, though she grew up in Boston and Toledo.

4. BREAKFAST TIME AT THE BOYLES' HOUSE ON LA FLORIDA STREET, ALAMEDA, CALIFORNIA, THE CHILDREN DEMAND SUGAR FROSTED FLAKES.

With some reluctance Sarah Boyle dishes out Sugar Frosted Flakes to her children, already hearing the decay set in upon the little milk-white teeth, the bony whine of the dentist's drill. The dentist is a short, gentle man with a moustache who sometimes reminds Sarah of an uncle who lives in Ohio. One bowl per child.

5. If one can imagine it considered as an abstract object by members of a totally separate culture, one can see that the cereal box might seem a beautiful

thing. The solid rectangle is neatly joined and classical in proportions, on it are squandered wealths of richest colours, virgin blues, crimsons, dense ochres, precious pigments once reserved for sacred paintings and as cosmetics for the blind faces of marble gods. Giant size. Net Weight 16 ounces, 250 grams. "They're tigeriffic!" says Tony the Tiger. The box blats promises: Energy, Nature's Own Goodness, an endless pubescence. On its back is a mask of William Shakespeare to be cut out, folded, worn by thousands of tiny Shakespeares in Kansas City, Detroit, Tucson, San Diego, Tampa. He appears at once more kindly and somewhat more vacant than we are used to seeing him. Two or more of the children lay claim to the mask, but Sarah puts off that Solomon's decision until such time as the box is empty.

6. A notice in orange flourishes states that a Surprise Gift is to be found somewhere in the package, nestled amongst the golden flakes. So far it has not been unearthed, and the children request more cereal than they wish to eat, great yellow heaps of it, to hurry the discovery. Even so, at the end of the meal, some layers of flakes remain in the box and the Gift must still be among them.

7. There is even a Special Offer of a secret membership, code and magic ring; these to be obtained by sending in the box top with 50¢.

8. Three offers on one cereal box. To Sarah Boyle this seems to be oversell. Perhaps something is terribly wrong with the cereal and it must be sold quickly, got off the shelves before the news breaks.

Perhaps it causes a special, cruel Cancer in little children. As Sarah Boyle collects the bowls printed with bunnies and baseball statistics, still slopping half full of milk and wilted flakes, she imagines *in her mind's eye* the headlines, "Nation's Small Fry Stricken, Fate's Finger Sugar-Coated, Lethal Sweetness Socks Tots."

9. Sarah Boyle is a vivacious and intelligent young wife and mother, educated at a fine Eastern college, proud of her growing family which keeps her busy and happy around the house.

10. BIRTHDAY.

Today is the birthday of one of the children. There will be a party in the late afternoon.

11. CLEANING UP THE HOUSE. ONE.

Cleaning up the kitchen. Sarah Boyle puts the bowls, plates, glasses and silverware into the sink. She scrubs at the stickiness on the yellow-marbled Formica table with a blue synthetic sponge, a special blue which we shall see again. There are marks of children's hands in various sizes printed with sugar and grime on all the table's surfaces. The marks catch the light, they appear and disappear according to the position of the observing eye. The floor sweepings include a triangular half of toast spread with grape jelly, bobby pins, a green Band-Aid, flakes, a doll's eye, dust, dog's hair and a button.

12. Until we reach the statistically likely planet and begin to converse with whatever green-faced, teleporting denizens thereof—considering only this shrunk and communication-ravaged world—can we

any more postulate a separate culture? Viewing the metastasis of Western Culture it seems progressively less likely. Sarah Boyle imagines a whole world which has become like California, all topographical imperfections sanded away with the sweet-smelling burr of the plastic surgeon's cosmetic polisher; a world populace dieting, leisured, similar in pink and mauve hair and rhinestone shades. A land Cunt Pink and Avocado Green, brassiered and girdled by monstrous complexities of Super Highways, a California endless and unceasing, embracing and transforming the entire globe, California, California!

13. INSERT ONE. ON ENTROPY.

ENTROPY: A quantity introduced in the first place to facilitate the calculations, and to give clear expressions to the results of thermodynamics. Changes of entropy can be calculated only for a reversible process, and may then be defined as the ratio of the amount of heat taken up to the absolute temperature at which the heat is absorbed. Entropy changes for actual irreversible processes are calculated by postulating equivalent theoretical reversible changes. The entropy of a system is a measure of its degree of disorder. The total entropy of any isolated system can never decrease in any change; it must either increase (irreversible process) or remain constant (reversible process). The total entropy of the Universe therefore is increasing, tending towards a maximum, corresponding to complete disorder of the particles in it (assuming that it may be regarded as an isolated system). See *heat death of the Universe.*

14. CLEANING UP THE HOUSE. TWO.

Washing the baby's diapers. Sarah Boyle writes notes to herself all over the house; a mazed wild script larded with arrows, diagrams, pictures; graffiti on every available surface in a desperate/heroic attempt to index, record, bluff, invoke, order and placate. On the fluted and flowered white plastic lid of the diaper bin she has written in Blushing Pink Nitetime lipstick a phrase to ward off fumy ammoniac despair. "The nitrogen cycle is the vital round of organic and inorganic exchange on earth. The sweet breath of the Universe." On the wall by the washing machine are Yin and Yang signs, mandalas, and the words, "Many young wives feel trapped. It is a contemporary sociological phenomenon which may be explained in part by a gap between changing living patterns and the accommodation of social services to these patterns." Over the stove she has written "Help, Help, Help, Help, Help."

15. Sometimes she numbers or letters the things in a room, writing the assigned character on each object. There are 819 separate moveable objects in the living room, counting books. Sometimes she labels objects with their names, or with false names; thus on her bureau the hair brush is labeled HAIR BRUSH, the cologne, COLOGNE, the hand cream, CAT. She is passionately fond of children's dictionaries, encyclopaedias, ABCs and all reference books, transfixed and comforted at their simulacra of a complete listing and ordering.

16. On the door of a bedroom are written two definitions from reference books, "GOD: An object of

worship"; HOMEOSTASIS: Maintenance of constancy of internal environment."

17. Sarah Boyle washes the diapers, washes the linen, Oh Saint Veronica, changes the sheets on the baby's crib. She begins to put away some of the toys, stepping over and around the organizations of playthings which still seem inhabited. There are various vehicles, and articles of medicine, domesticity and war; whole zoos of stuffed animals, bruised and odorous with years of love; hundreds of small figures, plastic animals, cowboys, cars, spacemen, with which the children make sub and supra worlds in their play. One of Sarah's favourite toys is the Baba, the wooden Russian doll which, opened, reveals a smaller but otherwise identical doll which opens to reveal, etc., a lesson in infinity at least to the number of seven dolls.

18. Sarah Boyle's mother has been dead for two years. Sarah Boyle thinks of music as the formal articulation of the passage of time, and of Bach as the most poignant rendering of this. Her eyes are sometimes the colour of the aforementioned kitchen sponge. Her hair is natural spaniel brown; months ago on an hysterical day she dyed it red, so now it is two-toned with a stripe in the middle, like the painted walls of slum buildings or old schools.

19. INSERT TWO. THE HEAT DEATH OF THE UNIVERSE. The second law of thermodynamics can be interpreted to mean that the ENTROPY of a closed system tends toward a maximum and that its available ENERGY tends toward a minimum. It has been held that the Universe constitutes a thermodynam-

ically closed system, and if this were true it would mean that a time must finally come when the Universe "unwinds" itself, no energy being available for use. This state is referred to as the "heat death of the Universe." It is by no means certain, however, that the Universe can be considered as a closed system in this sense.

20. Sarah Boyle pours out a Coke from the refrigerator and lights a cigarette. The coldness and sweetness of the thick brown liquid make her throat ache and her teeth sting briefly, sweet juice of my youth, her eyes glass with the carbonation, she thinks of the Heat Death of the Universe. A logarithmic of those late summer days, endless as the Irish serpent twisting through jewelled manuscripts forever, tail in mouth, the heat pressing, bloating, doing violence. The Los Angeles sky becomes so filled and bleached with detritus that it loses all colour and silvers like a mirror, reflecting back the fricasseeing earth. Everything becoming warmer and warmer, each particle of matter becoming more agitated, more excited until the bonds shatter, the glues fail, the deodorants lose their seals. She imagines the whole of New York City melting like a Dali into a great chocolate mass, a great soup, the Great Soup of New York.

21. CLEANING UP THE HOUSE. THREE.

Beds made. Vacuuming the hall, a carpet of faded flowers, vines and leaves which endlessly wind and twist into each other in a fevered and permanent ecstasy. Suddenly the vacuum blows instead of sucks, spewing marbles, dolls' eyes, dust, crackers. An old trick. "Oh my god," says Sarah. The baby yells on cue for attention/changing/food. Sarah kicks the vacuum cleaner and it retches and begins working again.

22. AT LUNCH ONLY ONE GLASS OF MILK IS SPILLED. At lunch only one glass of milk is spilled.

23. The plants need watering, Geranium, Hyacinth, Lavender, Avocado, Cyclamen. Feed the fish, happy fish with china castles and mermaids in the bowl. The turtle looks more and more unwell and is probably dying.

24. Sarah Boyle's blue eyes, how blue? Bluer far and of a different quality than the Nature metaphors which were both engine and fuel to so much of precedent literature. A fine, modern, acid, synthetic blue; the shiny cerulean of the skies on postcards sent from lush subtropics, the natives grinning ivory ambivalent grins in their dark faces; the promising, fat, unnatural blue of the heavy tranquillizer capsule; the cool, mean blue of that fake kitchen sponge; the deepest, most unbelievable azure of the tiled and mossless interiors of California swimming pools. The chemists in their kitchens cooked, cooled and distilled this blue from thousands of colourless and wonderfully constructed crystals, each one unique and nonpareil; and now that colour hisses, bubbles, burns in Sarah's eyes.

25. INSERT THREE. ON LIGHT.
    LIGHT: Name given to the agency by means of which a viewed object influences the observer's eyes. Consists of electro-magnetic radiation within the wave-length range 4×10^{-5} cm. to 7×10^{-5} cm. approximately; variations in the wave-length pro-

duce different sensations in the eye, corresponding to different colours. See *colour vision.*

26. LIGHT AND CLEANING THE LIVING ROOM.

All the objects (819) and surfaces in the living room are dusty, grey common dust as though this were the den of a giant, moulting mouse. Suddenly quantities of waves or particles of very strong sunlight speed in through the window, and everything incandesces, multiple rainbows. Poised in what has become a solid cube of light, like an ancient insect trapped in amber, Sarah Boyle realizes that the dust is indeed the most beautiful stuff in the room, a manna for the eyes. Duchamp, that father of thought, has set with fixative some dust which fell on one of his sculptures, counting it as part of the work. "That way madness lies, says Sarah," says Sarah. The thought of ordering a household on Dada principles balloons again. All the rooms would fill up with objects, newspapers and magazines would compost, the potatoes in the rack, the canned green beans in the garbage can would take new heart and come to life again, reaching out green shoots towards the sun. The plants would grow wild and wind into a jungle around the house, splitting plaster, tearing shingles, the garden would enter in at the door. The goldfish would die, the birds would die, we'd have them stuffed; the dog would die from lack of care, and probably the children—all stuffed and sitting around the house, covered with dust.

27. INSERT FOUR. DADA.

DADA (Fr., hobby-horse) was a nihilistic precursor of Surrealism, invented in Zurich during

World War I, a product of hysteria and shock lasting from about 1915 to 1922. It was deliberately anti-art and anti-sense, intended to outrage and scandalize, and its most characteristic production was the reproduction of the "Mona Lisa" decorated with a moustache and the obscene caption LHOOQ (read: *elle a chaud au cul*) "by" Duchamp. Other manifestations included Arp's collages of coloured paper cut out at random and shuffled, ready-made objects such as the bottle drier and the bicycle wheel "signed" by Duchamp, Picabia's drawings of bits of machinery with incongruous titles, incoherent poetry, a lecture given by 38 lecturers in unison, and an exhibition in Cologne in 1920, held in an annexe to a café lavatory, at which a chopper was provided for spectators to smash the exhibits with—which they did.

28. TIME PIECES AND OTHER MEASURING DEVICES.

In the Boyle house there are four clocks; three watches (one a Mickey Mouse watch which does not work); two calendars and two engagement books; three rulers, a yard stick; a measuring cup; a set of red plastic measuring spoons which includes a tablespoon, a teaspoon, a one-half teaspoon, one-fourth teaspoon and one-eighth teaspoon; an egg timer; an oral thermometer and a rectal thermometer; a Boy Scout compass; a barometer in the shape of a house, in and out of which an old woman and an old man chase each other forever without fulfilment; a bathroom scale; an infant scale; a tape measure which can be pulled out of a stuffed felt strawberry; a wall on which the children's heights are marked; a metronome.

29. Sarah Boyle finds a new line in her face after lunch while cleaning the bathroom. It is as yet barely visible, running from the midpoint of her forehead to the bridge of her nose. By inward curling of her eyebrows she can etch it clearly as it will come to appear in the future. She marks another mark on the wall where she has drawn out a scoring area. Face Lines and Other Intimations of Mortality, the heading says. There are thirty-two marks, counting this latest one.

30. Sarah Boyle is a vivacious and witty young wife and mother, educated at a fine Eastern college, proud of her growing family which keeps her happy and busy around the house, involved in many hobbies and community activities, and only occasionally given to obsessions concerning Time/Entropy/Chaos and Death.

31. Sarah Boyle is never quite sure how many children she has.

32. Sarah thinks from time to time; Sarah is occasionally visited with this thought; at times this thought comes upon Sarah, that there are things to be hoped for, accomplishments to be desired beyond the mere reproductions, mirror reproduction of one's kind. The babies. Lying in bed at night sometimes the memory of the act of birth, always the hue and texture of red plush theatre seats, washes up; the rending which always, at a certain intensity of pain, slipped into landscapes, the sweet breath of the sweating nurse. The wooden Russian doll has bright, perfectly round red spots on her cheeks, she splits in the centre to reveal a doll

smaller but in all other respects identical with round bright red spots on her cheeks, etc.

33. How fortunate for the species, Sarah muses or is mused, that children are as ingratiating as we know them. Otherwise they would soon be salted off for the leeches they are, and the race would extinguish itself in a fair sweet flowering, the last generation's massive achievement in the arts and pursuits of high civilization. The finest women would have their tubes tied off at the age of twelve, or perhaps refrain altogether from the Act of Love? All interests would be bent to a refining and perfecting of each febrile sense, each fluid hour, with no more cowardly investment in immortality via the patchy and too often disappointing vegetables of one's own womb.

34. INSERT FIVE. LOVE.

LOVE: A typical sentiment involving fondness for, or attachment to, an object, the idea of which is emotionally coloured whenever it arises in the mind, and capable, as Shand has pointed out, of evoking any one of a whole gamut of primary emotions, according to the situation in which the object is placed, or represented; often, and by psychoanalysts always, used in the sense of *sex-love* or even *lust* (q.v.).

35. Sarah Boyle has at times felt a unity with her body, at other times a complete separation. The mind/body duality considered. The time/space duality considered. The male/female duality considered. The matter/energy duality considered. Sometimes, at extremes, her Body seems to her an animal on a leash, taken for walks in the park by her Mind.

The lampposts of experience. Her arms are lightly freckled, and when she gets very tired the places under her eyes became violet.

36. Housework is never completed, the chaos always lurks ready to encroach on any area left unweeded, a jungle filled with dirty pans and the roaring of giant stuffed toy animals suddenly turned savage. Terrible glass eyes.

37. SHOPPING FOR THE BIRTHDAY CAKE.

Shopping in the supermarket with the baby in front of the cart and a larger child holding on. The light from the ice-cube-tray-shaped fluorescent lights is mixed blue and pink and brighter, colder, and cheaper than daylight. The doors swing open just as you reach out your hand for them, Tantalus, moving with a ghastly quiet swing. Hot dogs for the party. Potato chips, gum drops, a paper tablecloth with birthday designs, hot-dog buns, catsup, mustard, piccalilli, balloons, instant coffee Continental style, dog food, frozen peas, ice cream, frozen lima beans, frozen broccoli in butter sauce, paper birthday hats, paper napkins in three colours, a box of Sugar Frosted Flakes with a Wolfgang Amadeus Mozart mask on the back, bread, pizza mix. The notes of a just graspable music filter through the giant store, for the most part by-passing the brain and acting directly on the liver, blood and lymph. The air is delicately scented with aluminum. Half-and-half cream, tea bags, bacon, sandwich meat, strawberry jam. Sarah is in front of the shelves of cleaning products now, and the baby is beginning to whine. Around her are whole libraries of objects, offering themselves. Some of that same old hysteria that had incarnadined her hair rises up again, and she does not refuse it. There is one moment when she can choose direction, like standing on a chalk-drawn X, a hot cross bun, and she does not choose calm and measure. Sarah Boyle begins to pick out, methodically, deliberately and with a careful ecstasy, one of every cleaning product which the store sells. Window Cleaner, Glass Cleaner, Brass Polish, Silver Polish, Steel Wool, eighteen different brands of Detergent, Disinfectant, Toilet Cleanser, Water Softener, Fabric Softener, Drain Cleanser, Spot Remover, Floor Wax, Furniture Wax, Car Wax, Carpet Shampoo, Dog Shampoo, Shampoo for people with dry, oily and normal hair, for people with dandruff, for people with grey hair. Toothpaste, Tooth Powder, Denture Cleaner, Deodorants, Antiperspirants, Antiseptics, Soaps, Cleansers, Abrasives, Oven Cleaners, Makeup Removers. When the same products appear in different sizes Sarah takes one of each size. For some products she accumulates whole little families of containers: a giant Father bottle of shampoo, a Mother bottle, an Older Sister bottle just smaller than the Mother bottle, and a very tiny Baby Brother bottle. Sarah fills three shopping carts and has to have help wheeling them all down the aisles. At the check-out counter her laughter and hysteria keep threatening to overflow as the pale blonde clerk with no eyebrows like the "Mona Lisa" pretends normality and disinterest. The bill comes to $57.53 and Sarah has to write a check. Driving home, the baby strapped in the drive-a-cot and the paper bags bulging in the back seat, she cries.

38. BEFORE THE PARTY.

Mrs. David Boyle, mother-in-law of Sarah Boyle, is coming to the party of her grandchild. She brings a toy, a yellow wooden duck on a string, made in Austria; the duck quacks as it is pulled along the floor. Sarah is filling paper cups with gum drops and chocolates, and Mrs. David Boyle sits at the kitchen table and talks to her. She is talking about several things, she is talking about her garden which is flourishing except for a plague of rare black beetles, thought to have come from Hong Kong, which are undermining some of the most delicate growths at the roots, and feasting on the leaves of other plants. She is talking about a sale of household linens which she plans to attend on the following Tuesday. She is talking about her neighbour who has Cancer and is wasting away. The neighbour is a Catholic woman who had never had a day's illness in her life until the Cancer struck, and now she is, apparently, failing with dizzying speed. The doctor says her body's chaos, chaos, cells running wild all over, says Mrs. David Boyle. When I visited her she hardly *knew* me, can hardly *speak*, can't keep herself *clean*, says Mrs. David Boyle.

39. Sometimes Sarah can hardly remember how many cute, chubby little children she has.

40. When she used to stand out in center field far away from the other players, she used to make up songs and sing them to herself.

41. She thinks of the end of the world by ice.

42. She thinks of the end of the world by water.

43. She thinks of the end of the world by nuclear war.

44. There must be more than this, Sarah Boyle thinks, from time to time. What could one do to justify one's passage? Or less ambitiously, to change, even in the motion of the smallest mote, the course and circulation of the world? Sometimes Sarah's dreams are of heroic girth, a new symphony using laboratories of machinery and all invented instruments, at once giant in scope and intelligible to all, to heal the bloody breach; a series of paintings which would transfigure and astonish and calm the frenzied art world in its panting race; a new novel that would refurbish language. Sometimes she considers the mystical, the streaky and random, and it seems that one change, no matter how small, would be enough. Turtles are supposed to live for many years. To carve a name, date and perhaps a word of hope upon a turtle's shell, then set him free to wend the world, surely this one act might cancel out absurdity?

45. Mrs. David Boyle has a faint moustache, like Duchamp's "Mona Lisa."

46. THE BIRTHDAY PARTY.
Many children, dressed in pastels, sit around the long table. They are exhausted and overexcited from games fiercely played, some are flushed and wet, others unnaturally pale. This general agitation and the paper party hats they wear combine to make them appear a dinner party of debauched midgets. It is time for the cake. A huge chocolate cake in the shape of a rocket and launching pad and covered with blue and pink icing is carried in. In

the hush the birthday child begins to cry. He stops crying, makes a wish and blows out the candles.

47. One child will not eat hot dogs, ice cream or cake, and asks for cereal. Sarah pours him out a bowl of Sugar Frosted Flakes, and a moment later he chokes. Sarah pounds him on the back and out spits a tiny green plastic snake with red glass eyes, the Surprise Gift. All the children want it.

48. AFTER THE PARTY THE CHILDREN ARE PUT TO BED.

Bath time. Observing the nakedness of children, pink and slippery as seals, squealing as seals, now the splashing, grunting and smacking of cherry flesh on raspberry flesh reverberate in the pearl-tiled steamy cubicle. The nakedness of children is so much more absolute than that of the mature. No musky curling hair to indicate the target points, no knobbly clutch of plane and fat and curvature to ennoble this prince of beasts. All well-fed naked children appear edible. Sarah's teeth hum in her head with memory of bloody feastings, prehistory. Young humans appear too like the young of other species for smugness, and the comparison is not even in their favour, they are much the most peeled and unsupple of those young. Such pinkness, such utter nuded pinkness; the orifices neatly incised, rimmed with a slightly deeper rose, the incessant demands for breast, time, milks of many sorts.

49. INSERT SIX. WEINER ON ENTROPY.

In Gibbs' Universe order is least probable, chaos most probable. But while the Universe as a whole, if indeed there is a whole Universe, tends to run down, there are local enclaves whose direction seems opposed to that of the Universe at large and in which there is a limited and temporary tendency for organization to increase. Life finds its home in some of these enclaves.

50. Sarah Boyle imagines, in her mind's eye, cleaning and ordering the whole world, even the Universe. Filling the great spaces of space with a marvellous sweet-smelling, deep-cleansing foam. Deodorizing rank caves and volcanoes. Scrubbing rocks.

51. INSERT SEVEN. TURTLES.

Many different species of carnivorous Turtles live in the fresh waters of the tropical and temperate zones of various continents. Most northerly of the European Turtles (extending as far as Holland and Lithuania) is the European Pond Turtle (*Emys orbicularis*). It is from 8 to 10 inches long and may live a hundred years.

52. CLEANING UP AFTER THE PARTY.

Sarah is cleaning up after the party. Gum drops and melted ice cream surge off paper plates, making holes in the paper tablecloth through the printed roses. A fly has died a splendid death in a pool of strawberry ice cream. Wet jelly beans stain all they touch, finally becoming themselves colourless, opaque white like flocks of tamed or sleeping maggots. Plastic favours mount half-eaten pieces of blue cake. Strewn about are thin strips of fortune papers from the Japanese poppers. Upon them are printed strangely assorted phrases selected by apparently unilingual Japanese. Crowds of delicate yellow people spending great chunks of their lives in producing these most ephemeral of objects, and inscribing thousands of fine papers with absurd and incomprehensible messages. "The very hairs of your head are all numbered," reads one. Most of the balloons have popped. Someone has planted a hot dog in the daffodil pot. A few of the helium balloons have escaped their owners and now ride the celing. Another fortune paper reads, "Emperor's horses meet death worse, numbers, numbers."

53. She is very tired, violet under the eyes, mauve beneath the eyes. Her uncle in Ohio used to get the same marks under his eyes. She goes to the kitchen to lay the table for tomorrow's breakfast, then she sees that in the turtle's bowl the turtle is floating, still, on the surface of the water. Sarah Boyle pokes at it with a pencil but it does not move. She stands for several minutes looking at the dead turtle on the surface of the water. She is crying again.

54. She begins to cry. She goes to the refrigerator and takes out a carton of eggs, white eggs, extra large. She throws them one by one onto the kitchen floor which is patterned with strawberries in squares. They break beautifully. There is a Secret Society of Dentists, all moustached, with Special Code and Magic Rings. She begins to cry. She takes up three bunny dishes and throws them against the refrigerator, they shatter, and then the floor is covered with shards, chunks of partial bunnies, an ear, an eye here, a paw; Stockton, California, Acton, California, Chico, California, Redding, California, Glen Ellen, California, Cadiz, California, Angels Camp, California, Half Moon Bay. The total EN-

TROPY of the Universe therefore is increasing, tending towards a maximum, corresponding to complete disorder of the particles in it. She is crying, her mouth is open. She throws a jar of grape jelly and it smashes the window over the sink. Her eyes are blue. She begins to open her mouth. It has been held that the Universe constitutes a thermodynamically closed system, and if this were true it would mean that a time must finally come when the Universe "unwinds" itself, no energy being available for use. This state is referred to as the "heat death of the Universe." Sarah Boyle begins to cry. She throws a jar of strawberry jam against the stove, enamel chips off and the stove begins to bleed. Bach had twenty children, how many children has Sarah Boyle? Her mouth is open. Her mouth is opening. She turns on the water and fills the sinks with detergent. She writes on the kitchen wall, "William Shakespeare has Cancer and lives in California." She writes, "Sugar Frosted Flakes are the Food of the Gods." The water foams up in the sink, overflowing, bubbling onto the strawberry floor. She is about to begin to cry. Her mouth is opening. She is crying. She cries. How can one ever tell whether there are one or many fish? She begins to break glasses and dishes, she throws cups and cooking pots and jars of food which shatter and break and spread over the kitchen. The sand keeps falling, very quietly, in the egg timer. The old man and woman in the barometer never catch each other. She picks up eggs and throws them into the air. She begins to cry. She opens her mouth. The eggs arch slowly through the kitchen, like a baseball, hit high against the spring sky, seen from far away. They go higher and higher in the stillness, hesitate at the zenith, then begin to fall away slowly, slowly, through the fine, clear air.

∞

SONGS
OF WAR

KIT REED

Kit Reed lives in New England and has worked as a reporter and television editor. Her short fiction has appeared in Cosmopolitan, Transatlantic Review, The Magazine of Fantasy & Science Fiction, *and* Redbook. *She is the author of several novels, including* Tiger Rag *(Dutton),* Cry of the Daughter *(Dutton),* The Better Part *(Farrar, Straus & Giroux), and* Armed Camps *(Dutton). She was awarded a Guggenheim Fellowship in 1964. "Songs of War" is a sharply etched story of revolutionaries confronting both injustice and their own ambivalence about the roles they must play.*

For some weeks now a fire had burned day and night on a hillside just beyond the town limits; standing at her kitchen sink, Sally Hall could see the smoke rising over the trees. It curled upward in promise, but she could not be sure what it promised, and despite the fact that she was contented with her work and her family, Sally found herself stirred by the bright autumn air, the smoke emblem.

Nobody seemed to want to talk much about the fire, or what it meant. Her husband, Zack, passed it off with a shrug, saying it was probably just another commune. June Goodall, her neighbor, said it was coming from Ellen Ferguson's place; she owned the land and it was her business what she did with it. Sally said what if she had been taken prisoner. Vic Goodall said not to be ridiculous, if Ellen Ferguson wanted those people off her place, all she had to do was call the police and get them off, and in the meantime, it was nobody's business.

Still there was something commanding about the presence of the fire; the smoke rose steadily and could be seen for miles, and Sally, working at her drawing board, and a number of other women, going about their daily business, found themselves yearning after the smoke column with complex feelings. Some may have been recalling a primal past in which men conked large animals and dragged them into camp, and the only housework involved was a little gutting before they roasted the bloody chunks over the fire. The grease used to sink into the dirt and afterward the diners, smeared with blood and fat, would roll around in a happy tangle. Other women were stirred by all the adventure tales they had stored up from childhood; people would run away without even bothering to pack or leave a note, they always found food one way or another and they met new friends in the woods. Together they would tell stories over a campfire, and when they had eaten they would walk away from the bones to some high excitement that had nothing to do with the business of living from day to day. A few women, thinking of Castro and his happy guerrilla band, in the carefree, glamorous days before he came to power, were closer to the truth. Thinking wistfully of campfire camaraderie, of everybody marching together in a common cause, they were already dreaming of revolution.

Despite the haircut and the cheap suit supplied by the Acme Vacuum Cleaner company, Andy Ellis was an under-achiever college dropout who could care less about vacuum cleaners. Until this week he had been a beautiful, carefree kid, and now, with a dying mother to support, with the wraiths of unpaid bills and unsold Marvelvacs trailing behind him like Marley's chains, he was still beautiful, which is why the women opened their doors to him.

He was supposed to say, "Good morning, I'm from the Acme Vacuum Cleaner Company and I'm here to clean your living room, no obligation, absolutely free of charge." Then, with the room clean and the Marvelsweep with twenty attachments and ten optional features spread all over the rug, he was supposed to make his pitch.

The first woman he called on said he did good work but her husband would have to decide, so Andy sighed and began collecting the Flutesnoot, the Miracle Whoosher and all the other attachments and putting them back into the patented Bomb Bay Door.

"Well thanks anyway . . ."

"Oh, thank *you*," she said. He was astounded to discover that she was unbuttoning him here and there.

"Does this mean you want the vacuum after all?"

She covered him with hungry kisses. "Shut up and deal."

At the next house, he began again. "Good morning, I'm from the Acme Vacuum Cleaner company . . ."

"Never mind that. Come in."

At the third house, he and the lady of the house grappled in the midst of her unfinished novel, rolling here and there between the unfinished tapestry and the unfinished wire sculpture.

"If he would let me alone for a minute I would get some of these things done," she said. "All he ever thinks about is sex."

"If you don't like it, why are we doing this?"

"To get even," she said.

On his second day as a vacuum cleaner salesman, Andy changed his approach. Instead of going into his pitch, he would say, "Want to screw?" By the third day he had refined it to, "My place or yours?"

Friday his mother died so he was able to turn in his Marvelvac, which he thought was just as well, because he was exhausted and depressed, and, for all his efforts, he had made only one tentative sale, which was contingent upon his picking up the payments in person every week for the next twelve years. Standing over his mother's coffin, he could not for the life of him understand what had happened to women—not good old Mom, who had more or less liked her family and at any rate had died uncomplaining—but the others, all the women in every condition in all the houses he had gone to this week. Why weren't any of them happy?

Up in the hills, sitting around the fire, the women in the vanguard were talking about just that: the vagaries of life, and woman's condition. They had to think it was only that. If they were going to go on, they would have to be able to decide the problem was X, whatever X was. It had to be something they could name, so that, together, they could do something about it.

They were of a mind to free themselves. One of the things was to free themselves of the necessity of being thought of as sexual objects, which turned out to mean only that certain obvious concessions, like lipstick and pretty clothes, had by ukase been done away with. Still, there were those who wore their khakis and bandoliers with a difference. Whether or not they shaved their legs and armpits, whether or not they smelled, the pretty ones were still pretty and the others were not; the ones with good bodies walked in an unconscious pride and the others tried to ignore the differences and settled into their flesh, saying: Now, we are all equal.

There were great disputes as to what they were going to do, and which things they would do first. It was fairly well agreed that although the law said they were equal, nothing much was changed. There was still the monthly bleeding; Dr. Ora Fessenden, the noted gynecologist, had showed them a trick which was supposed to take care of all that, but nothing short of surgery or menopause would halt the process altogether; what man had to undergo such indignities? There was still pregnancy, but the women all agreed they were on top of that problem. That left the rest: men still looked down on them, in part because in the main, women were shorter; they were more or less free to pursue their careers, assuming they could keep a baby-sitter, but there were still midafternoon depressions, dishes, the wash; despite all the changes, life was much the same. More drastic action was needed.

They decided to form an army.

At the time, nobody was agreed on what they were going to do or how they would go about it, but they were all agreed that it was time for a change. Things could not go on as they were; life was often boring, and too hard.

She wrote a note:

Dear Ralph,

I am running away to realize my full potential. I know you have always said I could do anything I want but what you meant was, I could do anything as long as it didn't mess you up, which is not exactly the same thing now, is it? Don't bother to look for me.

No longer yours,
Lory

Then she went to join the women in the hills.

I would like to go, Suellen thought, *but what if they wouldn't let me have my baby?*

Jolene's uncle in the country always had a liver-colored setter named Fido. The name remained the same and the dogs were more or less interchangeable. Jolene called all her lovers Mike, and because they were more or less interchangeable, eventually she tired of them and went to join the women in the hills.

"You're not going," Herb Chandler said.

Annie said, "I am."

He grabbed her as she reached the door. "The hell you are, I need you."

"You don't need me, you need a maid." She slapped the side of his head. "Now let me go."

"You're mine," he said, aiming a karate chop at her neck. She wriggled and he missed.

"Just like your ox and your ass, huh." She had gotten hold of a lamp and she let him have it on top of the head.

"Ow," he said, and crumpled to the floor.

"Nobody owns me," she said, throwing the vase of flowers she kept on the side table, just for good measure. "I'll be back when it's over." Stepping around him, she went out the door.

After everybody left that morning, June mooned around the living room, picking up the scattered newspapers, collecting her and Vic's empty coffee cups and marching out to face the kitchen table, which looked the same way every morning at this time, glossy with spilled milk and clotted cereal, which meant that she had to go through the same motions every morning at this time, feeling more and more like that jerk, whatever his name was, who for eternity kept on pushing the same recalcitrant stone up the hill; he was never going to get it to the top because it kept falling back on him and she was never going to get to the top, wherever that was, because there would always be the kitchen table, and the wash, and the crumbs on the rug, and besides she didn't know where the top was because she had gotten married right after Sweetbriar and the next minute, bang, there was the kitchen table and, give or take a few babies, give or take a few

stabs at night classes in something or other, tha'
seemed to be her life. There it was in the morning,
there it was again at noon, there it was at night;
when people said, at parties, "What do you do?" she
could only move her hands helplessly because there
was no answer she could give that would please
either herself or them. *I clean the kitchen table*, she
thought, because there was no other way to describe
it. Occasionally she thought about running away,
but where would she go, and how would she live?
Besides, she would miss Vic and the kids and her
favorite chair in the television room. Sometimes she
thought she might grab the milkman or the next delivery boy, but she knew she would be too embarrassed, either that or she would start laughing, or
the delivery boy would, and even if they didn't, she
would never be able to face Vic. She thought she
had begun to disappear, like the television or the
washing machine; after a while nobody would see
her at all. They might complain if she wasn't working properly, but in the main she was just another
household appliance, and so she mooned, wondering if this was all there was ever going to be: herself
in the house, the kitchen table.

Then the notice came.

JOIN NOW

It was in the morning mail, hastily mimeographed
and addressed to her by name. If she had been in a
different mood she might have tossed it out with the
rest of the junk mail, or called a few of her friends
to see if they had gotten it too. As it was, she read
it through, chewing over certain catchy phrases in

this call to arms, surprised to find her blood quickening. Then she packed and wrote her note:

Dear Vic,

There are clean sheets on all the beds and three casseroles in the freezer and one in the oven. The veal one should do for two meals. I have done all the wash and a thorough vacuuming. If Sandy's cough doesn't get any better you should take her in to see Dr. Weixelbaum, and don't forget Jimmy is supposed to have his braces tightened on the 12th. Don't look for me.

Love,
June

Then she went to join the women in the hills.

Glenda Thompson taught psychology at the university; it was the semester break and she thought she might go to the women's encampment in an open spirit of inquiry. If she liked what they were doing she might chuck Richard, who was only an instructor while she was an assistant professor, and join them. To keep the appearance of objectivity, she would take notes.

Of course she was going to have to figure out what to do with the children while she was gone. No matter how many hours she and Richard taught, the children were her responsibility, and if they were both working in the house, she had to leave her typewriter and shush the children because of the way Richard got when he was disturbed. None of the sitters she called could come; Mrs. Birdsall, their regular sitter, had taken off without notice

again, to see her son the freshman in Miami, and
she exhausted the list of student sitters without any
luck. She thought briefly of leaving them at Richard's office, but she couldn't trust him to remember
them at the end of the day. She reflected bitterly
that men who wanted to work just got up and went
to the office. It had never seemed fair.

"Oh hell," she said finally, and because it was
easier, she packed Tommy and Bobby and took
them along.

Marva and Patsy and Betts were sitting around
in Marva's room; it was two days before the junior
prom and not one of them had a date, or even a
nibble; there weren't even any blind dates to be
had.

"I know what let's do," Marva said, "let's go up
to Ferguson's and join the women's army."

Betts said, "I didn't know they had an *army*."

"Nobody knows what they have up there," Patsy
said.

They left a note so Marva's mother would be
sure and call them in case somebody asked for a
date at the last minute and they got invited to the
prom after all.

Sally felt a twinge of guilt when she opened the
flier:

JOIN NOW

After she read it she went to the window and
looked at the smoke column in open disappoint-
ment: *Oh, so that's all it is.* Yearning after it in the
early autumn twilight, she had thought it might

represent something more: excitement, escape, but she supposed she should have guessed. There was no great getaway, just a bunch of people who needed more people to help. She knew she probably ought to go up and help out for a while, she could design posters and ads they could never afford if they went to a regular graphics studio. Still, all those women . . . She couldn't bring herself to make the first move.

"I'm not a joiner," she said aloud, but that wasn't really it; she had always worked at home, her studio took up one wing of the house and she made her own hours; when she tired of working she could pick at the breakfast dishes or take a nap on the lumpy couch at one end of the studio; when the kids came home she was always there and besides, she didn't like going places without Zack.

Instead she used the flier to test her colors, dabbing blues here, greens there, until she had more or less forgotten the message and all the mimeographing was obscured by color.

At the camp, Dr. Ora Fessenden was leading an indoctrination program for new recruits. She herself was in the stirrups, lecturing coolly while everybody filed by.

One little girl, lifted up by her mother, began to whisper: "Ashphasphazzzzz-pzz."

The mother muttered, "Mumumumummmmmmm. . . ."

Ellen Ferguson, who was holding the light, turned it on the child for a moment. "Well, what does *she* want?"

"She wants to know what a man's looks like."

Dr. Ora Fessenden took hold, barking from the stirrups. "With luck, she'll never have to see."

"Right on," the butch sisters chorused, but the others began to look at one another in growing discomfiture, which as the weeks passed would ripen into alarm.

By the time she reached the camp, June was already worried about the casseroles she had left for Vic and the kids. Would the one she had left in the oven go bad at room temperature? Maybe she ought to call Vic and tell him to let it bubble for an extra half hour just in case. Would Vic really keep an eye on Sandy, and if she got worse, would he get her to the doctor in time? What about Jimmy's braces? She almost turned back.

But she was already at the gate to Ellen Ferguson's farm, and she was surprised to see a hastily constructed guardhouse, with Ellen herself in khakis, standing with a carbine at the ready, and she said, "Don't shoot, Ellen, it's me."

"For God's sake, June, I'm not going to shoot you." Ellen pushed her glasses up on her forehead so she could look into June's face. "I never thought you'd have the guts."

"I guess I needed a change."

"Isn't it thrilling?"

"I feel funny without the children." June was trying to remember when she had last seen Ellen: over a bridge table? at Weight Watchers? "How did you get into this?"

"I needed something to live for," Ellen said.

By that time two other women with rifles had impounded her car and then she was in a jeep bouncing up the dirt road to headquarters. The

women behind the table all had on khakis, but
they looked not at all alike in them. One was tall
and tawny and called herself Sheena; there was a
tough, funny-looking one named Rap and the third
was Margy, still redolent of the kitchen sink. Sheena
made the welcoming speech, and then Rap took
her particulars while Margy wrote everything
down.

She lied a little about her weight, and was already on the defensive when Rap looked at her
over her glasses, saying, "Occupation?"

"Uh, household manager."

"Oh shit, another housewife. Skills?"

"Well, I used to paint a little, and . . ."

Rap snorted.

"I'm pretty good at conversational French."

"Kitchen detail," Rap said to Margy and Margy
checked off a box and flipped over to the next
sheet.

"But I'm tired of all that," June said.

Rap said, "Next."

Oh it was good sitting around the campfire,
swapping stories about the men at work and the
men at home; every woman had a horror story,
because even the men who claimed to be behind
them weren't really behind them, they were paying
lip service to avoid a higher price, and even the
best among them would make those terrible verbal
slips. It was good to talk to other women who
were smarter than their husbands and having to
pretend they weren't. It was good to be able to
sprawl in front of the fire without having to think
about Richard and what time he would be home.

The kids were safely stashed down at the day-care compound, along with everybody else's kids, and for the first time in at least eight years Glenda could relax and think about herself. She listened drowsily to that night's speeches, three examples of wildly diverging cant, and she would have taken notes except that she was full, digesting a dinner she hadn't had to cook, and for almost the first time in eight years she wasn't going to have to go out to the kitchen and face the dishes.

Marva, Patsy and Betts took turns admiring each other in their new uniforms and they sat at the edge of the group, hugging their knees and listening in growing excitement. Why, they didn't *have* to worry about what they looked like, that wasn't going to matter in the new scheme of things. It didn't *matter* whether or not they had dates. By the time the new order was established, they weren't even going to *want* dates. Although they would rather die than admit it, they all felt a little pang at this. Goodbye hope chest, goodbye wedding trip to Nassau and picture in the papers in the long white veil. Patsy, who wanted to be a corporation lawyer, thought: Why can't I have it *all*.

Now that his mother was dead and he didn't need to sell vacuum cleaners any more, Andy Ellis was thrown back on his own resources. He spent three hours in the shower and three days sleeping, and on the fourth day he emerged to find out his girl had left him for the koto player from across the hall. "Well shit," he said, and wandered into the street.

He had only been asleep for three days but everything was subtly different. The people in the corner market were mostly men, stocking up on TV dinners and chunky soups or else buying cooking wines and herbs, kidneys, beef liver and tripe. The usual girl was gone from the checkout counter, the butcher was running the register instead, and when Andy asked about it, Freddy the manager said, "She joined up."

"Are you kidding?"

"Some girl scout camp up at Ferguson's. The tails revolt."

Just then a jeep sped by in the street outside; there was a crash and they both hit the floor, rising to their elbows after the object that had shattered the front window did not explode. It was a rock with a note attached. Andy picked his way through the glass to retrieve it. It read:

WE WILL BURY YOU

"See?" Freddy said, ugly and vindictive. "See? See?"

The local hospital admitted several cases of temporary blindness in men who had been attacked by night with women's deodorant spray.

All over town the men whose wives remained lay next to them in growing unease. Although they all feigned sleep, they were aware that the stillness was too profound: the women were thinking.

The women trashed a porn movie house. Among them was the wife of the manager, who said, as

she threw an open can of film over the balcony,
watching it unroll, "I'm doing this for us."

So it had begun. For the time being, Rap and her
cadre, who were in charge of the military operation, intended to satisfy themselves with guerrilla
tactics; so far, nobody had been able to link the
sniping and matériel bombing with the women on
the hill, but they all knew it was only a matter of
time before the first police cruiser came up to Ellen Ferguson's gate with a search warrant, and
they were going to have to wage open war.

By this time one of the back pastures had been
converted to a rifle range, and even poor June had
to spend at least one hour of every day in practice.
She began to take an embarrassing pleasure in it,
thinking, as she potted away:

*Aha, Vic, there's a nick in your scalp. Maybe
you'll remember what I look like next time you
leave the house for the day.*

Okay, kids, I am not the maid.

*All right, Sally, you and your damn career. You're
still only the maid.*

Then, surprisingly: *This is for you, Sheena. How
dare you go around looking like that, when I have
to look like this.*

This is for every rapist on the block.

By the time she fired her last shot her vision was
blurred by tears. *June, you are stupid, stupid, you
always have been and you know perfectly well
nothing is going to make any difference.*

Two places away, Glenda saw Richard's outline
in the target. She made a bull's-eye. *All right, damn
you, pick up that toilet brush.*

Going back to camp in the truck they all sang "Up Women" and "The Internationale," and June began to feel a little better. It reminded her of the good old days at camp in middle childhood, when girls and boys played together as if there wasn't any difference. She longed for that old androgynous body, the time before sexual responsibility. Sitting next to her on the bench, Glenda sang along but her mind was at the university; she didn't know what she was going to do if she got the Guggenheim because Richard had applied without success for so long that he had given up trying. What should she do, lie about it? It would be in all the papers. She wondered how convincing she would be, saying, Shit, honey, it doesn't mean anything. She would have to give up the revolution and get back to her work; her book was only half-written; she would have to go back to juggling kids and house and work; it was going to be hard, hard. She decided finally that she would let the Guggenheim Foundation make the decision for her. She would wait until late February and then write and tell Richard where to forward her mail.

Leading the song, Rap looked at her group. Even the softest ones had callouses now, but it was going to be some time before she made real fighters out of them. She wondered why women had all buried the instinct to kill. It was those damn babies, she decided: grunt, strain, pain, *Baby*. Hand a mother a gun and tell her to kill and she will say, *After I went to all that trouble?* Well if you are going to make sacrifices you are going to have to make sacrifices, she thought, and led them in a chorus of the battle anthem, watching to see just

who did and who didn't throw herself into the last
chorus, which ended: kill, kill, *kill.*

Sally was watching the smoke again. Zack said,
"I wish you would come away from that window."
She kept looking for longer than he would have
liked her to, and when she turned, she said, "Zack,
why did you marry me?"
"Couldn't live without you."
"No, really."
"Because I wanted to love you and decorate you
and take care of you for the rest of your life."
"Why me?"
"I thought we could be friends for a long time."
"I guess I didn't mean why did you marry *me,*
I meant, why did you *marry* me."
He looked into his palms. "I wanted you to take
care of me too."
"Is that all?"
He could see she was serious and because she
was not going to let go he thought for a minute
and said at last, "Nobody wants to die alone."

Down the street, June Goodall's husband, Vic,
had called every hospital in the county without results. The police had no reports of middle-aged
housewives losing their memory in Sears or getting raped, robbed or poleaxed anywhere within
the city limits. The police sergeant said, "Mr. Goodall, we've got more serious things on our minds.
These bombings, for one thing, and the leaflets
and the rip-offs. Do you know that women have
been walking out of supermarkets with full shopping carts without paying a cent?" There seemed

to be a thousand cases like June's, and if the department ever got a minute for them it would have to be first come first served.

So Vic languished in his darkening house. He had managed to get the kids off to school by himself the past couple of days. He gave them money for hot lunches, but they were running out of clean clothes and he could not bring himself to sort through those disgusting smelly things in the clothes hamper to run a load of wash. They had run through June's casseroles and they were going to have to start eating out; they would probably go to the Big Beef Plaza tonight, and have pizza tomorrow and chicken the next night and Chinese the next, and if June wasn't back by that time he didn't know what he was going to do because he was at his wits' end. The dishes were piling up in the kitchen and he couldn't understand why everything looked so grimy; he couldn't quite figure out why, but the toilet had begun to smell. One of these days he was going to have to try and get his mother over to clean things up a little. It was annoying, not having any clean underwear. He wished June would come back.

For the fifth straight day, Richard Thompson, Glenda's husband, opened *The French Chef* to a new recipe and prepared himself an exquisite dinner. Once it was finished he relaxed in the blissful silence. Now that Glenda was gone he was able to keep things the way he liked them; he didn't break his neck on Matchbox racers every time he went to put a little Vivaldi on the record player. It was refreshing not to have to meet Glen-

da's eyes, where, to his growing dissatisfaction, he
perpetually measured himself. Without her demands, without the kids around to distract him,
he would be able to finish his monograph on Lyly's
Euphues. He might even begin to write his book.
Setting aside Glenda's half-finished manuscript
with a certain satisfaction, he cleared a space for
himself at the desk and tried to begin.

Castrated, he thought half an hour later. *Her and
her damned career, she has castrated me.*

He went to the phone and began calling names
on his secret list. For some reason most of them
weren't home, but on the fifth call he came up
with Jennifer, the biology major who wanted to
write poetry, and within minutes the two of them
were reaffirming his masculinity on the living room
rug, and if a few pages of Glenda's half-finished
manuscript got mislaid in the tussle, who was there
to protest? If she was going to be off there, farting
around in the woods with all those women, she
never would get it finished.

In the hills, the number of women had swelled,
and it was apparent to Sheena, Ellen and Rap that
it was time to stop hit-and-run terrorism and operate on a larger scale. They would mount a final
recruiting campaign. Once that was completed,
they would be ready to take their first objective.
Sheena had decided the Sunnydell Shopping Center would be their base for a sweep of the entire
country. They were fairly sure retaliation would be
slow, and to impede it further, they had prepared
an advertising campaign built on the slogan: YOU

WOULDN'T SHOOT YOUR MOTHER, WOULD YOU? As soon as they could, they would co-opt some television equipment and make their first nationwide telecast from Sunnydell. Volunteers would flock in from fifty states and in time the country would be theirs.

There was some difference of opinion as to what they were going to do with it. Rap was advocating a scorched-earth policy; the women would rise like phoenixes from the ashes and build a new nation from the rubble, more or less alone. Sheena raised the idea of an auxiliary made up of male sympathizers. The women would rule, but with men at hand. Margy secretly felt that both Rap and Sheena were too militant; she didn't want things to be completely different, only a little better. Ellen Ferguson wanted to annex all the land surrounding her place. She envisioned it as the capitol city of the new world. The butch sisters wanted special legislation that would outlaw contact, social or sexual, with men, with, perhaps, special provisions for social meetings with their gay brethren. Certain of the straight sisters were made uncomfortable by their association with the butch sisters and wished there were some way the battle could progress without them. At least half of these women wanted their men back, once victory was assured, and the other half were looking into ways of perpetuating the race by means of parthenogenesis, or, at worst, sperm banks and AI techniques. One highly vocal splinter group wanted mandatory sterilization for everybody, and a portion of the lunatic fringe was demanding transsexual operations. Because nobody

could agree, the women decided for the time being
to skip over the issues and concentrate on the war
effort itself.

By this time, word had spread and the volunteers
were coming in, so it was easy to ignore issues
because logistics were more pressing. It was still
warm enough for the extras to bunk in the fields,
but winter was coming on and the women were
going to have to manage food, shelters and uniforms for an unpredictable number. There had
been a temporary windfall when Rap's bunch hi-
jacked a couple of semis filled with frozen dinners
and surplus clothes, but Rap and Sheena and the
others could sense the hounds of hunger and need
not far away and so they worked feverishly to prepare for the invasion. Unless they could take the
town by the end of the month, they were lost.

"We won't have to hurt our *fathers*, will we?"
Although she was now an expert marksman and
had been placed in charge of a platoon, Patsy was
still not at ease with the cause.

Rap avoided her eyes. "Don't be ridiculous."

"I just couldn't do that to anybody I *loved*," Patsy
said. She reassembled her rifle, driving the bolt into
place with a click.

"Don't you worry about it," Rap said. "All you
have to worry about is looking good when you lead
that recruiting detail."

"Okay." Patsy tossed her hair. She knew how she
and her platoon looked, charging into the wind;
she could feel the whole wild group around her, on
the run with their heads high and their bright hair
streaming. *I wish the boys at school could see,* she

thought, and turned away hastily before Rap could guess what she was thinking.

I wonder if any woman academic can be happy. Glenda was on latrine detail and this always made her reflective. *Maybe if they marry garage mechanics.* In the old days there had been academic types: single, tweedy, sturdy in orthopedic shoes, but somewhere along the way these types had been supplanted by married women of every conceivable type, who pressed forward in wildly varied disciplines, having in common only the singular harried look which marked them all. The rubric was more or less set: if you were good, you always had to worry about whether you were shortchanging your family; if you weren't as good as he was, you would always have to wonder whether it was because of all the other duties: babies, meals, the house; if despite everything you turned out to be better than he was, then you had to decide whether to try and minimize it, or prepare yourself for the wise looks on the one side, on the other, his look of uncomprehending reproach. If you *were* better than he was, then why should you be wasting your time with *him?* She felt light years removed from the time when girls used to be advised to let *him* win the tennis match; everybody played to win now, but she had the uncomfortable feeling that there might never be any real victories. Whether or not you won, there were too many impediments: if he had a job and you didn't, then tough; if you both had jobs but he didn't get tenure, then you had to quit and move with him to a new place. She poured Lysol into the last toilet and turned her back on it, thinking: *Maybe that's why those Hollywood marriages are always breaking up.*

Sally finished putting the children to bed and came back into the living room, where Zack was waiting for her on the couch. By this time she had heard the women's broadcasts, she was well aware of what was going on at Ellen Ferguson's place and knew as well that this was where June was, and June was so inept, so soft and incapable that she really ought to be up there helping June, helping *them;* it was a job that ought to be done, on what scale she could not be sure, but the fire was warm and Zack was waiting; he and the children, her career, were all more important than that abstraction in the hills; she had negotiated her own peace—let them take care of theirs. Settling in next to Zack, she thought: *I don't love my little pink dishmop, I don't, but everybody has to shovel* some *shit.* Then: *God help the sailors and poor fishermen who have to be abroad on a night like this.*

June had requisitioned a jeep and was on her way into town to knock over the corner market, because food was already in short supply. She had on the housedress she had worn when she enlisted, and she would carry somebody's old pink coat over her arm to hide the pistol and the grenade she would use to hold her hostages at bay while the grocery boys filled up the jeep. She had meant to go directly to her own corner market, thinking, among other things, that the manager might recognize her and tell Vic, after which, of course, he would track her back to the camp and force her to come home to him and the children. Somehow or other she went right by the market and ended up at the corner of her street.

She knew she was making a mistake but she parked and began to prowl the neighborhood. The curtains in Sally's window were drawn but the light behind them gave out a rosy glow, which called up in her longings that she could not have identified; they had very little to do with her own home, or her life with Vic; they dated, rather, from her childhood, when she had imagined marriage, had prepared herself for it with an amorphous but unshakeable idea of what it would be like. Vic had forgotten to put out the garbage; overflowing cans crowded the back porch and one of them was overturned. Walking on self-conscious cat feet, June made her way up on the porch and peered into the kitchen: just as she had suspected, a mess. A portion of her was tempted to go in and do a swift, secret cleaning—*the phantom housewife strikes*—but the risk of being discovered was too great. Well, let him clean up his own damn messes from now on. She tiptoed back down the steps and went around the house, crunching through bushes to look into the living room. She had hoped to get a glimpse of the children, but they were already in bed. She thought about waking Juney with pebbles on her window, whispering: Don't worry, mother's all right, but she wasn't strong enough; if she saw the children she would never be able to walk away and return to camp. She assuaged herself by thinking she would come back for Juney and Victor Junior just as soon as victory was assured. The living room had an abandoned look, with dust visible and papers strewn, a chair overturned and Vic himself asleep on the couch, just another neglected object in this neglected house. Surprised at how little she felt, she shrugged and turned away. On her way back to the jeep she did stop to right the garbage can.

The holdup went off all right; she could hear distant sirens building behind her, but so far as she knew, she wasn't followed.

The worst thing turned out to be finding Rap, Sheena and Ellen Ferguson gathered around the stove in the main cabin; they didn't hear her come in.

". . . so damn fat and soft," Rap was saying.

Sheena said, "You have to take your soldiers where you can find them."

Ellen said, "An army travels on its stomach."

"As soon as it's over we dump the housewives," Rap said. "Every single one."

June cleared her throat. "I've brought the food."

"Politics may make strange bedfellows," Glenda said, "but this is ridiculous."

"Have it your way," she said huffily—whoever she was—and left the way she had come in.

Patsy was in charge of the recruiting platoon, which visited the high school, and she thought the principal was really impressed when he saw that it was her. Her girls bound and gagged the faculty and held the boys at bay with M-1s, while she made her pitch. She was successful but drained when she finished, pale and exhausted, and while her girls were processing the recruits (all but one per cent of the girl students, as it turned out) and waiting for the bus to take them all to camp, Patsy put Marva in charge and simply drifted away, surprised to find herself in front of the sweetie shop two blocks from school. The place was empty except for Andy Ellis, who had just begun work as a counter boy.

He brought her a double dip milkshake and lingered.

She tried to wave him away with her rifle. "We don't have to pay."

"That isn't it." He yearned, drawn to her.

She couldn't help seeing how beautiful he was. "Bug off."

Andy said, "Beautiful."

She lifted her head, aglow. "Really?"

"No kidding. Give me a minute, I'm going to fall in love with you."

"You can't," she said, remembering her part in the eleventh grade production of *Romeo and Juliet*. "I'm some kind of Montague."

"Okay, then, I'll be the Capulet."

"I . . ." Patsy leaned forward over the counter so they could kiss. She drew back at the sound of a distant shot. "I have to go."

"When can I see you?"

Patsy said, "I'll sneak out tonight."

Sheena was in charge of the recruiting detail that visited Sally's neighborhood. Although she had been an obscure first-year medical student when the upheaval started, she was emerging as the heroine of the revolution. The newspapers and television newscasters all knew who she was, and so Sally knew, and was undeniably flattered that she had come in person.

She and Sally met on a high level: if there was an aristocracy of achievement, then they spoke aristocrat to aristocrat. Sheena spoke of talent and obligation; she spoke of need and duty; she spoke of service. She said the women needed Sally's help, and when Sally said, Let them help themselves, she said: They can't. They were still arguing when the kids came home from school; they were still arguing when Zack came home. Sheena spoke of the common cause and a better world; she spoke once more of the relationship between gifts and service. Sally turned to Zack, murmuring, and he said, "If you think you have to do it, then I guess you'd better do it."

She said, "The sooner I go the sooner this thing will be over."

Zack said, "I hope you're right."

Sheena stood aside so they could make their goodbyes. Sally hugged the children, and when they begged to go with her she said, "It's no place for kids."

Climbing into the truck, she looked back at Zack and thought: *I could not love thee half so much loved I not honor more.* What she said was, "I must be out of my mind."

Zack stood in the street with his arms around the kids, saying, "She'll be back soon. Some day they'll come marching down our street."

In the truck, Sheena said, "Don't worry. When we occupy, we'll see that he gets a break."

They were going so fast now that there was no

jumping off the truck; the other women at the camp seemed to be so grateful to see her that she knew there would be no jumping off the truck until it was over.

June whipered, "To be perfectly honest, I was beginning to have my doubts about the whole thing, but with *you* along . . ."

They made Sally a member of the council.

The next day the women took the Sunnydell Shopping Center, which included two supermarkets, a discount house, a fast-food place and a cinema; they selected it because it was close to camp and they could change guard details with a minimum of difficulty. The markets would solve the food problem for the time being, at least.

In battle, they used M-1s, one submachine gun and a variety of sidearms and grenades. They took the place without firing a shot.

The truth was that until this moment, the men had not taken the revolution seriously.

The men had thought: After all, it's only women.

They had thought: Let them have their fun. We can stop this thing whenever we like.

They had thought: What difference does it make? They'll come crawling back to us.

In this first foray, the men, who were, after all, unarmed, fled in surprise. Because the women had not been able to agree upon policy, they let their vanquished enemy go; for the time being, they would take no prisoners.

They were sitting around the victory fire that night, already aware that it was chilly and when the flames burned down a bit they were going to have to go back inside. It was then, for the first time, that Sheena raised the question of allies.

She said, "Sooner or later we have to face facts. We can't make it alone."

Sally brightened, thinking of Zack: "I think you're right."

Rap leaned forward. "Are you *serious*?"

Sheena tossed her hair. "What's the matter with sympathetic men?"

"The only sympathetic man is a dead man," Rap said.

Sally rose. "Wait a minute . . ."

Ellen Ferguson pulled her down. "Relax. All she means is, at this stage we can't afford any risks. Infiltration. Spies."

Sheena said, "We could use a few men."

Sally heard herself, sotto voce: "You're not kidding."

Dr. Ora Fessenden rose, in stages. She said, with force, "Look here, Sheena, if you are going to take a stance, you are going to have to take a stance."

If she had been there, Patsy would have risen to speak in favor of a men's auxiliary. As it was, she had sneaked out to meet Andy. They were down in the shadow of the conquered shopping center, falling in love.

In the command shack, much later, Sheena paced moodily. "They aren't going to be satisfied with the shopping center for long."

Sally said, "I think things are going to get out of hand."

"They can't." Sheena kept on pacing. "We have too much to do."

"Your friend Rap and the doctor are out for blood. Lord knows how many of the others are going to go along." Sally sat at the desk, doodling on the roll sheet. "Maybe you ought to dump them."

"We need muscle, Sally."

Margy, who seemed to be dusting, said, "I go along with Sally."

"No." Lory was in the corner, transcribing Sheena's remarks of the evening. "Sheena's absolutely right."

It was morning, and Ellen Ferguson paced the perimeter of the camp. "We're going to need fortifications here, and more over here."

Glenda, who followed with the clipboard, said, "What are you expecting?"

"I don't know, but I want to be ready for it."

"Shouldn't we be concentrating on *off*ense?"

"Not me," Ellen said, with her feet set wide in the dirt. "This is my place. This is where I make my stand."

"Allies. That woman is a marshmallow. *Allies.*" Rap was still seething. "I think we ought to go ahead and make our play."

"We still need them," Dr. Ora Fessenden said. The two of them were squatting in the woods above the camp. "When we get strong enough, then . . ." She drew her finger across her throat. "Zzzzt."

"Dammit to hell, Ora." Rap was on her feet, punching a tree trunk. "If you're going to fight, you're going to have to kill."

"You know it and I know it," Dr. Ora Fessenden said. "Now try and tell that to the rest of the girls."

As she settled into the routine, Sally missed Zack more and more, and, partly because she missed him so much, she began making a few inquiries. The consensus was that women had to free themselves from every kind of dependence, both emotional and physical; sexual demands would be treated on the level of other bodily functions: any old toilet would do.

"Hello, Ralph?"

"Yes?"

'It's me, Lory. Listen, did you read about what we did?"

"About what *who* did?"

"Stop trying to pretend you don't know. Listen, Ralph, that was us that took over out at Sunny-dell. *Me.*"

"You and what army?"

"The women's army. Oh, I see, you're being sarcastic. Well listen, Ralph, I said I was going to realize myself as a person and I have. I'm a sublieutenant now. A sublieutenant, imagine."

"What about your novel you were going to write about your rotten marriage?"

"Don't pick nits. I'm Sheena's secretary now. You were holding me back, Ralph, all those years you were dragging me down. Well, now I'm a free agent. Free."

"Terrific."

"Look, I have to go; we have uniform inspection now and worst luck, I drew KP."

"Listen," Rap was saying to a group of intent women, "You're going along minding your own business and *wham*, he swoops down like the wolf on the fold. It's the ultimate weapon."

Dr. Ora Fessenden said, bitterly, "And you just try and rape him back."

Margy said, "I thought men were, you know, supposed to protect women from all that."

Annie Chandler, who had emerged as one of the militants, threw her knife into a tree. "Try and convince them it ever happened. The cops say you must have led him on."

Dr. Ora Fessenden drew a picture of the woman as ruined city, with gestures.

"I don't know what I would do if one of them tried to . . ." Betts said to Patsy. "What would you do?"

Oh Andy. Patsy said, "I don't know."

"There's only one thing *to* do," Rap said, with force. "Shoot on sight."

It was hard to say what their expectations had been after this first victory. There were probably almost as many expectations as there were women. A certain segment of the group was disappointed because Vic/Richard/Tom-Dick-Harry had not come crawling up the hill, crying, My God how I have misused you, come home and everything will be different. Rap and the others would have wished for more carnage, and as the days passed the thirst for blood heaped dust in their mouths; Sheena was secretly disappointed that there had not been wider coverage of the battle in the press and on nation-wide TV. The mood in the camp after that first victory was one of anticlimax, indefinable but growing discontent.

Petty fights broke out in the rank and file.

There arose, around this time, some differences between the rank-and-file women, some of whom had children, and the Mothers' Escadrille, an elite corps of women who saw themselves as profes-sional mothers. As a group, they looked down on people like Glenda, who sent their children off to the day-care compound. The Mothers' Escadrille would admit, when pressed, that their goal in band-ing together was the eventual elimination of the role of the man in the family, for man, with his incessant demands, interfered with the primary function of the mother. Still, they had to admit that, since they had no other profession, they were going to have to be assured some kind of financial support in the ultimate scheme of things. They also wanted more respect from the other women, who seemed to look down on them because they lacked technical or professional skills, and so they con-ducted their allotted duties in a growing atmo-sphere of hostility.

It was after a heated discussion with one of the mothers that Glenda, suffering guilt pangs and feel-ings of inadequacy, went down to the day-care compound to see her own children. She picked them out at once, playing in the middle of a tangle of preschoolers, but she saw with a pang that Bobby was reluctant to leave the group to come and talk to her, and even after she said, "It's Mommy," it took Tommy a measurable number of seconds before he recognized her.

The price, she thought in some bitterness. *I hope in the end it turns out to be worth the price.*

Betts had tried running across the field both with and without her bra, and except for the time when she wrapped herself in the Ace bandage, she definitely bounced. At the moment nobody in the camp was agreed as to whether it was a good or a bad thing to bounce; it was either another one of those things the world at large was going to have to, by God, learn to ignore, or else it was a sign of weakness. Either way, it was uncomfortable, but so was the Ace bandage uncomfortable.

Sally was drawn toward home but at the same time, looking around at the disparate women and their growing discontentment, she knew she ought to stay on until the revolution had put itself in order. The women were unable to agree what the next step would be, or to consolidate their gains, and so she met late into the night with Sheena, and walked around among the others. She had the feeling she could help, that whatever her own circumstance, the others were so patently miserable that she must help.

"Listen," said Zack, when Sally called him to explain, "it's no picnic being a guy, either."

The fear of rape had become epidemic. Perhaps because there had been no overt assault on the

women's camp, no army battalions, not even any
police cruisers, the women expected more subtle
and more brutal retaliation. The older women were
outraged because some of the younger women said
what difference did it make? If you were going to
make it, what did the circumstances matter? Still,
the women talked about it around the campfire and
at last it was agreed that regardless of individual
reactions, for ideological reasons it was important
that it be made impossible; the propaganda value
to the enemy would be too great, and so, at Rap's
suggestion, each woman was instructed to carry her
handweapon at all times and to shoot first and ask
questions later.

Patsy and Andy Ellis were finding more and
more ways to be together, but no matter how much
they were together, it didn't seem to be enough.
Since Andy's hair was long, they thought briefly of
disguising him as a woman and getting him into
camp, but a number of things: whiskers, figure,
musculature, would give him away and Patsy decided it would be too dangerous.

"Look, I'm in love with you," Andy said. "Why
don't you run away?"

"Oh, I couldn't do that," Patsy said, trying to hide
herself in his arms. "And besides . . ."

He hid his face in her hair. "Besides nothing."

"No, really. Besides. Everybody has guns now,
everybody has different feelings, but they all hate
deserters. We have a new policy."

"They'd never find us."

She looked into Andy's face. "Don't you want to
hear about the new policy?"

"Okay, what?"

"About deserters." She spelled it out, more than a little surprised at how far she had come. "It's hunt down and shave and kill."

"They wouldn't really do that."

"We had the first one last night, this poor old lady, about forty. She got homesick for her family and tried to run away."

Andy was still amused. "They shaved all her hair off."

"That wasn't all," Patsy said. "When they got finished they really did it. Firing squad, the works."

Although June would not have been sensitive to it, there were diverging feelings in the camp about who did what, and what there was to do. All she knew was she was sick and tired of working in the day-care compound and when she went to Sheena and complained, Sheena, with exquisite sensitivity, put her in charge of the detail that guarded the shopping center. It was a temporary assignment but it gave June a chance to put on a cartridge belt and all the other paraphernalia of victory, so she cut an impressive figure for Vic, when he came along.

"It's me, honey, don't you know me?"

"Go away," she said with some satisfaction. "No civilians allowed."

"Oh, for God's sake."

To their mutual astonishment, she raised her rifle. "Bug off, fella."

"You don't really think you can get away with this."

"Bug off or I'll shoot."

"We're just letting you do this, to get it out of your system." Vic moved as if to relieve her of the rifle. "If it makes you feel a little better . . ."

"This is your last warning."

"Listen," Vic said, a study in male outrage, "one step too far, and, *tschoom*, federal troops."

She fired a warning shot so he left.

Glenda was a little sensitive about the fact that various husbands had found ways to smuggle in messages, some had even come looking for their wives, but not Richard. One poor bastard had been shot when he came in too close to the fire; they heard an outcry and a thrashing in the bushes but when they looked for him the next morning there was no body, so he must have dragged himself away. There had been notes in food consignments and one husband had hired a skywriter, but so far she had neither word nor sign from Richard, and she wasn't altogether convinced she cared. He seemed to have drifted off into time past along with her job, her students and her book. Once her greatest hope had been to read her first chapter at the national psychological conference; now she wondered whether there would even be any more conferences. If she and the others were successful, that would break down, along with a number of other things. Still, in the end she would have her definitive work on the women's revolution, but so far the day-to-day talks had been so engrossing that she hadn't had a minute to begin. Right now, there was too much to do.

They made their first nationwide telecast from a specially erected podium in front of the captured shopping center. For various complicated reasons the leaders made Sally speak first, and, as they had anticipated, she espoused the moderate view: this was a matter of service, women were going to have to give up a few things to help better the lot of their sisters. Once the job was done everything would be improved, but not really different.

Sheena came next, throwing back her bright hair and issuing the call to arms. The mail she drew would include several spirited letters from male volunteers who were already in love with her and would follow her anywhere; because the women had pledged never to take allies, these letters would be destroyed before they ever reached her.

Dr. Ora Fessenden was all threats, fire and brimstone. Rap took up where she left off.

"We're going to fight until there's not a man left standing . . ."

Annie Chandler yelled, "Right on."

Margy was trying to speak: ". . . just a few concessions . . ."

Rap's eyes glittered. "Only sisters, and you guys . . ."

Ellen Ferguson said, "Up, women, out of slavery."

Rap's voice rose. "You guys are going to burn."

Sally was saying, "Reason with you . . ."

Rap hissed: "Bury you."

It was hard to say which parts of these messages reached the viewing public, as the women all interrupted and overrode each other and the cameramen concentrated on Sheena, who was to become the sign and symbol of the revolution. None of the women on the platform seemed to be listening to any of the others, which may have been just as well; the only reason they had been able to come this far together was because nobody ever did.

The letters began to come:

Dear Sheena, I would like to join, but I already have nine children and now I am pregnant again . . .

Dear Sheena, I am a wife and mother but I will throw it all over in an instant if you will only glance my way . . .

Dear Sheena, our group has occupied the town hall in Gillespie, Indiana, but we are running out of ammo and the water supply is low. Several of the women have been stricken with plague, and we are running out of food . . .

First I made him lick my boots and then I killed him but now I have this terrible problem with the body, the kids don't want me to get rid of him . . .

Who do you think you are running this war when you don't even know what you are doing, what you have to do is kill every last damn one of them and the ones you don't kill you had better cut off their Things . . .

Sheena, baby, if you will only give up this half-assed revolution you and I can make beautiful music together. I have signed this letter Maud to escape the censors but if you look underneath the stamp you can see who I really am.

The volunteers were arriving in dozens. The first thing was that there was not housing for all of them; there was not equipment, and so the women in charge had to cut off enlistments at a certain point and send the others back to make war in their own home towns.

The second thing was that, with the increase in numbers, there was an increasing bitterness about the chores. Nobody wanted to do them; in secret truth nobody ever had, but so far the volunteers had all borne it, up to a point, because they sincerely believed that in the new order there would be no chores. Now they understood that the more people there were banded together, the more chores there would be. Laundry and garbage were piling up. At some point around the time of the occupation of the shopping center, the women had begun to understand that no matter what they accomplished, there would always be ugly things to do: the chores, and now, because there seemed to be so *much* work, there were terrible disagreements as to who was supposed to do what, and as a consequence they had all more or less stopped doing any of it.

Meals around the camp were catch as catch can.

The time was approaching when nobody in the camp would have clean underwear.

The latrines were unspeakable.

The children were getting out of hand; some of them were forming packs and making raids of their

own, so that the quartermaster never had any clear
idea of what she would find in the storehouse.
Most of the women in the detail that had been put
in charge of the day-care compound were fed up.

By this time Sheena was a national figure; her
picture was on the cover of both newsmagazines in
the same week and there were nationally distrib-
uted lines of sweatshirts and tooth glasses bearing
her picture and her name. She received love mail
and hate mail in such quantity that Lory, who had
joined the women to realize her potential as an individual, had to give up her other duties to concentrate on Sheena's mail. She would have to admit
that it was better than KP, and besides, if Sheena
went on to better things, maybe she would get to
go along.

The air of dissatisfaction grew. Nobody agreed
any more, not even all those who had agreed to
agree for the sake of the cause. Fights broke out
like flash fires; some women were given to sulks and
inexplicable silences, others to blows and helpless
tears quickly forgotten. On advice from Sally,
Sheena called a council to try and bring everybody
together, but it got off on the wrong foot.

Dr. Ora Fessenden said, "Are we going to sit
around on our butts, or what?"

Sheena said, "National opinion is running in our
favor. We have to consolidate our gains."

Rap said, "Gains hell. What kind of war is this?
Where are the scalps?"

Sheena drew herself up. "We are not Amazons."

Rap said, "That's a crock of shit," and she and Dr. Ora Fessenden stamped out.

"Rape," Rap screamed, running from the far left to the far right and then making a complete circuit of the clearing. "Rape," she shouted, taking careful note of who came running and who didn't. "Raaaaaaaape."

Dr. Ora Fessenden rushed to her side, the figure of outraged womanhood. They both watched until a suitable number of women had assembled, and then she said, in stentorian tones, "We cannot let this go unavenged."

"My God," Sheena said, looking at the blackened object in Rap's hand. "What are you doing with that thing?"

Blood-smeared and grinning, Rap said, "When you're trying to make a point, you have to go ahead and make your point." She thrust her trophy into Sheena's face.

Sheena averted her eyes quickly; she thought it was an ear. "That's supposed to be a *rhetorical* point."

"Listen, baby, this world doesn't give marks for good conduct."

Sheena stiffened. "You keep your girls in line or you're finished."

Rap was smoldering; she pushed her face up to Sheena's, saying, "You can't do without us and you know it."

"If we have to, we'll learn."

"Aieee." One of Rap's cadre had taken the trophy

from her and tied it on a string; now she ran
through the camp, swinging it around her head,
and dozens of throats opened to echo her shout.
"Aiiiieeeee . . ."

Patsy and Andy were together in the bushes near
the camp; proximity to danger made their pleasure
more intense. Andy said, "Leave with me."

She said, "I can't. I told you what they do to
deserters."

"They'll never catch us."

"You don't know these women," Patsy said.
"Look, Andy, you'd better go."

"Just a minute more." Andy buried his face in her
hair. "Just a little minute more."

"Rape," Rap shouted again, running through the
clearing with her voice raised like a trumpet.
"*Raaaaaaaape.*"

Although she knew it was a mistake, Sally had
sneaked away to see Zack and the children. The
camp seemed strangely deserted, and nobody was
there to sign out the jeep she took. She had an un-
canny intimation of trouble at a great distance, but
she shook it off and drove to her house. She would
have expected barricades and guards: state of war,
but the streets were virtually empty and she
reached her neighborhood without trouble.

Zack and the children embraced her and wanted
to know when she was coming home.

"Soon, I think. They're all frightened of us now."

Zack said, "I'm not so sure."

"There doesn't seem to be any resistance."

"Oh," he said, "they've decided to let you have the town."

"What did I tell you?"

"Sop," he said. "You can have anything you want. Up to a point."

Sally was thinking of Rap and Dr. Ora Fessenden. "What if we take more?"

"Wipeout," Zack said. "You'll see."

"Oh Lord," she said, vaulting into the jeep. "Maybe it'll be over sooner than I thought."

She was already too late. She saw the flames shooting skyward as she came out the drive.

"It's Flowermont."

Because she had to make sure, she wrenched the jeep in that direction and rode to the garden apartments; smoke filled the streets for blocks around.

Looking at the devastation, Sally was reminded of Indian massacres in the movies of her childhood: the smoking ruins, the carnage, the moans of the single survivor who would bubble out his story in her arms. She could not be sure about the bodies: whether there were any, whether there were as many as she thought, but she was sure those were charred corpses in the rubble. Rap and Dr. Ora Fessenden had devised a flag and hoisted it from a tree: the symbol of the women's movement, altered to suit their mood—the crudely executed fist reduced to clenched bones and surrounded by flames. The single survivor died before he could bubble out his story in her arms.

In the camp, Rap and Dr. Ora Fessenden had a victory celebration around the fire. They had taken unspeakable trophies in their raid and could not understand why many of the women refused to wear them.

Patsy and Andy, in the bushes, watched with growing alarm. Even from their safe distance, Andy was fairly sure he saw what he thought he saw, and he whispered, "Look, we've got to get out of here."

"Not now," Patsy said, pulling him closer. "Tonight. The patrols."

By now the little girls had been brought up from the day-care compound and they had joined the dance, their fat cheeks smeared with blood. Rap's women were in heated discussion with the Mothers' Escadrille about the disposition of the boy children: would they be destroyed or reared as slaves? While they were talking, one of the mothers who had never felt at home in any faction sneaked down to the compound and freed the lot of them. Now she was running around in helpless tears, flapping her arms and sobbing broken messages, but no matter what she said to the children, she couldn't seem to get any of them to flee.

Sheena and her lieutenant, Margy, and Lory, her secretary, came out of the command shack at the same moment Sally arrived in camp; she rushed to join them, and together they extracted Rap and Dr. Ora Fessenden from the dance for a meeting of the council.

When they entered the shack, Ellen Ferguson hung up the phone in clattering haste and turned to confront them with a confusing mixture of expressions; Sally thought the foremost one was probably guilt.

Sally waited until they were all silent and then said, "The place is surrounded. They let me through to bring the message. They have tanks."

Ellen Ferguson said, "They just delivered their ultimatum. Stop the raids and pull back to camp or they'll have bombers level this place."

"Pull back hell," Rap said.

Dr. Ora Fessenden shook a bloody fist. "We'll show them."

"We'll fight to the death."

Ellen said, quietly, "I've already agreed."

Down at the main gate, Marva, who was on guard duty, leaned across the barbed wire to talk to the captain of the tank detail. She thought he was kind of cute.

"Don't anybody panic," Rap was saying. "We can handle this thing. We can fight them off."

"We can fight them in the hedgerows," Dr. Ora Fessenden said in rising tones. "We can fight them in the ditches, we can hit them with everything we've got . . ."

"Not from here you can't."

"We can burn and bomb and kill and . . . What did you say?"

"I said, not from here." Because they were all staring, Ellen Ferguson covered quickly, saying, "I mean, if I'm going to be of any value to the movement, I have to have this place in good condition."

Sheena said, quietly, "That's not what you mean."

Ellen was near tears. "All right, dammit, this place is all I have."

"My God," Annie Chandler shrieked. "Rape." She parted the bushes to reveal Patsy and Andy, who hugged each other in silence. "Rape," Annie screamed, and everybody who could hear above the din came running. "Kill the bastard, rape, rape, rape."

Patsy rose to her feet and drew Andy up with her, shouting to make herself heard. "I said, it isn't rape."

Rap and Dr. Ora Fessenden were advancing on Ellen Ferguson. "You're not going to compromise us. We'll kill you first."

"Oh," Ellen said, backing away. "That's another thing. They wanted the two of you. I had to promise we'd send you out."

The two women plunged, and then retreated, mute with fury. Ellen had produced a gun from her desk drawer and now she had them covered.

"Son of a bitch," Rap said. "Son of a bitch."

"Kill them."
"Burn them."
"Hurt them."
"Make an example of them."
"I love you, Patsy."
"Oh, Andy, I love you."

Sally said, softly, "So it's all over."

"Only parts of it," Ellen said. "It will never really be over as long as there are women left to fight. We'll be better off without these two and their cannibals; we can retrench and make a new start."

"I guess this is as good a time as any." Sheena got to her feet. "I might as well tell you, I'm splitting."

They turned to face her, Ellen being careful to keep the gun on Dr. Ora Fessenden and Rap.

"You're what?"

"I can do a hell of a lot more good on my new show. Prime time, nightly, nationwide TV."

Rap snarled. "The hell you say."

"Look, Rap, I'll interview you."

"Stuff it."

"Think what I can do for the movement, I can reach sixty million people, you'll see."

Ellen Ferguson said, with some satisfaction, "That's not really what you mean."

"Maybe it isn't. It's been you, you, you all this time." Sheena picked up her clipboard, her notebooks and papers; Lory and Margy both moved as if to follow her but she rebuffed them with a single sweep of her arm. "Well it's high time I started thinking about me."

Outside, the women had raised a stake and now Patsy and Andy were lashed to it, standing back to back.

In the shack, Rap and Dr. Ora Fessenden had turned as one and advanced on Ellen Ferguson, pushing the gun aside.

The good doctor said, "I knew you wouldn't have the guts to shoot. You never had any guts."

Ellen cried out. "Sheena, help me."

But Sheena was already in the doorway, and she

hesitated for only a moment, saying, "Listen, it's
sauve qui peut in this day and time, sweetie, and
the sooner you realize it the better."

Rap finished pushing Ellen down and took the
gun. She stood over her victim for a minute, grinning. "In the battle of the sexes, there are no allies."
Then she put a bullet through Ellen's favorite
moosehead so Ellen would have something to remember her by.

The women had collected twigs and they were
just about to set fire to Patsy and Andy when
Sheena came out, closely followed by Dr. Ora
Fessenden and a warlike Rap.

Everybody started shouting at once and in the
imbroglio that followed, Patsy and Andy escaped.
They would surface years later, in a small town in
Minnesota, with an ecologically alarming number
of children; they would both be able to pursue their
chosen careers in the law because they worked
hand in hand to take care of all the children and
the house, and they would love each other until
they died.

Ellen Ferguson sat with her elbows on her knees
and her head drooping, saying, "I can't believe it's
all over, after I worked so hard, I gave so
much. . . ."

Sally said, "It isn't over. Remember what you
said, as long as there are women, there will be a
fight."

"But we've lost our leaders."

"You could . . ."

"No, I couldn't."

"Don't worry, there are plenty of others."

As Sally spoke, the door opened and Glenda stepped in to take Sheena's place.

When the melee in the clearing was over, Dr. Ora Fessenden and Rap had escaped with their followers. They knew the lay of the land and so they were able to elude the troop concentration, which surrounded the camp, and began to lay plans to regroup and fight another day.

A number of women, disgusted by the orgy of violence, chose to pack their things and go. The Mothers' Escadrille deserted en masse, taking their children and a few children who didn't even belong to them.

Ellen said, "You're going to have to go down there and parley. I'm not used to talking to men."

And so Sally found herself going down to the gate to conduct negotiations.

She said, "The two you wanted got away. The rest of them—I mean us—are acting in good faith." She lifted her chin. "If you want to go ahead and bomb anyway, you'll have to go ahead and bomb."

The captain lifted her and set her on the hood of the jeep. He was grinning. "Shit, little lady, we just wanted to throw a scare into you."

"You don't understand." She wanted to get down off the hood but he had propped his arms on either side of her. She knew she ought to be furious, but instead she kept thinking how much she missed Zack. Speaking with as much dignity as she could under the circumstances, she outlined the women's complaints; she already knew it was hopeless to list them as demands.

"Don't you worry about a thing, honey." He lifted her down and gave her a slap on the rump to speed her on her way. "Everything is going to be real different from now on."

"I bet."

Coming back up the hill to camp, she saw how sad everything looked, and she could not for the life of her decide whether it was because the women who had been gathered here had been inadequate to the cause or whether it was, rather, that the cause itself had been insufficiently identified; she suspected that they had come up against the human condition, failed to recognize it and so tried to attack a single part, which seemed to involve attacking the only allies they would ever have. As for the specific campaign, as far as she could tell, it was possible to change some of the surface or superficial details but once that was done things were still going to be more or less the way they were, and all the best will in the world would not make any real difference.

In the clearing, Lory stood at Glenda's elbow. "Of course you're going to need a lieutenant."

Glenda said, "I guess so."

Ellen Ferguson was brooding over a row of birches that had been trashed during the struggle. If she could stake them back up in time, they might reroot.

June said, "Okay, I'm going to be mess sergeant."

Margy said, "The hell you will," and pushed her in the face.

Glenda said, thoughtfully, "Maybe we could mount a Lysistrata campaign."

Lory snorted. "If their wives won't do it, there are plenty of girls who will."

Zack sent a message:
> WE HAVE TO HELP EACH OTHER

Sally sent back:
> I KNOW

Before she went home, Sally had to say goodbye to Ellen Ferguson.

Ellen's huge, homely face sagged. "Not you too."

Sally looked at the desultory groups policing the wreckage, at the separate councils convening in every corner. "I don't know why I came. I guess I thought we could really *do* something."

Ellen made a half-turn, taking in the command shack, the compound, the women who remained. "Isn't this enough?"

"I have to get on with my *life*."

Ellen said, "This is mine."

"Oh, Vic, I've been so stupid." June was sobbing in Vic's arms. She was also lying in her teeth but she didn't care, she was sick of the revolution and she was going to have to go through this formula before Vic would allow her to resume her place at his kitchen sink. The work was still boring and stupid but at least there was less of it than there had been at camp; her bed was softer, and since it was coming on winter, she was grateful for the storm sashes, which Vic put up every November, and the warmth of the oil burner, which he took apart and cleaned with his own hands every fall.

Sally found her house in good order, thanks to Zack, but there was several weeks' work piled up in her studio, and she had lost a couple of commissions. She opened her drawer to discover, with a smile, that Zack had washed at least one load of underwear with something red.

"I think we do better together," Zack said.

Sally said, "We always have."

In the wake of fraternization with the military guard detail, Marva discovered she was pregnant. She knew what Dr. Ora Fessenden said she was supposed to do, but she didn't think she wanted to.

As weeks passed, the women continued to drift away. "It's nice here and all," Betts said apologetically, "but there's a certain *je ne sais quoi* missing; I don't know what it is, but I'm going back in there and see if I can find it."

Glenda said, "Yeah, well. So long as there is a Yang, I guess there is going to have to be a Yin."

"Don't you mean, so long as there is a Yin, there is going to have to be a Yang?"

Glenda looked in the general direction of town, knowing there was nothing there for her to go back to. "I don't know what I mean anymore."

Activity and numbers at the camp had decreased to the point where federal troops could be withdrawn. They were needed, as it turned out, to deal with wildcat raids in another part of the state. Those who had been on the scene came back with reports of incredible viciousness.

Standing at their windows in the town, the women could look up to the hills and see the camp fire still burning, but as the months wore on, fewer and fewer of them looked and the column of smoke diminished in size because the remaining women were running out of volunteers whose turn it was to feed the fire.

Now that it was over, things went on more or less as they had before.

∞

THE WOMEN MEN DON'T SEE

JAMES TIPTREE, JR.

James Tiptree, Jr., began publishing science fiction in 1968, and has won both the Hugo and Nebula awards. Two collections of Tiptree short fiction, Ten Thousand Light-Years from Home *(Ace) and* Warm Worlds and Otherwise *(Ballantine), have been published. It was known that Tiptree had served in the U.S. Army, had lived in India and Africa, worked for the government, and seemed to have a love of the outdoors; little else was known about the author and many assumed that the Tiptree pseudonym concealed a man. Early in 1977, Tiptree admitted to being Alice B. Sheldon, a retired psychologist who has also written under the name Raccoona Sheldon. In a letter, she wrote: "Actually all the Tiptree biog. stuff is true, it just sounds male to people who forget that women were in the Army in W.W. II . . ."*

I see her first while the Mexicana 727 is barrelling down to Cozumel Island. I come out of the can and lurch into her seat, saying, "Sorry," at a double female blur. The near blur nods quietly. The younger one in the window seat goes on looking out. I continue down the aisle, registering nothing. Zero. I never would have looked at them or thought of them again.

Cozumel airport is the usual mix of panicky Yanks dressed for the sand pile and calm Mexicans dressed for lunch at the Presidente. I am a used-up Yank dressed for serious fishing; I extract my rods and duffel from the riot and hike across the field to find my charter pilot. One Captain Estéban has contracted to deliver me to the bonefish flats of Bélise three hundred kilometers down the coast.

Captain Estéban turns out to be four feet nine of mahogany Maya *puro*. He is also in a somber Mayan snit. He tells me my Cessna is grounded somewhere and his Bonanza is booked to take a party to Chetumal.

Well, Chetumal is south; can he take me along and go on to Bélise after he drops them? Gloomily he concedes the possibility—*if* the other party permits, and *if* there are not too many *equipajes*.

The Chetumal party approaches. It's the woman and her young companion—daughter?—neatly picking their way across the gravel and yucca apron. Their Ventura two-suiters, like themselves, are small, plain and neutral-colored. No problem. When the captain asks if I may ride along, the mother says mildly, "Of course," without looking at me.

I think that's when my inner tilt-detector sends up its first faint click. How come this woman has already looked me over carefully enough to accept on her plane? I disregard it. Paranoia hasn't been useful in my business for years, but the habit is hard to break.

As we clamber into the Bonanza, I see the girl has what could be an attractive body if there was any spark at all. There isn't. Captain Estéban folds a serape to sit on so he can see over the cowling and runs a meticulous check-down. And then we're up and trundling over the turquoise Jello of the Caribbean into a stiff south wind.

The coast on our right is the territory of Quintana Roo. If you haven't seen Yucatán, imagine the world's biggest absolutely flat green-grey rug. An empty-looking land. We pass the white ruin of Tulum and the gash of the road to Chichén Itzá, a half-dozen coconut plantations, and then nothing but reef and low scrub jungle all the way to the horizon, just about the way the conquistadores saw it four centuries back.

Long strings of cumulus are racing at us, shadowing the coast. I have gathered that part of our pilot's gloom concerns the weather. A cold front is dying on the henequen fields of Mérida to the west, and the south wind has piled up a string of coastal storms: what they call *llovisnos*. Estéban detours methodically around a couple of small thunderheads. The Bonanza jinks, and I look back with a vague notion of reassuring the women. They are calmly intent on what can be seen of Yucatán. Well, they were offered the co-pilot's view, but they turned it down. Too shy?

Another *llovisno* puffs up ahead. Estéban takes the Bonanza upstairs, rising in his seat to sight his course. I relax for the first time in too long, savoring the latitudes between me and my desk, the week of fishing ahead. Our captain's classic Maya profile attracts my gaze: forehead sloping back from his predatory nose, lips and jaw stepping back below it. If his slant eyes had been any more crossed, he couldn't have made his license. That's a handsome combination, believe it or not. On the little Maya chicks in their minishifts with iridescent gloop on those cockeyes, it's also highly erotic. Nothing like the oriental doll thing; these people have stone bones. Captain Estéban's old grandmother could probably tow the Bonanza . . .

I'm snapped awake by the cabin hitting my ear. Estéban is barking into his headset over a drumming racket of hail; the windows are dark grey.

One important noise is missing—the motor. I realize Estéban is fighting a dead plane. Thirty-six hundred; we've lost two thousand feet.

He slaps tank switches as the storm throws us around; I catch something about *gasolina* in a snarl that shows his big teeth. The Bonanza reels down. As he reaches for an overhead toggle, I see the fuel gauges are high. Maybe a clogged gravity feed line, I've heard of dirty gas down here. He drops the set; it's a million to one nobody can read us through the storm at this range anyway. Twenty-five hundred—going down.

His electric feed pump seems to have cut in: the motor explodes—quits—explodes—and quits again for good. We are suddenly out of the bottom of the clouds. Below us is a long white line almost hidden by rain: The reef. But there isn't any beach behind it, only a big meandering bay with a few mangrove flats—and it's coming up at us fast.

This is going to be bad, I tell myself with great

unoriginality. The women behind me haven't made
a sound. I look back and see they're braced down
with their coats by their heads. With a stalling
speed around eighty, all this isn't much use, but I
wedge myself in.

Estéban yells some more into his set, flying a
falling plane. He is doing one jesus job, too—as the
water rushes up at us he dives into a hair-raising
turn and hangs us into the wind—with a long pale
ridge of sandbar in front of our nose.

Where in hell he found it I never know. The Bonanza mushes down, and we belly-hit with a tremendous tearing crash—bounce—hit again—and
everything slews wildly as we flat-spin into the mangroves at the end of the bar. Crash! Clang! The
plane is wrapping itself into a mound of strangler
fig with one wing up. The crashing quits with us
all in one piece. And no fire. Fantastic.

Captain Estéban prys open his door, which is
now in the roof. Behind me a woman is repeating
quietly, "Mother. Mother." I climb up the floor and
find the girl trying to free herself from her mother's
embrace. The woman's eyes are closed. Then she
opens them and suddenly lets go, sane as soap.
Estéban starts hauling them out. I grab the Bonanza's aid kit and scramble out after them into
brilliant sun and wind. The storm that hit us is already vanishing up the coast.

"Great landing, Captain."

"Oh, yes! It was beautiful." The women are shaky,
but no hysteria. Estéban is surveying the scenery
with the expression his ancestors used on the
Spaniards.

If you've been in one of these things, you know

the slow-motion inanity that goes on. Euphoria, first. We straggle down the fig tree and out onto the sandbar in the roaring hot wind, noting without alarm that there's nothing but miles of crystalline water on all sides. It's only a foot or so deep, and the bottom is the olive color of silt. The distant shore around us is all flat mangrove swamp, totally uninhabitable.

"Bahía Espíritu Santo." Estéban confirms my guess that we're down in that huge water wilderness. I always wanted to fish it.

"What's all that smoke?" The girl is pointing at plumes blowing around the horizon.

"Alligator hunters," says Estéban. Maya poachers have left burn-offs in the swamps. It occurs to me that any signal fires we make aren't going to be too conspicuous. And I now note that our plane is well-buried in the mound of fig. Hard to see it from the air.

Just as the question of how the hell we get out of here surfaces in my mind, the older woman asks composedly, "If they didn't hear you, Captain, when will they start looking for us? Tomorrow?"

"Correct," Estéban agrees dourly. I recall that air-sea rescue is fairly informal here. Like, keep an eye open for Mario, his mother says he hasn't been home all week.

It dawns on me we may be here quite some while.

Furthermore, the diesel-truck noise on our left is the Caribbean piling back into the mouth of the bay. The wind is pushing it at us, and the bare bottoms on the mangroves show that our bar is covered at high tide. I recall seeing a full moon this morning in—believe it, St. Louis—which means maximal tides. Well, we can climb up in the plane. But what about drinking water?

There's a small splat! behind me. The older woman has sampled the bay. She shakes her head, smiling ruefully. It's the first real expression on either of them; I take it as the signal for introductions. When I say I'm Don Fenton from St. Louis, she tells me their name is Parsons, from Bethesda, Maryland. She says it so nicely I don't at first notice we aren't being given first names. We all compliment Captain Estéban again.

His left eye is swelled shut, an inconvenience beneath his attention as a Maya, but Mrs. Parsons spots the way he's bracing his elbow in his ribs.

"You're hurt, Captain."

"*Roto*—I think is broken." He's embarrassed at being in pain. We get him to peel off his Jaime shirt, revealing a nasty bruise on his superb dark-bay torso.

"Is there tape in that kit, Mr. Fenton? I've had a little first-aid training."

She begins to deal competently and very impersonally with the tape. Miss Parsons and I wander to the end of the bar and have a conversation which I am later to recall acutely.

"Roseate spoonbills," I tell her as three pink birds flap away.

"They're beautiful," she says in her tiny voice. They both have tiny voices. "He's a Mayan Indian, isn't he? The pilot, I mean."

"Right. The real thing, straight out of the Bonampak murals. Have you seen Chichén and Uxmal?"

"Yes. We were in Mérida. We're going to Tikal in Guatemala . . . I mean, we were."

"You'll get there." It occurs to me the girl needs cheering up. "Have they told you that Maya mothers used to tie a board on the infant's forehead to get that slant? They also hung a ball of tallow over its nose to make the eyes cross. It was considered aristocratic."

She smiles and takes another peek at Estéban. "People seem different in Yucatán," she says thoughtfully. "Not like the Indians around Mexico City. More, I don't know, independent."

"Comes from never having been conquered. Mayas got massacred and chased a lot, but nobody ever really flattened them. I bet you didn't know that the last Mexican-Maya war ended with a negotiated truce in 1935?"

"No!" Then she says seriously, "I like that."

"So do I."

"The water is really rising very fast," says Mrs. Parsons gently from behind us.

It is, and so is another *llovisno*. We climb back into the Bonanza. I try to rig my parka for a rain catcher, which blows loose as the storm hits fast and furious. We sort a couple of malt bars and my bottle of Jack Daniel's out of the jumble in the cabin and make ourselves reasonably comfortable. The Parsons take a sip of whiskey each, Estéban and I considerably more. The Bonanza begins to bump soggily. Estéban makes an ancient one-eyed Mayan face at the water seeping into his cabin and goes to sleep. We all nap.

When the water goes down, the euphoria has gone with it, and we're very, very thirsty. It's also damn near sunset. I get to work with a bait-casting rod and some treble hooks and manage to foul-hook

four small mullets. Estéban and the women tie the
Bonanza's midget life raft out in the mangroves to
catch rain. The wind is parching hot. No planes go
by.

Finally another shower comes over and yields us
six ounces of water apiece. When the sunset envel-
opes the world in golden smoke, we squat on the
sandbar to eat wet raw mullet and Instant Breakfast
crumbs. The women are now in shorts, neat but
definitely not sexy.

"I never realized how refreshing raw fish is," Mrs.
Parsons says pleasantly. Her daughter chuckles,
also pleasantly. She's on Mamma's far side away
from Estéban and me. I have Mrs. Parsons figured
now: Mother Hen protecting only chick from male
predators. That's all right with me. I came here to
fish.

But something is irritating me. The damn women
haven't complained once, you understand. Not a
peep, not a quaver, no personal manifestations
whatever. They're like something out of a manual.

"You really seem at home in the wilderness, Mrs.
Parsons. You do much camping?"

"Oh goodness no." Diffident laugh. "Not since my
girl scout days. Oh, look—are those man-of-war
birds?"

Answer a question with a question. I wait while
the frigate birds sail nobly into the sunset.

"Bethesda . . . Would I be wrong in guessing you
work for Uncle Sam?"

"Why, yes. You must be very familiar with Washington, Mr. Fenton. Does your work bring you there
often?"

Anywhere but on our sandbar the little ploy would have worked. My hunter's gene twitches.

"Which agency are you with?"

She gives up gracefully. "Oh, just GSA records. I'm a librarian."

Of course. I know her now, all the Mrs. Parsonses in records divisions, accounting sections, research branches, personnel and administration offices. Tell Mrs. Parsons we need a recap on the external service contracts for fiscal '73. So Yucatán is on the tours now? Pity . . . I offer her the tired little joke. "You know where the bodies are buried."

She smiles deprecatingly and stands up. "It does get dark quickly, doesn't it?"

Time to get back into the plane.

A flock of ibis are circling us, evidently accustomed to roosting in our fig tree. Estéban produces a machete and a Maya string hammock. He proceeds to sling it between tree and plane, refusing help. His machete stroke is noticeably tentative.

The Parsons are taking a pee behind the tail vane. I hear one of them slip and squeal faintly. When they come back over the hull, Mrs. Parsons asks, "Might we sleep in the hammock, Captain?"

Estéban splits an unbelieving grin. I protest about rain and mosquitoes.

"Oh, we have insect repellent and we do enjoy fresh air."

The air is rushing by about force five and colder by the minute.

"We have our raincoats," the girl adds cheerfully.

Well, okay, ladies. We dangerous males retire

inside the damp cabin. Through the wind I hear the women laugh softly now and then, apparently cosy in their chilly ibis roost. A private insanity, I decide. I know myself for the least threatening of men; my non-charisma has been in fact an asset jobwise, over the years. Are they having fantasies about Estéban? Or maybe they really are fresh-air nuts . . . Sleep comes for me in invisible diesels roaring by on the reef outside.

We emerge dry-mouthed into a vast windy salmon sunrise. A diamond chip of sun breaks out of the sea and promptly submerges in cloud. I go to work with the rod and some mullet bait while two showers detour around us. Breakfast is a strip of wet barracuda apiece.

The Parsons continue stoic and helpful. Under Estéban's direction they set up a section of cowling for a gasoline flare in case we hear a plane, but nothing goes over except one unseen jet droning toward Panama. The wind howls, hot and dry and full of coral dust. So are we.

"They look first in the sea," Estéban remarks. His aristocratic frontal slope is beaded with sweat; Mrs. Parsons watches him concernedly. I watch the cloud blanket tearing by above, getting higher and dryer and thicker. While that lasts nobody is going to find us, and the water business is now unfunny.

Finally I borrow Estéban's machete and hack a long light pole. "There's a stream coming in back there, I saw it from the plane. Can't be more than two, three miles."

"I'm afraid the raft's torn." Mrs. Parsons shows

me the cracks in the orange plastic; irritatingly, it's a Delaware label.

"All right," I hear myself announce. "The tide's going down. If we cut the good end off that air tube, I can haul water back in it. I've waded flats before."

Even to me it sounds crazy.

"Stay by plane," Estéban says. He's right, of course. He's also clearly running a fever. I look at the overcast and taste grit and old barracuda. The hell with the manual.

When I start cutting up the raft, Estéban tells me to take the serape. "You stay one night." He's right about that, too; I'll have to wait out the tide.

"I'll come with you," says Mrs. Parsons calmly.

I simply stare at her. What new madness has got into Mother Hen? Does she imagine Estéban is too battered to be functional? While I'm being astounded, my eyes take in the fact that Mrs. Parsons is now quite rosy around the knees, with her hair loose and a sunburn starting on her nose. A trim, in fact a very neat shading-forty.

"Look, that stuff is horrible going. Mud up to your ears and water over your head."

"I'm really quite fit and I swim a great deal. I'll try to keep up. Two would be much safer, Mr. Fenton, and we can bring more water."

She's serious. Well, I'm about as fit as a marshmallow at this time of winter, and I can't pretend I'm depressed by the idea of company. So be it.

"Let me show Miss Parsons how to work this rod."

Miss Parsons is even rosier and more windblown, and she's not clumsy with my tackle. A good girl, Miss Parsons, in her nothing way. We cut another staff and get some gear together. At the last minute Estéban shows how sick he feels: he offers me the machete. I thank him, but, no; I'm used to my Wirkkala knife. We tie some air into the plastic tube for a float and set out along the sandiest looking line.

Estéban raises one dark palm. *"Buen viaje."* Miss Parsons has hugged her mother and gone to cast from the mangrove. She waves. We wave.

An hour later we're barely out of waving distance. The going is purely god-awful. The sand keeps dissolving into silt you can't walk on or swim through, and the bottom is spiked with dead mangrove spears. We flounder from one pothole to the next, scaring up rays and turtles and hoping to god we don't kick a moray eel. Where we're not soaked in slime, we're desiccated, and we smell like the Old Cretaceous.

Mrs. Parsons keeps up doggedly. I only have to pull her out once. When I do so, I notice the sandbar is now out of sight.

Finally we reach the gap in the mangrove line I thought was the creek. It turns out to open into another arm of the bay, with more mangroves ahead. And the tide is coming in.

"I've had the world's lousiest idea."

Mrs. Parsons only says mildly, "It's so different from the view from the plane."

I revise my opinion of the girl scouts, and we plow on past the mangroves toward the smoky haze that has to be shore. The sun is setting in our faces, making it hard to see. Ibises and herons fly up around us, and once a big permit spooks ahead, his fin cutting a rooster tail. We fall into more potholes. The flashlights get soaked. I am having fantasies of the mangrove as universal obstacle; it's hard to recall I ever walked down a street, for instance, without stumbling over or under or through mangrove roots. And the sun is dropping, down, down.

Suddenly we hit a ledge and fall over it into a cold flow.

"The stream! It's fresh water!"

We guzzle and gargle and douse our heads; it's the best drink I remember. "Oh my, oh my—!" Mrs. Parsons is laughing right out loud.

"That dark place over to the right looks like real land."

We flounder across the flow and follow a hard shelf, which turns into solid bank and rises over our heads. Shortly there's a break beside a clump of spiny bromels, and we scramble up and flop down at the top, dripping and stinking. Out of sheer reflex my arm goes around my companion's shoulder—but Mrs. Parsons isn't there; she's up on her knees peering at the burnt-over plain around us.

"It's so good to see land one can walk on!" The tone is too innocent. *Noli me tangere.*

"Don't try it." I'm exasperated; the muddy little woman, what does she think? "That ground out there is a crust of ashes over muck, and it's full of stubs. You can go in over your knees."

"It seems firm here."

"We're in an alligator nursery. That was the slide we came up. Don't worry, by now the old lady's doubtless on her way to be made into hand-bags."

"What a shame."

"I better set a line down in the stream while I can still see."

I slide back down and rig a string of hooks that may get us breakfast. When I get back Mrs. Parsons is wringing muck out of the serape.

"I'm glad you warned me, Mr. Fenton. It *is* treacherous."

"Yeah." I'm over my irritation; god knows I don't want to *tangere* Mrs. Parsons, even if I weren't beat down to mush. "In its quiet way, Yucatan is a tough place to get around in. You can see why the Mayas built roads. Speaking of which—look!"

The last of the sunset is silhouetting a small square shape a couple of kilometers inland: a Maya *ruina* with a fig tree growing out of it.

"Lot of those around. People think they were guard towers."

"What a deserted-feeling land."

"Let's hope it's deserted by mosquitoes."

We slump down in the 'gator nursery and share the last malt bar, watching the stars slide in and out of the blowing clouds. The bugs aren't too bad; maybe the burn did them in. And it isn't hot any more, either—in fact, it's not even warm, wet as we are. Mrs. Parsons continues tranquilly interested in Yucatan and unmistakably uninterested in togetherness.

Just as I'm beginning to get aggressive notions about how we're going to spend the night if she expects me to give her the serape, she stands up, scuffs at a couple of hummocks and says, "I expect this is as good a place as any, isn't it, Mr. Fenton?"

With which she spreads out the raft bag for a pillow and lies down on her side in the dirt with exactly half the serape over her and the other corner folded neatly open. Her small back is toward me.

The demonstration is so convincing that I'm halfway under my share of serape before the preposterousness of it stops me.

"By the way. My name is Don."

"Oh, of course." Her voice is graciousness itself. "I'm Ruth."

I get in not quite touching her, and we lie there like two fish on a plate, exposed to the stars and smelling the smoke in the wind and feeling things underneath us. It is absolutely the most intimately awkward moment I've had in years.

The woman doesn't mean one thing to me, but the obtrusive recessiveness of her, the defiance of her little rump eight inches from my fly—for two pesos I'd have those shorts down and introduce myself. If I were twenty years younger, if I wasn't so bushed . . . But the twenty years and the exhaustion are there, and it comes to me wryly that Mrs. Ruth Parsons has judged things to a nicety. If I *were* twenty years younger, she wouldn't be here. Like the butterfish that float around a sated barracuda, only to vanish away the instant his intent changes, Mrs. Parsons knows her little shorts are safe. Those firmly filled little shorts, so close . . .

A warm nerve stirs in my groin—and just as it does I become aware of a silent emptiness beside me. Mrs. Parsons is imperceptibly inching away. Did my breathing change? Whatever, I'm perfectly sure that if my hand reached, she'd be elsewhere—probably announcing her intention to take a dip. The twenty years bring a chuckle to my throat, and I relax.

"Good night, Ruth."

"Good night, Don."

And believe it or not, we sleep, while the armadas of the wind roar overhead.

Light wakes me—a cold white glare.

My first thought is 'gator hunters. Best to manifest ourselves as *turistas* as fast as possible. I scramble up, noting that Ruth has dived under the bromel clump.

"*Quién estás? A socorro!* Help, *señores!*"

No answer except the light goes out, leaving me blind.

I yell some more in a couple of languages. It stays dark. There's a vague scrabbling, whistling sound somewhere in the burn-off. Liking everything less by the minute, I try a speech about our plane having crashed and we need help.

A very narrow pencil of light flicks over us and snaps off.

"Eh-ep," says a blurry voice and something metallic twitters. They for sure aren't locals. I'm getting unpleasant ideas.

"Yes, help!"

Something goes crackle-crackle whish-whish, and all sounds fade away.

"What the holy hell!" I stumble toward where they were.

"Look." Ruth whispers behind me. "Over by the ruin."

I look and catch a multiple flicker which winks out fast.

"A camp?"

And I take two more blind strides. My leg goes down through the crust and a spike spears me just where you stick the knife in to unjoint a drumstick. By the pain that goes through my bladder I recognize that my trick kneecap has caught it.

For instant basket case you can't beat kneecaps. First you discover your knee doesn't bend any more, so you try putting some weight on it and a bayonet goes up your spine and unhinges your jaw. Little grains of gristle have got into the sensitive bearing surface. The knee tries to buckle and can't, and mercifully you fall down.

Ruth helps me back to the serape.

"What a fool, what a godforgotten imbecile—"

"Not at all, Don. It was perfectly natural." We strike matches; her fingers push mine aside, exploring. "I think it's in place, but it's swelling fast. I'll lay a wet handkerchief on it. We'll have to wait for morning to check the cut. Were they poachers, do you think?"

"Probably," I lie. What I think they were is smugglers.

She comes back with a soaked bandanna and drapes it on. "We must have frightened them. That light . . . it seemed so bright."

"Some hunting party. People do crazy things around here."

"Perhaps they'll come back in the morning."

"Could be."

Ruth pulls up the wet serape, and we say good-night again. Neither of us are mentioning how we're going to get back to the plane without help.

I lie staring south where Alpha Centauri is blinking in and out of the overcast and cursing myself for the sweet mess I've made. My first idea is giving way to an even less pleasing one.

Smuggling, around here, is a couple of guys in an outboard meeting a shrimp boat by the reef. They don't light up the sky or have some kind of swamp buggy that goes whoosh. Plus a big camp . . . paramilitary-type equipment?

I've seen a report of Guévaristo infiltrators operating on the British Honduran border, which is about a hundred kilometers—sixty miles—south of here. Right under those clouds. If that's what looked us over, I'll be more than happy if they don't come back . . .

I wake up in pelting rain, alone. My first move confirms that my leg is as expected—a giant misplaced erection bulging out of my shorts. I raise up painfully to see Ruth standing by the bromels, looking over the bay. Solid wet nimbus is pouring out of the south.

"No planes today."

"Oh, good morning, Don. Should we look at that cut now?"

"It's minimal." In fact the skin is hardly broken, and no deep puncture. Totally out of proportion to the havoc inside.

"Well, they have water to drink," Ruth says tranquilly. "Maybe those hunters will come back. I'll go see if we have a fish—that is, can I help you in any way, Don?"

Very tactful. I emit an ungracious negative, and she goes off about her private concerns.

They certainly are private, too; when I recover from my own sanitary efforts, she's still away. Finally I hear splashing.

"It's a big fish!" More splashing. Then she climbs up the bank with a three-pound mangrove snapper—and something else.

It isn't until the messy work of filleting the fish that I begin to notice.

She's making a smudge of chaff and twigs to singe the fillets, small hands very quick, tension in that female upper lip. The rain has eased off for the moment; we're sluicing wet but warm enough. Ruth brings me my fish on a mangrove skewer and sits back on her heels with an odd breathy sigh.

"Aren't you joining me?"

"Oh, of course." She gets a strip and picks at it, saying quickly, "We either have too much salt or too little, don't we? I should fetch some brine." Her eyes are roving from nothing to noplace.

"Good thought." I hear another sigh and decide the girl scouts need an assist. "Your daughter mentioned you've come from Mérida. Have you seen much of Mexico?"

"Not really. Last year we went to Mazatlán and Cuernavaca . . ." She puts the fish down, frowning.

"And you're going to see Tikal. Going to Bonampak too?"

"No." Suddenly she jumps up brushing rain off her face. "I'll bring you some water, Don."

She ducks down the slide, and after a fair while comes back with a full bromel stalk.

"Thanks." She's standing above me, staring restlessly round the horizon.

"Ruth, I hate to say it, but those guys are not coming back and it's probably just as well. Whatever they were up to, we looked like trouble. The most they'll do is tell someone we're here. That'll take a day or two to get around, we'll be back at the plane by then."

"I'm sure you're right, Don." She wanders over to the smudge fire.

"And quit fretting about your daughter. She's a big girl."

"Oh, I'm sure Althea's all right . . . They have plenty of water now." Her fingers drum on her thigh. It's raining again.

"Come on, Ruth. Sit down. Tell me about Althea. Is she still in college?"

She gives that sighing little laugh and sits. "Althea got her degree last year. She's in computer programming."

"Good for her. And what about you, what do you do in GSA Records?"

"I'm in Foreign Procurement Archives." She smiles mechanically, but her breathing is shallow. "It's very interesting."

"I know a Jack Wittig in Contracts, maybe you know him?"

It sounds pretty absurd, there in the 'gator slide.

"Oh, I've met Mr. Wittig. I'm sure he wouldn't remember me."

"Why not?"

"I'm not very memorable."

Her voice is factual. She's perfectly right, of course. Who was that woman, Mrs. Jannings, Janny, who coped with my per diem for years? Competent, agreeable, impersonal. She had a sick father or something. But dammit, Ruth is a lot younger and better-looking. Comparatively speaking.

"Maybe Mrs. Parsons doesn't want to be memorable."

She makes a vague sound, and I suddenly realize Ruth isn't listening to me at all. Her hands are clenched around her knees, she's staring inland at the ruin.

"Ruth. I tell you our friends with the light are in the next county by now. Forget it, we don't need them."

Her eyes come back to me as if she'd forgotten I was there, and she nods slowly. It seems to be too much effort to speak. Suddenly she cocks her head and jumps up again.

"I'll go look at the line, Don. I thought I heard something—" She's gone like a rabbit.

While she's away I try getting up onto my good leg and the staff. The pain is sickening; knees seem to have some kind of hot line to the stomach. I take a couple of hops to test whether the Demerol I have in my belt would get me walking. As I do so, Ruth comes up the bank with a fish flapping in her hands.

"Oh, no, Don! *No!*" She actually clasps the snapper to her breast.

"The water will take some of my weight. I'd like to give it a try."

"You mustn't!" Ruth says quite violently and instantly modulates down. "Look at the bay, Don. One can't see a thing."

I teeter there, tasting bile and looking at the mingled curtains of sun and rain driving across the water. She's right, thank god. Even with two good legs we could get into trouble out there.

"I guess one more night won't kill us."

I let her collapse me back onto the gritty plastic, and she positively bustles around, finding me a chunk to lean on, stretching the serape on both staffs to keep rain off me, bringing another drink, grubbing for dry tinder.

"I'll make us a real bonfire as soon as it lets up, Don. They'll see our smoke, they'll know we're all right. We just have to wait." Cheery smile. "Is there any way we can make you more comfortable?"

Holy Saint Stercuilius: playing house in a mud puddle. For a fatuous moment I wonder if Mrs. Parsons has designs on me. And then she lets out another sigh and sinks back onto her heels with that listening look. Unconsciously her rump wiggles a little. My ear picks up the operative word: *wait.*

Ruth Parsons is waiting. In fact, she acts as if she's waiting so hard it's killing her. For what? For someone to get us out of here, what else? . . . But why was she so horrified when I got up to try to leave? Why all this tension?

My paranoia stirs. I grab it by the collar and start idly checking back. Up to when whoever it was showed up last night, Mrs. Parson was, I guess, normal. Calm and sensible, anyway. Now's she's humming like a high wire. And she seems to want to stay here and wait. Just as an intellectual pastime, why?

Could she have intended to come here? No way. Where she planned to be was Chetumal, which is on the border. Come to think, Chetumal is an odd way round to Tikal. Let's say the scenario was that she's meeting somebody in Chetumal. Somebody who's part of an organization. So now her contact in Chetumal knows she's overdue. And when those types appeared last night, something suggests to her that they're part of the same organization. And she hopes they'll put one and one together and come back for her?

"May I have the knife, Don? I'll clean the fish."

Rather slowly I pass the knife, kicking my subconscious. Such a decent ordinary little woman, a good girl scout. My trouble is that I've bumped into too many professional agilities under the careful stereotypes. *I'm not very memorable . . .*

What's in Foreign Procurement Archives? Wittig handles classified contracts. Lots of money stuff; foreign currency negotiations, commodity price schedules, some industrial technology. Or—just as a hypothesis—it could be as simple as a wad of bills back in that modest beige Ventura, to be exchanged for a packet from say, Costa Rica. If she were a courier, they'd want to get at the plane. And then what about me and maybe Estéban? Even hypothetically, not good.

I watch her hacking at the fish, forehead knotted with effort, teeth in her lip. Mrs. Ruth Parsons of Bethesda, this thrumming, private woman. How crazy can I get? *They'll see our smoke . . .*

"Here's your knife, Don. I washed it. Does the leg hurt very badly?"

I blink away the fantasies and see a scared little woman in a mangrove swamp.

"Sit down, rest. You've been going all out."

She sits obediently, like a kid in a dentist chair.

"You're stewing about Althea. And she's probably

worried about you. We'll get back tomorrow under our own steam, Ruth."

"Honestly I'm not worried at all, Don." The smile fades; she nibbles her lip, frowning out at the bay.

"You know, Ruth, you surprised me when you offered to come along. Not that I don't appreciate it. But I rather thought you'd be concerned about leaving Althea alone with our good pilot. Or was it only me?"

This gets her attention at last.

"I believe Captain Estéban is a very fine type of man."

The words surprise me a little. Isn't the correct line more like "I trust Althea," or even, indignantly, "Althea is a good girl"?

"He's a man. Althea seemed to think he was interesting."

She goes on staring at the bay. And then I notice her tongue flick out and lick that prehensile upper lip. There's a flush that isn't sunburn around her ears and throat too, and one hand is gently rubbing her thigh. What's she seeing, out there in the flats? Oho.

Captain Estéban's mahogany arms clasping Miss Althea Parsons' pearly body. Captain Estéban's archaic nostrils snuffling in Miss Parsons' tender neck. Captain Estéban's copper buttocks pumping into Althea's creamy upturned bottom . . . The hammock, very bouncy. Mayas know all about it.

Well, well. So Mother Hen has her little quirks.

I feel fairly silly and more than a little irritated. *Now* I find out. But even vicarious lust has much to recommend it, here in the mud and rain. I settle back, recalling that Miss Althea the computer programmer had waved good-bye very composedly. Was she sending her mother to flounder across the bay with me so she can get programmed in Maya? The memory of Honduran mahogany logs drifting in and out of the opalescent sand comes to me. Just as I am about to suggest that Mrs. Parsons might care to share my rain shelter, she remarks serenely, "The Mayas seem to be a very fine type of people. I believe you said so to Althea."

The implications fall on me with the rain. *Type.* As in breeding, bloodline, sire. Am I supposed to have certified Estéban not only as a stud but as a genetic donor?

"Ruth, are you telling me you're prepared to accept a half-Indian grandchild?"

"Why, Don, that's up to Althea, you know."

Looking at the mother, I guess it is. Oh, for mahogany gonads.

Ruth has gone back to listening to the wind, but I'm not about to let her off that easy. Not after all that *noli me tangere* jazz.

"What will Althea's father think?"

Her face snaps around at me, genuinely startled.

"Althea's father?" Complicated semismile. "He won't mind."

"He'll accept it too, eh?" I see her shake her head as if a fly were bothering her, and add with a cripple's malice: "Your husband must be a very fine type of a man."

Ruth looks at me, pushing her wet hair back abruptly. I have the impresssion that mousy Mrs. Parsons is roaring out of control, but her voice is quiet.

"There isn't any Mr. Parsons, Don. There never

was. Althea's father was a Danish medical student
. . . I believe he has gained considerable promi-
nence."

"Oh." Something warns me not to say I'm sorry.
"You mean he doesn't know about Althea?"

"No." She smiles, her eyes bright and cuckoo.

"Seems like rather a rough deal for her."

"I grew up quite happily under the same circumstances."

Bang, I'm dead. Well, well, well. A mad image
blooms in my mind: generations of solitary Parsons
women selecting sires, making impregnation trips.
Well, I hear the world is moving their way.

"I better look at the fish line."

She leaves. The glow fades. *No.* Just no, no contact. Good-bye, Captain Estéban. My leg is very
uncomfortable. The hell with Mrs. Parsons' long-
distance orgasm.

We don't talk much after that, which seems to
suit Ruth. The odd day drags by. Squall after squall
blows over us. Ruth singes up some more fillets,
but the rain drowns her smudge; it seems to pour
hardest just as the sun's about to show.

Finally she comes to sit under my sagging serape,
but there's no warmth there. I doze, aware of her
getting up now and then to look around. My subconscious notes that she's still twitchy. I tell my
subconscious to knock it off.

Presently I wake up to find her penciling on the
water-soaked pages of a little notepad.

"What's that, a shopping list for alligators?"

Automatic polite laugh. "Oh, just an address. In
case we—I'm being silly, Don."

"Hey." I sit up, wincing. "Ruth, quit fretting. I

mean it. We'll all be out of this soon. You'll have a great story to tell."

She doesn't look up. "Yes . . . I guess we will."

"Come on, we're doing fine. There isn't any real danger here, you know. Unless you're allergic to fish?"

Another good-little-girl laugh, but there's a shiver in it.

"Sometimes I think I'd like to go . . . really far away."

To keep her talking I say the first thing in my head.

"Tell me, Ruth. I'm curious why you would settle for that kind of lonely life, there in Washington? I mean, a woman like you—"

"—should get married?" She gives a shaky sigh, pushing the notebook back in her wet pocket.

"Why not? It's the normal source of companionship. Don't tell me you're trying to be some kind of professional man-hater."

"Lesbian, you mean?" Her laugh sounds better. "With my security rating? No, I'm not."

"Well, then. Whatever trauma you went through, these things don't last forever. You can't hate all men."

The smile is back. "Oh, there wasn't any trauma, Don, and I *don't* hate men. That would be as silly as—as hating the weather." She glances wryly at the blowing rain.

"I think you have a grudge. You're even spooky of me."

Smooth as a mouse bite she says, "I'd love to hear about your family, Don."

Touché. I give her the edited version of how I

don't have one any more, and she says she's sorry, how sad. And we chat about what a good life a single person really has, and how she and her friends enjoy plays and concerts and travel, and one of them is head cashier for Ringling Brothers, how about that?

But it's coming out jerkier and jerkier like a bad tape, with her eyes going round the horizon in the pauses and her face listening for something that isn't my voice. What's wrong with her? Well, what's wrong with any furtively unconventional middle-aged woman with an empty bed. And a security clearance. An old habit of mind remarks unkindly that Mrs. Parsons represents what is known as the classic penetration target.

"—so much more opportunity now." Her voice trails off.

"Hurrah for women's lib, eh?"

"The lib?" Impatiently she leans forward and tugs the serape straight. "Oh, that's doomed."

The apocalyptic word jars my attention.

"What do you mean, doomed?"

She glances at me as if I weren't hanging straight either and says vaguely, "Oh . . ."

"Come on, why doomed? Didn't they get that equal rights bill?"

Long hesitation. When she speaks again her voice is different.

"Women have no rights, Don, except what men allow us. Men are more agressive and powerful, and they run the world. When the next real crisis upsets them, our so-called rights will vanish like—like that smoke. We'll be back where we always were: property. And whatever has gone wrong will be blamed on our freedom, like the fall of Rome was. You'll see."

Now all this is delivered in a grey tone of total conviction. The last time I heard that tone, the speaker was explaining why he had to keep his file drawers full of dead pigeons.

"Oh, come on. You and your friends are the backbone of the system; if you quit, the country would come to a screeching halt before lunch."

No answering smile.

"That's fantasy." Her voice is still quiet. "Women don't work that way. We're a—a toothless world." She looks around as if she wanted to stop talking. "What women do is survive. We live by ones and twos in the chinks of your world-machine."

"Sounds like a guerrilla operation." I'm not really joking, here in the 'gator den. In fact, I'm wondering if I spent too much thought on mahogany logs.

"Guerrillas have something to hope for." Suddenly she switches on the jolly smile. "Think of us as opossums, Don. Did you know there are opossums living all over? Even in New York City."

I smile back with my neck prickling. I thought I was the paranoid one.

"Men and women aren't different species, Ruth. Women do everything men do."

"Do they?" Our eyes meet, but she seems to be seeing ghosts between us in the rain. She mutters something that could be "My Lai" and looks away. "All the endless wars . . ." Her voice is a whisper. "All the huge authoritarian organizations for doing unreal things. Men live to struggle against each other; we're just part of the battlefield. It'll never change unless you change the whole world. I dream sometimes of—of going away—" She checks and abruptly changes voice. "Forgive me, Don, it's so stupid saying all this."

"Men hate wars too, Ruth," I say as gently as I can.

"I know." She shrugs and climbs to her feet. "But that's your problem, isn't it?"

End of communication. Mrs. Ruth Parsons isn't even living in the same world with me.

I watch her move around restlessly, head turning toward the ruins. Alienation like that can add up to dead pigeons, which would be GSA's problem. It could also lead to believing some joker who's promising to change the whole world. Which could just probably be my problem if one of them was over in that camp last night, where she keeps looking. *Guerrillas have something to hope for . . . ?*

Nonsense. I try another position and see that the sky seems to be clearing as the sun sets. The wind is quieting down at last too. Insane to think this little woman is acting out some fantasy in this swamp. But that equipment last night was no fantasy; if those lads have some connection with her, I'll be in the way. You couldn't find a handier spot to dispose of the body. Maybe some Guévaristo is a fine type of man?

Absurd. Sure. The only thing more absurd would be to come through the wars and get myself terminated by a mad librarian's boyfriend on a fishing trip.

A fish flops in the stream below us. Ruth spins around so fast she hits the serape. " I better start the fire," she says, her eyes still on the plain and her head cocked, listening.

All right, let's test.

"Expecting company?"

It rocks her. She freezes, and her eyes come swiveling around at me like a film take captioned Fright. I can see her decide to smile.

"Oh, one never can tell!" She laughs weirdly, the eyes not changed. "I'll get the—the kindling." She fairly scuttles into the brush.

Nobody, paranoid or not, could call *that* a normal reaction.

Ruth Parsons is either psycho or she's expecting something to happen—and it has nothing to do with me; I scared her pissless.

Well, she could be nuts. And I could be wrong, but there are some mistakes you only make once.

Reluctantly I unzip my body-belt, telling myself that if I think what I think, my only course is to take something for my leg and get as far as possible from Mrs. Ruth Parsons before whoever she's waiting for arrives.

In my belt also is a .32-caliber asset Ruth doesn't know about—and it's going to stay there. My longevity program leaves the shoot-outs to TV and stresses being somewhere else when the roof falls in. I can spend a perfectly safe and also perfectly horrible night out in one of those mangrove flats . . . Am I insane?

At this moment Ruth stands up and stares blatantly inland with her hand shading her eyes. Then she tucks something into her pocket, buttons up and tightens her belt.

That does it.

I dry-swallow two 100-mg tabs, which should get me ambulatory and still leave me wits to hide. Give

it a few minutes. I make sure my compass and some
hooks are in my own pocket and sit waiting while
Ruth fusses with her smudge fire, sneaking looks
away when she thinks I'm not watching.

The flat world around us is turning into an un-
earthly amber and violet light-show as the first
numbness seeps into my leg. Ruth has crawled
under the bromels for more dry stuff; I can see her
foot. Okay. I reach for my staff.

Suddenly the foot jerks, and Ruth yells—or
rather, her throat makes that *Uh-uh-hhh* that means
pure horror. The foot disappears in a rattle of
bromel stalks.

I lunge upright on the crutch and look over the
bank at a frozen scene.

Ruth is crouching sideways on the ledge, clutching her stomach. They are about a yard below,
floating on the river in a skiff. While I was making
up my stupid mind, her friends have glided right
under my ass. There are three of them.

They are tall and white. I try to see them as men
in some kind of white jumpsuits. The one nearest
the bank is stretching out a long white arm toward
Ruth. She jerks and scuttles farther away.

The arm stretches after her. It stretches and
stretches. It stretches two yards and stays hanging
in air. Small black things are wiggling from its tip.

I look where their faces should be and see black
hollow dishes with vertical stripes. The stripes move
slowly . . .

There is no more possibility of their being human
—or anything else I've ever seen. What has Ruth
conjured up?

The scene is totally silent. I blink, blink—this cannot be real. The two in the far end of the skiff are writhing those arms around an apparatus on a tripod. A weapon? Suddenly I hear the same blurry voice I heard in the night.

"Guh-give," it groans. "G-give . . ."

Dear God, it's real, whatever it is. I'm terrified. My mind is trying not to form a word.

And Ruth—Jesus, of course—Ruth is terrified too; she's edging along the bank away from them, gaping at the monsters in the skiff, who are obviously nobody's friends. She's hugging something to her body. Why doesn't she get over the bank and circle back behind me?

"G-g-give." That wheeze is coming from the tripod. "Pee-eeze give." The skiff is moving upstream below Ruth, following her. The arm undulates out at her again, its black digits looping. Ruth scrambles to the top of the bank.

"Ruth!" My voice cracks. "Ruth, get over here behind me!"

She doesn't look at me, only keeps sidling farther away. My terror detonates into anger.

"Come back here!" With my free hand I'm working the .32 out of my belt. The sun has gone down.

She doesn't turn but straightens up warily, still hugging the thing. I see her mouth working. Is she actually trying to *talk* to them?

"Please . . ." She swallows. "Please speak to me. I need your help."

"RUTH!!"

At this moment the nearest white monster whips into a great S-curve and sails right onto the bank at her, eight feet of snowy rippling horror.

And I shoot Ruth.

I don't know that for a minute—I've yanked the
gun up so fast that my staff slips and dumps me as
I fire. I stagger up, hearing Ruth scream "No! No!
No!"

The creature is back down by his boat, and Ruth
is still farther away, clutching herself. Blood is running down her elbow.

"Stop it, Don! They aren't attacking you!"

"For god's sake! Don't be a fool, I can't help you
if you won't get away from them!"

No reply. Nobody moves. No sound except the
drone of a jet passing far above. In the darkening
stream below me the three white figures shift uneasily; I get the impression of radar dishes focusing.
The word spells itself in my head: *Aliens*.

Extraterrestrials.

What do I do, call the President? Capture them
single-handed with my peashooter? . . . I'm alone in
the arse end of nowhere with one leg and my brain
cuddled in meperidine hydrochloride.

"Prrr-eese," their machine blurs again. "Wa-wat
hep . . ."

"Our plane fell down," Ruth says in a very distinct, eerie voice. She points up at the jet, out towards the bay. "My—my child is there. Please take
us *there* in your boat."

Dear god. While she's gesturing, I get a look at
the thing she's hugging in her wounded arm. It's
metallic, like a big glimmering distributor head.
What—?

Wait a minute. This morning: when she was gone
so long, she could have found that thing. Something
they left behind. Or dropped. And she hid it, not
telling me. That's why she kept going under that

bromel clump—she was peeking at it. Waiting. And the owners came back and caught her. They want it. She's trying to bargain, by god.

"—Water," Ruth is pointing again. "Take us. Me. And him."

The black faces turn toward me, blind and horrible. Later on I may be grateful for that "us." Not now.

"Throw your gun away, Don. They'll take us back." Her voice is weak.

"Like hell I will. You—who are you? What are you doing here?"

"Oh god, does it matter? He's frightened," she cries to them. "Can you understand?"

She's as alien as they, there in the twilight. The beings in the skiff are twittering among themselves. Their box starts to moan.

"Ss-stu-dens," I make out. "S-stu-ding . . . not—huh-arm-ing . . . w-we . . . buh . . ." It fades into garble and then says "G-give . . . we . . . g-go . . ."

Peace-loving cultural-exchange students—on the interstellar level now. Oh, no.

"Bring that thing here, Ruth—right now!"

But she's starting down the bank toward them saying, "Take me."

"Wait! You need a tourniquet on that arm."

"I know. Please put the gun down, Don."

She's actually at the skiff, right by them. They aren't moving.

"Jesus Christ." Slowly, reluctantly, I drop the .32. When I start down the slide, I find I'm floating; adrenaline and Demerol are a bad mix.

The skiff comes gliding toward me, Ruth in the bow clutching the thing and her arm. The aliens stay in the stern behind their tripod, away from me. I note the skiff is camouflaged tan and green. The world around us is deep shadowy blue.

"Don, bring the water bag!"

As I'm dragging down the plastic bag, it occurs to me that Ruth really is cracking up, the water isn't needed now. But my own brain seems to have gone into overload. All I can focus on is a long white rubbery arm with black worms clutching the far end of the orange tube, helping me fill it. This isn't happening.

"Can you get in, Don?" As I hoist my numb legs up, two long white pipes reach for me. *No you don't.* I kick and tumble in beside Ruth. She moves away.

A creaky hum starts up, it's coming from a wedge in the center of the skiff. And we're in motion, sliding toward dark mangrove files.

I stare mindlessly at the wedge. Alien technological secrets? I can't see any, the power source is under that triangular cover, about two feet long. The gadgets on the tripod are equally cryptic, except that one has a big lens. Their light?

As we hit the open bay the hum rises, and we start planing faster and faster still. Thirty knots? Hard to judge in the dark. Their hull seems to be a modified trihedral much like ours, with a remarkable absence of slap. Say twenty-two feet. Schemes of capturing it swirl in my mind. I'll need Estéban.

Suddenly a huge flood of white light fans out over us from the tripod, blotting out the aliens in the stern. I see Ruth pulling at a belt around her arm, still hugging the gizmo.

"I'll tie that for you."

"It's all right."

The alien device is twinkling or phosphorescing slightly. I lean over to look, whispering, "Give that to me, I'll pass it to Estéban."

"No!" She scoots away, almost over the side. "It's theirs, they need it!"

"What? Are you crazy?" I'm so taken aback by this idiocy I literally stammer. "We have to, we—"

"They haven't hurt us. I'm sure they could." Her eyes are watching me with feral intensity; in the light her face has a lunatic look. Numb as I am, I realize that the wretched woman is poised to throw herself over the side if I move. With the alien thing.

"I think they're gentle," she mutters.

"For Christ's sake, Ruth, they're *aliens*!"

"I'm used to it," she says absently. "There's the island! Stop! Stop here!"

The skiff slows, turning. A mound of foliage is tiny in the light. Metal glints—the plane.

"Althea! Althea! Are you all right?"

Yells, movement on the plane. The water is high, we're floating over the bar. The aliens are keeping us in the lead with the light hiding them. I see one pale figure splashing toward us and a dark one behind, coming more slowly. Estéban must be puzled by that light.

"Mr. Fenton is hurt, Althea. These people brought us back with the water. Are you all right?"

"A-okay." Althea flounders up, peering excitedly. "You all right? Whew, that light!" Automatically I start handing her the idiotic water bag.

"Leave that for the captain," Ruth says sharply. "Althea, can you climb in the boat? Quickly, it's important."

"Coming."

"No, no!" I protest, but the skiff tilts as Althea swarms in. The aliens twitter, and their voice box starts groaning. "Gu-give . . . now . . . give . . ."

"*Qué llega?*" Estéban's face appears beside me, squinting fiercely into the light.

"Grab it, get it from her—that thing she has—" but Ruth's voice rides over mine. "Captain, lift Mr. Fenton out of the boat. He's hurt his leg. Hurry, please."

"Goddamn it, wait!" I shout, but an arm has grabbed my middle. When a Maya boosts you, you go. I hear Althea saying, "Mother, your arm!" and fall onto Estéban. We stagger around in water up to my waist; I can't feel my feet at all.

When I get steady, the boat is yards away. The two women are head-to-head, murmuring.

"Get them!" I tug loose from Estéban and flounder forward. Ruth stands up in the boat facing the invisible aliens.

"Take us with you. Please. We want to go with you, away from here."

"Ruth! Estéban, get that boat!" I lunge and lose my feet again. The aliens are chirruping madly behind their light.

"Please take us. We don't mind what your planet is like; we'll learn—we'll do anything! We won't cause any trouble. Please. Oh *please*." The skiff is drifting farther away.

"Ruth! Althea! Are you crazy? Wait—" But I can only shuffle nightmarelike in the ooze, hearing that damn voice box wheeze, "N-not come . . . more . . . not come . . ." Althea's face turns to it, open-mouthed grin.

"Yes, we understand," Ruth cries. "We don't want to come back. Please take us with you!"

I shout and Estéban splashes past me shouting too, something about radio.

"Yes-s-s," groans the voice.

Ruth sits down suddenly, clutching Althea. At that moment Estéban grabs the edge of the skiff beside her.

"Hold them, Estéban! Don't let her go."

He gives me one slit-eyed glance over his shoulder, and I recognize his total uninvolvement. He's had a good look at that camouflage paint and the absence of fishing gear. I make a desperate rush and slip again. When I come up Ruth is saying, "We're going with these people, Captain. Please take your money out of my purse, it's in the plane. And give this to Mr. Fenton."

She passes him something small; the notebook. He takes it slowly.

"Estéban! No!"

He has released the skiff.

"Thank you so much," Ruth says as they float apart. Her voice is shaky; she raises it. "There won't be any trouble, Don. Please send the cable. It's to a friend of mine, she'll take care of everything." Then she adds the craziest touch of the entire night. "She's a grand person, she's director of nursing training at N.I.H."

As the skiff drifts out I hear Althea add something that sounds like "Right on."

Sweet Jesus . . . Next minute the humming has started; the light is receding fast. The last I see of Mrs. Ruth Parsons and Miss Althea Parsons is two small shadows against that light, like two opossums. The light snaps off, the hum deepens— and they're going, going, gone away.

In the dark water beside me Estéban is instructing everybody in general to *chingarse* themselves.

"Friends, or something," I tell him lamely. "She seemed to want to go with them."

He is pointedly silent, hauling me back to the plane. He knows what could be around here better than I do, and Mayas have their own longevity program. His condition seems improved. As we get in I notice the hammock has been repositioned.

In the night—of which I remember little—the wind changes. And at seven thirty next morning a Cessna buzzes the sandbar under cloudless skies.

By noon we're back in Cozumel. Captain Estéban accepts his fees and departs laconically for his insurance wars. I leave the Parsons' bags with the Caribe agent, who couldn't care less. The cable goes to a Mrs. Priscilla Hayes Smith, also of Bethesda. I take myself to a medico and by three P.M. I'm sitting on the Cabañas terrace with a fat leg and a double Margarita, trying to believe the whole thing.

The cable said: ALTHEA AND I TAKING EXTRAORDINARY OPPORTUNITY FOR TRAVEL. GONE SEVERAL YEARS. PLEASE TAKE CHARGE OUR AFFAIRS. LOVE, RUTH.

She'd written it that afternoon, you understand.

I order another double, wishing to hell I'd gotten a good look at that gizmo. Did it have a label, Made by Betelgeusians? No matter how weird it was, *how* could a person be crazy enough to imagine—?

Not only that but to hope, to plan? *If I could only go away* . . . That's what she was doing, all day. Waiting, hoping, figuring how to get Althea. To go sight unseen to an alien world . . .

With the third Margarita I try a joke about alienated women, but my heart's not in it. And I'm certain there won't be any bother, any trouble at all. Two human women, one of them possibly pregnant, have departed for, I guess, the stars; and the fabric of society will never show a ripple. I brood: do all Mrs. Parsons' friends hold themselves in readiness for any eventuality, including leaving Earth? And will Mrs. Parsons somehow one day contrive to send for Mrs. Priscilla Hayes Smith, that grand person?

I can only send for another cold one, musing on Althea. What suns will Captain Estéban's sloe-eyed offspring, if any, look upon? "Get in, Althea, we're taking off for Orion." "A-okay, Mother." Is that some system of upbringing? *We survive by ones and twos in the chinks of your world-machine* . . . *I'm used to aliens* . . . She'd meant every word. Insane. How could a woman choose to live among unknown monsters, to say good-bye to her home, her world?

As the Margaritas take hold, the whole mad scenario melts down to the image of those two small shapes sitting side by side in the receding alien glare.

Two of our opossums are missing.

∞

DEBUT
CAROL EMSHWILLER

Carol Emshwiller studied art at the University of Michigan and in France on a Fulbright scholarship. Her stories have appeared in New Worlds, Orbit, Transatlantic Review, *and other magazines and anthologies. Recently she wrote the narrations for two PBS specials,* Pilobus and Joan *and* Family Focus, *created by her husband, filmmaker Ed Emshwiller. A collection of her fiction,* Joy in Our Cause *(Harper & Row), was published in 1974, winning her praise for her unique talent from many reviewers.*

There are always the helping hands of my sisters and everywhere the rustle of soft silk and the tinkle of iced drinks, so being blind is no hardship. All is dark and calm and cool with the flutter of fans. Hands touch me, guide me. My sisters talk in soft voices and sometimes they sing. Their hands are thin and dry. Their long fingernails seldom scratch, only now and then when they can't help it.

Sometimes I say, "I wish I could see," yet never really wanting to, for I have all I could wish for now. I don't need to see with their hands always about me and their fans fanning me. "Better not to see," they answer. "The world is a black place. The days are sharp with thorns. Better not to see the world," and they sing me a slow song.

Mara says the world is blacker even than anything I see now, but I don't believe it. Also I don't see black always, but red sometimes and sometimes purple stripes, sometimes white pricks of light.

Mara and Netta take me to the banks of the stream to listen to the water. "It's nice to hear water over stones," they say, and, "sound is better than sight." Mara combs my hair and Netta washes my feet. I lie on my side with my knees drawn up and play with my blunted daggers, thick as fingers on the string of my belt. I put my hands down sometimes to rub my knees or across to feel how my breasts have grown. I think: There's a change coming. I'm nervous. I'm not sure, today, if I like my hair combed or not or my feet washed. Perhaps I do. Perhaps I don't. (One of these days the daggers won't be so blunt. I wonder if, under their thick shells, there might not be needle points, with poison perhaps, to kill or put asleep. I hope so, but what a strange hope and what a strange thought that comes from nowhere unless from the sound of the pines which also have needles.) This time I won't tell Mara my thoughts, but shall I tell her to stop combing? I don't believe I can ask it gently. I don't feel gentle. I turn onto my other side. By mistake I kick Netta.

"Dear Princess," Mara says, "listen to the music of the stream. It sings just for you." She combs my hair faster and puts her hand on my forehead. Now I know that I don't like the combing. "Stop," I shout. "Don't you ever get enough hair combing? This is the last of it . . . ever." I bang down one fat dagger and it does break open. I hear it shatter and I feel with my finger that it's now a needle shape just as I guessed and almost as long as my hand. I don't yet know if it's poison.

My sisters are quiet and I don't feel their touch. I wonder have they gone off quietly on their bare tiptoes and left me, poor blind thing, alone in the forest? But I don't call out or make any move. I sit with my head up and listen. There's the sound of leaves and of water flowing. I've never been without the rustle of my sisters' sounds or their touch before. Their hands that hold my cup of milk and feed me my bread and honey, my strawberries, my plums, would they now, silently, suddenly, desert me? But have I ever spoken so harshly to them before?

Then some other sister comes. I hear her humming from somewhere across the stream, and then I hear Mara, still quiet near me, say to the one coming, "Thus the Princess," and I turn my face toward her sound. The other comes. It's Mona. "Ah," she says, "I'll go on ahead and tell the Queen." What she says frightens me, but the tone of her voice makes me angry. If she's talking about the Queen, I think, why doesn't she sound grander, or if not grander then more servile. But I was never angry at Mona's voice before. She is one, with Lula and others too, who comes to sing me to sleep.

Now that I know my sisters haven't left me alone, I get to my knees by myself and put my arms above my head and feel how strong I seem today. I stretch and then gather my hair behind my shoulders. I loop it in my necklace like my sisters do when they go hunting. I think how my sisters say I'm beautiful. How they say the Queen doesn't like beauty or strength like mine and I wonder will the sisters stand by me with the Queen. They've been sweet and loving, all with their hands coming to feed me and wash me and cover me with my silk, but will they stand by me as I come, so blind and helpless, to see the Queen? I'm not sure that they will. The world is black, they say. Mara sometimes would hold me in her arms. "Never see it," she would say. "I hope you never see the black world." "Woman child," she called me. Mara is my closest sister, but even so I'm not sure she'll stand by me. Perhaps, after all, the world is as black as what I can see now, perhaps with purple stripes and frightening pricks of light.

I feel the sisters' hands help me to my feet. This time they don't ask me if I'd like to swim before going back. This irritates me, for at least they could ask even though I would say no. Haven't they any respect for my feelings? Can't they let me refuse for myself? Do they, perhaps, think me so stupid, so ignorant, that I might say yes? I don't think I want them on my side before the Queen if that's how they feel about me. I, helpless as I am, will stand up to the Queen alone. But why am I so angry?

Though I'm blind, I know our house well. I've walked along its wide verandas and, when I was younger, played on its steps. I know its many open doors, its porches. I know its stone, its wood, its cushions, curtains, tassels, tapestries. I've heard sounds echo through high-ceilinged rooms. I've put my arms around fat pillars and could not touch my fingertips at the other side, and always I've heard the steps of sisters, upstairs and down, night and day, their rustlings and tinklings, their songs, their humming and sometimes the sound of their spears.

Yet, though the house is big, the doors and porches wide, my own world is always close about me. Sometimes I seem to walk in a ball of dark hardly wider than my fingertips can reach. The world comes to me as I feel it and mostly from the hands of my sisters.

I don't think I was born blind. I have dim memories of once having seen. I remember it best in dreams. Faces come to me, all of them pale, all with long hair. I think I know what lace looks like, and white and pink coverlets, beds that hang from the ceiling on thin golden cords. In my dreams I can see tall, narrow windows with misty light coming in. I see lamps on the walls with fringe hiding their brilliance, but only in the dreams have these things any meaning for me now.

The sisters lead me into the house and into a back room I don't remember having been in before. From here I can smell bread baking and rabbit or perhaps pig cooking, but I know none will be for me. I'm not hungry, but still it makes me angry that none will be for me. I sit stiffly as the sisters take off the soft, light clothes I wear and give me softer, lighter ones. They give me shoes and I'm not used to shoes but they tie them on tightly with knots so I can't take them off. They have thick, soft soles as though I walked on moss or one of our rugs, but the strings around my ankles make me furious. Before they've finished dressing me, I begin to tremble and I touch my shattered dagger and the other blunt one. I feel very strong.

They take me down long halls and then up the central stairway to the top to see the Queen. The Queen calls me "my dear." "My dear," she says and her voice is very old and ugly. "My sweet, my dear," she says, "you've come to me at last, my prettiest one." Does she think I came for compliments? Has she no dignity at all? She's too old. I can tell by her voice. I turn my head toward her. She isn't far from me. I take my one true dagger and leap toward her and, just as I feared, my sisters don't stand by me. Their hands hold me back just when they should be helping. One has her arm across my throat, choking me. Mara, I suppose.

"See, my sweet one, see!" screams the Queen and someone rips my mask from my face and I do see, I see the brilliant world at last. My sisters let me go but now I can't kill the Queen because I don't know anymore where she is. No one moves and gradually I come to understand that there's a mirror along the back wall. I even remember that mirror though I had forgotten it, and I know it's a mirror, and I see now that the Queen sits, or rather reclines before me twice, once in her reflection, and she's not quite as old as her voice seems. And I stand here, and there behind the Queen too, and I know this one in shoes and green scarves with her hair tied up behind is I. And all along I see my sisters, pale ladies, gentle warriors, some leaning toward their spears. Now I'm among strangers, for I don't even know which one is Mara. Now I see how the world is. I still tremble, but from sight.

The Queen is smiling. "Take her," she says and they take me, not bothering now if their fingernails dig and scratch. They take me down the long stairways, across the halls and out the wide doors, away across the meadow and then the stream, away into the forest until we come to a hill. We climb this hill and at the top one sister says, "Sit down." She brings out mead and a little bread. "You must stay here now," she says. "You must wait." They all turn to leave, but one, no different from the others, turns back. "I'm Mara," she says, "and you must stay and wait," and then she goes.

I sit and look. I think they've left me to die. I've seen how the Queen hates me, but still to be able to look is a wonderful thing. I look and recognize and even remember the squirrel, the bird and the beetle.

Soon the sun gets low and the birds sing louder. It's cool. A rabbit comes out to feed not far from where I sit. Then suddenly something drops from a tree not far from me, silent as a fox, but I see him. I jump to my feet. I've never seen a creature like this but I know what it is. I've not heard the word except in whispers in the hallways. I've hardly believed they could exist. Taller, thicker than I, than any of us. Brother to the goat spirit. It is Man. Now I know what the shoes are for. I turn and run, but away from our house and into the hills.

It grows dark as I run and then the moon comes up and I run on and on, back where the hills are steeper and there are more rocks and fewer trees. In my shoes I don't worry about the sharp stones or the long, steep, slippery climbs, for the shoes stick like flies on the wall and I go up or down like a lizard. I've never run like this in my life. I'm supple as water. Nothing can stop me. My steps are like wind in summer. My eyes fly with me and they see everything.

Then there's the steepest climb of all. He can't be close behind me now, for even I, with my magic shoes, am winded, but I keep on to the top where the trees are twisted and small from the wind. There's a hollow, soft with pine needles. I lie down there to hide and turn to face the moon. I'm not afraid of the forest or the night. It's not as dark as blindness.

I lie panting and when my own breathing quiets I hear panting still. I look away from the moon and I see the creature, Man, lying as I lie, exhausted. I watch him until his eyes close, then I close my own. I've run a long way. I don't think or even dream anymore now.

In the first light of dawn the brother to the goat's ghost touches me on my breast and wakes me. My anger of yesterday has changed. I tremble. Man's fingers are strong as the golden bed cords. His hands aren't dry and cool like my sister's hands. He tears away a green scarf and I feel there, at my neck, the coarse hairs by his mouth. I shut my eyes and for a moment I think that I'm being eaten, but then I feel again that I'm running like a lizard on the mountainsides, and Man breathes like a lion in my ear.

Afterward he rolls away and looks at the morning sky. Quickly, before it's too late, I smash the other dagger open, grasp the two and stab him twice with each hand. He makes a big bird sound and curls like a caterpillar. Then I rest a little while.

I understand now. Of course the Queen hates me, but she'll care for me, and all those like me, well. And I hate her, but I don't feel irritable any longer. I'm happy and relaxed. I rest, and later I hear my sisters coming for me, singing in the hills. How I love my sisters. Someday they might stand by me before the Queen, so I'll let them comb my hair. I'll drink milk from their cups and I'll eat strawberries out of their hands even though I'm no longer blind.

Now Mara and Netta will be the first to come to me. I'll kiss them and they'll feed me. We'll stay on this hill and in this hollow all night and we'll pray together by moonlight to the goat's ghost for the birth of a girl.

∞

WHEN IT CHANGED

JOANNA RUSS

Joanna Russ teaches science fiction and creative writing at the University of Colorado and is currently working on a sword-and-sorcery novel for young people. She studied English at Cornell University and playwriting at Yale. She is the author of many short stories and the novels And Chaos Died *(Ace),* Picnic on Paradise *(Ace),* The Female Man *(Bantam), and* We Who Are About To . . . *(Dell). "When It Changed," which became the subject of controversy when it first appeared in 1972, won a Nebula Award in 1973.*

Katy drives like a maniac; we must have been doing over 120 kilometers per hour on those turns. She's good, though, extremely good, and I've seen her take the whole car apart and put it together again in a day. My birthplace on Whileaway was largely given to farm machinery and I refuse to wrestle with a five-gear shift at unholy speeds, not having been brought up to it, but even on those turns in the middle of the night, on a country road as bad as only our district can make them, Katy's driving didn't scare me. The funny thing about my wife, though: she will not handle guns. She has even gone hiking in the forests above the forty-eighth parallel without firearms, for days at a time. And that *does* scare me.

Katy and I have three children between us, one of hers and two of mine. Yuriko, my eldest, was asleep in the back seat, dreaming twelve-year-old dreams of love and war: running away to sea, hunting in the North, dreams of strangely beautiful people in strangely beautiful places, all the wonderful guff you think up when you're turning twelve and the glands start going. Some day soon, like all of them, she will disappear for weeks on end to come back grimy and proud, having knifed her first cougar or shot her first bear, dragging some abominably dangerous dead beastie behind her, which I will never forgive for what it might have done to my daughter. Yuriko says Katy's driving puts her to sleep.

For someone who has fought three duels, I am afraid of far, far too much. I'm getting old. I told this to my wife.

"You're thirty-four," she said. Laconic to the point of silence, that one. She flipped the lights on, on the dash—three kilometers to go and the road getting worse all the time. Far out in the country. Electric-green trees rushed into our headlights and around the car. I reached down next to me where we bolt the carrier panel to the door and eased my rifle into my lap. Yuriko stirred in the back. My height but Katy's eyes, Katy's face. The car engine is so quiet, Katy says, that you can hear breathing in the back seat. Yuki had been alone in the car when the message came, enthusiastically decoding her dot-dashes (silly to mount a wide-frequency transceiver near an I. C. engine, but most of Whileaway is on steam). She had thrown herself out of the car, my gangly and gaudy offspring, shouting at the top of her lungs, so of course she had had to come along. We've been intellectually prepared for this ever since the Colony was founded, ever since it was abandoned, but this is different. This is awful.

"Men!" Yuki had screamed, leaping over the car door. "They've come back! Real Earth men!"

We met them in the kitchen of the farmhouse near the place where they had landed; the windows were open, the night air very mild. We had passed all sorts of transportation when we parked outside—steam tractors, trucks, an I. C. flatbed, even a bicycle. Lydia, the district biologist, had come out of her Northern taciturnity long enough to take blood and urine samples and was sitting in a corner of the kitchen shaking her head in astonishment over the results; she even forced herself (very big, very fair, very shy, always painfully blushing) to dig up the old language manuals—though I can talk the old tongues in my sleep. And do. Lydia is uneasy with us; we're Southerners and too flamboyant. I counted twenty people in that kitchen, all the brains of North Continent. Phyllis Spet, I think, had come in by glider. Yuki was the only child there.

Then I saw the four of them.

They are bigger than we are. They are bigger and broader. Two were taller than I, and I am extremely tall, one meter eighty centimeters in my bare feet. They are obviously of our species but *off*, indescribably off, and as my eyes could not and still cannot quite comprehend the lines of those alien bodies, I could not, then, bring myself to touch them, though the one who spoke Russian—what voices they have—wanted to "shake hands," a custom from the past, I imagine. I can only say they were apes with human faces. He seemed to mean well, but I found myself shuddering back almost the length of the kitchen—and then I laughed apologetically—and then to set a good example (*interstellar amity*, I thought) did "shake hands" finally. A hard, hard hand. They are heavy as draft horses. Blurred, deep voices. Yuriko had sneaked in between the adults and was gazing at *the men* with her mouth open.

He turned *his* head—those words have not been in our language for six hundred years—and said, in bad Russian, "Who's that?"

"My daughter," I said, and added (with that irrational attention to good manners we sometimes employ in moments of insanity), "My daughter, Yuriko Janetson. We use the patronymic. You would say matronymic."

He laughed, involuntarily. Yuki exclaimed, "I thought they would be *good-looking!*" greatly disappointed at this reception of herself. Phyllis Helgason Spet, whom someday I shall kill, gave me across the room a cold, level, venomous look, as if to say: *Watch what you say. You know what I can do.* It's true that I have little formal status, but Madam President will get herself in serious trouble with both me and her own staff if she continues to consider industrial espionage good clean fun. Wars and rumors of wars, as it says in one of our ancestors' books. I translated Yuki's words into *the man's* dog-

Russian, once our lingua franca, and *the man* laughed again.

"Where are all your people?" he said conversationally.

I translated again and watched the faces around the room; Lydia embarrassed (as usual), Spet narrowing her eyes with some damned scheme, Katy very pale.

"This is Whileaway," I said.

He continued to look unenlightened.

"Whileaway," I said. "Do you remember? Do you have records? There was a plague on Whileaway."

He looked moderately interested. Heads turned in the back of the room, and I caught a glimpse of the local professions-parliament delegate; by morning every town meeting, every district caucus, would be in full session.

"Plague?" he said. "That's most unfortunate."

"Yes," I said. "Most unfortunate. We lost half our population in one generation."

He looked properly impressed.

"Whileaway was lucky," I said. "We had a big initial gene pool, we had been chosen for extreme intelligence, we had a high technology and a large remaining population in which every adult was two-or-three experts in one. The soil is good. The climate is blessedly easy. There are thirty millions of us now. Things are beginning to snowball in industry —do you understand?—give us seventy years and we'll have more than one real city, more than a few industrial centers, full-time professions, full-time radio operators, full-time machinists, give us seventy years and not everyone will have to spend three-

quarters of a lifetime on the farm." And I tried to
explain how hard it is when artists can practice full-
time only in old age, when there are so few, so very
few who can be free, like Katy and myself. I tried
also to outline our government, the two houses, the
one by professions and the geographic one; I told
him the district caucuses handled problems too big
for the individual towns. And that population control was not a political issue, not yet, though give
us time and it would be. This was a delicate point
in our history; give us time. There was no need to
sacrifice the quality of life for an insane rush into
industrialization. Let us go our own pace. Give us
time.

"Where are all the people?" said that monoma-
niac.

I realized then that he did not mean people, he
meant *men*, and he was giving the word the meaning it had not had on Whileaway for six centuries.

"They died," I said. "Thirty generations ago."

I thought we had poleaxed him. He caught his
breath. He made as if to get out of the chair he was
sitting in; he put his hand to his chest; he looked
around at us with the strangest blend of awe and
sentimental tenderness. Then he said, solemnly and
earnestly:

"A great tragedy."

I waited, not quite understanding.

"Yes," he said, catching his breath again with that
queer smile, that adult-to-child smile that tells you
something is being hidden and will be presently
produced with cries of encouragement and joy, "a
great tragedy. But it's over." And again he looked

around at all of us with the strangest deference. As if we were invalids.

"You've adapted amazingly," he said.

"To what?" I said. He looked embarrassed. He looked inane. Finally he said, "Where I come from, the women don't dress so plainly."

"Like you?" I said. "Like a bride?" for the men were wearing silver from head to foot. I had never seen anything so gaudy. He made as if to answer and then apparently thought better of it; he laughed at me again. With an odd exhilaration—as if we were something childish and something wonderful, as if he were doing us an enormous favor—he took ones shaky breath and said, "Well, we're here."

I looked at Spet, Spet looked at Lydia, Lydia looked at Amalia, who is the head of the local town meeting, Amalia looked at I don't know whom. My throat was raw. I cannot stand local beer, which the farmers swill as if their stomachs had iridium linings but I took it anyway, from Amalia (it was her bicycle we had seen outside as we parked), and swallowed it all. This was going to take a long time. I said, "Yes, here you are," and smiled (feeling like a fool), and wondered seriously if male-Earth-people's minds worked so very differently from female-Earth-people's minds, but that couldn't be so or the race would have died out long ago. The radio network had got the news around planet by now and we had another Russian speaker, flown in from Varna; I decided to cut out when *the man* passed around pictures of his wife, who looked like the priestess of some arcane cult. He proposed to question Yuki, so I barreled her into a back room in spite of her furious protests, and went out on the front porch. As I left, Lydia was explaining the difference between parthenogenesis (which is so easy that anyone can practice it) and what we do, which is the merging of ova. That is why Katy's baby looks like me. Lydia went on to the Ansky Process and Katy Ansky, our one full-polymath genius and the great-great-I don't know how many times great-grandmother of my own Katharina.

A dot-dash transmitter in one of the outbuildings chattered faintly to itself: operators flirting and passing jokes down the line.

There was a man on the porch. The other tall man. I watched him for a few minutes—I can move very quietly when I want to—and when I allowed him to see me, he stopped talking into the little machine hung around his neck. Then he said calmly, in excellent Russian, "Did you know that sexual equality has been reestablished on Earth?"

"You're the real one," I said, "aren't you? The other one's for show." It was a great relief to get things cleared up. He nodded affably.

"As a people, we are not very bright," he said. "There's been too much genetic damage in the last few centuries. Radiation. Drugs. We can use Whileaway's genes, Janet." Strangers do not call strangers by the first name.

"You can have cells enough to drown in," I said. "Breed your own."

He smiled. "That's not the way we want to do it." Behind him I saw Katy come into the square of light that was the screened-in door. He went on, low and urbane, not mocking me, I think, but with the self-confidence of someone who has always had money and strength to spare, who doesn't know what it is to be second-class or provincial. Which is very odd, because the day before, I would have said that was an exact description of me.

"I'm talking to you, Janet," he said, "because I suspect you have more popular influence than anyone else here. You know as well as I do that parthenogenetic culture has all sorts of inherent defects, and we do not—if we can help it—mean to use you for anything of the sort. Pardon me; I should not have said 'use.' But surely you can see that this kind of society is unnatural."

"Humanity is unnatural," said Katy. She had my rifle under her left arm. The top of that silky head does not quite come up to my collarbone, but she is as tough as steel; he began to move, again with that queer smiling deference (which his fellow had showed to me but he had not), and the gun slid into Katy's grip as if she had shot with it all her life.

"I agree," said the man. "Humanity is unnatural. I should know. I have metal in my teeth and metal pins here." He touched his shoulder. "Seals are harem animals," he added, "and so are men; apes are promiscuous and so are men; doves are monogamous and so are men; there are even celibate men and homosexual men. There are homosexual cows, I believe. But Whileaway is still missing something." He gave a dry chuckle. I will give him the credit of believing that it had something to do with nerves.

"I miss nothing," said Katy, "except that life isn't endless."

"You are—?" said the man, nodding from me to her.

"Wives," said Katy. "We're married." Again the dry chuckle.

"A good economic arrangement," he said, "for working and taking care of the children. And as good an arrangement as any for randomizing heredity, if your reproduction is made to follow the same pattern. But think, Katharina Michaelason, if there isn't something better that you might secure for your daughters. I believe in instincts, even in Man, and I can't think that the two of you—a machinist, are you? and I gather you are some sort of chief of police—don't feel somehow what even you must miss. You know it intellectually, of course. There is only half a species here. Men must come back to Whileaway."

Katy said nothing.

"I should think, Katharina Michaelason," said the man gently, "that you, of all people, would benefit most from such a change," and he walked past Katy's rifle into the square of light coming from the door. I think it was then that he noticed my scar, which really does not show unless the light is from the side: a fine line that runs from temple to chin. Most people don't even know about it.

"Where did you get that?" he said, and I answered with an involuntary grin. "In my last duel." We stood there bristling at each other for several seconds (this is absurd but true) until he went inside and shut the screen door behind him. Katy said in a brittle voice, "You damned fool, don't you know when we've been insulted?" and swung up the rifle to shoot him through the screen, but I got to her before she could fire and knocked the rifle out of aim; it burned a hole through the porch floor.

Katy was shaking. She kept whispering over and over, "That's why I never touched it, because I knew I'd kill someone. I knew I'd kill someone." The first man—the one I'd spoken with first—was still talking inside the house, something about the grand movement to recolonize and rediscover all that Earth had lost. He stressed the advantages to Whileaway: trade, exchange of ideas, education. He, too, said that sexual equality had been reestablished on Earth.

Katy was right, of course; we should have burned them down where they stood. Men are coming to Whileaway. When one culture has the big guns and the other has none, there is a certain predictability about the outcome. Maybe men would have come eventually in any case. I like to think that a hundred years from now my great-grandchildren could have stood them off or fought them to a standstill, but even that's no odds; I will remember all my life those four people I first met who were muscled like bulls and who made me—if only for a moment—feel small. A neurotic reaction, Katy says. I remember everything that happened that night; I remember Yuki's excitement in the car, I remember Katy's sobbing when we got home as if her heart would break, I remember her lovemaking, a little peremptory as always, but wonderfully soothing and comforting. I remember prowling restlessly around the house after Katy fell asleep with one bare arm flung into a patch of light from the hall. The muscles of her forearms are like metal bars from all that driving and testing of her machines. Sometimes I dream about Katy's arms. I remember wandering into the nursery and picking up my wife's baby, dozing for a while with the poignant, amazing warmth of an infant in my lap, and finally returning to the kitchen to find Yuriko fixing herself a late snack. My daughter eats like a Great Dane.

"Yuki," I said, "do you think you could fall in love with a man?" and she whooped derisively. "With a ten-foot toad!" said my tactful child.

But men are coming to Whileaway. Lately I sit up nights and worry about the men who will come to this planet, about my two daughters and Betta Katharinason, about what will happen to Katy, to me, to my life. Our ancestors' journals are one long cry of pain and I suppose I ought to be glad now, but one can't throw away six centuries, or even (as I have lately discovered) thirty-four years. Sometimes I laugh at the question those four men hedged about all evening and never quite dared to ask, looking at the lot of us, hicks in overalls, farmers in canvas pants and plain shirts: *Which of you plays the role of the man?* As if we had to produce a carbon copy of their mistakes! I doubt very much that sexual equality has been reestablished on Earth. I do not like to think of myself mocked, of Katy deferred to as if she were weak, of Yuki made to feel unimportant or silly, of my other children cheated of their full humanity or turned into strangers. And I'm afraid that my own achievements will dwindle from what they were—or what I thought they were—to the not-very-interesting curiosa of the human race, the oddities you read about in the back of the book, things to laugh at sometimes because they are so exotic, quaint but not impressive, charming but not useful. I find this more painful than I can say. You will agree that for a woman who has fought three duels, all of them kills, indulging in such fears is ludicrous. But what's around the corner now is a duel so big that I don't think I have the guts for it; in Faust's words: *Verweile doch, du bist so schoen!* Keep it as it is. Don't change.

Sometimes at night I remember the original name of this planet, changed by the first generation of our ancestors, those curious women for whom, I suppose, the real name was too painful a reminder after the men died. I find it amusing, in a grim way, to see it all so completely turned around. This, too, shall pass. All good things must come to an end.

Take my life but don't take away the meaning of my life.

For-A-While.

∞

DEAD IN IRONS

CHELSEA QUINN YARBRO

Chelsea Quinn Yarbro is the author of the novels Ogilvie, Tallant & Moon *(Berkley-Putnam),* Time of the Fourth Horseman *(Doubleday),* Hotel Transylvania *(St. Martin), and* False Dawn *(Doubleday). A collection of her short fiction will be published by Doubleday in 1978. She teaches voice and is a tarot-card reader at San Francisco's Magic Cellar. She is also a serious composer; her most recent compositions are "Cinque Ritratti" for piano and "The Sayre Cycle" for cello. Her story "Dead in Irons" shows us spacefarers in a bleak future society.*

They all hated steerage, every steward in the *Babel Princess*. Mallory made that plain when he showed Shiller around the ship for the first time.

"Hell of a place," she agreed, looking at the narrow, dark corridors that connected the cold storage rooms.

Mallory chuckled, a sound of marbles falling on tin. "Worse'n that. Don't let 'em stick you back here, Shiller. They're gonna try, but don't you do it. You being the newest one, they think they can get away with it, making you do steerage. But this damn duty has to be shared." He cast a sideways look at Shiller. "Wranswell's the worst. You keep an eye out for him."

"It's like cold storage for food," Shiller said, peering through the viewplate at the honeycomb of quiet, frosted cocoons.

"Sure is," Mallory said, contempt darkening his voice.

"I wonder why they do it, considering the risks?" Shiller mused, not really talking to Mallory. "You couldn't pay me to do that."

A white grin split Mallory's black face. "Cause they're stinking poor and dumb. Remember that, Shiller; they're dumb."

Shiller turned her gaze once again to the figures stacked in the coffinlike tiers. "Poor bastards," she said before she moved away from the hatch that closed the steerage section away from the life of the rest of the ship.

"It's not that bad," Mallory said, running his eyes over the dials that monitored the steerage cargo. Some of the indicators were perilously low, but Mallory only grunted and shook his head. "Hell, Shiller, this way we don't have to feed 'em, except for that minimal support glop they get. We don't have a lot of crap to get rid of. We don't have to keep a shrink around for 'em the way we do for first class. We don't have to worry about space. It could be a lot worse. Imagine all of 'em running around loose down here."

"Yeah," Shiller nodded, following Mallory down the corridor to the drive shield. But she added one last question. "Why don't they buy into a generation ship instead of this? They're slow but they're safe."

Mallory shrugged. "Generation ships cost money; maybe they can't afford it. Maybe they figure that this way they'll be alive when they get where they going, *if* they get where they're going."

"If," Shiller repeated, frowning. "But what happens if we drop out wrong? Where would we be? What would we do with them?" She sounded upset, her face was blank but her dark eyes grew wide.

"Hasn't happened yet. Maybe it won't. It's only a seven percent chance, Shiller. That's not bad odds. Besides, we couldn't keep operating if we lost more'n that. Don't worry about it." He swung open the hatch to the small, low-ceilinged cubicle beside the core of the ship. "I'll show you what to look for if we get into trouble."

Although she had been to school and had been told these things before, Shiller followed him through the lock, turning to look one last troubled time at the hatch to the cold room.

"Shiller. Pay attention," Mallory's voice snapped at her. "I got to get back on deck watch."

"Yeah," she answered and stepped into the little room.

Wranswell posted the watches later in the day, and Shiller saw she had been assigned to steerage. Mallory's warning rang in her mind, but she shrugged it off. "Can't hurt to do it once," she said to the air as she thumb-printed the order.

"Don't let them get frisky," Wranswell said with

ponderous humor. He loomed at the end of the corridor, filling it with his bulk. He was a gathering of bigness. His body, his head, his eyes, all were out-sized, massive, more like some mythic creature than chief steward of a cargo jump ship.

Inwardly Shiller shrank back from the man. Small and slight herself, she distrusted the big man. She knew that stewards rose in rank by their ability to control other stewards, and Wranswell's bulk clearly dominated the others.

"Got nothing to say? Well, that'll be good in steerage. All you got to do is sit there and wait for nothing to happen." He chortled his huge, rumbling chortle as he started down the corridor. "You haven't been to see me, Shiller," he complained as he grew nearer.

"I've been stowing my gear."

"Of course you have. It's a pity you didn't let me inspect it first. Now it's all over your cabin. And some of it got torn. You got to have tougher things, Shiller." He was close to her now. He leaned on the order board and smiled down at her. "You got to remember what my job is. And you're the new steward. I got to be sure of you, you know."

"My watch is about to begin," Shiller said in a small tight voice.

"Oh. Yes. It's too bad your cold gear got ripped. You'll get cold for those four hours." He grinned at the fear in her face. "I'd loan you some others, but it's against the rules. And you don't want me to break the rules, do you?"

Shiller said no, hating herself for fearing the big

man, and for letting him see her fear. He was the sort who would turn it against her.

"Of course, Shiller. The rules shouldn't be broken. But I make the rules. They're my rules." He reached down and touched her arm. "I make 'em and I can break 'em. Because they're mine. Remember that, Shiller."

"I'll remember." Her fists were hard knots at her sides.

"Do you want me to break them for you? Hum?" His smile had no warmth, no humor. "What do you think, Shiller? What do you want me to do?"

She moved back from him. "I think a rule is a rule, Wranswell. I wouldn't want you to make an exception for a new steward like me." Then she turned and fled, followed by Wranswell's huge laughter.

Steerage was icy; the cold cut through Shiller's torn gear with an edge as keen and penetrating as steel. Her hands, inadequately protected by ripped gloves, were brittle and stiff, and her fingers moved slowly and clumsily as she adjusted the valves on the tiers.

The monitor showed that the indicators which had been near critical were now back within tolerable limits. The silent, cocoon-like figures stacked in the tiers drifted on in their sleep that was not sleep, their bodies damped with cold and drugs. One day they would be warm again, would breathe deeply the air of another planet, their hearts would beat a familiar seventy-two beats a minute. But at the moment, they were like so much meat stored for the butcher.

Shiller was horrified with herself as the thought rose unbidden in her mind. She had been determined to treat steerage passengers as the people they were, not as cold cargo. Yet in less than a day, she had found herself slipping, seeing steerage as meat only. She forced herself to pause as she worked, to talk to each of the passengers, to learn their names and destinations.

"How's it going?" Mallory's voice asked on the speaker.

"It's cold."

"Sure." He paused. "You're cold or it's cold?"

"Both," she said shortly, wishing she could ask him for help and knowing that she must not.

"You got your gear on, don't you?"

"Sure. But turns out some of it's ripped." She was too near telling him what Wranswell had done, and what he had said.

"Don't you know enough not to go in there in ripped gear?"

"It's all the gear I have," she said. The cold had gathered on her face and made it hard to talk.

"Ripped gear? Where'd you buy crap like that?"

"It got ripped after I came aboard." She thought it was safe to say that much, that Mallory would understand and hold his peace.

"Wranswell?" said the voice from the speaker.

"I'm not accusing anyone of anything." Her hands were so cold they felt hot. Carefully she rubbed them together and waited to hear what more Mallory had to say.

"I'll talk to you later." The speaker clicked once and was dead.

Shiller sat looking at the monitors, feeling the

cold seeping into her body. It was too cold and too long. She knew that her hands would need treatment when she got off watch. It would go on her report, and she would be docked for improper maintenance of her gear. Bitterly she realized that Wranswell had engineered things very well. All he had to do was be sure that her gear was faulty, and he would be able to order her to do anything. She would have no choice but to obey, or the company would leave her stranded on some two-bit agricultural planet. It had happened before, she thought. Wranswell was too good at his game to be a novice player. Shuddering, she forced her attention on the tiers.

"You're the new one." The steward who confronted Shiller was an older woman, one whose face was hardened with her job and made tight with worry. "I heard we'd got you."

Shiller felt the hostility of the other steward engulf her, hot, a vitriolic pulse. "I'm sorry," she faltered. "I haven't learned who everyone is yet."

"No. Only the one that counts." The woman barred her way, one muscular arm across the door.

"Look," Shiller said, tired of riddles and anger, "my name is Shiller. I only came aboard last night, I don't know the ropes around here. If I've done something wrong, I wish you'd tell me, then I won't have to do it again."

"Shiller," the other said, looking her over measuringly. "Wranswell told me about you. You're the reason he's kicking me out." She waited to see what effect this announcement would have.

"No," said Shiller, closing her eyes, feeling the

bile touch the back of her mouth. She dreaded what Wranswell had planned, and now she had made an enemy of his former mate. "I didn't do anything. I don't want him."

The laughter was unpleasant. "You're not serious," the other said, stating a fact. "On these tubs, you take everything you can get, and if you can get the chief steward, don't you tell me you'd refuse."

"I don't want Wranswell," Shiller repeated, very tired now, her hands beginning to ache now that they were warm again.

"Sure. Sure, Shiller." The woman leaned toward her, one hand balling into a fist, her face distorted with rage.

"Dandridge!" Wranswell's voice echoed down the hall, and in a moment he appeared, his big body moving effortlessly, swiftly to stop the woman's hands as she rushed Shiller.

"Oh, no, Wranswell," she cried out, turning to see his fist as it smashed the side of her face. Clutching at the sudden well of blood, she sank to her knees, a soft moan escaping her before she began to sob.

"Looks like you need someone to take care of you, Shiller," Wranswell said, ignoring Dandridge on the floor.

"Not you, Wranswell." Shiller had begun to back up, feeling her face go ashen under Wranswell's mocking eyes. "Not after what you did to Dandridge."

The woman on the floor was bleeding freely, her hands leaking red around the fingers. Her breath was choked now, and when she coughed there was blood on her lips.

"Dandridge is nothing," Wranswell said.

"She was your mate," Shiller said tensely, still hoping to break away from him, from the bloody woman on the floor.

"Was, Shiller. Not now. Now you're here and I got plans for you."

Shiller shook her head, sensing the hurt he would give her if he could.

"No? There's a lot of time you can spend in steerage. Hours and hours, Shiller. In torn gear. Think about it."

In spite of herself, she said, "Mallory said that watch was shared."

"Mallory ain't chief steward. I am. You'll do all the steerage watches I say you will. That could be quite a lot. Until you get sensible, Shiller."

Dandridge stumbled to her feet and, hiding her face, pushed down the hall toward the medic room. Shiller watched her go, her hands leaving red marks where they touched the wall.

"Think about what I said, Shiller." For a moment Wranswell studied her with arrogant calm, then he turned and followed Dandridge to the medic room.

The skin on her left hand was unhealthily mottled. Shiller studied it under her bunk light, feeling a worry that was not reflected in her face. Four days of steerage watch had brought her to this. She flexed her fingers uncertainly and found that even a simple movement hurt and left her hand weak and trembling. Taking the packet of ointment Mallory had left for her, she smeared it over the livid spot. The pain eased.

Out in the hall she could hear Dandridge talking

to Briggs. Shiller knew what Dandridge was saying, that she was angry, taking vengeance where she could, the hurt and damage done to her much worse than the ruin of her face. Leaning back, Shiller tried to shut out the words, the spite that came through palpably.

A warning buzzer sounded the change of watch. Hearing it, Shiller felt a surge of rebellion, but she was too tired to ride it through. With tired acceptance she rose and pulled on her cold gear, checking all the temporary seals with more hope than trust. It would be a little better, but there was no way they could keep the cold out entirely, there was no way they could save her from the ache and the numbness.

Mallory's friendly face appeared around the frame of her door. "Ready?" he asked brightly.

"I guess."

"I'll walk you down." He waited in the door, his hands blocking the passage and the cruel words Dandridge spewed out at Briggs.

"Thanks," Shiller said, summoning the ghost of a smile. She had not smiled often since coming to the *Babel Princess*. Draping her headgear over her arm she joined Mallory in the narrow corridor.

"Too bad Wranswell's being shitty about steerage," Mallory was saying loudly enough for Dandridge and Briggs to hear them. He was still in his first-class uniform: tight breeches, loose shirt, half jacket and jaunty cuffed blue boots. Shiller looked at him with envy, her body made shapeless and clumsy in the cold gear. Mallory gave her clothes one uncertain look, then went on, "Say, Shiller, it's none of my business, but why fight it?"

"Fight what?" she asked, wishing he had not spoken.

"Wranswell. He's not interested in Dandridge anymore. You could be his mate. It's obvious he wants you."

"You're right, it's none of your business."

Mallory did not pay any attention to this. "What he's trying to do is wear you down, Shiller. He can do it."

"We're not out here all the time. Sometime we have to drop out and come into port. When we do, there's company officials . . ."

"Be reasonable, Shiller," Mallory said patiently. "We're in port maybe one day in twenty, then we're gone again. You can't begin to get to one of the officials of the Babel line. That takes weeks."

"Then I'd transfer to another ship." She was speaking recklessly and she knew it. If Mallory decided to, he could tell Wranswell, and then there would be no escape for her.

"Don't kid yourself, Shiller. It's no different on the other ships. We run by our own law out here. And if we break the rules now and then, who's going to come after us. And how?" He smiled at her, his dark eyes showing a gentle concern. "This is our universe. And Wranswell runs it."

"I'll think of something," Shiller said, not to Mallory. "I won't be his mate. I can't stand him." She turned, suddenly afraid. "Mallory, don't tell him I said that. Please."

He made a dismissing gesture, hands wide. "You don't want me to know, don't tell me. I probably won't tell Wranswell. But he's a tough man. Maybe I'll have to." He shrugged fatalistically.

"But Mallory . . . You wouldn't tell him." She felt suddenly desperate. Under the heavy wrap of her gear she felt a cold hard lump gather under her ribs.

Seeing her panic he said, "No, of course not, Shiller."

They were almost at the cold room. Shiller pulled her headgear off her arm and began to secure it. Her gloves made her hands awkward, and in a moment she asked Mallory to do it for her.

"Sure, glad to," he said, pulling the gear into place and sealing it. "Keep what I said in mind," he told her as they reached steerage. With a cuff on her arm for luck, he opened the hatch.

Shiller hesitated inside the hatch, dreading the four hours to come. She was still close enough to hear Wranswell stop Mallory outside.

"Well, Mallory, how did it go?" asked the hated voice.

"Well, I talked to her," Mallory said, hedging.

"Any headway?"

"Not so far." There was contrition in his tone, and embarrassment.

"Keep trying, Mallory. Or you can do your watches in there."

Mallory laughed uneasily. "You don't have to worry about that. You won't get me in there for anything." He paused. "I can talk to her again in the morning, when she's had some rest. Maybe she'll think it over while she's standing watch."

"I hope so, for your sake."

"It's gonna take time, Wranswell. The thing is, you got her real scared."

"That," Wranswell said, "is the general idea."

"You rotten traitor!" Shiller shouted when Mallory appeared in her door the next morning. "You can fucking well bet I thought about it!"

"Thought about what?" Mallory asked warily.

"You know. I heard you talking to Wranswell. I heard what you said, Mallory."

Mallory hesitated, indecisive. His face was a mixture of aggravation and loss. "Then you know how things stand," he said at last.

Shiller swung off her bunk. "No, I do not know how things stand. I thought I did, but obviously I was wrong." She found suddenly that it was hard to speak, and the difficulty was only partly due to the cold in steerage.

"Ah, Shiller." If he meant to be conciliatory, he failed.

"Don't you talk that way to me. Why did you do it, Mallory? I thought you gave a damn. I thought you were my friend."

"I am your friend," he said, speaking with a caution he might have used with a child. "Why else would I do this?"

"To save your hide, that's why."

"Look, Shiller, I told you the day you came aboard to be careful of Wranswell. He's the boss here. Why didn't you listen to me then? You dumb, or something?"

"I didn't think you meant this," she shot back at him, finding a strength in her that she did not know she had. "You never said a damn thing about what Wranswell wants, or what he's like. You never told me he'd want this of me." There was a burning behind her eyes and Shiller was shocked to realize that she was on the verge of tears.

"I figured you knew. What else would it be?"

"You were very careful about that, Mallory. You warned me to watch out for Wranswell. You said that when you showed me around the ship. But that wasn't what you meant, was it? And you didn't come out and tell me what I had to deal with. And you didn't tell me you were following Wranswell's orders."

Mallory was getting angry. "Who the hell else's orders would I follow? This is Wranswell's world, and he makes the decisions. More'n that, he's the one who makes sure things get done. You can't fight that, Shiller. And I can't fight it either."

"That's shit," she spat at him.

"Fuck you, Shiller." He turned away from the door, then looked back. "You keep this up, you're gonna be as dead as the stuff outside this ship. Wranswell ain't gonna wait forever. You gotta give in sometime."

Shiller grabbed her cold gear and hurled it at Mallory.

"You're as dumb as steerage. You belong there!" Casting the heavy gear aside, Mallory stormed off, his steps sounding like explosions along the corridor.

As Shiller listened to the sounds die away, she felt part of herself die with them. Mallory was right, and Wranswell waited inexorably for her, to possess her and break her. She did not recognize the terrible grating sounds as her own sobs.

By the time the *Babel Princess* dropped out for

its first stop, Shiller had got used to the steerage routine. She figured out the colonists bound for Grady's Hole and prepared them for shipping to the surface. It was a long tedious job, but now she welcomed it, for at least in steerage she was safe from Wranswell.

"It's okay, Harper," she said to one of the co-coons, addressing it by the name stenciled across it. "You're gonna like Grady's Hole. It's sunny and warm, and the soil is good. The Babel line has an outpost there already, so you know you won't starve." She hooked the support tubes into his shipping capsule, noticing as she did that the color of the fluid was wrong. Quickly she checked the feeders to see if she had confused the line, but no, it was the correct one. And the solution that should have been mulberry was a pale pink.

Cautiously she tapped the feeder, drawing out a sample of the fluid for later examination. "Hope you're okay, Harper," she said to the cocoon. "Don't want you to get down there and find out they can't thaw you out." She put the sample into one of her capacious pockets and moved on to the next tier.

"Crawleigh, Matson, Ewings and Marmer," she read from her list, as if calling roll. "You're the last of the lot. The consignment says fourteen, and you make it fourteen." She moved the tiers into position for capsule loading, making a final check of the list.

When she was finished she stamped the invoices and relayed them up to the bridge for verification. In her pocket there were now four samples, the other three drawn from Marmer, Ewings and from one of the earlier capsules which she had gone back to check after seeing Harper's feeder.

The invoices came back with the Babel seal and the captain's sigil on them. Shiller took them and put each in the capsule it belonged to. Then she sealed the capsules one after the other, checking each seal in the manner prescribed.

"Shiller." The voice on the speaker was Briggs. "I got something you have to ship down with the capsules."

"What?" she asked, not caring.

"Something important."

"It's against regulations," she said, speaking by rote. She no longer trusted anyone on the ship. "Sorry."

"Wranswell said to tell you that he'd count it as a favor. He said he might find some other work for you to do if you can get this stuff down for him."

"What is it?" She found that to her disgust, she was interested. She hesitated on the seals of the capsule.

"It goes with Baily. You seal it up yet?" Briggs sounded urgent, as if he too had some consideration riding on her agreement.

"Not yet," she admitted. She hesitated, thinking. If it were found out that she had added something not on the invoice, she could be stranded out on some distant planet where she could be a common laborer or a prostitute. But if she failed to do this for Wranswell, her life would continue to be a nightmare.

"Hurry up," Briggs prodded. "I got it right here. It's small. Wranswell really wants it, Shiller."

"Okay," she said. She went to the hatch and held out her gloved hand. To her surprise the thing Briggs dropped into it was only a small dark vial, weighing no more than a couple of ounces. "Is this all?" she asked, turning the thing over in her gloved hand.

"That's it. And remember, it has to go in Baily," Briggs said, sounding relieved.

"You can tell Wranswell it's done," she said and closed the hatch.

But she wondered idly what it was Wranswell was smuggling—for surely he was smuggling—that was so small and so precious.

"I haven't thanked you yet for that service you did me," Wranswell said to Shiller as they sat in the mess. "You're coming around. Perhaps all the way?"

Shiller did not even look up from her plate.

"You might be interested to learn what I am up to. No? Not the least curiosity?"

"No."

"No? But do you really have so little concern for your fate? You, Shiller?"

"I'm not interested, Wranswell," she said, and knew she was lying.

"But you might be arrested for this. Don't you want to know what the charge will be?" Wranswell was being funny again. His deep rumbling laughter filled the mess room. "We could all be arrested for this, certainly. But then, to arrest us, they would have to catch us. Out here." A few of the other stewards took up his laugh.

Shiller bit her lip and remained silent.

"Here we are, engaged in secret smuggling. Babel policy would condemn us all and most of you know nothing about it." He looked contemptuously over his underlings. "How many of you are like Shiller here, and don't want to know?"

"It's steerage," said Dandridge from across the room. "Wranswell smuggles the bodies. He waters down the feeders so the cargo is just getting cold and drugs; it makes 'em hard to thaw out that way. He ships along the feeder solution so his bunch in customs on the ground can keep 'em going until they can sell the cargo to slavers." Her voice was loud in a room suddenly still.

"Dandridge, is, of course, right," Wranswell allowed, spreading his huge hands on the table. "She is also very foolish. But then, I don't imagine anyone heard her very well."

Conversation erupted in the mess, the eleven stewards trying to shut out the accusation that would condemn them all.

Under the racket, Wranswell said to Shiller, "I would put it differently, but essentially Dandridge is right. From time to time I'll expect a little help from you. In exchange, you may be allowed to stand something other than steerage watches. Is your first-class uniform clean?"

"And if I don't cooperate?" In spite of herself, she knew she was striking a bargain with Wranswell, giving her consent to his terrible scheme. She had heard enough about the slavers to make her shudder, for they were far worse than anything Wranswell could hope to be.

"I think you will. In the next few days you might have a few words with Dandridge about it. She can tell you what to expect."

"Why Dandridge? What should I ask her?"

"Shiller, you will know when the time is right." He turned away from her then and spoke softly to Mallory.

Dandridge's body was stiff by the time Shiller found it. She had been struck many times, and even the ugly lividity of death could not disguise the large bruises on her arms and back. She lay now crammed between two rows of tiers at the back of steerage, her dead eyes blackened, horrified. She had not died easily.

"Briggs, you and Carstairs get in here," Shiller said to the speaker. She was feeling curiously light-headed, as if Dandridge's death had spared her.

"Want some company, Shiller?" Briggs asked with an audacity he had learned from Wranswell. "Come outside here."

"I've got company. Dandridge's body's in here. You gonna come in and get it out or do I call the bridge?" It was a bluff: Shiller knew she could never call the bridge and risk the ostracism it would bring, or maybe an end like Dandridge's.

"You don't have to do that," Briggs said quickly. "You said Dandridge's body?"

"Yes. She's dead. Somebody killed her. You better tell Wranswell. He might be anxious about her." Shiller heard Briggs whisper to someone, then he said, 'It'll take a couple of minutes. We'll get her out."

It was longer than that when they at last came through the hatch, shapeless in their cold gear, a stretcher slung between them. Shiller saw that the other steward was Mallory, and that he was calm.

"She's at the back under tier number five. You

won't be able to lay her flat; she's got stiff."

When they got to the place, Briggs stopped, his eyes widening behind his mask. "Come on, Briggs," Mallory said. "We gotta get 'er out of here. Wranswell's waiting."

Briggs pulled himself together, grabbing the outthrust elbows. "Look at her. She sure got hit," Briggs said. Mallory only grunted.

They wrestled the body onto the stretcher and lashed it down as best they could. Then, without a word to Shiller, they left steerage, carrying their grim trophy between them.

Shiller watched them go, remembering what Wranswell had said. The warning was plain. If she talked, she, too, would be killed. If she did not cooperate with Wranswell's smuggling, she would find herself beaten and frozen at the back of steerage.

"It's too bad that we'd already gone hyper when this happened," Wranswell announced to the stewards. "If we were still in port we could report this to the Babel home office and they could investigate. But since we've gone hyper and we aren't due to touch port for another fifteen days, even preserving the body might be difficult."

Gathering her anger and her courage, Shiller said, "Why not put her in steerage? She'll keep in there."

Wranswell chuckled at the idea. 'Well, it's a novel approach," he said as he loomed over her. "But it's not practical. We'll put her in one of the spare capsules and ship her off."

Briggs had got noticeably paler. "Off *where?*"

he demanded. "Out there? We don't even know where that is. We won't know where's she's gone."

From his side of the room Mallory gave Briggs an impatient sign. "Don't worry about it, Briggs. It's better this way. More'n that, there won't be any hassle at the other end of the line. Nobody'll investigate and we'll all be safe. Captain'll file a report and that'll be the end of it."

"Mallory's right, you know," Wranswell agreed. "Much less trouble for everyone. Believe me, the Babel line doesn't like these occurrences any better than we do. We'll prepare her for burial and send her off tomorrow."

When the others got up to leave, he motioned Shiller to stay behind. "I trust your talk was constructive? I know these one-sided conversations can be trying, but I'm sure she had some information for you." He reached out one hand and tugged at Shiller's hair. "Be reasonable, Shiller. You won't get anywhere if you antagonize me."

"I got the message. Can I go now?" She refused to look at Wranswell, at his bloated, smiling face and his eyes that raked her body like nails.

"Not quite yet. I want to explain about the next drop out. On Archer Station, the next port, we play the game a little differently."

"I hear you," Shiller said, wishing she could scream.

"There, one capsule more or less makes little difference to my agent's clients. And I find it hard to justify keeping a steward on who is only good for steerage work. Unless I find out you're more versatile, there might be an extra capsule. Archer

Station deals with Ranyion slavers. I understand they're most unpleasant."

Shiller felt her teeth grind as she held her mouth shut. There was little she could say now. Archer Station was two weeks away, and they would be her last two weeks of freedom.

In the end they had to break Dandridge's bones to fit her into the capsule. But at last her stiff, distorted body was closed away, sealed for a journey into nothing that would lead nowhere. The stewards gathered at the lock, as Wranswell had ordered.

Briggs arrived last, looking haggard. He watched Mallory through exhausted eyes, fingering a lean statue which he clutched to his chest. Mallory deliberately ignored him, turning away when Briggs started his way.

Wranswell, his big body looking out of place in his first-class uniform, arrived to deliver his eulogy before sending the capsule on its way. He wore a secret smile that grated on Shiller's nerves. Wranswell was obviously satisfied.

"For our comrade who has died in the line of duty," Wranswell began the traditional benediction as the rest of the stewards shifted on their feet and felt awkward, "we praise her now for all she accomplished while she worked among us and did her tasks. . . ."

Before Wranswell could continue, Briggs shouted out, "You killed her!" And he lunged at Mallory, the statue he had been holding at the ready. "I loved her and you killed her!"

Mallory shouted and leaped aside, bringing his arm down on Briggs' back. Briggs staggered under the blow, but turned, his face filled with loathing. "You're Wranswell's errand boy. He gave her to you and when she wouldn't take you, you killed her!" He sloughed around on Wranswell. "You're as bad a slaver as the ones you sell to."

This time it was Wranswell who hit him, sinking his balled-up fists deep into Briggs' gut. Retching, Briggs fell to his knees. Beside him the little black statue lay broken. "You can hit me till I'm dead. It doesn't change anything. You still killed her."

"When you're finished, Briggs, we'll get on with this ceremony." Wranswell turned to Mallory. "You're okay?"

"Sure. Briggs's just upset. He don't know what he's saying. Why, when this is all over, he's gonna forget all about it." Mallory was straightening his uniform as he spoke, adjusting it with strangely finicky gestures.

Briggs looked up. His face was ashen and his voice hoarse, but there was no mistaking his words. "You hear me, Wranswell. So long as Dandridge is out there, we're gonna stay hyper, too."

"Go away, Briggs. If you can't conduct yourself right, go away." Then Wranswell turned from him, ignoring him now. He began the ceremony once more in impressive, sonorous tones. No one but Wranswell spoke.

Above decks the captain played back Wranswell's report, shaking his head, not caring about what went on below decks. He heard the thing out, then connected it to his log, giving his formal acceptance to the report. It was too bad that the steward had died. They would have to lay over a couple extra days at Archer Station while a new one was sent.

It was several hours later when there was the first indication that something was wrong. The *Babel Princess* gave a lurch, like a boat riding over choppy water. But in hyper there were no waves, and there was no reason for the ship to lurch. Alarms began to sound all over the ship.

Shiller tumbled out of the bunk, still half-asleep, knowing that something had wakened her. The shrilling of the alarm broke through and she began to dress automatically. The cold of steerage was still on her and she trembled as she pulled herself into her clothes.

The alarms grew louder. Down the corridor there were other stewards stumbling about, shouting to each other.

Suddenly the ship's master address system came on. "This is the captain. This is the captain," the system announced. "We have encountered unfamiliar turbulence. For that reason we are going to drop out and see if there is any reason for it. I apologize in advance to our passengers for this inconvenience. I ask your indulgence while we complete this maneuver. The stewards are standing by to take care of you should you experience any discomfort. We will drop out in ten minutes. For that reason, please remain in your quarters. If you need assistance, buzz for a steward. Thank you."

Mallory pounded on Shiller's door. "Get your

ass above decks, Shiller. First-class uniform so the
tourists can throw up on somebody neat and clean."

"Shut up," she answered.

"The passengers are waiting," he said in a brusque
voice.

Sarcastically she asked, "And are you looking
after steerage? I thought that regulations required
that steerage be manned during every drop out
and every pass to hyper. Don't tell me you're going
in there, Mallory."

"Not me, but you are," Mallory said, taking cruel
delight in this change of orders. "You can take
care of the cargo in steerage. You been doing it so
long, you're real good at it. Maybe you can snuggle
up to 'em and keep 'em warm." He laughed in
imitation of Wranswell, then hurried down the hall.

Slowly Shiller changed into her cold gear, a deep
worry settling over her with gloom. Unlike the
others, she suspected that Briggs was behind the
trouble. And when the others discovered it, what
would happen to him? Mutiny brought with it an
automatic death sentence. Shiller had seen a formal
execution once, and it had not been pretty. To
watch poor, crazy Briggs die that way . . .

"Hurry up, Shiller," Langly shouted from down
the hall. "Time's short! Three minutes!"

"Coming," she answered, and went out into the
corridor still pulling on her gloves. When the one-
minute warning sounded she began to run.

The drop out did not work. The drive whined,
the ship bucked and slid like a frightened horse, the
shield room grew unbearably hot, the core reached
its danger point, but they failed to drop out.

There was a wait then, while the core cooled down, and then they tried once more. Above decks the tourists in first class watched each other uneasily, not willing to admit that their pleasure jaunt could end this way. The stewards kept to their assigned posts, not daring to show the panic they felt. For if the tourists did not know they were in trouble, the stewards did.

The fear did not touch steerage. Shiller braced the cocoons, strapping the tiers to their stanchions on the walls. She steadied herself between them and stoically rode out the first attempt to drop, and the second. She knew a morose satisfaction: if they were stranded in hyper, she would be free of Wranswell, free of Mallory. She glanced around the familiar bleakness of steerage, thinking of the names stenciled on the cocoons with a certain affection, as she might have thought of plants.

"Don't let this worry you, Ander," she said to the nearest one. "This doesn't matter. If we don't get where you're going, you'll never know about it anyway." Idly she wondered if Ander were male or female. There was nothing on the invoice that mentioned sex. Was Ander a great strapping lad with huge shoulders and hands the size of dinner plates? Was she a strong farm woman who could carry a sheep slung over her shoulders? Was he a small ferocious man with bright eyes and boundless energy? Did she work handily, driving her small frame to greater feats . . . ?

She tightened the cocoon in place and moved on to the next one.

This was Taslit, bound for Dreuten's Spot, an out-of-the-way agricultural planet, the last on their outward run. "Taslit, never mind," she spoke gently, easing the cocoon more firmly into place. "Two to one Wranswell would have sold you to some slaver anyway. You won't have lost anything this way."

Then the alarm sounded once more and another futile attempt to drop out began. As the heat mounted in the core, steerage began to warm up, the temperature rising almost five degrees. Shiller watched with concern as more and more indicators moved into the critical zones. If they kept this up long it would kill her cargo. She couldn't let that happen.

She went like a drunken man across steerage, reaching for the speaker button as she was thrown against the wall. She grabbed for a brace and held on as the *Babel Princess* sunfished about her. At last the attempt was broken off, the core stopped its maddened hum and the ship righted itself in the vastness of hyper.

Again the speaker came to life. "This is the captain speaking. This is the captain speaking." There was silence following that announcement. "We appear to be having some difficulty returning to normal space. As it will take time to effect the necessary repairs, we will continue our journey in hyper until we can drop out without endangering the ship or her passengers . . ."

Shiller stared at the speaker, incredulous. "We're never gonna drop out; you know that," she told it, shaking her head.

"We may be delayed in arriving at Archer's Station . . ."

"We sure will. Forever."

"But the Babel Company will gladly refund part

of your fare to compensate for this delay. I trust
we will proceed without incident."

When the sound died away, Shiller sank onto
the monitor bench. She wondered if the others in
the seven percent who never came out of hyper
did this, lied to the passengers and to themselves,
pretending that everything was all right, promising
an end to the voyage they would never live to see.

Shiller started to laugh. In the eerie cold the
walls echoed her laughter, making it louder.

Wranswell was left to deal with Briggs; the captain had decided that it was a matter for the chief
steward because Briggs was a steward. Wranswell
had smiled, accepted the responsibility and sought
out Mallory. Together they decided what had to
be done.

They attached burners to Briggs' hands and feet
and lit them. Then they locked him in steerage,
alone with the cocoons. Wranswell and Mallory
took turns at the hatch window, watching him as
he died. They watched for a long time.

And when at last they dragged the body out, it
had burned-off hands and feet, leaving charred,
bleeding stumps on a corpse rimed with frost,
seared with cold, the skin mottled blue where it
was not black.

On Wranswell's orders it was left in the corridor
for a day, a silent ghastly reminder of Wranswell's
power. Then it was loaded into a capsule and sent
out to join Dandridge in the lost places.

There had been trouble above decks. Rations
had been shortened again and a fight had broken

out, the stronger taking what little food there was from the weak. Now that most of them knew there would be no escape from hyper they cared less what became of one another. There had been several injuries and medicine was running as short as food.

"Look," said Mallory to a general meeting of the stewards, "we can take the ones that are worst hurt and we can stick 'em in cocoons and hook 'em up like the rest of steerage. We won't have to feed 'em, they won't get any worse, and if we ever get out of this, they'll be alive. They'll be grateful."

"And if we don't get out of this?" Shiller asked, the fear of Mallory all but gone. She had not bothered to change out of her cold gear.

"Then it won't matter, Shiller," Wranswell said from the head of the table. He had lost weight and his flesh hung in folds about him like a garment that no longer fit.

"Then who's supposed to look after 'em?" Shiller went on, seeing with contempt that the other stewards did not challenge him.

"You are."

"What? No more flattering offers?" She barked out a laugh, and found that it no longer hurt to laugh, or to die.

Stung, Wranswell retorted. "I've made other arrangements. You lose, Shiller. Too bad." His greedy eyes fastened on the slender grace of Langly, and the boy pouted in response.

"Lucky you," Shiller said before she walked out.

She woke to the smell of cooking meat. She sat up slowly, for hunger had made her faint. The light over her bunk was off but she did not bother to turn it on; she knew it was dead. More awake, she sniffed again. Yes, it was meat, fresh meat broiling. She felt her way to the door and pulled it open.

"Hey, Shiller, come on down and have some breakfast," Langly called when he caught sight of her. His bony face was wreathed in smiles and grease.

Shiller shook her head as if to clear it. "Where'd that come from?"

"It was Mallory's idea." He turned into the mess to answer a question, then said to her, "You're entitled to two pounds of meat a day so long as you're working."

"What'd you do, kill someone?" she asked without thinking.

Langly's answering giggle told her what she did not know.

"Oh, shit," she cried, ducking back into her room and pulling on her cold gear as fast as she could. It was a slow business in the dark, and she had to pause often to regain her strength. When she was done she stumbled down the corridor, oblivious to the mocking words that Langly sent with her.

When she pulled open the hatch, she knew.

The tiers had been raided, the cocoons pulled apart and the bodies harvested for the stewards. Here and there a few of the cocoons remained intact, awaiting the time when the others would be hungry again. Some held the injured passengers, their new seals not quite dry.

Shiller stood in the door, swaying on her feet. That they had done this to her steerage, that they had damaged her cargo . . . She moved into the cold room, unbelieving. Ander was gone. So was Taslit. And Ettinger. And Swansleigh. Nathan. Cort. Fairchild. Vaudillion. Desperately she searched the tiers for the cocoons and found them empty. Gone, gone, gone . . . She thought of Wranswell, his sagging face full of meat, smiling, gesturing as he ate, his thick hands caressing Langly and his dinner alternately.

Vomit spewed from her before she could stop it, and she sank to her knees until there was nothing left for her to cast up.

"There she is." Mallory's soft words reached across steerage to Shiller as she lay exhausted on the floor.

"Good work," Wranswell said, a contented grin spreading over his shiny face. "I was afraid we'd lost her."

Shiller turned her head slowly, filth and ice clinging to her face. Dully she watched as the two men came nearer.

"Hello, Shiller," Mallory beamed down at her. "We've been looking for you." He was much closer now. He put his boot on the side of her face and pushed.

Shiller gasped and was silent.

"Come now, Shiller. You aren't going to spoil this for us, are you?" Wranswell leaned down next to her. "Let me hear you, Shiller. It's much quicker if you do." He sank his hands in her hair and pulled sharply back. Shiller left blood and skin on Mallory's boot.

Mallory was good at his job. Each time a fist or a boot struck her, Shiller remembered the way Dandridge had looked when she found her. Now she knew how it had happened. She tried to let go, to ride with the punishment and the pain, but she knew that she fought back. In some remote part of her mind she knew that she struck at Mallory, trying desperately to stop him, to give him back hurt for hurt. Once she had the satisfaction of connecting with his eye, and as he beat her into unconsciousness, she could see the slow drip of blood down his face, and she was satisfied.

When she woke it was warm. Her cocoon had thawed around her and the room reeked of putrefaction. Of the few remaining bodies in steerage, only she was alive. Numbly she felt for the feeder lines and found none. They must not have had time to attach them.

Carefully she eased herself off the tier, her hands shaking when she tried to close them around the lip of the tier.

Then she heard the sound. "Wranswell? Wranswell? Where are you?"

The voice was Mallory's, but so changed. Now it was a quavering thread, coming on uneven breaths like an old man's.

"Wranswell?"

Shiller listened for the answer, hardly daring to breathe. She did not want to be discovered, not by Mallory, not by Wranswell. She was not alive for that. Discovering that she was trembling, she willed herself to relax.

"I know you're down here," Mallory went on, his voice reverberating in the still corridors. "I'm hungry, Wranswell."

At the words Shiller felt her own hunger rage in her with fangs as sharp and demanding as some beast's. She knew that her trembling weakness was from hunger, that her bony hands were the face of hunger.

Something stumbled near the shield room. Then lumbering footsteps came down the hall, wallowing, blundering into the walls, no longer careful or cautious, wanting only escape.

Now Shiller understood, and it was what she had feared. It was the hunt. The last hunt. She lay back on the tier, very still, hearing her heart very loud in the stinking room.

There was a scuffle now, flesh meeting flesh, and a mingled panting of voices, senseless sounds that neither Mallory nor Wranswell knew they made.

Then came the heavy, final sound, as though something large and moist had burst.

"Got you. Got you," Mallory chanted in ragged victory. He was not good to hear. "Got you. Got you. Got you, Wranswell." His high crowing made the hackles on Shiller's neck rise.

Now the sounds were different, a chopping and tearing as Mallory set about his grisly work.

This was her chance then. Her hunger was gone and her mind had become clear as her terror dissolved. After this, there could be no more terror, no more fear.

Carefully, very carefully Shiller eased herself off the tier. Slowly, so slowly she slid across the room, no longer seeing the slime that oozed underfoot, or seeing the things that rotted on the other tiers, or the wreckage in steerage. That was over and done. That she could not change. There was only one thing now that she wanted, one last act she could perform.

She reached the monitor bench, raising the lid so that it made no sound.

In the hall Mallory began to sing.

Then Shiller had it, the long wedged blade that opened the capsules. Its edge shone purposefully. It had been designed to cut through seventeen inches of steel without slowing down.

Ander was dead, and Taslit. Dandridge, Briggs. Langly, too, she supposed. Wranswell. Cort. Ettinger. Harper. All of them.

The *Babel Princess* was dead, lost in uncharted darkness, derelict, drifting on unknown tides, its last energies draining into emptiness.

She was dead, too.

Shiller fondled the blade with care, testing the edge against her thumb, sucking the blood, tasting the salt. Weak as she was, she would not fail.

In the corridor Mallory was almost finished.

And in steerage, on the other side of the hatch, Shiller was waiting.

∞

BUILDING BLOCK

SONYA DORMAN

Sonya Dorman lives in Connecticut, where she raises and shows Akita dogs. Her fiction has appeared in The Magazine of Fantasy & Science Fiction, Orbit, Analog, *and other magazines and anthologies. She has also published three collections of poetry,* Poems, Stretching Fence, *and* A Paper Raincoat, *and is working on a fourth,* The Lost Traveller. *She is the author of a novel for young people,* Roxy Rimidon *(Coward-McCann & Geoghegan). In "Building Block," she writes of a future artist-businesswoman faced with some unusual yet familiar problems.*

"Count to ten in French," Dr. Elaine Bassey told me, and I could hear my voice: "*Un, deux, trois . . .*" and feel the needle in my arm. Before closing my eyes, I took a last look at the recall-specialist, attractive, tall, with a strong, inquisitive face.

Closing my eyes didn't help. Dr. Bassey had said she would have trouble with me because I was the type who wouldn't willingly surrender my "executive brain." She was so right. Owner, manager, and chief architect of Sky Castles, Incorporated, I wasn't about to give up my mind. Yet if I didn't give up a portion of it to this session, to the tape recording, I'd be broke and out of business.

"Six, sept, huit . . ."

In the last few years I'd designed and built half a dozen fabulous private space homes, from my own innovative plans. My mock name had become Arachne, spoken with respect, even while other space architects were doing their best to drive me out of competition.

Dr. Bassey asked me a question, and automatically I began a commercial response, indicating I hadn't yet given up enough of myself to her drug. "It's amazing," I began to spiel, "how designers with no imagination continue to use the solar-power units in vanes, sticking the ugly shapes all over the buildings. What you want is a home that is your castle, a beautiful dwelling that's uniquely yours . . ."

"No," Dr. Bassey said, interrupting me. "I am Dr. Bassey, not a customer. We won't have any of this custom-built stuff. Frankly, I don't care for the space-home concept, no matter what the status."

It seemed odd she was talking like that, but possibly it was in order to get through my defenses, to the lost Star Cup concept. The papers were gone. Stolen. Perhaps shredded by a competitor, or misplaced in a file, or, less likely, never in existence outside of my mind. I'd been suffering from exhaustion, followed by depression, and after my last terrific booze had put myself on vitamins and plenty of sleep, but too late: my most radical and innovative house design, along with the blue-

prints I swore I'd seen, was not even a memory.
Or rather, it was a memory, but not reachable in
ordinary conditions.

I was scared. Maybe I had lost so many neurons
my brain would never be as good. Maybe I'd
wind up on Pluto, another bum, working a day a
month in the mines to pay for my daily bowl of
soup. And no more castles in the sky. It would be
worth my last credit if a recall doctor could draw
out and record the basic concept for the Star Cup.
From that, I could work up the rest. Just get me
the root, and I'd make the tree flower.

"Yes, that's it," Dr. Bassey said. I'd missed my
own words. I now became conscious of consciousness and began to fight the situation. Too much of
the drug, and I'd be out cold; too little, and I
couldn't cooperate. It was a delicate business, and
probably worth the enormous fee I paid her.

"The web shape?" she suggested. "The spider in
the cup?"

For a glorious instant the finished building glittered in lunar blue. I was seated at the drawing
board, dead center, with the marvelous geometry
spun from my brain spreading out around me. Facing the star of planetary life. Solar fire pouring
energy through the web. There was nothing else
like it in the known universe. Quite aside from the
worth in credits, it was the functional beauty of
the Star Cup building that I wanted to retrieve.
No artist can bear to lose a vision.

"You're all right," Dr. Bassey said. My eyes
opened to the numerals on the ceiling. An hour
had passed.

"Did you get it?" I asked, sitting up and rubbing the inside of my arm where the needle had been.

Dr. Bassey was sitting at her desk, a cup of tea steaming near her left hand. The soft burr of the tape recorder was extinguished. "Feel okay?" she asked me.

"Did you get it?" I yelled impatiently, rolling off the couch to my feet. I picked up my tunic from the chair where I'd dropped it before the session began. Dr. Bassey had suggested being physically comfortable, and for me, that meant no shoes and no tunic, only the short skirt.

"I'm not at all sure," the doctor replied, leaning back in her swivel chair. There was something in her voice that was all too familiar; the assurance, the arrogance, of a person who has done you in, shafted you, fused your relays. I pressed the tunic seam shut, and looked at her through my eyelashes. I was wearing the blonde ones, and they obscured far too much. Throw them out, I advised myself silently.

"You know damn well you got something," I said to Dr. Bassey, keeping a good grip on my rage while I struggled with my incredulity. Doctors simply don't do things like this. Or do they?

"It might be worth your while to examine what I did get," she said, and took a big swig of the hot tea.

"Dr. Bassey, I told you before we began that in order to pay your fee, I took out every credit I had banked. You know I haven't worked in a year, I'm not able to work, I'm blocked. Or I wouldn't be here."

"I'm sure someone with your reputation could raise more for an emergency," she said calmly. "It might be well worth your while."

Oh, you irresponsible, unprofessional fool, I thought, but not sure whether I meant it for her or myself. I put on the dark-purple shoes that matched my tunic, trying to think but making no progress. Permanent brain damage, I assumed.

"How much?" I asked.

"Let's say—a quarter of a million?"

"Malpractice!" I shouted. "Outrageous! How do you think I'm going to raise that much? Look, Doctor, you see before you a beaten and broken woman, who not long ago worked miracles in the sky around this planet. I'm an artist. I contribute to the psychic well-being of our species, as much if not more than you do. In effect, we both work toward the same purpose."

"Quite," she said.

"You can't do this."

"Of course I can, Norja. You told me the Star Cup concept is worth millions. I could ask you to build me one, and let it go at that, except as I told you, I don't care to revolve in space and I sincerely believe that anyone who wishes to live that way is sick. A sick escapist. A sick egotist. Draining off the sun's power before it reaches the planet at all. Living in luxury above the middle-class masses who could never in their wildest dreams afford one of those spectacular and rather ridiculous Sky Castles of yours. No, thank you. I'll take my returns in credits, the way normal, healthy people do."

The woman was obviously worse off than her

patients. Yet she had been highly recommended, and in her field was as well known and successful as I was in mine.

"You'll have to give me time," I said.

"Any time," Dr. Bassey said. "I'll keep your tape in the vault. Any time to the end of the month will be fine."

"After that, I suppose you'll sell it to the highest bidder, and I can predict that will be Simons and Emory. For all I know, they bought you off the day I phoned for an appointment."

She frowned severely. "Absolutely not. I don't operate in that fashion."

"Strictly out for yourself, then."

"Certainly. Aren't you?"

Well, of course. But not by dishonorable means. I'd never cut a corner at a client's expense, and didn't intend to ever. Not that I had any clients left. The last booze had been damn near interstellar, according to gossip, anyway. Nobody seemed to understand that between the boozes, I was more lucid, talented, and productive than ten other architects put together nose to nose in a pentagon. Oh dear, no, I thought, you'd have to double the number . . . something was amiss in my mind. More vitamins? A truly tender lover? A short cruise to the moons and back? I couldn't afford the cruise, I was taking the vitamins, and a lover would, at the moment, distract me from work. I could look forward to him after the Star Cup was completed. If I found the right one, I would, by God, build us our own Star Cup and nestle there in the center of it with him until every last credit was gone, slowly sipping love and champagne—no, Norja, I said to myself, that's exactly what happened last time. You see where it got you.

"You have more than two weeks until the end of the month," Dr. Bassey said. "If you'll excuse me now, I have another patient."

As I left the building, I thought how I wouldn't excuse her for anything, or forgive her. Of course I could report her to the Medical Corporation, but I had no proof, it was her word against mine, and I was broke and a scandal. The fact that I'd gone to her at all was admission of at least a temporary incompetence. Aside from not wanting to publish such an admission, I felt I'd do better to handle this on my own. However, I indulged in a few revenge fantasies; how I'd use her brown left eye, frozen and ground to a distance lens, or decorate a lock panel with strands of her brunette hairs.

Home is the best place for me to think things out, so I went directly to my four big light rooms. I like sparse surroundings, and what few stark pieces furnished my home were individually chosen. The only luxury was a huge, squashy couch that gripped you like warm flesh. Two serographs on the living-room wall offered tawny colors in the otherwise neutral scheme. The one object I liked best was in my study—an old-fashioned artifact, quite genuine. Inside the wooden box hung on the wall there was a painted view through a worn old wooden window frame to nothing but cold blue sky. Provocative, melancholy, infinitely restful.

I like my home. It really is my castle, my second skin, and a reflection of part of my personality the public never gets to see.

For half a day, lying around at home, I contemplated immediate action, another booze, a visit to friends, or one of my follow-up trips. The latter made the most sense. Every six months for five years after completing a Sky Castle home, I took an Electric Boat cruiser out and checked with the client to make sure everything was to his taste, functioning properly, needing no adjustment. If adjustments were required, I had them taken care of. My clients paid a lot for their homes; they got perfect service and genuine care; my reputation was not just that of an artist and craftswoman, but that of a fine, dependable businessperson as well. I did not build a house and then vanish. Anyone who bought a Sky Castle that I designed knew I was on call afterward, that I came through on the guarantees. None of them understood what it cost me in terms of emotional drain and surviving the pressure of emergencies, but that was okay. I didn't ask them to think about such things. You count on friends for that kind of understanding and concern; it would not be fair to expect it from clients.

Even routine checkups were better than not working at all. I went alone this trip, though often I took with me Joe Andressi, my foreman. He had such a lovely sense of humor and easy manner. I enjoyed his company, and he enjoyed looking over a completed job. I'd once offered him a partnership, which he in his kindly manner refused, explaining how much he dreaded being desked. What he wanted for the rest of his life was the best building equipment and someone yelling for action. I could understand perfectly. Anyhow, this trip I felt like being alone.

The Copleys' docking carriage was warped, and that was the only repair job I found during the four-day sweep. They didn't even realize how much it needed attention, or they pretended not to, but when I said goodbye, Mrs. Copley came to the lock with me and murmured something about how Sherwood got pretty reckless with his shuttle car, and she gave me a tolerant wink, so I winked back, and we understood each other.

I gave Joe a call, and he said he'd send maintenance out right away with a new carriage frame. Business taken care of, I was left to think about Dr. Bassey. In the midst of one of these red rage bouts, I thought maybe if I went to another recall specialist —but no, what would I pay with? Personal care can't be written off as business expense. That's an artist's problem, of course. Business people get all kinds of medical coverage; action people can be insured for thousands against broken bones or ruptured spleens. A playwright or an architect, a painter or choreographer, artistically blocked and unable to produce, must pay credit on the line and in advance for any kind of medical help. It isn't fair and it ought to be changed. Someday maybe I would organize a big group and lobby the change through.

On the way home I thought of Dr. Moons, and wondered if he was still alive. I hadn't seen him since he retired, to live in a modest earthside home, his reputed millions donated to the research center named for him, The Moons Psychic Alliance Corporation. He'd been a friend of my parents' and a sort of unofficial godfather to me as I grew up, but after retirement he'd become moody and reclusive, so I stopped going to visit.

My transmitter finally raised him. He didn't sound any happier to hear from me now than he had those years ago when I'd last contacted him, but that could be my own fault, for not being more persistent.

"No," he told me, "I don't give consultations any more. I do not work. I am entitled to my peace and quiet. All I want is to be left alone with my bees and mesquite and if you have a problem there are any number of working physicians you can call on."

But I need a friend, I told him.

"Why me?" he grumbled. "I'm an old man, and you haven't so much as called me in five years."

"Last time I called you were just plain disagreeable," I reminded him.

"I remember it, Norja. You called at a very inconvenient time." There was a long pause. He cleared his throat. Then he said, "I was younger, at that time. It's not as inconvenient right now. As a matter of fact, I'm not doing anything. The cold has put the bees into dormancy and the last batch of honey has clarified nicely. Would you like to come to dinner, Norja?"

Good old Moons, I thought. "Save me the whole comb," I said. It was an old family joke, going back to my tenth birthday when he had come to visit, bringing his usual honey jar for a gift and including in it the comb, more valuable than diamonds. It was the beeswax-based healing salve which had given him leisure to establish his Psychic Alliance Corporation. Of course I ate the comb in the kitchen while the grownups were having drinks before dinner, and of course I was so sick from it I couldn't look at honey again for ten years.

The transmitter said "Bleep," or something like that, just as I switched off. Was he being funny, or was he making that sound himself? I wondered. Well, I'd find out at dinnertime. And also satisfy my curiosity as to what he was doing, because certainly a man who'd been head of a corporation for many years didn't really quit business just because he announced retirement; he simply exchanged an office desk for the easier pace of working out of his home. Moons was a good businessman, as his Corporation showed more and more profits. Bees and honey must be only toys.

Dr. Moons's adobe house looked deceptively simple. I noticed lots of sagebrush growing around it, and imagined he was getting some nice honeys from the sage, as well as from the prized mesquite, one of the most delicate and pale honeys available. His semi-wild bees were tucked away to drowse out the cold months in a row of Tudor arched hives, in hot weather shaded by a lath roof, now open to the fine blue sky.

We had a pleasant dinner while I opened up and explained the nature of my problem, beginning with a common enough artist's block and extending to a swindle and hold-up. He hum'd and yeah'd and nodded in his contemplative way, now and then giving me a sharp look. The dessert was Natilla with sage honey added to the cream-sherry sauce, a daring innovation of his own, and entirely successful. Though I suppose a Spanish chef would be taken aback, perhaps even angry, at this departure from tradition.

When we had sipped the last cup of Café Atómico, that mixture of cognac and espresso he served to his favorite people, he asked, "Well, what is it you want? A few cc's of sodium pentothal? I'm not a recallist, but I could probably do it."

"Advice, advice," I begged. "Do it yourself or send me to someone I can pay later, or suggest an alternative. For God's sake, Henry, you can see how desperate I am."

"Slowly," he said. "Softly." He poured cognac into a snifter and offered it to me. I only like cognac with coffee, so he sipped it himself.

"But the problem is, who can you trust," Henry Moons murmured. "I don't have any pentothal here, but can get some similar stuff delivered. Why don't you stay over?"

On second thought I poured some of the cognac into another snifter, for myself. We sat up for a while, talking about the old days when my mother ran an independent political machine in a southern industrial sector. She'd been of considerable use to Henry Moons at one time.

The moonlight illuminated the grounds surrounding Dr. Moons's house, drawing horizontal shadows at the edge of every gully and dip, throwing down a network of black lace shadow from the thorny mesquite. He lived in a stony, somewhat hilly area, for the sake of the variety, he said.

As I went toward the guest room I said to Dr. Moons, "It's hell when I'm not working."

He chuckled in his dry way. "Yes, I know. I'll see what I can do."

I went to bed, planning to dream of the Star Cup, but all night I was engaged in archaic activities like galloping a horse over the desert, and it was a wonder I woke refreshed. After breakfast we went through what he called The Pantry, a windowless, temperature-controlled room where his honeys were worked and stored, to the big sunny den at the other side of the house.

"I don't like using sodium pentothal," he said. "I've had my own mixture made up."

"That's just what Dr. Bassey said. It seems as if no one uses the pentothal any more."

"There's much better stuff for recall on the market. Take off your shoes, Norja. Lie down. Relax. Do some deep breathing. Relax."

He put on a show of mumbling and puttering, exactly as he used to do when I was a child and in an uproar over something. It was awfully soothing. The pitch of his voice dropped lower and lower, it became a dreamlike grumble; by the time he swabbed my arm and inserted the needle I was in a drowsy, confidential state.

"Count to ten in German," Henry Moons said.

"*Ein, zwei . . .*" I began, closing my eyes against the sunshine and trying to focus on the Star Cup blueprints.

"Now," he said, and a long pause followed. Then some intricate nonsense. "No, no, Norja, you're going under," he said. I became conscious that I was losing consciousness of what was happening. I was going back to sleep. I trusted him entirely too much, that was the trouble. It was like being back in the cradle, totally assured of everything. If I'd gone to a stranger, the sharp edge of alertness, of being on guard, would have kept me in the proper condition. His voice went on, and my voice replied, though I didn't understand what either of us said. When a blueprint came to my mind's eye, it was squinty and streaked with bright sunshine. Whatever I said fell from my lips like drops of Henry Moons's special honey, ever so slow and sweet, tumbling down a drop at a time, and melting off into the distances of desert, or space.

The sound of my own snoring brought me to. "Henry, did I sleep?" I asked, sitting up. I was alone in the room. He'd left me a note at the foot of the couch: "Norja, I'm in The Pantry and do not wish to be disturbed until noon. Make yourself comfortable. We'll talk at lunch. Uncle Henry."

Uncle Henry, indeed, I thought. He may have all the time in the world, but I can't just lie around here while he extracts honey from the comb—well, but I would have to. I took a beekeeping journal from his desk and curled up on the couch with it. The time passed like dust drifting down; I alternated between hope and dreary boredom. At one moment I was sure he'd gotten the plans from me and by lunch time I'd be back in business; the next moment I was convinced it was a waste of time and I might as well forget my life's work.

"Lunch," Henry Moons said, coming to the door. I went back through The Pantry after him and emerged into the larger part of the house, where beer and sandwiches waited on trays for us.

"Did you get it?" I asked, allowing myself to hope.

"I'm not sure," Henry Moons said. He licked beer foam from his upper lip. "I'm not quite sure, but it might be worth your while to find out."

"Hey, wait," I said, putting down my untasted glass of beer. "Now hold on, Dr. Moons. That's not very funny."

"No? Norja, the concept is worth millions. I've

been retired for some time, and as you know, in a
moment of mad generosity I gave my money to the
Psychic Alliance Corporation, in which, it is true,
I still hold many shares. But there's maintenance
right here—"

"I'll guarantee you five years of maintenance," I
screamed.

"Thank you, but I have my own arrangements. Do
try the one on rice bread, it's calf's liver with sage
honey and apricots."

"I'll choke first," I replied, getting up and going
to the windows, just to turn my back on him and
regain some control. It's one thing to be screwed by
a stranger, and quite another to be screwed by a
friend of the family. Good Lord, I'd known him
since I was a baby. How could he do this to me
thirty years later?

"Well," I said, without turning around to face
him, "there's two of you bastards now, so you'll have
to hope that Simons and Emory buy from you rather
than from the other doctor."

"My dear Norja, I'd never do anything like that.
I'd so much rather build the Star Cup myself. You
know, I'm getting restless. There are four or five
months at this time of the year when I have nothing
serious to occupy me. If you'd like to buy the tape,
I'll be able to take a trip. If you prefer me to keep
the tape for my own use, I'll buy a building company."

I grabbed the honey-liver-apricot sandwich from
the plate and began to savagely demolish it with
my teeth. Even managed to register the flavor, exotic, agreeable, richly soothing. Just like Henry
Moons himself, and all on the surface. Deep down

lay ulcers, I thought. Deep lay cancer of the conscience. The world was filled with liars, thieves, sick
egotists and poor traitors. I was born too late, or
maybe three generations too early. There was no
room for an honest businessperson or a dedicated
artist; no place to turn for advice and trust in a society that was self-seeking and so consumed with
greed that a life-long friendship could dissolve in
the temptation to accumulate a little more. I hated
becoming embittered, for that would lead me toward the same kind of behavior. But how to keep
myself intact, and still survive?

"Goodbye, Dr. Moons," I said. "Thank you for
some delicious food, if nothing else." May your
honeys all crystallize, I thought.

I went home and brooded. Two hours later I
called Joe Andressi at one of the warehouses. "Joe,
if I don't call back in two hours, will you come over
here and check on me?"

"Hey, you got trouble? I'll come over now," he
offered.

"Uh-uh. Just wait for my call, or call me back."

"Right. Two hours."

I took off my clothes, psychologically freeing
myself from all restrictions, and lay down on my
bed. Star Cup. A solar-power web. Shimmering lines
in space, darker than blueprints. Faces came and
went, too, as well as plans, lists of construction materials, routes for work shuttles. The tape recorder
wound itself around. I took another sip of Hot Bird
and lay back. Somewhere in my mind the concept
still existed; just because I couldn't remember it
didn't mean it had vanished. Once created, it must
continue to exist.

After nearly two hours, I got up, looked at the empty Hot Bird bottle, put on a robe, and rewound the tape. Then I punched the PLAY button, and listened.

". . . take the empiric out of the basement and put it in a glass jar to clarify . . ." I shut the damn thing off. Of course it hadn't worked. If it had, the recall specialists would be out of business.

Wearily I made my call to Joe, told him to go home to dinner and forget the whole thing. He lingered on the line, saying, "You sure you don't want some help? You okay? You just want a voice to lean on? A pecan-butter sandwich?"

"Thanks, Joe, but I have to do this one myself."

"Yeah. Well, you can get me at home if you need me."

For a while after, I sat by the windows with the lights out, looking north toward the city. I lived in the best outer ring, twenty-three stories up. I liked to look across the lighted rings, though I couldn't avoid seeing the small dark core of the city where people were so poor they couldn't afford to pay the power rates after nine at night. There weren't as many of them these days, and they were taken for granted, one of society's nagging but insoluble problems, always with us and never considered, part of our past history. The solution, if there was one, lay in a vague future. Most of the people I knew donated time, and professional help, or credits, to alleviate the worst of the poverty; they kept hope alive with small regular feedings of promise; they handed out reward goodies to whole families, or even went so far as to move them out to one of the more prosperous rings, where they could have lights all night if they wanted. This created the incentive in those left behind to continue the struggle, but nicely contained and comfortably out of our sight.

For the first time, I had to consider how I'd survive if I had to live there myself. It gave me a stunned, unreal sensation. The probability of its happening was strong enough to shrivel my gut, now that I was forced to think about it.

I'd have to move into one bleak room, cold or steamy according to the season; dark after nine at night; surrounded by desperate, unhappy people, and no escape, no hope, no ambition. Anything would be better than that, I decided. Even, for the moment, putting aside art in favor of business, though all my life I'd tried to combine the two, and keep them balanced. Now my thoughts were giving me a different view onto my world, just as that starkly painted window inside the box on my study wall sometimes did. Perhaps most people are, at some point, faced with this choice between hunger for beauty and hunger for food and shelter.

There was absolutely no question in my mind about which had precedence. I went into my study and began to draft some rough plans, and as I did so, I realized how, like so many before me in our world's history, I might benefit other people by resolving my own immediate problem.

When the plans were sketchily finished I nearly called the banker, Elliot Green, at his home, but decided the early dawn hour would find him in a sleepy stupor. For a while I sat and contemplated my new move.

It meant stepping out, literally, like a rope dancer, without a clear idea of what the other end of the

rope was attached to. It gave me the frights. Nobody can do that. No painter can stand in front of
a new board without any idea of what he's going to
make, and just make it. Could he? Could I? Would
it be possible, in the act of doing, to do?

Even if I had the nerve to try, without advance
payment I'd run out of credits halfway through, and
for whom would I be building if I had no client?
Elliot Green was my only hope.

At what might be called a decent hour of dawn
I called Joe Andressi. "How soon can we get the
work shuttles operating?" I asked.

"Two days. Maybe a day and a half. You got a list
of materials you want? Who's the client? Norja, you
don't know how glad I'll be to get back on a job."

Not any gladder than I. "Joe, I can't give you the
details now. Just get those shuttles ready to go. I'll
come by with the list this afternoon."

"But I don't have the specs," Joe protested.

"You'll have the building specs by the time you
really need them. Trust me."

"I do," he said. It was true. We trusted each other,
and that was half the secret of our progress.

I had already abandoned the degrading notion of
breaking into Dr. Bassey's office and stealing the
tape. I didn't want to start in that direction because
there'd be no end to what I'd do. We were all honest
once. I believe we were all honest and decent when
we were born, even though that's directly contrary
to contemporary mercantile theory as taught in our
business schools.

Before I left home I called Elliot Green's office
for an appointment; then went over to my own
office. Spectacular view through stone-colored glass;

filtered, clean air. As I opened the third bank of microreels, I thought how I could keep the lights and air on all night here, as well as at home, if I cared to. Push a button, screen a file; a small gesture with one finger and the power poured in. Power and love and beauty, I'd worked for them all my life and never gotten enough. Now I was going to risk what I had, run out on that rope and dance. Irrelevant, I told myself. These artsy thoughts are the equivocations of a coward. Get rid of them, because there's work to do.

By the time I'd flown over the residential rings, over the central core of the city, and over more rings, to the other side and Elliot Green's bank, I had firmed my mind. The look on my face seemed to unnerve his secretary; he barely mumbled hello.

Elliot was aimlessly sharpening the felt pens when I went in. "Hi there," I said, sitting in his lounge chair. "How long since you've been off this planet?"

"About five years. Why? What's to space for?" He had a kind of skinny charm, a good sharp mind, and a swift wit that I'd always appreciated.

"How'd you like to come along with me on a new job?"

"Don't be ridiculous, Norja. I'm a solid businessman, not one of you winged builders."

"You once said I was a good businesswoman. Don't you believe in crossover?"

He put the yellow pen down and started to sharpen the rouge one, doing it by hand with a little knife, to amuse himself. Fortunately, he didn't have many such affectations. "Yes, I believe in it, for those lucky enough to have it."

"Come try your luck, then, Elliot. Things have

changed since you were last out there. I've built six
Sky Castles. Several other firms have also built
space homes. Come and take a look. There are new
concepts abrewing."

"Like what?" he asked.

"Like something for the ordinary man."

He put the rouge pen down by the yellow one.
"What's in it for me?"

"Fun. Thrills. A look at the contemporary world
of architecture. And a chance to get your name in
space."

"My name!" he snorted.

Leaning toward him, I said, "I mean literally.
Your name in space, and also on the rolls of history."
I told him what I hoped to achieve. At intervals he
mumbled, and once shouted, that I was crazy. But
he listened.

At last Elliot Green picked up both pens together
and began to inscribe two-colored doodles on his
desk slate. When he was thinking hard, his nostrils
flared. I watched, intrigued, as they flared with his
breath. Just like a race horse at the end of six fur-
longs, I thought. Beautiful, fast, worth a million,
and good for nothing else if I couldn't stir him.

He asked, "How much is this going to cost me?"

"Us. It will cost us half a million, and worth it,
and you know it."

"Risky. I don't take risks like that any more."

"Not since your hair turned gray?"

His nostrils flared again, this time with resentment. "It's dyed gray. I'm told it's very becoming."

"That's a new one, for you. Come on, Elliot. Suit
up and space with me for a couple of days, you've
forgotten how good it feels to get out there."

His eyelids flickered as he turned his gaze down toward some invisible account or oracle on his desk. He was asking himself if it was worth it, weighing the risks, the credits, the time, against his business tradition of stability, of going slowly. Weighing the publicity against the days out of the office, the credits out of his bank. Weighing the inappropriateness of space building, the rope-dancing act, for a man of his position. He had been one hell of a companion some years ago. I was counting on the nerve not being buried too deep in brain-fat.

"Oh, Norja," he sighed. "Not more than half a million?"

"You'll never regret it," I promised.

"If we pull it off, I won't," Elliot Green said, and I was delighted to hear him already saying "we." It meant he had accepted half the responsibility. "I'm not sure it can be done, but all right, I'll back you, provided you can prove out your plans for my associates. If you can, I'll have the permits ready to co-sign within three days. You can use our computer complex on the eighteenth floor."

There was a long wait before he rounded up two vice-presidents and various other officials for a briefing, but I was glad enough of the time to think about such details as stress, extra facilities, and whether a nursery school should be housed above or below the older students. I had just decided that all the pre-puberty children should have free run of a certain area when the last bank official came in, looking as if his ulcer hurt terribly. He sat down as soon as the introductions were over.

I went to the computer control board and began, with one of the most difficult and newest objects to be put into the sky. The first of its kind, it was a double power-conversion core. Whether it would bear the building stress along the H-bars that connected the two single cores remained to be seen. It would be shuttled out before any other equipment and put into rotation to wait for the spools of cable, the solar panels, the space tractors.

During one pause, when I became conscious again of a room full of people, fidgety, bored, drinking coffee, talking, an attack of insecurity caught me off guard. But I told myself: None of that. This is how you make a living, remember? You run out on the rope and never mind the other end, because the rope is you, and you'll fasten it when you get there.

So, step by step, I went, and the further along I built, the more clearly the next phase came to me. The geometric patterns, ten times the size I'd ever used before. Behind me, the waiting group fell quiet; I'd gotten their attention for the moment. Me, the spider, spinning the power web. Establishing the lower bank of rooms. Watching the H-bars stand up well, taking the stress. Solar panels in a fan-light shape. Light all the time, day or night, whenever the tenant wanted. Light, heat, space, a view of the earth, that lovely marble, at appointed times.

Later on, Joe Andressi, whom I'd called before entering the computer complex, came in and forced me to sit down and eat some food. At the same time he tried to protect me from questions and talk that would take my mind too far away from the job. He was a great buffer, and handled the bank people with a kind of gloomy tact that earned their respect. I was grateful for the break and the nourishment, but even so, I resented the interference because it was hard to get back to work again.

The Star Cup haunted me, though much less on a full belly than an empty one, perhaps proving it a hallucination, I thought. Then, for a time, I was bewildered; stood in front of the computer and tried deep-breathing exercises. My shoulder muscles ached and I felt so dismal I thought perhaps this job couldn't be done and I'd never persuade any of them. I heard the soft voice of one woman, a vice-president, chatting with Elliot Green about a special type of mortgage for Sky Castles.

What am I doing here? I asked myself, as thousands of others ask all the time. Suffering the common woe, feeling confused, inadequate, even desperate. I plugged away at the work without much hope, but as I watched the building grow on the plan board that stretched from wall to wall above the computer banks, a little surety came back to me.

Joe Andressi murmured, "Crazy insane fabulous," and it wasn't just to keep my spirits up; I knew he really meant it.

"Champagne all around," I muttered to him when he was standing close to my shoulder.

"Knock that off, we have work to do," he said from the side of his mouth. But he grinned, and our eyes met for a moment, making me realize how pleased we both were with the way things were going.

"By God, she's doing it," someone said from the back of the room. There were voices, the sound of people coming in, going out. All this preliminary sweat and misery bored them, they just wanted the finished plan, and then they'd decide if it was worth the risk.

It took me another hour to run through two levels of shops, schools, and other facilities, and then to check the specs from start to finish. All done. The end of the rope attached to the beginning. And all I wanted to do was sleep for days.

They crowded around me now, Elliot Green shaking my hand, the others asking questions that Joe and I tried to answer without getting too deep into the technology of space building which would only baffle them.

"Come in day after tomorrow," Elliot said to me as we went into the lobby. "I'll have the papers and permits ready for you to co-sign."

I wondered if fifty years from now, some clerk would look at the nonfadable ink and not recognize whose signature it was. Or would they know, fifty years from now, who I was, and what I had been able to do?

At home I stocked up on vitamins, sleep, and decent food. Work to do! My God, how happy I was. If I'd pulled off this one, there was no end to my marvelous future, and I needn't dwell any more on the bad chance of being forced to live in the drab, powerless center of the city.

After the papers were signed and Joe Andressi took the work crew out to the site the Federal Building Corporation had allotted us, out past the spindle castle I'd built for Jim Mac a year ago, I felt that the tough part was over. Though each time I put in a call to Joe, I suffered some anxiety. Guessing what can go wrong is usually worse than watching it actually happen. But the troubles on the job were ordinary; no one was injured; Joe's time-saving bonus credits piled up and the tenth bank of rooms was completed. Soon a lot of weary workers could celebrate.

I began to dream of what the opening ceremonies would be like. Of course, I'd attend them in space, with Joe and those of the crew who wanted to make the trip again. It was nice to think of Elliot Green, and perhaps Dr. Elaine Bassey, if she accepted the invitation, standing with the city mayor and watching the satellite broadcast.

I took an Electric Boat Cruiser out for the ceremony. As the Cruiser approached the huge complex, even I was dazzled. By God, it wasn't bad at all. One hundred and forty compact high-power dwellings, bigger and better than anything ever built in space before, way beyond the means and dreams of Simons and Emory. The first shuttleload of tenants from the dark city core was standing by. Joe and I shook hands in front of the main lock. With a flourish, he branded the alloy plate over the lock: THE ELLIOT GREEN HOUSING PROJECT. I cut the cable, and the first shuttleload of tenants came in.

While their shuttle docked and the house was opened for moving in and living in, I clambered over the face of the building to sign my work on the edges facing earth: *Norja I*. Elliot Green wasn't going to get all the glory. He only paid half our way; the other half was mine, and *Norja II* already planned, and filed with the Space Builders Corporation.

I invited Joe and a couple of the others to ride home with me in the comparative luxury of the Electric Boat Cruiser. It was commodious, and it was fast, driven by the Electric Boat Company's reactor pile designed a century or so before to power nuclear submarines. Wonderful. From undersea to outerspace, though not as outer as I'd go to build in a few more years.

Joe and I took our shoes off and put our feet up on the empty seats in front of us. I said, "Take a couple of weeks off, or even a month. You sure did earn it on this one."

"You did, too. Only, if you don't mind my saying it, I wish you'd lay off the booze. You don't want to lose another design."

"Well, look, I can recoup, Joe. It wasn't easy, but I can do it."

He gave me a peculiar look, sharp and sideways, as if I'd just said something very strange. But I thought perhaps he was just overtired, as I was.

The Cruiser swung through the southeast sector to give us another view of the housing complex. "Nice," Joe said, in a subdued voice.

"Yeah," I agreed, with satisfaction.

Then someone up front yelled, "Hey, what the hell is that out there?" and we all rushed to look out the port.

A Simons and Emory work hut, suspended between two of their standard shuttles, was swarming with activity. A cup-shaped shell was already in rotation. It was one-family size, but like no other design ever seen in the universe before.

"Gawd," Joe breathed over my shoulder. "Look at that. It's a beauty."

"It's the Star Cup," I said, swallowing knives and feeling them grate and cut inside me. "It's the real thing. The one I lost."

"You gonna lay off the stuff now?" he demanded.

"Hell no, I'm going to celebrate. There's no future in one-family units, this sector is already overbuilt. You know how much the Housing Authority Corporation offered me for *Norja II?*"

"I can guess," Joe said dryly. "You're not ready to retire, huh?"

"Retire? Never. I'm just going to move out a little farther, and build a little bigger. Space is space, Joe. Plenty of room to move out the whole city core to a choice sector, and give them work, too. I'm starting light-industry plans next week."

Just the same, as we swam past the Star Cup I felt so terrible I couldn't look at it again. But the design was mine and it would operate; they could sign their names all over it but I knew who'd thought of it first, who'd lain awake nights sweating out the details. And maybe . . . someday . . . meanwhile, the offers were pouring in. So far, the best was from Curtis Titanium Flange Corporation, and I was seriously considering it.

First thing I saw when I got home and pressed the power on was a big transparent jar on my coffee table. Inside sat a complete honeycomb. Courtesy of Dr. Moons, who after all was not a sore winner. Wrenching off the lid, I dipped in two fingers and broke off an edge of the comb. Delicious. Pure mesquite honey. Nature's own energy. I sat down and broke off another waxy piece, and put it on my tongue to melt sweetly.

Now, if every third cell contained a solar panel, I thought, and you could stabilize rotation for that kind of shape, wouldn't it shine nicely out beyond the moon? As soon as they opened up that sector.

I uncorked a bottle of Asti Spumanti, dipped in a piece of honeycomb, and put my bare feet up on the coffee table. By next year, perhaps, I'd come up with something as good, if not better, than the Star Cup . . . meanwhile, the *Norja-Curtis Honeycomb I* began to take shape in my fertile mind.

∞

EYES OF AMBER

JOAN D. VINGE

*Joan D. Vinge lives in California and is the
author of several stories that have appeared
in* Analog, Orbit, *and other publications.
Her first novel,* The Outcasts of Heaven
Belt, *is being serialized in* Analog, *and she
is working on a second novel,* Carbuncle.
*She has worked as a salvage archeologist
and has a degree in anthropology. She
brings this background to "Eyes of Amber,"
the story of a man seeking to understand an
alien female and her culture.*

The beggar woman shuffled up the silent evening street to the rear of Lord Chwiul's town
house. She hesitated, peering up at the softly glowing towers, then clawed at the watchman's arm. "A
word with you, master—"

"Don't touch me, hag!" The guard raised his spear
butt in disgust.

A deft foot kicked free of the rags and snagged
him off balance. He found himself sprawled on his
back in the spring melt, the spear tip dropping
toward his belly, guided by a new set of hands. He
gaped, speechless.

The beggar tossed an amulet onto his chest.
"Look at it, fool! I have business with your lord."

The beggar woman stepped back, the spear tip tapped him impatiently.

The guard squirmed in the filth and wet, holding the amulet up close to his face in the poor light. "You . . . you are the one? You may pass."

"Indeed!" Muffled laughter. "Indeed I may pass— for many things, in many places. The Wheel of Change carries us all." She lifted the spear. "Get up, fool . . . and no need to escort me. I'm expected."

The guard climbed to his feet, dripping and sullen, and stood back while she freed her wing membranes from the folds of cloth. He watched them glisten and spread as she gathered herself to leap effortlessly to the tower's entrance, twice his height above. He waited until she had vanished inside before he even dared to curse her.

"Lord Chwiul?"

"T'uupieh, I presume." Lord Chwiul leaned forward on the couch of fragrant mosses, peering into the shadows of the hall.

"*Lady* T'uupieh." T'uupieh strode forward into the light, letting the ragged hood slide back from her face. She took a fierce pleasure in making no show of obeisance, in coming forward directly as nobility to nobility. The sensuous ripple of a hundred tiny *miih* hides underfoot made her calloused feet tingle. *After so long, it comes back too easily . . .*

She chose the couch across the low waterstone table from him, stretching languidly in her beggar's rags. She extended a finger claw and picked a juicy *kelet* berry from the bowl in the table's scroll-carven surface; let it slide into her mouth and down her throat, as she had done so often, so long ago. And then, at last, she glanced up, to measure his outrage.

"You dare to come to me in this manner—"

Satisfactory. *Yes, very* . . . "*I* did not come to you.
You came to me . . . you sought my services." Her
eyes wandered the room with affected casualness,
taking in the elaborate frescoes that surfaced the
waterstone walls even in this small private room
. . . particularly in this room? she wondered. How
many midnight meetings, for what varied intrigues,
were held in this room? Chwiul was not the wealthi-
est of his family or clan; and appearances of wealth
and power counted in this city, in this world—for
wealth and power were everything.

"I sought the services of T'uupieh the Assassin.
I'm surprised to find that the Lady T'uupieh dared
to accompany her here." Chwiul had regained his
composure; she watched his breath frost, and her
own, as he spoke.

"Where one goes, the other follows. We are in-
separable. You should know that better than most,
my lord." She watched his long pale arm extend to
spear several berries at once. Even though the
nights were chill, he wore only a body-wrapping
tunic, which let him display the intricate scaling of
jewels that danced and spiraled over his wing surfaces.

He smiled; she saw the sharp fangs protrude
slightly. "Because my brother made the one into the
other, when he seized your lands? I'm surprised you
would come at all—how did you know you could
trust me?" His movements were ungraceful; she remembered how the jewels dragged down fragile,
translucent wing membranes and slender arms, until
flight was impossible. Like every noble, Chwiul was
normally surrounded by servants who answered his

every whim. Incompetence, feigned or real, was one
more trapping of power, one more indulgence that
only the rich could afford. She was pleased that the
jewels were not of high quality.

"I don't trust you," she said. "I trust only myself.
But I have friends who told me you were sincere
enough—in this case. And of course, I did not come
alone."

"Your outlaws?" Disbelief. "That would be no
protection."

Picking up the rag pouch at her side, she calmly
separated the folds of cloth that held her secret
companion.

"It is true." Chwiul trilled softly. "They call you
Demon's Consort . . ."

She turned the amber lens of the demon's precious
eye so that it could see the room, as she had seen it,
and then settled its gaze on Chwiul. He drew back
slightly, fingering moss. "'A demon has a thousand
eyes, and a thousand thousand torments for those
who offend it.'" She quoted from the Book of Ngoss,
whose rituals she had used to bind the demon to
her.

Chwiul stretched nervously, as if he wanted to fly
away. But he only said, "Then I think we understand each other. And I think I have made a good
choice: I know how well you have served the Overlord, and other court members . . . I want you to
kill someone for me."

"Obviously."

"I want you to kill Klovhiri."

T'uupieh started, very slightly. "You surprise me
in return, Lord Chwiul. Your own brother?" *And*

the usurper of my lands. How I have ached to kill him slowly, so slowly, with my own hands . . . But always he is too well guarded.

"And your sister, too—my lady." Faint overtones of mockery. "I want his whole family eliminated; his mate, his children . . ."

Klovhiri . . . and Ahtseet. Ahtseet, her own younger sister, who had been her closest companion since childhood, her only family since their parents had died. Ahtseet, whom she had cherished and protected; dear, conniving, traitorous little Ahtseet, who could forsake pride and decency and family honor to mate willingly with the man who had robbed them of everything . . . Anything to keep the family lands, Ahtseet had shrilled; anything to keep her position. But that was not the way! Not by surrendering, but by striking back— T'uupieh became aware that Chwiul was watching her reaction with unpleasant interest. She fingered the dagger at her belt.

"Why?" She laughed, wanting to ask, *"How?"*

"That should be obvious. I'm tired of coming second. I want what he has—your lands and all the rest. I want him out of my way, and I don't want anyone else left with a better claim to his inheritance than I have."

"Why not do it yourself? Poison them, perhaps . . . it's been done before."

"No. Klovhiri has too many friends, too many loyal clansmen, too much influence with the Overlord. It has to be an 'accidental' murder. And no one would be better suited than you, my lady, to do it for me."

T'uupieh nodded vaguely, assessing. No one could be better chosen for a desire to succeed than she . . . and also, for a position from which to strike. All she had lacked until now was the opportunity. From the time she had been dispossessed, through the fading days of autumn and the endless winter—for nearly a third of her life, now—she had haunted the wild swamp and fenland of her estate. She had gathered a few faithful servants, a few malcontents, a few cutthroats, to harry and murder Klovhiri's retainers, ruin his *phib* nets, steal from his snares and poach her own game. And for survival, she had taken to robbing whatever travelers took the roads that passed through her lands.

Because she was still nobility, the Overlord had at first tolerated and then secretly encouraged her banditry. Many wealthy foreigners traveled the routes that crossed her estate, and for a certain commission, he allowed her to attack them with impunity. It was a sop, she knew, thrown to her because he had let his favorite, Klovhiri, have her lands. But she used it to curry what favor she could, and after a time the Overlord had begun to bring her more discreet and profitable business—the elimination of certain enemies. And so she had become an assassin as well—and found that the calling was not so very different from that of noble: both required nerve, and cunning, and an utter lack of compunction. And because she was T'uupieh, she had succeeded admirably. But because of her vendetta, the rewards had been small . . . until now.

"You do not answer," Chwiul was saying. "Does that mean your nerve fails you, in kith-murder, where mine does not?"

She laughed sharply. "That you say it proves twice that your judgment is poorer than mine . . . No, my nerve does not fail me. Indeed, my blood burns with desire! But I hadn't thought to lay Klovhiri under the ice just to give my lands to his brother. Why should I do that favor for you?"

"Because obviously you cannot do it alone. Klovhiri hasn't managed to have you killed in all the time you've plagued him, which is a testament to your skill. But you've made him too wary—you can't get near him when he keeps himself so well protected. You need the cooperation of someone who has his trust—someone like myself. I can make him yours."

"And what will be my reward if I accept? Revenge is sweet, but revenge is not enough."

"I will pay what you ask."

"My estate." She smiled.

"Even you are not so naïve—"

"No." She stretched a wing toward nothing in the air. "I am not so naïve. I know its value . . ." The memory of a golden-clouded summer's day caught her—of soaring, soaring on the warm updrafts above the steaming lake . . . seeing the fragile rose-red of the manor towers spearing light far off above the windswept tide of the trees . . . the saffron and crimson and aquamarine of ammonia pools, bright with dissolved metals, that lay in the gleaming melt-surface of her family's land, the land that stretched forever, like the summer . . . "I know its value." Her voice hardened. "And that Klovhiri is still the Overlord's pet. As you say, Klovhiri has many powerful friends, and they will become your friends when he dies. I need more strength, more wealth, before I

can buy enough influence to hold what is mine
again. The odds are not in my favor—now."

"You are carved from ice, T'uupieh. I like that."
Chwiul leaned forward. His amorphous red eyes
moved along her outstretched body, trying to guess
what lay concealed beneath the rags in the shadowy
foxfire light of the room. His eyes came back to her
face.

She showed him neither annoyance nor amusement. "I like no man who likes that in me."

"Not even if it meant regaining your estate?"

"As a mate of yours?" Her voice snapped like a
frozen branch. "My lord, I have just about decided
to kill my sister for doing as much. I would sooner
kill myself."

He shrugged, lying back on the couch. "As you
wish." He waved a hand in dismissal. "Then, what
will it take to be rid of my brother—and of you as
well?"

"Ah." She nodded, understanding more. "You
wish to buy my services, and to buy me off, too.
That may not be so easy to do. But . . ." *But I will
make the pretense, for now.* She speared berries
from the bowl in the tabletop, watched the silky
sheet of emerald-tinted ammonia water that cur-
tained one wall. It dropped from heights within the
tower into a tiny plunge basin, with a music that
would blur conversation for anyone who tried to
listen outside. Discretion, and beauty . . . The
musky fragrance of the mossy couch brought back
her childhood suddenly, disconcertingly: the memory of lying in a soft bed, on a soft spring night . . .
"But as the seasons change, change moves me in

new directions. Back into the city, perhaps. I like your tower, Lord Chwiul. It combines discretion and beauty."

"Thank you."

"Give it to me, and I'll do what you ask.".

Chwiul sat up, frowning. "My town house!" Recovering: "Is that all you want?"

She spread her fingers, studied the vestigial webbing between them. "I realize it is rather modest." She closed her hand. "But considering what satisfaction will come from earning it, it will suffice. And you will not need it, once I succeed."

"No . . ." He relaxed somewhat. "I suppose not. I will scarcely miss it, after I have your lands."

She let it pass. "Well then, we are agreed. Now, tell me, where is the key to Klovhiri's lock? What is your plan for delivering him—and his family—into my hands?"

"You are aware that your sister and the children are visiting here, in my house, tonight? And that Klovhiri will return before the new day?"

"I am aware." She nodded, with more casualness than she felt, seeing that Chwiul was properly, if silently, impressed at her nerve in coming here. She drew her dagger from its sheath beside the demon's amber eye and stroked the serrated blade of waterstone-impregnated wood. "You wish me to slit their throats while they sleep under your very roof?" She managed the right blend of incredulity.

"No!" Chwiul frowned again. "What sort of fool do you—" he broke off. "With the new day, they will be returning to the estate by the usual route. I have promised to escort them, to ensure their safety along the way. There will also be a guide, to lead us through the bogs. But the guide will make a mistake—"

"And I will be waiting." T'uupieh's eyes brightened. During the winter the wealthy used sledges for travel on long journeys, preferring to be borne over the frozen melt by membranous sails or dragged by slaves where the surface of the ground was rough and crumpled. But as spring came and the surface of the ground began to dissolve, treacherous sinks and pools opened like blossoms to swallow the unwary. Only an experienced guide could read the surfaces, tell sound waterstone from changeable ammonia-water melt. "Good," she said softly. "Yes, very good . . . Your guide will see them safely foundered in some slush hole, and then I will snare them like changeling *phibs*."

"Exactly. But I want to be there when you do; I want to watch. I'll make some excuse to leave the group, and meet you in the swamp. The guide will mislead them only if he hears my signal."

"As you wish. You've paid well for the privilege. But come alone. My followers need no help, and no interference." She sat up, let her long webbed feet down to rest again on the sensuous hides of the rug.

"And if you think that I'm a fool, and playing into your hands myself, consider this: you will be the obvious suspect when Klovhiri is murdered. I'll be the only witness who can swear to the Overlord that your outlaws weren't the attackers. Keep that in mind."

She nodded. "I will."

"How will I find you, then?"

"You will not. My thousand eyes will find you." She rewrapped the demon's eye in its pouch of rags.

Chwiul looked vaguely disconcerted. "Will—*it* take part in the attack?"

"It may, or it may not; as it chooses. Demons are not bound to the Wheel of Change like you and me. But you will surely meet it face to face—although it has no face—if you come." She brushed the pouch at her side. "Yes—do keep in mind that I have my safeguards too, in this agreement. A demon never forgets."

She stood up at last, gazing once more around the room. "I shall be comfortable here." She glanced back at Chwiul. "I will look for you, come the new day."

"Come the new day." He rose, his jeweled wings catching light.

"No need to escort me. I shall be discreet." She bowed, as an equal, and started toward the shadowed hall. "I shall definitely get rid of your watchman. He doesn't know a lady from a beggar."

"The Wheel turns once more for me, my demon. My life in the swamps will end with Klovhiri's life. I shall move into town . . . and I shall be lady of my manor again, when the fishes sit in the trees!"

T'uupieh's alien face glowed with malevolent joy as she turned away, on the display screen above the computer terminal. Shannon Wyler leaned back in his seat, finished typing his translation, and pulled off the wire headset. He smoothed his long blond slicked-back hair, the habitual gesture helping him reorient to his surroundings. When T'uupieh spoke he could never maintain the objectivity he needed to help him remember he was still on Earth, and not really on Titan, orbiting Saturn, some fifteen hundred million kilometers away. *T'uupieh, whenever I think I love you, you decide to cut somebody's throat . . .*

He nodded vaguely at the congratulatory murmurs of the staff and technicians, who literally hung on his every word waiting for new information. They began to thin out behind him as the computer reproduced copies of the transcript. Hard to believe he'd been doing this for over a year now. He looked up at his concert posters on the wall, with nostalgia but with no regret.

Someone was phoning Marcus Reed; he sighed, resigned.

" 'Vhen the fishes sit in the trees'? Are you being sarcastic?"

He looked over his shoulder at Dr. Garda Bach's massive form. "Hi, Garda. Didn't hear you come in."

She glanced up from a copy of the translation, tapped him lightly on the shoulder with her forked walking stick. "I know, dear boy. You never hear anything vhen T'uupieh speaks . . . But vhat do you mean by this?"

"On Titan that's summer—when the triphibians metamorphose for the third time. So she means maybe five years from now, our time."

"Ah! Of course. The old brain is not vhat it vas . . ." She shooked her gray-white head; her black cloak swirled out melodramatically.

He grinned, knowing she didn't mean a word of it. "Maybe learning Titanese on top of fifty other languages is the straw that breaks the camel's back."

"*Ja, ja,* maybe it is . . ." She sank heavily into the

next seat over, already lost in the transcript. He had never, he thought, expected to like the old broad so well. He had become aware of her Presence while he studied linguistics at Berkeley—she was the *grande dame of* linguistic studies, dating back to the days when there had still been unrecorded languages here on Earth. But her skill at getting her name in print and her face on television, as an expert on what everybody "really meant," had convinced him that her true talent lay in merchandising. Meeting her at last, in person, hadn't changed his mind about that, but it had convinced him forever that she knew her stuff about cultural linguistics. And that, in turn, had convinced him her accent was a total fraud. But despite the flamboyance, or maybe even because of it, he found that her now archaic views on linguistics were much closer to his own feelings about communication than the views of either one of his parents.

Garda sighed. "Remarkable, Shannon! You are simply remarkable—your feel for a wholly alien language amazes me. Vhatever vould ve have done if you had not come to us?"

"Done without, I expect." He savored the special pleasure that came of being admired by someone he respected. He looked down again at the computer console, at the two shining green-lit plates of plastic thirty centimeters on a side, which together gave him the versatility of a virtuoso violinist and a typist with a hundred thousand keys—his link to T'uupieh, his voice: the new IBM synthesizer, whose touch-sensitive control plates could be manipulated to re-create the impossible complexities of her language. God's gift to the world of linguistics . . . except that it required the sensitivity and inspiration of a musician to fully use its range.

He glanced up again and out the window, at the now familiar fog-shrouded skyline of Coos Bay. Since very few linguists were musicians, their resistance to the synthesizer had been like a brick wall. The old guard of the aging New Wave—which included His Father the Professor and His Mother the Communications Engineer—still clung to a fruitless belief in mathematical computer translation. They still struggled with ungainly programs weighed down by endless morpheme lists, that supposedly would someday generate any message in a given language. But even after years of refinement, computer-generated translations were still uselessly crude and sloppy.

At graduate school there had been no new languages to seek out, and no permission for him to use the synthesizer to explore the old ones. And so— after a final bitter family argument—he had quit graduate school. He had taken his belief in the synthesizer into the world of his second love, music; into a field where, he hoped, real communication still had some value. Now, at twenty-four, he was Shann the Music Man, the musician's musician, and a hero to an immense generation of aging fans, and a fresh new one that had inherited their love for the ever-changing music called "rock." And neither of his parents had willingly spoken to him in years.

"No false modesty," Garda was chiding. "Vhat could ve have done vithout you? You yourself have complained enough about your mother's methods. You know ve vould not have a tenth of the information about Titan ve have gained from T'uupieh if she had gone on using that damned computer translation."

Shannon frowned faintly, at the sting of secret guilt. "Look, I know I've made some cracks—and I meant most of them—but I'd never have gotten off the ground if she hadn't done all the preliminary analysis before I even came." His mother had already been on the mission staff, having worked for years at NASA on the esoterics of computer communication with satellites and space probes, and because of her linguistic background, she had been made head of the newly pulled-together staff of communications specialists by Marcus Reed, the Titan projector director. She had been in charge of the initial phonic analysis: using the computer to compress the alien voice range into one audible to humans, then breaking up the complex sounds into more, and simpler, human phones, she had identified phonemes, separated morphemes, fitted them into a grammatical framework, and assigned English sound equivalents to it all. Shannon had watched her on the early TV interviews, looking unhappy and ill at ease while Reed held court for the spellbound press. But what Dr. Wyler the Communications Engineer had had to say, at last, had held him on the edge of his seat; unable to resist, he had taken the next plane to Coos Bay.

"Vell, I meant no offense," Garda said. "Your mother is obviously a skilled engineer. But she needs a little more . . . flexibility."

"You're telling me." He nodded ruefully. "She'd still love to see the synthesizer drop through the floor. She's been out of joint ever since I got here. At least Reed appreciates my 'value.'" Reed had

welcomed him like a long-lost son when he first arrived at the institute: Wasn't he a skilled linguist as
well as an inspired musician, didn't he have some
time between gigs, wouldn't he like to extend his
visit, and get an insider's view of his mother's work?
He had agreed, modestly, to all three—and then the
television cameras and reporters had sprung up as
if on cue, and he understood clearly enough that
they were not there to record the visit of Dr. Wyler's kid, but Shann the Music Man.

But he had gotten his first session with a voice
from another world. And with one hearing he had
become an addict . . . because their speech was
music. Every phoneme was formed of two or three
superposed sounds, and every morpheme was a
blend of phonemes, flowing together like water.
They spoke in chords, and the result was a choir,
crystal bells ringing, the shattering of glass chan-
deliers.

And so he had stayed on and on, at first only able
to watch his mother and her assistants with ago-
nized frustration. His mother's computer-analysis
methods had worked well in the initial transphone-
micizing of T'uupieh's speech, and they had learned
enough very quickly to send back clumsy responses,
using the probe's echo-locating device, to keep
T'uupieh's interest from wandering. But typing in-
put at a keyboard, and expecting even the most
sophisticated programming to transform it into another language, still would not work even for known
human languages. And he knew, with an almost religious fervor, that the synthesizer had been designed for just this miracle of communication, and
that he alone could use it to capture directly the

nuances and subtleties a machine translation could never supply. He had tried to approach his mother about letting him use it, but she had turned him down flat: "This is a research center, not a recording studio."

And so he had gone over her head to Reed, who had been delighted. And when at last he felt his hands moving across the warm, faintly tingling plates of light, tentatively re-creating the speech of another world, he had known that he had been right all along. He had let his music commitments go to hell, without a regret, almost with relief, as he slid back into the field that had always come first.

Shannon watched the display, where T'uupieh had settled back with comfortable familiarity against the probe's curving side, half obscuring his view of the camp. Fortunately both she and her followers treated the probe with obsessive care, even when they dragged it from place to place as they constantly moved camp. He wondered what would have happened if they had inadvertently set off its automatic defense system, which had been designed to protect it from aggressive animals; it delivered an electric shock that varied from merely painful to fatal. And he wondered what would have happened if the probe and its "eyes" hadn't fit so neatly into T'uupieh's beliefs about demons. The idea that he might never have known her, or heard her voice . . .

More than a year had passed already since he, and the rest of the world, had heard the remarkable news that intelligent life existed on Saturn's major moon. He had no memory at all of the first two fly-bys of Titan, back in '79 and '81—although he could clearly remember the 1990 orbiter that had

caught fleeting glimpses of the surface through
Titan's swaddling of opaque golden clouds. But the
handful of miniprobes it had dropped had proved
that Titan profited from the same "greenhouse effect" that made Venus a boiling hell. And even
though the seasonal temperatures never rose above
two hundred degrees Kelvin, the few photographs
had shown, unquestionably, that life existed there.
The discovery of life, after so many disappointments
throughout the rest of the solar system, had been
enough to initiate another probe mission, one designed to actually send back data from Titan's
surface.

That probe had discovered a life-form with human intelligence, or rather, the life-form had discovered the probe. And T'uupieh's discovery had
turned a potentially ruined mission into a success:
the probe had been designed with a main, immobile
data-processing unit and ten "eyes," or subsidiary
units, that were to be scattered over Titan's surface
to relay information. The release of the subsidiary
probes during landing had failed, however, and all
of the "eyes" had come down within a few square
kilometers of its own landing in the uninhabited
marsh. But T'uupieh's self-interested fascination
and willingness to appease her "demon" had made
up for everything . . .

Shannon looked up at the flat wall screen again,
at T'uupieh's incredible, inhuman face—a face that
was as familiar now as his own in the mirror. She
sat waiting with her boundless patience for a reply
from her "demon": she would have been waiting
for over an hour by the time her transmission
reached him across the gap between their worlds;

and she would have to wait as long again while they discussed a response and he created the new translation. She spent more time now with the probe than she did with her own people. *The loneliness of command* . . . he smiled. The almost flat profile of her moon-white face turned slightly toward him— toward the camera lens; her own fragile mouth smiled gently, not quite revealing her long, sharp teeth. He could see one red pupilless eye, and the crescent nose-slit that half ringed it; her frosty cyanide breath shone blue-white, illuminated by the ghostly haloes of St. Elmo's fire that wreathed the probe all through Titan's interminable eight-day nights. He could see balls of light hanging like Japanese lanterns on the drooping snarl of icebound branches in a distant thicket.

It was unbelievable . . . or perfectly logical, depending on which biological expert was talking, that the nitrogen- and ammonia-based life on Titan should have so many analogues with oxygen- and water-based life on Earth. But T'uupieh was not human, and the music of her words time and again brought him messages that made a mockery of any ideals he tried to harbor about her, and their relationship. So far in the past year she had assassinated eleven people, and with her outlaws had murdered God knew how many more, in the process of robbing them. The only reason she cooperated with the probe, she had as much as said, was because only a demon had a more bloody reputation; only a demon could command her respect. And yet, from what little she had been able to show them and tell them about the world she lived in, she was no better or no worse than anyone else—only more competent.

Was she a prisoner of an age, a culture, where blood was something to be spilled instead of shared? Or was it something biologically innate that let her philosophize brutality, and brutalize philosophy—

Beyond T'uupieh, around the nitrogen campfire, some of her outlaws had begun to sing—the alien folk melodies that in translation were no more than simple, repetitive verse. But heard in their pure, untranslated form, they layered harmonic complexity on complexity: musical speech in a greater pattern of song. Shannon reached out and picked up the headset again, forgetting everything else. He had had a dream, once, where he had been able to sing in chords . . .

Using the long periods of waiting between their communications, he had managed, some months back, to record a series of the alien songs himself, using the synthesizer. They had been spare and uncomplicated versions compared to the originals, because even now his skill with the language couldn't match that of the singers, but he couldn't help wanting to make them his own. Singing was a part of religious ritual, T'uupieh had told him. "But they don't sing because they're religious; they sing because they like to sing." Once, privately, he had played one of his own human compositions for her on the synthesizer and transmitted it. She had stared at him (or into the probe's golden eye) with stony, if tolerant, silence. She never sang herself, although he had sometimes heard her softly harmonizing. He wondered what she would say if he told her that her outlaws' songs had already earned him his first Platinum Record. Nothing, probably . . . but knowing her, if he could make the concepts clear, she would probably be heartily in favor of the exploitation.

He had agreed to donate the profits of the record to NASA (and although he had intended that all along, it had annoyed him to be asked by Reed), with the understanding that the gesture would be kept quiet. But somehow, at the next press conference, some reporter had known just what question to ask, and Reed had spilled it all. And his mother, when asked about her son's sacrifice, had murmured, "Saturn is becoming a three-ring circus," and left him wondering whether to laugh or swear.

Shannon pulled a crumpled pack of cigarettes out of the pocket of his caftan and lit one. Garda glanced up, sniffing, and shook her head. She didn't smoke, or anything else (although he suspected she ran around with men), and she had given him a long wasted lecture about it, ending with, "Vell, at least they're not tobacco."

He shook his head back at her. "What do you think about T'uupieh's latest victims, then?"

Garda flourished the transcript, pulling his thoughts back. "Vill she kill her own sister?"

He exhaled slowly around the words "Tune in tomorrow, for our next exciting episode! I think Reed will love it; that's what I think." He pointed at the newspaper lying on the floor beside his chair. "Did you notice we've slipped to page three?" T'uupieh had fed the probe's hopper some artifacts made of metal—a thing she had said was only known to the "Old Ones"—and the scientific speculation about the existence of a former technological culture had boosted interest in the probe to front-page status again. But even news of that discovery couldn't last forever . . . "Gotta keep those ratings up, folks. Keep those grants and donations rolling in."

Garda clucked. "Are you angry at Reed or at T'uupieh?"

He shrugged dispiritedly. "Both of 'em. I don't see why she won't kill her own sister—" He broke off as the subdued noise of the room's numerous project workers suddenly intensified, and concentrated. Marcus Reed was making an entrance, simultaneously solving everyone else's problems, as always. Shannon marveled at Reed's energy, even while he felt something like disgust at the way he spent it. Reed exploited everyone and everything with charming cynicism, in the ultimate hype for Science—and watching him at work had gradually drained away whatever respect and good will Shannon had brought with him to the project. He knew that his mother's reaction to Reed was close to his own, even though she had never said anything to him about it; it surprised him that there was something they could still agree on.

"Dr. Reed—"

"Excuse me, Dr. Reed, but—"

His mother was with Reed now as they all came down the room; she looked tight-lipped and resigned, her lab coat buttoned up as if she was trying to avoid contamination. Reed was straight out of *Manstyle* magazine, as usual. Shannon glanced down at his own loose gray caftan and jeans, which had led Garda to remark, "Are you planning to enter a monastery?"

"We'd really like to—"

"Senator Foyle wants you to call him back—"

". . . yes, all right; and tell Dinocci he can go ahead and have the probe run another sample. Yes, Max, I'll get to that . . ." Reed gestured for quiet as Shannon and Garda turned in their seats to face him. "Well, I've just heard the news about our 'Robin Hood's' latest hard contract."

Shannon grimaced quietly. He was the first one to have, facetiously, called T'uupieh "Robin Hood." Reed had snapped it up and dubbed her ammonia swamps "Sherwood Forest" for the press. After the truth about her bloodthirsty body counts began to come out, and it even began to look as if she was collaborating with "the Sheriff of Nottingham," some reporter had pointed out that T'uupieh bore no more resemblance to Robin Hood than she did to Rima the Bird-Girl. Reed had said, laughing, "Well, after all, the only reason Robin Hood stole from the rich was because the poor didn't have any money!" That, Shannon thought, had been the real beginning of the end of his tolerance.

". . . this could be used as an opportunity to show the world graphically the harsh realities of life on Titan—"

"*Ein Moment*," Garda said. "You're telling us you vant to let the public vatch this atrocity, Marcus?" Up until now they had never released to the media the graphic tapes of actual murders; even Reed had not been able to argue that that would have served any real scientific purpose.

"No, he's not, Garda." Shannon glanced up as his mother began to speak. "Because we all agreed that we would *not* release any tapes just for purposes of sensationalism."

"Carly, you know that the press has been after me to release those other tapes, and that I haven't, because we all voted against it. But I feel this situation is different—a demonstration of a unique, alien sociocultural condition. What do you think, Shann?"

Shannon shrugged, irritated and not covering it up. "I don't know what's so damn unique about it: a snuff flick is a snuff flick, wherever you film it. I think the idea stinks." Once, at a party while he was still in college, he had watched a film of an unsuspecting victim being hacked to death. The film, and what all films like it said about the human race, had made him sick to his stomach.

"*Ach*—there's more truth than poetry in that!" Garda said.

Reed frowned, and Shannon saw his mother raise her eyebrows.

"I have a better idea." He stubbed out his cigarette in the ashtray under the panel. "Why don't you let me try to talk her out of it?" As he said it he realized how much he wanted to try, and how much success could mean to his belief in communication—to his image of T'uupieh's people, and maybe his own.

They both showed surprise this time. "How?" Reed said.

"Well . . . I don't know yet. Just let me talk to her, try to really communicate with her, find out how she thinks and what she feels—without all the technical garbage getting in the way for a while."

His mother's mouth thinned; he saw the familiar worry-crease form between her brows. "Our job here is to collect that 'garbage.' Not to begin imposing moral values on the universe. We have too much to do as it is."

"Vhat's 'imposing' about trying to stop a murder?" A certain light came into Garda's faded blue eyes. "Now, that has real . . . social implications. Think about it, Marcus."

Reed nodded, glancing at the patiently attentive faces that still ringed him. "Yes—it does. A great deal of human interest." Answering nods and murmurs. "All right, Shann. There are about three days left before morning comes again in 'Sherwood Forest.' You can have them to yourself, to work with T'uupieh. The press will want reports on your progress . . ." He glanced at his watch and nodded toward the door, already turning away. Shannon looked away from his mother's face as she moved past him.

"Good luck, Shann." Reed threw it back at him absently. "I wouldn't count on reforming 'Robin Hood,' but you can still give it a good try."

Shannon hunched down in his chair, frowning, and turned back to the panel. "In your next incarnation may you come back as a toilet."

T'uupieh was confused. She sat on the hummock of clammy waterstone beside the captive demon, waiting for it to make a reply. In the time that had passed since she'd found it in the swamp, she had been surprised again and again by how little its behavior resembled all the demon-lore she knew. And tonight . . .

She jerked, startled, as its grotesque, clawed arm came to life suddenly and groped among the icy-

silver spring shoots pushing up through the melt at
the hummock's foot. The demon did many incomprehensible things (which was fitting) and it demanded offerings of meat and vegetation and even
stone—even, sometimes, some part of the loot she
had taken from passers-by. She had given it those
things gladly, hoping to win its favor and its aid;
she had even, somewhat grudgingly, given it precious metal ornaments of the Old Ones that she had
stripped from a whining foreign lord. The demon
had praised her effusively for that; all demons
hoarded metal, and she supposed that it must need
metals to sustain its strength; its domed carapace,
gleaming now with the witchfire that always
shrouded it at night, was an immense metal jewel
the color of blood. And yet she had always heard
that demons preferred the flesh of men and women.
But when she had tried to stuff the wing of the
foreign lord into its maw, it spit him out with a
few dripping scratches and told her to let him go.
Astonished, she had obeyed, and let the fool run
screaming off to be lost in the swamp.

And then, tonight . . . "You are going to kill your
sister, T'uupieh," it had said to her tonight, "and
two innocent children. How do you feel about that?"
She had spoken what had come first, and truthfully,
into her mind: "That the new day cannot come
soon enough for me! I have waited so long—too
long—to take my revenge on Klovhiri! My sister
and her brats are a part of his foulness, better slain
before they multiply." She had drawn her dagger
and driven it into the mushy melt, as she would
drive it into their rotten hearts.

The demon had been silent again, for a long time,

as it always was. (The lore said that demons were immortal, and so she had always supposed that it had no reason to make a quick response; she had wished, sometimes, that it would show more consideration for her own mortality.) Then at last it had said, in its deep voice filled with alien shadows, "But the children have harmed no one. And Ahtseet is your only sister, she and the children are your only blood kin. She has shared your life. You say that once you"—the demon paused, searching its limited store of words—"cherished her, for that. Doesn't what she once meant to you mean anything now? Isn't there any love left, to slow your hand as you raise it against her?"

"Love!" she had said, incredulous. "What speech is that, oh Soulless One? You mock me—" Sudden anger had bared her teeth. "Love is a toy, my demon, and I have put my toys behind me. And so has Ahtseet . . . she is no kin of mine. Betrayer, betrayer!" The word hissed like the dying embers of the campfire; she had left the demon in disgust, to rake in the firepit's insulating layer of sulphury ash and lay on a few more soggy branches. Y'lirr, her second in command, had smiled at her from where he lay in his cloak on the ground, telling her that she should sleep. But she had ignored him and gone back to her vigil on the hill.

Even though this night was chill enough to re-crystallize the slowly thawing limbs of the *safilil* trees, the equinox was long past, and now the fine mist of golden polymer rain presaged the golden days of the approaching summer. T'uupieh had wrapped herself more closely in her own cloak and pulled up the hood, to keep the clinging, sticky mist from fouling her wings and ear membranes, and she had remembered last summer, her first summer, which she would always remember . . . Ahtseet had been a clumsy, flapping infant as that first summer began, and T'uupieh the child had thought her new sister was silly and useless. But summer slowly transformed the land and filled her wondering eyes with miracles, and her sister was transformed too, into a playful, easily led companion who could follow her into adventure. Together they learned to use their wings and to use the warm updrafts to explore the boundaries and the freedoms of their heritage.

And now, as spring moved into summer once again, T'uupieh clung fiercely to the vision, not wanting to lose it, or to remember that childhood's sweet, unreasoning summer would never come again, even though the seasons returned, for the Wheel of Change swept on, and there was never a turning back. No turning back . . . she had become an adult by the summer's end, and she would never soar with a child's light-winged freedom again. And Ahtseet would never do anything again. Little Ahtseet, always just behind her, like her own fair shadow. *No! She would not regret it! She would be glad—*

"Did you ever think, T'uupieh," the demon had said suddenly, "that it is wrong to kill anyone? You don't want to die, no one wants to die too soon. Why should they have to? Have you ever wondered what it would be like if you could change the world into one where you—where you treated everyone else as you wanted them to treat you, and they treated you the same? If everyone could . . . live and let live."

Its voice slipped into blurred overtones that she couldn't make out.

She had waited, but it said no more, as if it were waiting for her to consider what she'd already heard. But there was no need to think about what was obvious: "Only the dead 'live and let live.' I treat everyone as I expect them to treat me, or I would quickly join the peaceful dead! Death is a part of life. We die when fate wills it, and when fate wills it, we kill.

"You are immortal, you have the power to twist the Wheel, to turn destiny as you want. You may toy with idle fantasies, even make them real, and never suffer the consequences. We have no place for such things in our small lives. No matter how much I might try to be like you, in the end I die like all the rest. We can change nothing, our lives are preordained. That is the way among mortals." And she had fallen silent again, filled with unease at this strange wandering of the demon's mind. But she must not let it prey on her nerves. Day would come very soon, she must not be nervous; she must be totally in control when she led this attack on Klovhiri. No emotion must interfere, no matter how much she yearned to feel Klovhiri's blood spill bluely over her hands, and her sister's, and the children's . . . Ahtseet's brats would never feel the warm wind lift them into the sky, or plunge, as she had, into the depths of her rainbow-petaled pools, or see her towers spearing light far off among the trees. *Never! Never—*

She had caught her breath sharply then, as a fiery pinwheel burst through the wall of tangled brush behind her, tumbling past her head into the clearing of the camp. She watched it circle the fire—spitting sparks, hissing furiously in the quiet air—three and a half times before it spun on into the darkness. No sleeper wakened, and only two stirred. She clutched one of the demon's hard angular legs, shaken, knowing that the circling of the fire had been a portent—but not knowing what it meant. The burning silence it left behind oppressed her; she stirred restlessly, stretching her wings.

And utterly unmoved, the demon had begun to drone its strange, dark thoughts once more: "Not all you have heard about demons is true. We can suffer"—it groped for words again—"the . . . the consequences of our acts; among ourselves we fight and die. We *are* vicious, and brutal, and pitiless, but we don't like to be that way. We want to change into something better, more merciful, more forgiving. We fail more than we win, but we believe we *can* change. And you are more like us than you realize. You can draw a line between—trust and betrayal, right and wrong, good and evil; you can choose never to cross that line."

"How, then?" She had twisted to face the amber eye as large as her own head, daring to interrupt the demon's speech. "How can one droplet change the tide of the sea? It's impossible! The world melts and flows, it rises into mist, it returns again to ice, only to melt and flow once more. A wheel has no beginning, and no end; no starting place. There is no 'good,' no 'evil'—no line between them. Only acceptance. If you were a mortal, I would think you were mad!"

She had turned away again, her claws digging

shallow runnels in the polymer-coated stone as she struggled for self-control. *Madness . . .* Was it possible? she wondered suddenly. Could her demon have gone mad? How else could she explain the thoughts it had put into her mind? Insane thoughts, bizarre, suicidal—but thoughts that would haunt her.

Or could there be a method in its madness? She knew that treachery lay at the heart of every demon. It could simply be lying to her when it spoke of trust and forgiveness—knowing she must be ready for tomorrow, hoping to make her doubt herself, make her fail. Yes, that was much more reasonable. But then, why was it so hard to believe that this demon would try to ruin her most cherished goals? After all, she held it prisoner, and though her spells kept it from tearing her apart, perhaps it still sought to tear apart her mind, to drive her mad instead. Why shouldn't it hate her, and delight in her torment, and hope for her destruction?

How could it be so ungrateful! She had almost laughed aloud at her own resentment, even as it formed the thought. As if a demon ever knew gratitude! But ever since the day she had netted it in spells in the swamp, she had given it nothing but the best treatment. She had fetched and carried, and made her fearful followers do the same. She had given it the best of everything—anything it desired. At its command she had sent out searchers to look for its scattered eyes, and it had allowed, even encouraged, her to use the eyes as her own, as watchers and protectors. She had even taught it to understand her speech (for it was as ignorant as a baby about the world of mortals) when she realized that it wanted to communicate with her. She had done all those things to win its favor because she knew that it had come into her hands for a reason, and if she could gain its co-operation, there would be no one who would dare to cross her.

She had spent every spare hour in keeping it company, feeding its curiosity, and her own, as she fed its jeweled maw, until gradually those conversations with the demon had become an end in themselves, a treasure worth the sacrifice of even precious metals. Even the constant waiting for its alien mind to ponder her questions and answers had never tired her; she had come to enjoy sharing even the simple pleasures of its silences, and resting in the warm amber light of its gaze.

T'uupieh looked down at the finely woven fiber belt which passed through the narrow slits between her side and wing, and held her tunic to her. She fingered the heavy, richly amber beads which decorated it—metal-dyed melt trapped in polished waterstone by the jewelsmith's secret arts—and which reminded her always of her demon's thousand eyes. *Her* demon . . .

She looked away again, toward the fire, toward the cloak-wrapped forms of her outlaws. Since the demon had come to her she had felt both the physical and the emotional space that she had always kept between herself as leader and her band of followers gradually widening. She was still completely their leader, perhaps more firmly so because she had tamed the demon, and their bond of shared danger and mutual respect had never weakened.

But there were other needs which her people might fill for each other, but never for her.

She watched them sleeping like the dead—as she should be sleeping now—preparing themselves for tomorrow. They took their sleep sporadically, when they could, as all commoners did—as she did now, too, instead of hibernating the night through like proper nobility. Many of them slept in pairs, man and woman, even though they mated with a commoner's chaotic lack of discrimination whenever a woman felt the season come upon her. T'uupieh wondered what they must imagine when they saw her sitting here with the demon far into the night. She knew what they believed, what she encouraged all to believe: that she had chosen it for a consort, or that it had chosen her. Y'lirr, she saw, still slept alone. She trusted and liked him as well as she did anyone; he was quick and ruthless, and she knew that he worshiped her. But he was a commoner, and more important, he did not challenge her. Nowhere, even among the nobility, had she found anyone who offered the sort of companionship she craved . . . until now, until the demon had come to her. No, she would not believe that all its words had been lies—

"T'uupieh!" The demon called her name buzzingly in the misty darkness. "Maybe you can't change the pattern of fate, but you can change your mind. You've already defied fate by turning outlaw and by defying Klovhiri. Your sister was the one who accepted"—unintelligible words—"only let the Wheel take her. Can you really kill her for that? You must understand why she did it, how she *could* do it. You don't have to kill her for that . . . you don't have to kill any of them. You have the strength, the courage, to put vengeance aside, and find another way to your goals. You can choose to be merciful—you can choose your own path through life, even if the ultimate destination of all life is the same."

She stood up resentfully, matching the demon's height, and drew her cloak tightly around her. "Even if I wished to change my mind, it is too late. The Wheel is already in motion, and I must get my sleep if I am to be ready for it." She started away toward the fire, stopped, looking back. "There is nothing I can do now, my demon. I cannot change tomorrow. Only you can do that. Only you . . ."

She heard it, later, calling her name softly as she lay sleepless on the cold ground. But she turned her back toward the sound and lay still, and at last sleep came.

Shannon slumped back into the embrace of the padded chair, rubbing his aching head. His eyelids were sandpaper, his body was a weight. He stared at the display screen, at T'uupieh's back turned stubbornly toward him as she slept beside the nitrogen campfire. "Okay, that's it. I give up. She won't even listen. Call Reed and tell him I quit."

"That you've quit trying to convince T'uupieh?" Garda said. "Are you sure? She may yet come back. Use a little more emphasis on—spiritual matters. Ve must be certain ve have done all ve can to . . . change her mind."

To save her soul, he thought sourly. Garda had gotten her early training at an institute dedicated to translating the Bible; he had discovered in the past few hours that she still had a hidden desire to proselytize. *What soul?* "We're wasting our time. It's been six hours since she walked out on me. She's not coming back . . . And I mean quit everything. I don't want to be around for the main event. I've had it."

"You don't mean that," Garda said. "You're tired, you need the rest too. Vhen T'uupieh vakes, you can talk to her again."

He shook his head, pushing back his hair. "Forget it. Just call Reed." He looked out the window, at dawn separating the mist-wrapped silhouette of seaside condominiums from the sky.

Garda shrugged, disappointed, and turned to the phone.

He studied the synthesizer's touchboards again, still bright and waiting, still calling his leaden, weary hands to try one more time. At least when he made this final announcement it wouldn't have to be direct to the eyes and ears of a waiting world; he doubted that any reporter was dedicated enough to still be up in the glass-walled observation room at this hour. Their questions had been endless earlier tonight, probing his feelings and his purpose and his motives and his plans, asking about "Robin Hood's" morality, or lack of it, and his own, about a hundred and one other things that were nobody's business but his own.

The music world had tried to do the same thing to him once, but then there had been buffers—agents, publicity staffs—to protect him. Now, when he'd had so much at stake, there had been no protection, only Reed at the microphone eloquently turning the room into a side show, with Shann the

Man as chief freak, until Shannon had begun to feel like a man staked out on an ant hill and smeared with honey. The reporters gazed down from on high, critiquing T'uupieh's responses and criticizing his own, and filled the time gaps when he needed quiet to think with infuriating interruptions. Reed's success had been total in wringing every drop of pathos and human interest out of his struggle to prevent T'uupieh's vengeance against the Innocents . . . and by that, had managed to make him fail.

No. He sat up straighter, trying to ease his back. No, he couldn't lay it on Reed . . . By the time what he'd had to say had really counted, the reporters had given up on him. The failure belonged to him, only him: his skill hadn't been great enough, his message hadn't been convincing enough—he was the one who hadn't been able to see through T'uupieh's eyes clearly enough to make her see through his own. He had had his chance to really communicate, for once in his life—to communicate something important. And he'd sunk it.

A hand reached past him to set a cup of steaming coffee on the shelf below the terminal. "One thing about this computer," a voice said quietly, "it's programmed for a good cup of coffee."

Startled, he laughed without expecting to and glanced up. His mother's face looked drawn and tired; she held another cup of coffee in her hand. "Thanks." He picked up the cup and took a sip, felt the hot liquid slide down his throat into his empty stomach. Not looking up again, he said, "Well, you got what you wanted. And so did Reed. He got his pathos, and he gets his murders, too."

She shook her head. "This isn't what I wanted. I don't want to see you give up everything you've done here just because you don't like what Reed is doing with part of it. It isn't worth that. Your work means too much to this project, and it means too much to you."

He looked up.

"*Ja,* she is right, Shannon. You can't quit now—we need you too much. And T'uupieh needs you."

He laughed again, not meaning it. "Like a cement yo-yo. What are you trying to do, Garda, use my own moralizing against me?"

"She's telling you what any blind man could see tonight, if he hadn't seen it months ago . . ." His mother's voice was strangely distant. "That this project would never have had this degree of success without you. That you were right about the synthesizer. And that losing you now might—"

She broke off, turning away to watch as Reed came through the doors at the end of the long room. He was alone this time, for once, and looking rumpled. Shannon guessed that he had been asleep when the phone call came, and was irrationally pleased at having awakened him.

Reed was not so pleased. Shannon watched the frown that might be worry or displeasure, or both, forming on his face as he came down the echoing hall toward them. "What did she mean, you want to quit? Just because you can't change an alien mind?" He entered the cubicle and glanced down at the terminal—to be sure that the remote microphones were all switched off, Shannon guessed. "You knew it was a long shot, probably hopeless. You have to accept that she doesn't want to reform, accept that the values of an alien culture are going to be different from your own."

Shannon leaned back, feeling a muscle begin to twitch with fatigue along the inside of his elbow. "I can accept that. What I can't accept is that you want to make us into a bunch of damn panderers. Christ, you don't even have a good reason! I didn't come here to play sound track for a snuff flick. If you go ahead and feed the world those murders, I'm laying it down. I don't want to give all this up, but I'm not staying for a kill-porn carnival."

Reed's frown deepened; he glanced away. "Well? What about the rest of you? Are you still privately branding me an accessory to murder too? Carly?"

"No, Marcus—not really." She shook her head. "But we all feel that we shouldn't cheapen and weaken our research by making a public spectacle of it. After all, the people of Titan have as much right to privacy and respect as any culture on Earth."

"*Ja*, Marcus, I think ve all agree about that."

"And just how much privacy does anybody on Earth have today? Good God—remember the Tasaday? And that was thirty years ago. There isn't a single mountaintop or desert island left that the all-seeing eye of the camera hasn't broadcast all over the world. And what do you call the public crime surveillance laws—our own lives are one big peep show."

Shannon shook his head. "That doesn't mean we have to—"

Reed turned cold eyes on him. "And I've had a little too much of your smartass piety, Wyler. Just what do you owe your success as a musician to, if not publicity?" He gestured at the posters on the walls. "There's more hard sell in your kind of music than any other field I can name."

"I have to put up with some publicity push or I couldn't reach the people. I couldn't do the thing that's really important to me—communicate. That doesn't mean I like it."

"You think I enjoy this?"

"Don't you?"

Reed hesitated. "I happen to be good at it, which is all that really matters. Because you may not believe it, but I'm still a scientist, and what I care about most of all is seeing that research gets its fair slice of the pie. You say I don't have a good reason for pushing our findings. Do you realize that NASA lost all the data from our Neptune probe just because somebody in effect got tired of waiting for it to get to Neptune and cut off our funds? The real problem on these long outer-planet missions isn't instrumental reliability, it's financial reliability. The public will pay out millions for one of your concerts, but not one cent for something they don't understand."

"I don't make—"

"People want to forget their troubles, be entertained . . . and who can blame them? So in order to compete with movies, and sports, and people like you—not to mention ten thousand other, worthy government and private causes—we have to give the public what it wants. It's my responsibility to deliver that, so that the 'real scientists' can sit in their neat bright institutes with half a billion dollars' worth of equipment around them, and talk about 'respect for research.' "

He paused; Shannon kept his gaze stubbornly. "Think it over. And when you can tell me how what you did as a musician is morally superior to or more valuable than what you're doing now, you can come to my office and tell me who the real hypocrite is. But think it over, first—all of you." Reed turned and left the cubicle.

They watched in silence until the double doors at the end of the room hung still. "Vell . . ." Garda glanced at her walking stick, and down at her cloak. "He does have a point."

Shannon leaned forward, tracing the complex beauty of the synthesizer terminal, feeling the combination of chagrin and caffeine pushing down his fatigue. "I know he does, but that isn't the point I was trying to get at! I didn't want to change T'uupieh's mind, or quit either, just because I objected to selling this project. It's the way it's being sold, like some kind of kill–porn-show perversion, that I can't take—" When he was a child, he remembered, rock concerts had had a kind of notoriety, but they were as respectable as a symphony orchestra now, compared to the "thrill shows" that had eclipsed them as he was growing up: where "experts" gambled their lives against a million-dollar pot, in front of a crowd who came to see them lose; where masochists made a living by self-mutilation; where they ran *cinéma vérité* films of butchery and death.

"I mean, is that what everybody really wants? Does it really make everybody feel good to watch somebody else bleed? Or are they going to get some kind of moral-superiority thing out of watching it happen on Titan instead of here?" He looked up at

the display, at T'uupieh, who still lay sleeping, unmoving and unmoved. "If I could have changed
T'uupieh's mind, or changed what happens here,
then maybe I could have felt good about something. At least about myself. But who am I kidding . . ." T'uupieh had been right all along, and
now he had to admit it to himself: that there had
never been any way he could change either one.
"T'uupieh's just like the rest of them, she'd rather
cut off your hand than shake it . . . and doing it
vicariously means we're no better. And none of us
ever will be." The words to a song older than he
was slipped into his mind, with sudden irony:
" 'One man's hands can't build' "—he began to
switch off the terminal—" 'anything.' "

"You need to sleep . . . ve all need to sleep."
Garda rose stiffly from her chair.

" '. . . but if one and one and fifty make a million . . .' " his mother matched his quote softly.

Shannon turned back to look at her, saw her
shake her head; she felt him looking at her, glanced
up. "After all, if T'uupieh could have accepted that
everything she did was morally evil, what would
have become of her? She knew: it would have
destroyed her—we would have destroyed her. She
would have been swept away and drowned in the
tide of violence." His mother looked away at Garda,
back at him. "T'uupieh is a realist, whatever else
she is."

He felt his mouth tighten against the resentment
that sublimated a deeper, more painful emotion; he
heard Garda's grunt of indignation.

"But that doesn't mean that you vere wrong, or
that you failed . . ."

"That's big of you." He stood up, nodding at Garda, and toward the exit. "Come on."

"Shannon."

He stopped, still facing away.

"I don't think you failed. I think you did reach T'uupieh. The last thing she said was 'Only you can change tomorrow.' I think she was challenging the demon to go ahead, to do what she didn't have the power to do herself. I think she was asking you to help her."

He turned, slowly. "You really believe that?"

"Yes, I do." She bent her head, freed her hair from the collar of her sweater.

He moved back to his seat, his hands brushed the dark, unresponsive touchplates on the panel. "But it wouldn't do any good to talk to her again. Somehow the demon has to stop the attack itself. If I could use the 'voice' to warn them . . . Damn the time lag!" By the time his voice reached them, the attack would have been over for hours. How could he change anything tomorrow if he was always two hours behind?

"I know how to get around the time-lag problem."

"How?" Garda sat down again, mixed emotions showing on her broad, seamed face. "He can't send a varning ahead of time; no one knows when Klovhiri will pass. It vould come too soon, or too late."

Shannon straightened up. "Better to ask, 'Why?' Why are you changing your mind?"

"I never changed my mind," his mother said mildly. "I never liked this either . . . When I was a girl, we used to believe that our actions *could* change the world; maybe I've never stopped wanting to believe that."

"But Marcus is not going to like us meddling behind his back, anyvay." Garda waved her staff. "And vhat about the point that perhaps ve do need this publicity?"

Shannon glanced back irritably. "I thought you were on the side of the angels, not the devil's advocate."

"I am!" Garda's mouth puckered. "But—"

"Then what's such bad news about the probe making a last-minute rescue? It'll be a sensation."

He saw his mother smile, for the first time in months. "Sensational . . . if T'uupieh doesn't leave us stranded in the swamp for our betrayal."

He sobered. "Not if you really think she wants our help. And I know she wants it . . . I *feel* it. But how do we beat the time lag?"

"I'm the engineer, remember? I'll need a recorded message from you, and some time to play with that." His mother pointed at the computer terminal.

He switched on the terminal and moved aside. She sat down and started a program documentation on the display; he read, REMOTE OPERATIONS MANUAL. "Let's see . . . I'll need feedback on the approach of Klovhiri's party . . ."

He cleared his throat. "Did you really mean what you said, before Reed came in?"

She glanced up; he watched one response form on her face and then fade into another smile. "Garda, have you met My Son the Linguist?"

"And when did you ever pick up on that Pete Seeger song?"

"And My Son the Musician . . ." The smile came back to him. "I've listened to a few records in my day." The smile turned inward, toward a memory. "I don't suppose I ever told you that I fell in love with your father because he reminded me of Elton John?"

T'uupieh stood silently, gazing into the demon's unwavering eye. A new day was turning the clouds from bronze to gold; the brightness seeped down through the glistening, snarled hair of the treetops, glanced from the green translucent cliff-faces and sweating slopes, to burnish the demon's carapace with light. She gnawed the last shreds of flesh from a bone, forcing herself to eat, scarcely aware that she did. She had already sent out watchers in the direction of the town, to keep watch for Chwiul . . . and Klovhiri's party. Behind her the rest of her band made ready now, testing weapons and reflexes or feeding their bellies.

And still the demon had not spoken to her. There had been many times when it had chosen not to speak for hours on end, but after its mad ravings of last night, the thought obsessed her that it might never speak again. Her concern grew, lighting the fuse of her anger, which this morning was already short enough, until at last she strode recklessly forward and struck it with her open hand. "Speak to me, *mala'ingga!*"

But as her blow landed, a pain like the touch of fire shot up the muscles of her arm. She leaped back with a curse of surprise, shaking her hand. The demon had never lashed out at her before, never

hurt her in any way. But she had never dared to
strike it before; she had always treated it with
calculated respect . . . *Fool!* She looked down at
her hand, half afraid to see it covered with burns
that would make her a cripple in the attack today.
But the skin was still smooth and unblistered, only
bright with the smarting shock.

"T'uupieh! Are you all right?"

She turned, to see Y'lirr, who had come up behind her looking half frightened, half grim. "Yes."
She nodded, controlling a sharper reply at the sight
of his concern. "It was nothing." He carried her
double-arched bow and quiver; she put out her
smarting hand and took them from him casually,
slung them at her back. "Come, Y'lirr, we must—"

"T'uupieh." This time it was the demon's eerie
voice that called her name. "T'uupieh, if you believe in my power to twist fate as I like, then you
must come back and listen to me again."

She turned back, felt Y'lirr hesitate behind her.
"I believe truly in all your powers, my demon!"
She rubbed her hand.

The amber depths of its eye absorbed her expres-
sion and read her sincerity, or so she hoped.
"T'uupieh, I know I did not make you believe what
I said. But I want you to"—its words blurred un-
intelligibly—"in me. I want you to know my name.
T'uupieh, my name is—"

She heard a horrified yowl from Y'lirr behind her.
She glanced around—seeing him cover his ears—
and back, paralyzed by disbelief.

"—Shang'ang."

The word struck her like the demon's fiery lash,

but the blow this time struck only in her mind. She cried out, in desperate protest, but the name had already passed into her knowledge, *too late!*

A long moment passed; she drew a breath and shook her head. Disbelief still held her motionless as she let her eyes sweep the brightening camp, as she listened to the sounds of the wakening forest and breathed in the spicy acridness of the spring growth. And then she began to laugh. She had heard a demon speak its name, and she still lived—and was not blind, not deaf, not mad . . . The demon had chosen her, joined with her, surrendered to her at last!

Dazed with exaltation, she almost did not realize that the demon had gone on speaking to her. She broke off the song of triumph that rose in her, listening:

". . . then I command you to take me with you when you go today. I must see what happens, and watch Klovhiri pass."

"Yes! Yes, my—Shang'ang. It will be done as you wish. Your whim is my desire." She turned away down the slope, stopped again as she found Y'lirr still prone where he had thrown himself down when the demon spoke its name. "Y'lirr?" She nudged him with her foot. Relieved, she saw him lift his head, watched her own disbelief echoing in his face as he looked up at her.

"My lady . . . it did not—?"

"No, Y'lirr," she said softly; then more roughly, "Of course it did not! I am truly the Demon's Consort now; nothing shall stand in my way." She pushed him again with her foot, harder. "Get up. What do

I have, a pack of sniveling cowards to ruin the morning of my success?"

Y'lirr scrambled to his feet, brushing himself off. "Never that, T'uupieh! We're ready for any command . . . ready to deliver your revenge." His hand tightened on his knife hilt.

"And my demon will join us in seeking it out!" The pride she felt rang in her voice. "Get help to fetch a sledge here, and prepare it. And tell them to move it *gently*."

He nodded, and for a moment as he glanced at the demon she saw both fear and envy in his eyes. "Good news." He moved off then with his usual brusqueness, without glancing back at her.

She heard a small clamor in the camp and looked past him, thinking that word of the demon had spread already. But then she saw Lord Chwiul, come as he had promised, being led into the clearing by her escorts. She lifted her head slightly, in surprise—he had indeed come alone, but he was riding a *bliell*. They were rare and expensive mounts, being the only beast she knew of large enough to carry so much weight, and being vicious and difficult to train as well. She watched this one snapping at the air, its fangs protruding past slack, dribbling lips, and grimaced faintly. She saw that the escort kept well clear of its stumplike webbed feet, and kept their spears ready to prod. It was an amphibian, being too heavy ever to make use of wings, but buoyant and agile when it swam. T'uupieh glanced fleetingly at her own webbed fingers and toes, at the wings that could only lift her body now for bare seconds at a time; she wondered, as she had so many times, what strange turns of fate had formed, or transformed, them all.

She saw Y'lirr speak to Chwiul, pointing her out, saw his insolent grin and the trace of apprehension that Chwiul showed looking up at her; she thought that Y'lirr had said, "She knows its name."

Chwiul rode forward to meet her, with his face under control as he endured the demon's scrutiny. T'uupieh put out a hand to casually—gently—stroke its sensuous, jewel-facet side. Her eyes left Chwiul briefly, drawn by some instinct to the sky directly above him, and for half a moment she saw the clouds break open . . .

She blinked, to see more clearly, and when she looked again it was gone. No one else, not even Chwiul, had seen the gibbous disc of greenish gold, cut across by a line of silver and a band of shadow-black: the Wheel of Change. She kept her face expressionless, but her heart raced. The Wheel appeared only when someone's life was about to be changed profoundly—and usually the change meant death.

Chwiul's mount lunged at her suddenly as he stopped before her. She held her place at the demon's side, but some of the *bliell*'s bluish spittle landed on her cloak as Chwiul jerked at its heavy head. "Chwiul!" She let her emotion out as anger. "Keep that slobbering filth under control, or I will have it struck dead!" Her hand fisted on the demon's slick hide.

Chwiul's near-smile faded abruptly, and he pulled his mount back, staring uncomfortably at the demon's glaring eye.

T'uupieh took a deep breath and produced a

smile of her own. "So you did not quite dare to come to my camp alone, my lord."

He bowed slightly, from the saddle. "I was merely hesitant to wander in the swamp on foot, alone, until your people found me."

"I see." She kept the smile. "Well then, I assume that things went as you planned this morning. Are Klovhiri and his party all well on their way into our trap?"

"They are. And their guide is waiting for my sign, to lead them off safe ground into whatever mire you choose."

"Good. I have a spot in mind that is well ringed by heights." She admired Chwiul's self-control in the demon's presence, although she sensed that he was not as easy as he wanted her to believe. She saw some of her people coming toward them with a sledge to carry the demon on their trek. "My demon will accompany us, by its own desire. A sure sign of our success today, don't you agree?"

Chwiul frowned as if he wanted to question that but didn't quite dare. "If it serves you loyally, then yes, my lady. A great honor and a good omen."

"It serves me with true devotion." She smiled again, insinuatingly. She stood back as the sledge came up onto the hummock, watched as the demon was settled onto it, to be sure her people used the proper care. The fresh reverence with which her outlaws treated it, and their leader, was not lost on either Chwiul or herself.

She called her people together then, and they set out for their destination, picking their way over the steaming surface of the marsh and through the slimy slate-blue tentacles of the fragile, thawing underbrush. She was glad that they covered this ground often because the pungent spring growth and the ground's mushy unpredictability changed the pattern of their passage from day to day. She wished that she could have separated Chwiul from his ugly mount, but she doubted that he would cooperate, and she was afraid that he might not be able to keep up on foot. The demon was lashed securely onto its sledge, and its sweating bearers pulled it with no hint of complaint.

At last they reached the heights overlooking the main road—though it could hardly be called one now—that led past her family's manor. She had the demon positioned where it could look back along the overgrown trail in the direcetion of Klovhiri's approach, and sent some of her followers to secrete its eyes farther down the track. She stood then gazing down at the spot below where the path seemed to fork, but did not: the false fork followed the rippling yellow bands of the cliff-face below her, directly into a sink caused by ammonia-water melt seeping down and through the porous sulphide compounds of the rock. There they would all wallow while she and her band picked them off like swatting *ngips*—she thoughtfully swatted a *ngip* that had settled on her hand—unless her demon . . . unless her demon chose to create some other outcome.

"Any sign?" Chwiul rode up beside her.

She moved back slightly from the cliff's crumbly edge, watching him with more than casual interest. "Not yet. But soon." She had outlaws posted on the lower slope across the track as well, but not even her demon's eye could pierce too deeply into the foliage along the road. It had not spoken since

Chwiul's arrival, and she did not expect it to reveal its secrets now. "What livery does your escort wear, and how many of them do you want killed for effect?" She unslung her bow and began to test its pull.

Chwiul shrugged. "The dead carry no tales; kill them all. I shall have Klovhiri's soon. Kill the guide, too—a man who can be bought once, can be bought twice."

"Ah—" She nodded, grinning. "A man with your foresight and discretion will go far in the world, my lord." She nocked an arrow in the bowstring before she turned away, to search the road again. Still empty. She looked away restlessly, at the spiny silver-blue-green of the distant fog-clad mountains; at the hollow fingers of upthrust ice, once taller than she was, stubby and diminishing now along the edge of the nearer lake. The lake where last summer she had soared . . .

A flicker of movement, a small unnatural noise, pulled her eyes back to the road. Tension tightened the fluid ease of her movement as she made the trilling call that would send her band to their places along the cliff's edge. *At last—* Leaning forward eagerly for the first glimpse of Klovhiri, she spotted the guide, and then the sledge that bore her sister and the children. She counted the numbers of the escort, saw them all emerge into her unbroken view on the track. But Klovhiri . . . where was Klovhiri? She turned back to Chwiul, her whisper struck out at him, "Where is he? Where is Klovhiri?"

Chwiul's expression lay somewhere between guilt and guile. "Delayed. He stayed behind, he said there were still matters at court—"

"Why didn't you tell me that?"

He jerked sharply on the *bliell*'s rein. "It changes nothing! We can still eradicate his family. That will leave me first in line to the inheritance, and Klovhiri can always be brought down later."

"But it's Klovhiri I want, for myself . . ." T'uupieh raised her bow, the arrow tracked toward his heart.

"They'll know who to blame if I die!" He spread a wing defensively. "The Overlord will turn against you for good; Klovhiri will see to that. Avenge yourself on your sister, T'uupieh—and I will still reward you well if you keep the bargain!"

"This is not the bargain we agreed to!" The sounds of the approaching party reached her clearly now from down below; she heard a child's high notes of laughter. Her outlaws crouched, waiting for her signal, and she saw Chwiul prepare for his own signal call to his guide. She looked back at the demon, its amber eye fixed on the travelers below. She started toward it. It could still twist fate for her. *Or had it already?*

"*Go back, go back!*" The demon's voice burst over her, down across the silent forest, like an avalanche. "Ambush . . . trap . . . you have been betrayed!"

"—betrayal!"

She barely heard Chwiul's voice below the roaring; she looked back in time to see the *bliell* leap forward, to intersect her own course toward the demon. Chwiul drew his sword; she saw the look of white fury on his face, not knowing whether it was for her or the demon itself. She ran toward the demon's sledge, trying to draw her bow, but the *bliell* covered the space between them in two great bounds. Its head swung toward her, jaws gaping.

Her foot skidded on the slippery melt and she went down; the dripping jaws snapped futilely shut above her face. But one flailing leg struck her heavily and knocked her sliding through the melt to the demon's foot.

The demon. She gasped for the air that would not fill her lungs, trying to call its name; saw with incredible clarity the beauty of its form, and the ululating horror of the *bliell* bearing down on them to destroy them both. She saw it rear above her, above the demon; saw Chwiul, either leaping or thrown, sail out into the air—and at last her voice came back to her and she screamed the name, a warning and a plea, "Shang'ang!"

And as the *bliell* came down, lightning lashed out from the demon's carapace and wrapped the *bliell* in fire. The beast's ululations rose off the scale; T'uupieh covered her ears against the piercing pain of its cry. But not her eyes: the demon's lash ceased with the suddenness of lightning, and the *bliell* toppled back and away, rebounding lightly as it crashed to the ground, stone dead. T'uupieh sank back against the demon's foot, supported gratefully as she filled her aching lungs, and looked away—

To see Chwiul, trapped in the updrafts at the cliff's edge, gliding, gliding . . . and she saw the three arrows that protruded from his back, before the currents let his body go and it disappeared below the rim. She smiled and closed her eyes.

"T'uupieh! T'uupieh!"

She blinked them open again, resignedly, as she felt her people cluster around her. Y'lirr's hand drew back from the motion of touching her face as she opened her eyes. She smiled again at him, at them

all, but not with the smile she had had for Chwiul.
"Y'lirr . . ." She gave him her hand and let him help
her up. Aches and bruises prodded her with every
small movement, but she was certain, reassured, that
the only real damage was an oozing tear in her wing.
She kept her arm close to her side.

"T'uupieh—"

"My lady—"

"What happened? The demon—"

"The demon saved my life." She waved them silent. "And—for its own reasons—it foiled Chwiul's
plot." The realization, and the implications, were
only now becoming real in her mind. She turned,
and for a long moment gazed into the demon's un-
readable eye. Then she moved away, going stiffly to
the edge of the cliff to look down.

"But the contract—" Y'lirr said.

"Chwiul broke the contract! He did not give me
Klovhiri." No one made a protest. She peered
through the brush, guessing without much difficulty
the places where Ahtseet and her party had gone to
earth below. She could hear a child's whimpered
crying now. Chwiul's body lay sprawled on the flat,
in plain view of them all, and she thought she saw
more arrows bristling from his corpse. Had Ahtseet's
guard riddled him too, taking him for an attacker?
The thought pleased her. And a small voice inside
her dared to whisper that Ahtseet's escape pleased
her much more . . . She frowned suddenly at the
thought.

But Ahtseet had escaped, and so had Klovhiri—
and so she might as well make use of that fact, to
salvage what she could. She paused, collecting her
still-shaken thoughts. "Ahtseet!" Her voice was not

the voice of the demon, but it echoed satisfactorily. "It's T'uupieh! See the traitor's corpse that lies before you—your own mate's brother, Chwiul! He hired murderers to kill you in the swamp—seize your guide, make him tell you all. It is only by my demon's warning that you still live."

"Why?" Ahtseet's voice wavered faintly on the wind.

T'uupieh laughed bitterly. "Why, to keep the roads clear of ruffians. To make the Overlord love his loyal servant more, and reward her better, dear sister! And to make Klovhiri hate me. May it eat his guts out that he owes your lives to me! Pass freely through my lands, Ahtseet; I give you leave—this once."

She drew back from the ledge and moved wearily away, not caring whether Ahtseet would believe her. Her people stood waiting, gathered silently around the corpse of the *bliell*.

"What now?" Y'lirr asked, looking at the demon, asking for them all.

And she answered, but made her answer directly to the demon's silent amber eye, "It seems I spoke the truth to Chwiul after all, my demon. I told him he would not be needing his town house after today . . . Perhaps the Overlord will call it a fair trade. Perhaps it can be arranged. The Wheel of Change carries us all, but not with equal ease. Is that not so, my beautiful Shang'ang?"

She stroked its day-warmed carapace tenderly, and settled down on the softening ground to wait for its reply.

FURTHER READING

NOVELS

BRADLEY, MARION ZIMMER. *The Shattered Chain*. New York, Daw, 1976.

BROWN, ROSEL GEORGE. *Sibyl Sue Blue*. Garden City, N.Y., Doubleday, 1966.

———. *The Waters of Centaurus*. Garden City, N.Y., Doubleday, 1970.

BRYANT, DOROTHY. *The Kin of Ata Are Waiting for You*. New York and San Francisco, Moon Books–Random House, 1976.

BUSBY, F.M. *Rissa Kerguelen*. New York, Berkley, 1977. (Published in two volumes, *Rissa Kerguelen* and *The Long View*, by Berkley–Putnam, 1976.)

BUTLER, OCTAVIA E. *Mind of My Mind*. Garden City, N.Y., Doubleday, 1977.

CHERRYH, C.J. *Gate of Ivrel*. New York, Daw, 1976.

———. *Hunter of Worlds*. New York, Daw, 1977.

DELANY, SAMUEL R. *Babel-17*. New York, Ace, 1966.

———. *Triton*. New York, Bantam, 1976.

DORMAN, SONYA. *Roxy Rimidon*. New York, Coward-McCann & Geoghegan, 1977.

GRAY, CURME. *Murder in Millennium VI*. Chicago, Shasta, 1951.

GOTLIEB, PHYLLIS. *Sunburst*. Greenwich, Conn., Fawcett, 1964.

GOULD, LOIS. *A Sea Change*. New York, Avon Books, 1977.

HARNESS, CHARLES. *The Rose*. New York, Berkley, 1969.

HENDERSON, ZENNA. *The People: No Different Flesh.* Garden City, N.Y., Doubleday, 1967.

————. *Pilgrimage: The Book of the People.* Garden City, N.Y., Doubleday, 1961.

HOLLAND, CECELIA. *Floating Worlds.* New York, Knopf, 1976.

KAUAN, ANNA. *Ice.* New York, Popular Library, 1970.

LEE, TANITH. *The Birthgrave.* New York, Daw, 1975.

LESSING, DORIS. *The Memoirs of a Survivor.* New York, Knopf, 1975.

MCCAFFREY, ANNE. *Dragonflight.* New York, Walker, 1968.

————. *The Ship Who Sang.* New York, Walker, 1969.

MCINTYRE, VONDA. *The Exile Waiting.* Greenwich, Conn., Fawcett, 1975.

MOORE, C. L. *Judgment Night.* New York, Paperback Library, 1965.

NORTON, ANDRE. *Spell of the Witch World.* New York, Daw, 1972.

————. *Year of the Unicorn.* New York, Ace, 1965.

PIERCY, MARGE. *Woman on the Edge of Time.* New York, Knopf, 1976.

PISERCHIA, DORIS. *Star Rider.* New York, Bantam, 1975.

RANDALL, MARTA. *Islands.* New York, Pyramid, 1976.

RUSS, JOANNA. *We Who Are About To . . .* New York, Dell, 1977.

SAXTON, JOSEPHINE. *The Hieros Gamos of Sam and An Smith.* Garden City, N.Y., Doubleday, 1969.

SCHMITZ, JAMES H. *The Demon Breed.* New York, Ace, 1968.

————. *The Witches of Karres.* Philadelphia, Pa., Chilton, 1966.

WILHELM, KATE. *The Clewiston Test.* New York, Farrar, Straus, Giroux, 1976.

————. *Margaret and I.* Boston, Little, Brown, 1971.

WYNDHAM, JOHN. *Trouble with Lichen.* New York, Ballantine, 1960.

YARBRO, CHELSEA QUINN. *Time of the Fourth Horseman*. Garden City, N.Y., Doubleday, 1976.

ANTHOLOGIES AND COLLECTIONS

HAMILTON, EDMOND, ED. *The Best of Leigh Brackett*. New York, Ballantine, 1977.

HENDERSON, ZENNA. *Holding Wonder*. Garden City, N.Y., Doubleday, 1971.

LE GUIN, URSULA K. *Orsinian Tales*. New York, Harper & Row, 1976.

MERRIL, JUDITH. *The Best of Judith Merril*. New York, Warner, 1976.

MOORE, C. L. *Jirel of Joiry*. New York, Paperback Library, 1969.

NORTON, ANDRE. *The Book of Andre Norton*. New York, Daw, 1975.

REED, KIT. *Mr. da V. and Other Stories*. New York, Berkley, 1973.

RUSS, JOANNA. *Alyx*. Boston, Gregg Press, 1977. (Includes the novel *Picnic on Paradise*.)

ST. CLAIR, MARGARET. *Change the Sky and Other Stories*. New York, Ace, 1974.

SILVERBERG, ROBERT, ED. *The Crystal Ship*. New York, Thomas Nelson, 1976.

TIPTREE, JAMES, JR. *Warm Worlds and Otherwise*. New York, Ballantine, 1975.

SHORT FICTION

ASHWELL, PAULINE. "Unwillingly to School," 1958. Appeared in *Astounding Science Fiction* (January 1958).

BUCK, DORIS PITKIN. "The Giberel," 1971. Appeared in *New Dimensions 1*, ed. by Robert Silverberg (Garden City, N.Y., Doubleday, 1971).

CARR, CAROL. "Inside," 1970. Appeared in *Orbit 8*, ed. by Damon Knight (New York, Putnam, 1970).

DAVIS, CHAIN. "The Star System," 1958. Appeared (in altered form under the title "It Walks in Beauty") in *Star Science Fiction* (January 1958).

EMSHWILLER, CAROL. "Escape Is No Accident," 1977. Appeared in *The American Tricentennial*, ed. by Edward Bryant (New York, Pyramid, 1977).

GOULD, LOIS. "X: A Fabulous Child's Story," 1972. Appeared in *MS Magazine*, December, 1972.

HENDERSON, ZENNA. "Something Bright," 1959. Reprinted in *Sixth Annual of the Year's Best SF*, ed. by Judith Merril (New York, Simon & Schuster, 1961).

LE GUIN, URSULA K. "The Diary of the Rose," 1976. Appeared in *Future Power*, ed. by Jack Dann and Gardner R. Dozois (New York, Random House, 1976).

————. "The New Atlantis," 1975. Appeared in *The New Atlantis*, ed. by Robert Silverberg (New York, Hawthorn, 1975).

McINTYRE, VONDA N. "Aztecs," 1977. Appeared in *The American Tricentennial*.

————. "The Genius Freaks," 1973. Appeared in *Orbit 12*, ed. by Damon Knight (New York, Putnam, 1973).

MACLEAN, KATHERINE. "And Be Merry," 1950. Reprinted in *Omnibus of Science Fiction*, ed. by Groff Conklin (New York, Crown, 1952).

MITCHISON, NAOMI. "Mary and Joe," 1962. Reprinted in *Nova 1*, ed. by Harry Harrison (New York, Delacorte, 1970).

MOORE, C. L. "No Woman Born," 1944. Reprinted in *Human-Machines*, ed. by Thomas N. Scortia and George Zebrowski (New York, Vintage, 1975).

NORTON, ANDRE. "Toads of Grimmerdale," 1973. Appeared in *Flashing Swords #2*, ed. by Lin Carter (New York, Dell, 1973).

PLAUGER, P. J. "Child of All Ages," 1975. Reprinted in *The Best Science Fiction of the Year #5*, ed. by Terry Carr (New York, Ballantine, 1976).

PIPER, H. BEAM. "Omnilingual," 1958. Appeared in *Astounding Science Fiction* (1958).

RANDALL, MARTA. "Secret Rider," 1976. Appeared in *New Dimensions 6*, ed. by Robert Silverberg (New York, Harper & Row, 1976).

REED, KIT. "In Behalf of the Product," 1973. Appeared in *Bad Moon Rising*, ed. by Thomas M. Disch (New York, Harper & Row, 1973).

———. "The Wait," 1958. Reprinted in *Apeman, Spaceman*, ed. by Harry Harrison and Leon E. Stover (Garden City, N.Y., Doubleday, 1968).

ROSMOND, BABETTE. "Error Hurled," 1976. Appeared in *Science Fiction Discoveries*, ed. by Carol and Frederik Pohl (New York, Bantam, 1976).

SEABRIGHT, IDRIS. "Short in the Chest," 1954. Reprinted in *Alpha 6*, ed. by Robert Silverberg (New York, Berkley, 1976).

TIPTREE, JAMES, JR. "Houston, Houston, Do You Read?," 1976. Appeared in *Aurora: Beyond Equality*, ed. by Vonda N. McIntyre and Susan Janice Anderson (Greenwich, Conn., Fawcett, 1976).

TUTTLE, LISA. "The Family Monkey," 1977. Appeared in *New Voices in Science Fiction*, ed. by George R. R. Martin (New York, Macmillan, 1977).

———, and George R. R. Martin. "The Storms of Windhaven," 1975. Reprinted in *The Best Science Fiction of the Year #5*, ed. by Terry Carr (New York, Ballantine, 1976).

VINGE, JOAN D. "Media Man," 1976. Appeared in *Analog*, October 1976.

———. "Mother and Child," 1975. Appeared in *Orbit 16*, ed. by Damon Knight (New York, Harper & Row, 1975).

WEINBAUM, STANLEY G. "The Adaptive Ultimate,"

1935. Reprinted in *The Best of Stanley G. Weinbaum* (New York, Ballantine, 1974).

————. "The Red Peri," 1935. Reprinted in *The Red Peri*, by Stanley G. Weinbaum (Reading, Pa., Fantasy Press, 1952).

WILHELM, KATE. "The Encounter," 1970. Appeared in *Orbit 8*, ed. by Damon Knight (New York, Putnam, 1970).

————. "Somerset Dreams," 1969. Appeared in *Orbit 5*, ed. by Damon Knight (New York, Putnam, 1969).

WYNDHAM, JOHN. "Consider Her Ways," 1956. Reprinted in *A Science Fiction Argosy*, ed. by Damon Knight (New York, Simon & Schuster, 1972).

ABOUT THE EDITOR

<small>PAMELA SARGENT</small> is the author of three novels, *Cloned Lives*, *The Sudden Star*, and *Watchstar*. She is also the author of *Starshadows*, a collection of her short fiction. She has edited the anthologies of *Bio-Futures*, *Women of Wonder*, and *More Women of Wonder*. She lives in upstate New York.